Under the gentle str... by's back, she felt her tight muscles begin to loosen. His murmured words next to her ear were reassuring. She wasn't sure what to make of this new, unsuspected side of him, but she liked it—very much. So when his hand slid from her back to her jaw, as though he'd willed her to do so, she tilted her head and received his kiss.

Such a simple thing, a kiss. But it had been so long since Ty had tasted one, and to him it felt like his first—as if he were a kid again, as if this were the first kiss he'd always waited for. Her hand emerged from the folds of the blanket to press flat against his chest, just over the place where his heart thundered. He reached up and quickly unbuttoned his shirt halfway down, then tucked her hand inside and held it against his bare skin.

Instantly a fierce heat sprang up between them. Ty's lips were lush, warm, thrilling. His breathing grew heavier and her own heart beat faster. Libby's head told her to resist, to end this now. But her foolish heart refused to obey. . . .

# A Taste of Heaven

## ALEXIS HARRINGTON

A TOPAZ BOOK

TOPAZ
Published by the Penguin Group
Penguin Books USA Inc., 375 Hudson Street,
New York, New York 10014, U.S.A.
Penguin Books Ltd, 27 Wrights Lane,
London W8 5TZ, England
Penguin Books Australia Ltd, Ringwood,
Victoria, Australia
Penguin Books Canada Ltd, 10 Alcorn Avenue,
Toronto, Ontario, Canada M4V 3B2
Penguin Books (N.Z.) Ltd, 182-190 Wairau Road,
Auckland 10, New Zealand

Penguin Books Ltd, Registered Offices:
Harmondsworth, Middlesex, England

First published by Topaz, an imprint of Dutton Signet,
a division of Penguin Books USA Inc.

First Printing, January, 1996
10  9  8  7  6  5  4  3  2

 REGISTERED TRADEMARK—MARCA REGISTRADA

## Printed in Canada

*To Janet Brayson—*
*It all started with a picture*
*from a magazine . . .*

## ACKNOWLEDGMENTS

*My thanks to my dear friend
and medical adviser,
Margaret A. Vajdos, M.D.
and
Loyce Gilpin,
a true American cowgirl*

# *Prologue*

*March 1887*

Liberty Garrison Ross momentarily straightened from her task and leaned on the shovel handle, flexing her back. Her skirt was solid mud from waist to hem. Wincing at the fire in her hands, she lifted them to look at the blisters forming on her palms. She hadn't thought to put on her worn gloves before she came out here. Small wonder.

A chill breeze came up and caught the long ends of her hair, flapping them across her face. The late March sun glared off blinding patches of snow that remained on the ground and still blanketed the surrounding hills. Out there, she knew, lay the rotting carcasses of thawing cattle, frozen on their hooves by successive blizzards that had howled over this land continually since November. She was a stranger here, but still, by this time of year, she would have expected to detect the scent of spring. It wasn't there.

She glanced down at the open trench in front of her. In one corner, a bit of white sheet protruded through the dark soil. It gleamed up from the bottom of the pit under the noon sun. Creeping hysteria closed in, making her heart jump, and the threat of tears burned behind her eyelids again. She dashed a shaking, muddy hand across them. She had to hold together a little longer; the worst part was over. She had only to finish filling the hole.

Don't think, she ordered herself, just dig. If she gave this too much thought, she'd run screaming through the winter-beaten range lands. Here, death and hardship lurked like the vultures circling the lifeless cattle.

Libby sank the shovel blade into the dwindling pile of heavy, water-soaked dirt that she'd erected while digging Ben Ross's grave. It was hard to remember that he had been her husband—she had never felt married to him. And not just because she'd been his wife for only four months before he died of pneumonia.

She lifted the shovel with effort. She had never buried anyone before. In Chicago, there were people whose business it was to handle such matters as funerals and interment. But this wasn't the city. It was the frontier. And since coming to Montana last September, Libby had done a lot of things she'd never expected to do.

Try though she might to make her mind a blank, she couldn't shut out the reality of what she was doing, and what had led her to this. Shuddering sobs began working their way up her throat, and she frantically pushed soil into the hole, working faster and faster.

She'd get away from this uncivilized, godforsaken place if it was the last thing she did. Life in Chicago had been a heartache.

In Montana, it was hell.

# Chapter 1

Libby Ross stepped out and carefully closed the door behind her, making certain it latched. It was a senseless exercise, she knew, but she performed it just the same.

At this early hour, it was cold here on the rough, narrow porch. During the winter, this side of the house had remained in shadows most of the day, even when the sun shone. That fact had served her well for the past month, especially when the ground had still been frozen—

At the thought, her hand tightened spasmodically on her satchel, the one she'd arrived with last September. She hadn't come here with much except hope, and in some ways, it felt as though she were leaving with even less.

Overhead, in a sky that seemed to have no end, clouds crowded out the sun. Libby took away with her only those personal items she'd brought last fall, and packed them in her trunk after hoisting it on the rickety buckboard. She also carried Ben's Winchester, which she would keep for protection. She didn't have much skill with the weapon, but she supposed if faced with the need to use it, she'd figure it out fast enough. Nothing else in the house was of any interest or help to her. A few broken pieces of furniture, and a hodgepodge of worthless stuff collected over Ben's lifetime of austere bachelorhood—these were her widow's dower.

She climbed onto the buckboard and picked up the lines, looking down at the skinny roan it had taken her over an hour to hitch. He was a sorry-looking thing, and she worried about him making the trip to the town of Heavenly. That the gelding had survived the winter was a miracle for which she was profoundly grateful; he was her only transportation out of here.

But Libby knew she would have walked, even crawled on her knees if she'd had to, just to escape from here, and Montana. She didn't have much money, but surely she had enough to buy a stage-coach ticket to *somewhere* outside this territory. That was her immediate goal. Where she was going, and what she'd do when she got there were worries to put off for later.

It wasn't much of a plan, but it was the best her numbed mind could devise. Her first destination was Heavenly, the nearest town, fifteen miles to the east. She'd seen it only once, and that had been last fall when she arrived on the stage. As she stood in the street blinking against the sun, to her city-bred eyes it had been a crude, disappointing outpost with a saloon and a few stores that rose from the sagebrush. But after months of seeing no other landscape but empty, snow-covered prairie, in her mind's eye Heavenly, Montana, had achieved the stature of its namesake.

Pointing the horse toward the road, she didn't look back at the shabby hovel where she'd spent the grueling, interminable winter. But she spared just a brief glance at Ben's grave. Yesterday, after finishing his burial, she'd marked it with a clumsy cross. It was made from two wooden spoons, lashed at their intersection with a tie from one of her aprons. It wasn't fancy, but it was the best she could do, and as much as he deserved for the lies he'd told her to bring her here.

On both sides of the road leading away from the ranch, the grassland was sparsely dotted with the mangy brown coats of dead cattle, revealed by the melting snow. She shivered in the face of the chill wind. It seemed like she never was warm enough anymore.

She bowed her head for an instant against the pain of knowing she was totally alone in the world. Then she flapped the reins on the horse's back to hurry her leave-taking from this place.

Under the halfhearted sun, Heavenly, Montana, was a disappointing sight. Libby glanced around as her tired horse stumbled down the street, and her inflated notion of the town fizzled away like a drop of water on a hot stove. Many of the buildings were tall and narrow, a design she'd found peculiar to the western towns she'd seen on her way out here. It made no sense to her; they had more room out here than they could use, but the structures were high and cramped. These were made from rough-sawn planking, and looked neglected.

It was late afternoon, and her arms felt as heavy as granite. They'd already ached from digging Ben's grave yesterday. Driving the horse fifteen miles over rough, nearly nonexistent roads had just about finished her off. She had no experience with reins and several times all three of them—horse, buckboard, and she—would have left the path had the gelding not been smart enough to correct Libby's errors. At least she'd remembered to wear gloves today, and it was a good thing—inside the leather, her hands were still raw.

Still, she thought, looking around again, there was life here, and people. She hadn't talked to another person besides Ben since last fall. And he hadn't been very talkative, at that. Especially toward the end.

Signs along the muddy street marked the establishments of a barber, a gunsmith, a feed store, an assay office, a "painless" dentist, a hotel, and the saloon. At least the town had a hotel, although what little money she possessed wouldn't last long if she had to spend more than one night there.

At the halfway point of the thoroughfare, Libby's eyes lit on Osmer's Dry Goods. She remembered the stage driver telling her that Osmer's sold the tickets. With clumsy maneuvering, she pulled the wobbling buckboard to a stop, and sighed with relief. Wrapping the lines around the brake handle, she climbed down. Every muscle she owned was stiff.

God only knew what she looked like after her day-long trip. She hadn't secured her hat very well and somewhere along the way, it had blown off, taking her best hat pin with it. She glanced down at her clothes. At least the roads hadn't been dusty, and aside from being wrinkled, her dark skirt was still fairly clean. She smoothed the front of her jacket and, taking a deep, steadying breath, set off toward Osmer's.

Three cowboys lounged at the hitching rail in front of the place, apparently engaged in a deep discussion. As she approached them, snatches of their conversation floated to her.

"—and I hope we can do somethin' about it before Mr. Hollins gets back. Elsewise, he's like to have a fit when he hears what we done," one of them reflected glumly. He leaned his tall, spare frame against the rail and crossed his ankles, making his spurs clink.

"Aw, he woulda done the same thing if he was here," the second cowboy replied. He had the bushiest mustache Libby had ever seen. He looked up from the cigarette he was rolling, his hat shifting when he raised his brows. "Maybe worse—he mighta shot that damned potato-head."

"Charlie's right. Tyler will understand," the youngest of the three offered, sounding the most confident. "I don't know why you two think he's so fearsome. It ain't like he'll flay our hides off."

The mustachioed one licked the seam of the tidy roll of tobacco and twisted the ends. "Yours, he won't, Sass. You ain't old enough yet to really get him riled, but he expects the rest of us to know better. If we don't, we're up to our asses in—

"—oh, a-afternoon ma'am!"

Catching sight of Libby, the two older ones lurched to attention and turned a ripe shade of crimson. They scraped their hats off their heads and held them against their chests as though watching a funeral cortege pass. Their spurs rang and there was general shuffling as they made a path for her on the sidewalk. The youngster gawked at her with respectful awe until the lean, leathery cowboy reached over and whipped off the youngster's hat impatiently. He shoved it into the boy's hands, and delivered a sharp poke to his ribs. With this silent reprimand, he shut his gaping mouth and straightened like the other two.

Libby nodded in acknowledgment and continued

to Osmer's door, unable to suppress her smile. The West was a crude, uncivilized wilderness, but at least some of the people were polite.

"Passed away? Old Ben Ross?" Nort Osmer stared at Libby across his counter, slack-jawed. "I know he's been poorly in the last year or so, but— Well, I swan . . ."

The general store was redolent with the clashing odors of jerked beef, tobacco, tanned leather, coffee, and a vague floral scent. A row of jars filled with colorful candy sat on the counter. Libby's eyes lingered on the candy; she hadn't eaten since noon, and the skimpy meal had consisted of only a piece of bread and a hunk of dried beef. Sneaking a surreptitious glance around her, Libby noted a jumble of merchandise on display, some items with fur still attached. This was all so different from the elegant department stores in Chicago—not that she'd had the money to shop in them. But she'd looked in their windows often enough over the years.

"Had you known my husband long, Mr. Osmer?" she inquired, more out of politeness than real interest. The word *husband* stuck in her throat.

He blinked at her, obviously still assimilating the news of Ben's death. He was a mild-looking man with small, pale eyes and reddish brown hair.

"Yes'm, since I was a boy. He's been coming in from the time my pa owned this place. We were surprised as all get-out when we heard he took a wife."

Libby wasn't sure who "we" were, but assumed he meant the townspeople. Osmer paused here, looking at her with curiosity.

"No offense intended, ma'am—uh, Mrs. Ross, but

an old cowhand like Ben, set in his ways and all, well, he didn't seem like the type to marry. Especially to a lady so much younger than him."

His remark only reinforced Libby's suspicions. Ben Ross had been looking for a nurse, not a wife. And how could she respond to the shopkeeper's observation? Admit that she'd been so desperate to leave her hometown that she'd traveled over thirteen hundred miles to meet a man who'd duped her? No. She merely nodded.

"It all happened so suddenlike," he went on, "you coming to town and getting married at the sheriff's office. We didn't get to meet you before Ben whisked you back to his place. Then winter set in, snowing blue murder. Did the weather treat Ben's place badly?"

Again, a grim picture of death—dead cattle, dead horses, dead land—wound tiredly through her mind. Libby nodded. "I don't believe I'd seen another living thing besides my horse till I got to town." She thought a sympathetic look crossed the man's bland face.

Nort Osmer straightened and put out his hand. "Well, welcome to Heavenly, ma'am. I'm mighty sorry we're meeting in sadness, but I hope you'll be staying on."

Libby was touched by his simple sentiment, despite her weariness, and shook hands with him. "Actually, Mr. Osmer, I'm here to buy a stagecoach ticket. Nothing much was left of Ben's place, and I can't live there."

He nodded understandingly. "To be honest, ma'am, he never had a lot of luck with that spread. I suppose the winter was just the last straw, so to speak." His tone became brisk and merchantlike.

"So, that'll be one ticket to Miles City? The stage will be here at noon tomorrow. From Miles City, you can catch the train for wherever you're bound."

"Yes, that would be fine." Just saying the words made her feel better. And suddenly she realized where she was headed: home, back to Chicago. She'd left in bitterness and hurt, an impetuous decision that had cost her far more than she'd gained. True, she was no longer welcome in the Brandauer home, but surely her prospects would be better there than in this wilderness.

She opened her bag and brought out five dollars. She was certain it wouldn't be enough for a train ticket, too, but at least she'd be closer to her goal. With the other five dollars she held, she'd have enough to get a room at the hotel and buy a couple of meals. "Please take it out of this."

Nort stared at the gold coin lying on the counter between them as though it were a nice button she'd offered for payment. He lifted his eyes to her face. "Mrs. Ross—you'll need more than five dollars. A stage ticket to Miles City is a lot more than that."

Libby gaped back at him. She hadn't a clue as to how much the trip out here had cost. Ben had sent her both train and stagecoach tickets, and she'd never traveled anywhere in her twenty-six years till last fall. "B-but I only have ten dollars total." She cast about in her mind, trying to think of an alternative. "Can I buy a ticket to another town?"

The shopkeeper shook his head. "No, ma'am, you can't go anywhere on the stagecoach for five dollars. Or even ten."

Libby found her problems to be piling up quickly. Where could she go? She couldn't drive back to Ben's place; night would be falling in another couple of hours. She was hungry and tired and discouraged. Besides, to return to that tiny, confining hovel—a shudder ran through her at the very thought. No, no, no. She couldn't go back there again, not for any reason. If she did, she'd lose her mind. She'd rather scrub every floor in Heavenly *twice* than go back to that place. Her head came up. Work. She needed to find work.

Libby picked up the gold coin and put it back in her bag. She took another quick glance around the shop, trying to decide how to broach the subject of a job. "You must know a lot about Heavenly, Mr. Osmer. It looks as though I'll be needing to, that is, maybe I can find work here in town." She gestured at the pine counter, feeling very awkward. "Could you use help here in the store? I-I don't have any experience with keeping shop, but I'm trustworthy and I can learn."

Nort looked like he'd swallowed one of the big sourballs in the jar next to his hand. "Well, uh, ma'am, I mean Mrs. Ross, after the beating we took this winter, things are pretty quiet. I wish I could help but I don't do enough business here to pay a clerk. And my wife, well, she wouldn't—" He stammered a few more words, until Libby took pity on him.

"Maybe you've heard of other work I could do?" she asked, struggling to maintain hope. It was a formidable task; everything about the last few months had seemed hopeless.

"I wish I could say I had, but Heavenly is just a little burp of a place and the only work in town for a woman would be down at the Big Dipper."

Libby drew a quiet breath. "The Big Dipper is the saloon?"

He looked apologetic. "Yes, ma'am. Miss Callie is always looking for ladies, well, that is—" Suddenly, his attention caught on something beyond Libby's shoulder. She turned to see him eyeing the three cowboys outside his window. Then he looked her over speculatively, his hand at his chin. "Say, now that you mention it, I just might know of something."

An apprehensive, uncomfortable feeling brushed Libby. To be a woman alone in the world, and in a strange place, was a chancy circumstance at best. But without resources, she was prey to any number of dangers. A fleeting memory of a warm, fragrant kitchen flickered through her mind, then it was gone, like the afterglow image of lightning. Libby glanced at the door, thinking that perhaps she should leave— while she could.

"Please don't trouble yourself, Mr. Osmer. I'm sorry to have taken your time."

Osmer leaned toward her, both hands on the counter. "Wait a minute, wait a minute. Can you cook? I mean, do you think you could cook for a bunch of people?"

She smiled. "Cook? Oh, yes! I have a lot of experience with that." For a nice little restaurant, she envisioned, or maybe at the hotel.

"All right, then. Let's go talk to those boys." He nodded toward the figures on the other side of the window. "They're with the Lodestar outfit and they're looking to replace the cook they run off last week." He stepped out from behind the counter.

"Lodestar outfit," Libby echoed hollowly. "You mean a ranch?"

"Yes, ma'am. It's a big spread over near the Musselshell River, one of the few around here that came through the winter in passable shape. Tyler Hollins owns the place. He's due back tomorrow and if there's no one to put three squares on the table, well—" Nort lifted his brows expressively. "He won't be too happy."

"But, uh—they ran off their last cook?" Libby found herself being herded toward the door with Nort Osmer's hand firmly under her elbow.

"Now, don't you fret. They're good boys, most of the time, and they need someone to fix them decent meals. No fancy food, mind you, just lots of it. Cowboying is hard work."

He opened the door to his shop and stepped out on the walk. At the sound of the overhead bell, the three glum men turned. Seeing Libby, once again they yanked off their hats, and watched her with a kind of mystified fascination.

"I believe I've got your problem solved, boys, but you can thank me later." He gestured at the three cowhands and presented them to her. Charlie Ryerson seemed to be about her age; he was the one with the mustache. Noah Bradley, a slightly older man, looked like he was made from hard-tanned leather and bones. Rory Egan had an earnest young face and a light scattering of freckles.

Nort held a hand out toward Libby. "This here is Mrs. Libby Ross, Ben's widow. Old Ben passed away from the pneumonia."

There was a murmur of self-conscious how-do ma'ams.

"Ben Ross is gone?" Noah asked Nort, with sidelong glances at her. He spoke in a hushed voice, as though he were in a museum, and Libby was the exhibit.

"Ben got hitched?" Charlie asked. "Old Ben?"

"Yeah, just before the snows commenced. The

winter was pretty hard on their place. Now Mrs. Ross needs a job for a while and she knows her way around a stove. Ain't that so, ma'am?"

Libby smiled uncertainly into their curious, respectful faces. "Before I came to Montana, I cooked for a family in Chicago."

After a brief exchange of looks among themselves, the men's reticence fell away. Apparently this information elevated her to a professional status. They drew a bit closer and all began talking at once, relating a confused but vehement account of lousy cooking, food poisoning, and the fate of the "potato-head" responsible for sending them all to the bunkhouse for two days.

Charlie winced. "Yeah, we was a pitiful sight, that's for sure. The only reason someone didn't shoot that dadblasted cook is 'cause we was all too puny and weak to get out of our bunks. It wasn't much comfort that he got sick, too."

"See, Mrs. Ross?" Rory spoke up. "We really need someone to take his place. We're not faring too good on our own."

"What about Mrs. Hollins? Can't she help with the cooking?"

The three cowboys shuffled and stammered before Nort said, "There ain't no Mrs. Hollins, ma'am."

"Well, but—" Libby knew she couldn't be picky, but neither was she certain that working for a bunch of cowboys on an isolated ranch was the best choice she could make. And she hated the idea of leaving this scrap of civilization to return to the loneliness of the grasslands.

"Mr. Bradley, is it far to your ranch?" It was hard to tell, since he was so weathered, but Libby could have sworn the lanky man blushed.

"Aw, shoot, ma'am, my pa was Mr. Bradley. You can call me Noah. And the Lodestar's about five or six miles that way." He pointed back over his shoulder toward the northwest.

Five or six miles wasn't nearly as bad as fifteen. And the job was a means to her eventual escape. "Well . . ." she wavered.

"Mr. Hollins is gonna have a flat-out conniption if he comes back and there's no cook," Charlie put in. Libby could barely see his mouth move for the luxuriant brush on his upper lip. "Ma'am, we're powerful sorry to hear about Ben, but we'd be much obliged if you'd help us out."

She looked around at the three expectant faces, then back at Nort Osmer. The shopkeeper nodded his approval.

"I guess we'll be doing each other a favor," she pondered, more to herself than to them. "You need someone to cook for you and I certainly need the work. I don't know how long I'll—" But with this implied acceptance, the rest of her words were drowned in the wild whoops from her new coworkers.

"Come on, ma'am, we've got to get back to the Lodestar. We've got hungry men to feed. Is that your buckboard over there?" Not waiting for her answer, Charlie took her by the elbow with great enthusiasm, practically lifting her feet from the plank sidewalk with each step. "Rory, you ride on ahead and tell Joe we're having supper tonight. Noah, tie your horse to the back of Mrs. Ross's wagon, and climb up there to drive it," he directed.

Before Libby knew it, she was perched on her wagon seat again, where she'd spent the hardest part of the long day. Now, though, Noah sat next to her and took her roan's lines. She had just enough time to wave good-bye to Nort Osmer before the wagon lurched forward and pulled away from his store.

She must have lost her mind, she thought, to be traipsing off into the wilderness again with three men she'd just met, based on the endorsement of a dry goods clerk, whom she'd also just met. Tyler Hollins—what was he like, the owner of the Lodestar ranch? And how would he react when he found a strange woman in his kitchen?

In a moment, the tall, funny buildings of Heavenly were receding behind her. And once more, Libby, with a dozen questions in her mind, found herself heading for an unknown destination and a future that was a complete mystery to her.

Libby shifted on the hard seat, gripping its edge as the buckboard bounced along. Charlie Ryerson led the little contingent. He was the Lodestar's top hand, he'd informed her with a bit of a swagger. Noah sat next to Libby, handling the reins expertly. Overhead the clouds were closing in, and chill gusts ruffled the short buffalo grass growing on either side of the road. She hoped they reached shelter before it started raining.

In her view, it seemed like days ago that she'd set out for Heavenly instead of just this morning. The months of nursing Ben in the confinement of his cabin had been enervating and unpleasant, but not always as physically demanding as the tasks she'd had to perform in the last two days. She tightened her grip on the edge of the seat as the vehicle jounced over a rock.

"Is the ranch much farther, Mr. Brad—um, Noah?"

"We'll be coming to the Lodestar in another mile, ma'am," he replied.

That was a relief, Libby thought. "Tell me about your ranch," she said to the leathery cowhand. "Mr. Osmer said it's a big place."

Noah raised his voice to be heard over the jingle of bridle and horses' hooves. "Well, ma'am, the Lodestar's got about five thousand acres, and about thirty thousand head of cattle grazing on open rangeland. Leastways, we did till this winter. We figure we lost more than three-quarters of the herd."

Five thousand acres, Libby marveled. She didn't know much about vast land measurements like that, but it had to be a lot. And they still had what—about seven thousand cattle? Ben Ross had begun the winter with two hundred cattle, and his ranch consisted of three hundred acres.

"It must take several men to run a place that big," she said.

"Yes'm, there's nigh on to twenny of us helpin' out."

Libby felt her eyes widen. She'd imagined she'd be cooking for maybe eight or ten people. It was a highly worrisome prospect to be stuck out on the emptiness of the prairie with twenty men. Everything about this ranch seemed larger than life. That is, life in Montana as she'd seen it so far.

"Guess you ain't used to cookin' for so many folks," he said, rightly reading part of her thoughts.

She shook her head. "No, the family I worked for had just four people."

"Was it in one of them big dressy houses?" Noah asked. "I seen a few of them when I worked in the Chicago stockyards for a while."

Oh, yes, it had been, she remembered, with

creamy walls and deep carpets. She hadn't seen the main floors very often. Mrs. Brandauer hadn't liked the kitchen help to stray from below stairs, and Libby always followed her edict. Until Wesley . . .

"It was a very nice home," she replied, struggling to keep the emotion out of her voice. It was difficult. If not for Wesley Brandauer, she wouldn't have married Ben. She wouldn't have come to Montana at all.

Suddenly curious about her new employer, Libby asked, "What about Mr. Hollins? Is he easy to work for?"

Noah squinted at the horizon. "Well, he don't like change, that's for sure. That's why me and the boys was so worried about runnin' off that cook."

Libby turned slightly to study Noah's weathered face. The three cowboys had been so persuasive, she hadn't thought to question their authority to hire her. "Do you think my coming to work will be all right with him?"

Noah didn't respond and she wondered if he'd heard her. The only sound was the clopping of the horses' hooves on the rain-softened earth. She was about to repeat her question when he answered. "We just have to hope so, but I couldn't say for certain. Mr. Hollins, he ain't an easy one to figure. He likes to keep to himself. Fact is, I never seen a man so bound to hold other folks at a distance."

Libby looked at the horizon, too, forced to be content this time with both Noah's answer and his ensuing silence. Desperation had driven her from Chicago; she'd had nothing left to lose then, and despite her great hopes for a new start, she'd gained nothing since. Only a job offer that could be withdrawn as soon as Tyler Hollins met her.

Still, this Mr. Hollins didn't sound so bad. When

the cowboys had mentioned their difficult boss, she imagined a man who was fault-finding and impossible to please.

But a man who simply wanted to be left alone sounded like no trouble at all. In fact, Libby thought that would be a real asset.

# Chapter 2

Joe Channing, Lodestar's foreman, was standing in the corral feeding an apple to his favorite horse when Rory Egan galloped into the yard, followed by Charlie Ryerson.

Joe walked over to the split-rail fence and looked at Rory, then at Charlie. "About time you boys got back. What did you do with Noah, lose him in town?"

Rory and Charlie exchanged idiotic grins. "No, he ain't lost," Charlie went on, "but I think we maybe found the answer to our prayers."

Joe watched them suspiciously for a moment, then lifted his hat and resettled it on his head. "Yeah? Well, if you've been tryin' to pray the roof back onto the woodshed, I can tell you it ain't worked yet." The woodshed roof had collapsed during one of the blizzards and Charlie was given the job of repairing it. He hadn't gotten around to that chore yet.

Rory's grin faded slightly and he slid down from his horse. If he'd been expecting a more favorable reaction from Joe, he wasn't getting it.

Charlie crooked one leg around his saddle horn. "I guess we better tell him what we did," he said to Rory.

The youngster turned to look over his shoulder. "I don't think we'll have to."

Just then Noah came through the gateway, driving a slat-sided horse and buckboard that didn't belong to the Lodestar. On the seat with him rode a young woman.

Joe looked at them, then back to Charlie, and scowled. "Charlie, goddamn it—"

"Now, Joe, don't go jumpin' on the wrong idea," the cowboy put in hastily. "She's our new cook."

"New cook, my Aunt Amelia. The last time you pulled some prank like this, Ty just about had my head. That woman goes back to the Big Dipper, or wherever she came from, before sundown."

But Charlie and Rory weren't listening. They had rushed to the girl's side to help her from the wagon. Joe's gaze traveled from the besotted cowhands to the young woman. Well, she didn't look like a saloon girl. Her dress was modest, and she wasn't wearing any paint that he could see. His view was obscured as she disappeared behind the circle of men that was growing by the second.

Joe swore and slammed open the corral gate with the heel of his hand. Tyler wasn't going to like this. Not one little bit.

He stomped toward the group, his strides lengthening with each irritated step. As he approached, the men parted before him like thistledown in the wind.

Charlie lifted his hand as if to forestall him and spoke to the girl. "Here's Mr. Channing now."

Joe raised a brow at the "Mr. Channing" and turned to look at the woman. She lifted large gray eyes to him and whatever angry words he'd planned to say died unspoken.

"Ma'am, Joe Channing is the foreman of this outfit. Joe, this here's Mrs. Libby Ross. We met her in town." Charlie's voice dropped to a whisper, as though she wouldn't hear him. "She's Ben Ross's widow. The winter was hard on them—Ben got carried off with the pneumonia and she needs a job."

Joe swiveled his head to look at her again. That was stunning news. This woman had married old Ben? It sure as hell couldn't have been for his money: he'd been on his last chip for years. Love? Naw. But why else would a young woman marry a man who was run down and nearly old enough to be her grandfather? She herself couldn't be any older than twenty-four or twenty-five. He gaped at Charlie before recovering his reserve.

"She knows how to cook, so we brought her back with us." Charlie's last words were lost in the overriding buzz of comments from the men. They stammered and shuffled in front of her like green schoolboys. Joe had to admit it was good to see a woman on this place again. Her hair was the color of clover honey, red and yellow and light browns all mixed together, and it hung down her back in a thick braid. Her eyes were clear gray, and her skin smooth. But most distracting of all was her faint, guileless smile.

Joe cleared his throat and this time all eyes turned to him. "The day ain't over yet. You men get back to your chores while I talk to Mrs. Ross, here. Rory, you unhitch her horse and take care of him. He looks wore out."

With much hat-tipping and backward glances, the men departed. Noah untied his own horse from the buckboard and Rory scuffed his boots in the dirt as he led her weary animal away.

Joe turned a meaningful glare on Noah and Charlie. "I'll talk to you two later." The pair backed away with great reluctance, pulling their horses with them.

Charlie turned, then over his shoulder he added, "Don't you light into her, Joe. She's a cook, just like I said."

He nodded after them impatiently, then turned to her as he gestured at the house. "Why don't we talk on the porch?"

"All right, Mr. Channing," she replied softly.

How had this woman ended up in a one-saloon town like Heavenly, married to an ailing old man? Joe wondered again. Oh, hell, the West was full of people with sad stories. It would be much easier to send her on her way if he didn't know hers. And send her he would. Tyler Hollins would never allow this woman to disrupt the routine of the Lodestar.

Libby had a feeling of impending doom. She sensed that, for one reason or another, she would not be allowed to stay here. And though she had no desire to stay in Montana any longer than she had to, at this moment in time she had nowhere else to go. Lifting her skirts from the damp earth, she allowed the rangy foreman to guide her across the open yard to the wide front porch.

The ranch house, a big, two-story dwelling, had a rustic look that matched its surroundings. It was built of logs, but they were small and fit together snugly. Along the front edge of the porch were what appeared to have once been flower beds, but Libby was too distracted to give them much notice. The front yard was a ratty tangle of winter-bleached weeds and wild grass that were coming to life in the feeble spring weather. But compared to Ben's shack, it was a grand home.

Settled on the porch swing, she folded her hands

in her lap and looked up at Joe Channing, waiting for him to commence. He was a tall, rawboned man, with a big mustache like Charlie's. Although she suspected that he was probably no older than thirty-two or -three, his dark hair was graying ever so slightly at the temples, as if this hard, unforgiving country and climate had stolen its color. When he spoke, his low, quiet voice rumbled up out of his chest like thunder rolling across a distant valley.

"You'll have to forgive those boys for dragging you out here, ma'am. They don't always use their heads." He leaned against one of the uprights and considered her. "I'm real sorry to hear about Ben. I know he was sickly for a long spell."

It seemed to her that everyone had known that about Ben Ross except her. Although the foreman studied her, he was apparently too polite to ask any questions, and that was fine with her. She didn't want to discuss the details leading to her brief marriage. "Mr. Channing, the men said you need a cook. Is there a problem with my being here?" She hoped he didn't hear the desperation in her voice.

He pulled off a glove and massaged the back of his neck. "Not a problem, exactly. It's just not up to me who gets hired at the Lodestar." She noticed his eyes slide away from her on this last statement.

Maybe if he realized what her skills were, he wouldn't be as hesitant to give her the job. "I really am a very good cook. I worked for a family in Chicago for years. I even have references." Oh, yes, the Brandauers had provided adequate references, on proper stationery. Their bequest to her in exchange for twelve years of her life and a piece of her heart.

Joe lifted his hat and plowed a big hand through his hair. "Excuse me for saying so, ma'am, but maybe you should go back to Chicago. This is rough territory, especially for city-born women."

She clenched her hands in the folds of her skirt. "I can't go anywhere, Mr. Channing, until I earn enough money to buy a ticket. That's why I need a job."

"Do you have kin you could wire for the money?"

Libby shook her head, feeling more distinctly unwelcome with each passing minute. She let her gaze drift across the yard to the empty range beyond. "There is no one else. And I need work." They assessed each other. She was out of options, and apparently, so was the foreman.

Finally, he pushed away from the post and shrugged. "You're welcome to stay, at least until Ty Hollins gets back. The boys probably told you he owns this place, and he'll be along in a day or two. After that, it will be up to him." He glanced down at her and Libby saw a trace of regret in his dark eyes. "It's nothing personal, Mrs. Ross, but I have to tell you straight out that he probably ain't gonna go along with this."

She suppressed a sigh, then straightened and turned to look at the house behind her. "If you'll let me, I'd like to fix supper for you and your men in payment for your hospitality."

He smiled at her, his grin creeping up a bit higher on one side of his face, then stretched out his hand to help her to her feet. "That would be a real pleasure. If an outfit can't feed its cowboys, they'll either leave or shoot the cook."

She couldn't help but smile back. "Then it would seem that keeping them happy is the smart thing to do."

"Come on, I'll show you the kitchen."

He led her down the long porch that ran the length of the house to the kitchen. Libby noted a pair of cattle horns hanging over the door.

Joe ushered her inside. "It's pretty messed up in here," he said apologetically. "The boys were right— the last cook wasn't the best. We haven't helped any, either."

This structure was also made of logs, chinked tightly against the elements. Was *everything* in this wilderness primitive? Libby wondered. She looked around at the clutter of dishes and open sacks of meal and flour. Coffee was scattered on the worktable and a big kettle steamed on the stove top.

"Rory and Dust had to make our coffee this morning. It really ain't their fault they left the place looking like this. I pulled them off this job—we've still got a lot of winter cleanup chores to take care of on the range. There's horses to break, dead cattle to count, roofs to mend. I figured we'd get to this later."

Libby raised her brows at the sight, a little overwhelmed by the clutter. "Yes, I suppose . . ."

"You'll be needing a place to sleep, too. Usually the cooks have stayed with the boys in the bunkhouse. Of course, we can't ask you to do that. You come on this way."

She followed him through the kitchen to a door that, it turned out, opened into the dining room of the main house. As they walked through the house to the stairway, she was astonished by the hominess of the place, despite its roughhewn construction. The touches were definitely masculine, with heavy, leather-upholstered furniture, and big paintings on the walls of range scenes. In the parlor, a huge stone fireplace dominated one wall and was big enough to cook in. But the place looked, well, comfortable, and that surprised her. When they reached the second floor, she realized that its hallway was a gallery that overlooked the parlor.

"This house is a lot bigger than it looks outside," she commented as she followed Joe Channing.

"Tyler's pa built it when they came up from Texas after the war. He cut down every one of the logs himself."

He stopped and opened the door to a large bedroom that had a preserved look, as though it had been waiting in readiness for years, but had remained unused. Lace curtains hung at the windows, and the bed was big. She thought of her third-floor room in Chicago. Located under the roof, it had been ice cold in the winter and like an oven in the summer. And compared to her cot by the stove at Ben's place, this was heaven.

It wasn't until the foreman spoke again that she realized she'd been standing there wide-eyed.

"Will this be all right, Mrs. Ross?"

"Oh, yes." She sighed. "It's just fine."

"Then I'll tell Rory to bring your trunk in for you," he said.

She thanked him and after a moment's awkward silence, he tipped his hat and let himself out. When the door closed behind him, she heard his boot steps in the hall as he walked away. She couldn't help but wish that he was the boss here, and that her immediate future was settled.

After Rory brought her trunk a minute later, she knelt in front of it, and lifted the lid. Her throat tightened momentarily at the faint lavender scent that reminded her of another time and place. She quickly lifted out a long white apron and closed the lid again, pushing the memories back in. Tying the starched cotton around her waist she took a deep breath and went back downstairs.

The kitchen was as roughhewn as the house. The Brandauers, always eager to be the first with the best, had bought a gas stove three years earlier, and Libby was accustomed to the predictability of gas cooking. Now she faced a huge black iron beast that had a low fire banked in its belly. She'd also had an icebox in the Chicago kitchen, but no such convenience would be found here, either. Of course not, she reminded herself as she poked through the shelves, looking for spices. There was no iceman.

Libby stoked the fire in the stove, then inspected the supplies. She peered into big dark bins of rice, flour, beans, sugar, and other staples. Mice had been into most of them, and the flour had turned weevily. The perishables—meat, eggs, and butter—were spoiled. If they had ham or bacon, these were nowhere to be found. Nearly everything bore a film of grease and dust. She shook her head as she wiped her hands on her apron. Whoever had run this kitchen before her had been lazy and very careless; no wonder everyone had come down sick. It would take a lot of hard scrubbing to bring the place up to her standards.

How much food did a person prepare for twenty hungry men? she wondered as she measured the best of the flour. She'd cooked for dinner parties in the past, but the numbers had been smaller, and she'd had help. All she could do was make her best guess. She shrugged and brought out a big enamel bowl and cast-iron skillet. With the salvageable provisions she put together a quick meal of biscuits and a good, peppery gravy. There was no baking powder, only saleratus, and that meant the biscuits would have an alkaline taste. After locating jars of canned cherries, she made three pies. Bacon or sausage would have gone well with all of this but there was nothing more she could do. If she stayed on, this kitchen would have to be stocked decently.

Two hours later, as dusk purpled the valley, she stepped out to the porch intending to ring the iron triangle that called the men to meals. But when she looked up, she saw most of them already waiting along the porch rail. Charlie Ryerson stood at the front of the line, as befitted the top hand. The scent of bay rum drifted to her. Scrubbed and combed like they were going to church, the cowboys stared at her with anticipation.

"It surely smells good, ma'am," Charlie ventured from behind his mustache.

Libby wasn't particularly proud of the results but she raised her voice a bit to be heard by those in the back. It was intimidating to address a group of strange men. "I-I wish I could've fixed something a little more hearty, but I couldn't find any meat in the pantry that wasn't spoiled." She gestured behind her in the general direction of the kitchen. "The best I could do was biscuits and gravy, with cherry pie for dessert."

When they didn't move, Libby felt her cold hands grow icy. Maybe biscuits and gravy weren't acceptable? Mr. Osmer had told her they didn't need fancy food. If she didn't make a good impression on these men, she certainly wouldn't be able to win over Tyler Hollins. Well, there was no helping it now; the supper was cooling on the long tables inside, and it was all she had for them tonight.

"Well, gentlemen, supper is served."

It was as though she'd fired a gun. She jumped out of the way as they stampeded through the door. There was a lot of jostling for seats, and the sounds of bench legs scraping over the plank flooring and tin plates clanking against the silverware. Libby stood in the doorway, her mouth open slightly as she watched the men fall on the food like starving refugees. There was no conversation at the tables; the business of eating took precedence over everything else. But as she passed among them, pouring coffee, nods and bashful smiles were directed at her, and any doubts she may have had about the meal evaporated.

As soon as each man had finished, he left the table. Libby wasn't used to that—where she came from, people lingered after meals, wanting more coffee, more tea, more service. Most of all, she wasn't accustomed to being thanked.

"Much obliged, ma'am. That was a good supper."

"Thanks, Mrs. Ross."

"I ain't had cherry pie since I can't remember."

By the time Libby sat down with her own biscuits and gravy, she was almost too tired to eat. With the plate in front of her, she stopped to massage the back of her neck and rub her temples. Even her braid felt heavy resting on her back. She swore this had been the longest day of her life, and she still had dishes to wash. Cleaning the kitchen itself would have to wait until tomorrow.

Just then, the door opened and Joe Channing walked in. He hadn't been part of the original rush of diners, but had come in later.

"Thanks again for supper, Mrs. Ross. You did a fine job on such short notice."

Libby never thought of herself as Mrs. Ross. It was

hard enough for her to remember to introduce herself with that last name instead of Garrison. The only other name she'd ever imagined for herself was Brandauer. "You can call me, Libby, Mr. Channing."

"I'll do that ma'am, uh, Miss Libby, if you'll call me Joe."

She gave him a tired smile. "All right, Joe."

Later that night, Libby lay in the big bed upstairs. She was bone weary but sleep wouldn't come. Until last summer, her life had had a relentless sameness. She hadn't been happy, but there had been security in the monotony, knowing that today would be the same as yesterday, the same as tomorrow. Then Mrs. Brandauer had discovered the secret of Wesley and her.

That had led her to Ben Ross's shack, and the horrible months that followed. Now she slept under a strange roof that belonged to a man she hadn't met, a man who might put her out on the road as soon as he returned.

She pulled the linen sheet closer to her chin and closed her eyes, hoping she wouldn't see Ben's shroud in her dreams.

It was almost midnight when Tyler Hollins pushed through the swinging doors of the Big Dipper Saloon, tired, saddle-sore, and dirty. A few late-night customers lingered in the smoky retreat, and a listless card game was underway at one table. The primary goals on his mind were a beer and a bed. He got his beer and settled at the corner table, crossing his ankle over his knee.

"By God, Ty, you look good enough to eat," Callie Michaels called across the room. Callie owned the saloon and she considered him to be one of her special customers. She made her way to him, her rust-colored hair shining like a dark penny under the kerosene lamps, her hips swaying in her garnet dress. Unhooking his ankle, she wiggled into his dusty lap.

She snaked an alabaster arm around his neck and leaned toward his ear to be heard over the clanking piano. "How about if we tell the rest of these bums good night and go upstairs for a midnight snack?"

He chuckled. No one could accuse her of being shy. "You're a shameless female, Callie, but that's part of your charm."

"I'd say it's about half," she replied, and looked him over with a gaze of candid appreciation. "It's good to have you back—things just aren't the same when you're gone. You give those gals in Miles City a sample of *your* charm?"

"You aren't going to start getting jealous after all this time, are you?" he asked, going along with the game. She had a smile that unsettled some people and, in fact, had once unsettled him. It made her look as though she had a secret that no one else knew. Hell, maybe she did.

She waved a smooth, white hand in a dismissing gesture. "Me? No, sir. But I know your habits, and I just got to wondering if you strayed from them when you're away from home."

He bounced her once on his knee. "The only thing I did in Miles City was sit through a lot of meetings with cattle buyers. I'm dead tired and I want to go to bed."

Her whiskey-colored eyes darkened with promised sensuality and she rubbed a breast against his shoulder. "Well then, come on, Ty. Let's go up to my room."

On another night he might have. His relationship with Callie was straightforward and uncomplicated, just the way he wanted it. She satisfied his physical needs and appeared pleased with his ability to do the same for her, and with the twenty dollars he gave her. But it was late and he was too tired for the amount of energy she burned up.

Suddenly, nothing was more appealing than getting back to the private solitude of the ranch. He'd been gone less than two weeks but it felt like an eternity, and something in his soul was left wanting by his absence. He reached for his beer and drained it.

"Next time, honey. Tonight you'd probably kill me." He patted her backside to move her off his lap.

Pouting in her disappointment, she stood slowly and raked his form with a sultry gaze. Running a hand over her hip, she gave him a slow smile. "But, darlin', can you think of a better way to leave this life?"

He laughed then and shook his head. Walking to the doors, he threw a good night to her over his shoulder.

It was five miles to the house and only a half-moon lit the way, but Tyler and his pinto knew every inch of the wagon-rutted road.

When he cleared the last rise, he reined in his horse and looked at his home. The meetings in Miles City left him feeling like vultures had picked at his bones. The buyers were eager to take advantage of the winter-borne disaster that had befallen cattlemen all over the Great Plains. At the railhead in Miles City they were calling it the Big Die-up, and the cigar-smoking opportunists knew it. A couple of times, he'd almost walked away from them. He'd wanted nothing more than to get back on his horse and come home. But he'd known he couldn't do that; he needed fast cash to rebuild the herds. So he'd hidden his anger and tempered his pride, and he'd agreed to the piddling offers. Because this land spread out before him made it all worth it.

His hands braced on the pommel, he leaned forward slightly in his saddle. As far as his vision could reach, the grass lay frosted in moonlight, accented with lingering traces of snow. The house and outbuildings were quiet in the midnight hush. This belonged to him. He was its master; he was its son.

It was hard for him to believe now that he'd once walked away from it. That only a promise made to his father in the last hours of his life had brought him back to stay. But that had been a long time ago. Tyler had been young and idealistic then, with no experience to make him value what he already had. He'd also had no idea of the grief that lay ahead.

He urged the horse forward, down the slope to the last quarter mile home. The ranch slept, but he was met by his dog, Sam, who gave one loud bark in greeting. Sam's tail wagged with joy that shook his entire length.

Ty got off his horse and patted the front of his shirt. The delighted dog stood to put his two huge forefeet on his master's chest. He laughed at the canine smile, then pulled his head back as his dog's tongue lapped at his chin. "Okay, Sam, that's enough. I can get my own bath."

After he unsaddled the pinto, fed him, and turned him loose in the paddock, Ty went to the kitchen for a piece of soap and bucket of warm water from the reservoir on the stove. Standing on the back porch, he was filled with the contentment of homecoming. The only sound was the wind sighing through the miles of rich grassland that surrounded him on this landlocked island he loved.

He pulled off his clothes, then lifted the bucket and poured some water over his head to rinse off the travel dirt. The breeze that stirred the grass felt like a winter gust on his wet skin. Shivering, he hurried with his makeshift bath. He hadn't remembered to get a towel and he looked inside the kitchen door for one. What he found instead was a white apron on a hook by the stove and he dried himself off with that.

A delicate scent whispered to him, giving rise to a fleeting memory of windblown sheets flapping on a clothesline. A face he hadn't seen in years flashed through his mind, then was gone. Puzzled, he decided the fragrance must be Callie's perfume on his shirt. He picked up his clothes off the porch rail and padded naked through the kitchen to the stairway. He didn't bother with a candle. He knew there would be enough moonlight coming through the hall window to let him find his bed.

When he came up to his room and fell on the big four-poster, he only had time to pull a corner of the quilt over himself before he was asleep.

Libby Ross carefully closed her door and tiptoed back to her bed. Sitting on the edge of the mattress, she put her hands to her hot face.

Being a stranger in the house, and thus alert to every sound, she'd heard the dog bark outside and a noise in the kitchen. When she detected the quiet creaking on the stairs, with her heart stuck in her throat she got up and opened her door a crack to peek into the hallway.

She was unprepared for the sight of the long-muscled, naked man who passed her room and went into the one next to hers. An oblong shaft of moonlight fell across his lean body, leaving his face in the shadows.

But she had no doubt as to his identity.

# Chapter 3

Ty rolled over and burrowed into the feather mattress, pulling the quilt with him. His eyes still closed, he was caught in the comfortable void between sleep and wakefulness that is sometimes more satisfying than sleep itself. He knew he was back in his own bed, and after ten days of hard travel and rented rooms, it was sweet luxury he could have wallowed in for hours. But responsibility prodded him, forcing him to full consciousness. He trusted Joe to keep the operation running in his absence but there was so much to be done, and he knew human nature made the men slack off if he wasn't around. He needed to see what had happened while he was gone.

Shoving back the quilt, he sat up in the chill blackness and scratched the stubble on his jaw. The suggestion of a fragrance drifted past him again, as subtle as a memory. It faded so quickly he wondered if he'd dreamed it. Shaking off the feeling, he groped around the big bedroom in the last few minutes of night and found his clothes.

A crimson ribbon of light edged the eastern horizon when he pulled open his bedroom door and walked out to the gallery and down to the kitchen. Intent on meeting with Joe before breakfast, he headed down the passageway toward the stairs, his thoughts on cattle and branding.

Ranching was a hard life in the best of times, but this year they really had their work cut out for them, he thought grimly. After a summer of drought and the worst winter on record, spring had brought with it one heavy rain after another. Even now, somewhere on the open range his thin, spent cattle might be drifting if the crew hadn't rounded them up yet. The ones that had survived, he added to himself.

On his way out, the smell of perking coffee tempted him, and he decided to stop for a cup. The boys grumbled that they couldn't tell the difference between what the cook was giving them and what he threw to the hogs, but if he got the coffee going first thing, Tyler saw that as a saving grace. His hand was on the doorknob to the kitchen when it was yanked out of his grip, and a woman stepped into his path.

Libby had a jumbled impression of a tall, slender man with brown hair just as he crashed into her. He reached out and gripped her arms to keep her from falling. She was startled, but he looked shocked. He stared at her as though she'd dropped in through the roof.

Even without benefit of introduction, Libby knew this was Tyler Hollins. He stood glaring at her, his frame stiff. Obviously caught off guard, he was just as obviously trying to conceal that fact.

He broke the physical contact with decisive speed. Stepping back, he demanded, "Who the hell are you and what are you doing in my house?"

After the diligent politeness of Joe Channing and the other cowboys, she was stunned by his lack of manners, and by the coldness in his blue eyes. "I-

I'm Liberty Ross. Mr. Channing hired me to cook. You're Mr. Hollins?" It was all she could do to look him in the face after seeing him naked, and carrying his clothes and boots down the dark hall last night. She felt her cheeks grow warm again.

He ignored the question and raised his hand as if to stop any others. "Wait a minute, what do you mean Mr. Channing hired you to cook? We already have a cook."

His indignation was palpable. She lifted her hand to rest it at the base of her throat. With that unnerving blue glare fixed on her, she began to babble. "W-well, you did but your men ran him off."

"What the hell for?"

"It was food poisoning, they said."

For a long moment he said nothing. Then he swore, once, the single word blunt and baldly stated. He half turned from her, looking away, his mouth tight.

Libby flinched at both the word and the low, fierce intensity with which he said it. How could her presence provoke such a response? Nothing of the sketchy information she'd heard about him prepared her for this. "I'm sorry. I'm sure it's a surprise to find a complete stranger in—"

"You can't stay." He started to brush past her, his tone ending the matter. "I don't know why Joe thought I'd go along with this."

"But I have experience, and letters of reference from a family in Chicago—"

"You don't have experience with ranching. The Lodestar is no place for a woman anyway, and if Joe didn't tell you that, I'm telling you."

Libby stepped back against the wall to avoid being shouldered out of the way. She felt a bite of anger at the man's hostility. He was behaving as if he'd caught her trying to steal the silverware.

Her gaze followed him, taking in the powerful stretch of his shoulders. Watching his angry strides carry him to the front door, she thought of yesterday's optimism when she'd believed this might be a good place to work.

She didn't know what to do next. If she was going to feed the hands this morning, she'd have to start now. "There's no one to cook breakfast for your men," she called after him. "You wouldn't want them to starve, would you?"

"It's physically impossible for a healthy human to starve to death because of one missed meal," he threw back without turning. "You get your belongings together. I'll have someone drive you to town within a half hour."

When he reached the front door he turned back to her abruptly. He actually saw her for the first time then, and inspected her from hair to hem in one lingering, assessing glance. The sensation that followed this scrutiny moved through her like a low vibration. It made her uncomfortably warm although she couldn't say why. But she did know the man was obnoxious.

With a last look, he turned from her. His heavy footsteps took him out the door and into the gray dawn.

Found guilty of an unnamed crime, Libby was helpless to defend herself. And she had no grounds on which to build a case to make Mr. Hollins let her stay. She turned back to her room to collect her things.

She'd come to Heavenly, hoping for a new start, for a home and a family of her own; for children

and a good place to raise them. A place to *belong*.
Ben Ross had promised all that and more to her to
get her to come west.

Now what, now what? she asked herself frantically
as she scooped up her hairbrush and comb from the
dresser top with shaking hands. After she spent what
little money she had on a hotel room and food, what
would she do? She could pound on every door in
Heavenly and ask for a job, but if no one would
hire her—

She envisioned knocking on the door of last resort,
and as she did, tears threatened behind her eyelids.
On that door, in her mind's eye she read the gilded
letters: BIG DIPPER.

No, she wouldn't do it, she thought, her hand
clenched in a fist at her bosom. Not if she had to
sleep in her wagon by the side of the road and steal
food. No one would ever make her feel cheap again.

"Joe!"
From the bunkhouse, Joe Channing heard the
shout and winced. At the sound, the eyes of the men
around him grew wide. Mr. Hollins usually maintained an icy control and that was intimidating
enough. But at those rare times when he lost his
temper it seemed as though the jaws of hell opened,
ready to swallow anyone with the bad luck to be
nearby. Of course, he chewed them some first.

Charlie paused, one boot on, the other in his
hand. He looked at Joe as though he didn't expect
to see him ever again. "I reckon Mr. Hollins is
home," he said. It sounded like a farewell.

Joe nodded with a sigh. Damn, Ty was back early
and by the sound of it, he'd discovered their new
cook. He'd hoped to work up to the story, to get

Ty used to the idea of Libby Ross, but any chance for that had just gone up in flames. He stuffed his shirttails into his jeans and went out to face the furious owner of the Lodestar.

Tyler was pacing back and forth in front of the porch, his hands jammed in his pockets, shoulders hunched, head down. The gray dawn was cold but he wore no coat, and his breath made vaporous clouds.

When Joe reached Ty the air around him nearly crackled with his wrath. "I guess you met Miss Libby."

Tyler stopped his marching on the last turn and stood in front of his foreman. "I'd like to know why I can't go away for a few days without coming home to find a strange woman in my house. A woman who tells me she's the new cook that Mr. Channing hired. Why is that, Joe?"

Joe remained calm and low-voiced in the face of Ty's question, then explained how Libby had come to be there.

"I don't care what the situation was. I won't have her in the house."

"For chrissakes, Tyler, what was I supposed to do?" Joe asked. "Night was coming on, she was all alone. I couldn't very well put her out on the road. She's Ben Ross's widow and I figured you'd—"

Ty cut him off. "Damn it, Joe, I want her out of my house and on her way."

Joe shifted his weight to his other hip. Even though this is what he'd expected from Tyler, he'd *hoped* for more tolerance. But when a man got his hopes mixed up with his expectations, the usual result was disappointment. Joe missed the open, easygoing man who'd been his friend.

He shrugged. "She's got nowhere to go, Ty. No family, no job, nothing."

"Then give her enough money to last her awhile. I'm not running a home for females in distress." He threw out his hands to emphasize the simplicity of his wishes. "I don't want her here. I don't like depending on women. You know that."

"Who's gonna cook for us when she's gone?"

Tyler looked at him as though he'd asked what day of the week Saturday falls on. "Well, hire another cook, Joe. I count on you to handle these things."

Joe's patience was evaporating. "It'll be nigh on to impossible to find someone this season, Ty. After last winter, just about everybody who could went west to Oregon, and south to the spreads in Nevada and Colorado. We did the best we could to get along on our own but these men don't know anything about food except how to eat it. And if we can't give them decent meals, they'll move on, too, and *you* know that."

"And am I supposed to bring her along on the trail drive, too?" Tyler inquired with obvious exasperation. "Fifteen men and one city woman out on the prairie with a thousand cattle? The first time she sees a snake she'll probably hide in the chuck wagon and refuse to come out."

Joe gestured toward the house. "I think Miss Libby is a lot tougher than that, Ty. Anyway, she cooked for us last night and even on short notice it was the best supper I've had in a long time. At least let her stay while we try to find someone to do the job."

The muscles along Tyler's jaw tightened and Joe knew he was battling with his urge to be rid of Libby

Ross right now, no matter what. In the end, practicality won out.

"All right, damn it! She can stay till the drive starts in two or three weeks, but after that I want her gone whether you find someone else or not." Ty turned on his heel and stalked back into the house, leaving Joe feeling like he'd just spent a whole day being pummeled by an especially stubborn bronco.

Upstairs, Libby pushed her trunk to the gallery and closed the bedroom door softly behind her. Adjusting her jacket, she tried to formulate a plan as she reviewed her assets. But she came up with mostly liabilities. She was a lone woman in a vast, wild country where man or nature could harm her, or destroy her, with a swift, uncaring stroke. Tyler Hollins might be an ogre but she'd been relieved just to hope that she had a place here. She was pulling on her dusty gloves when she heard her name.

"You, there—Mrs. Ross," he called brusquely.

Libby peered over the railing and saw him standing in the parlor below. He was looking up at her, his face still a mask of frustration.

"Those men need to eat and I don't have any choice but to keep you here for the time being. So get some breakfast going." He stormed away, his boots thundering as he went out the front door again.

The heel! The lowdown cad! Libby nearly strangled with indignation. She raised her skirts and swiftly descended the stairs. Her feet were carrying her to the door to search for him, to tell him what he could do with his graceless demand, when the cold hand of reason stopped her. He had no choice? She had less than no choice. At this moment in her life she was without options, money, or friends. And as rude and unpleasant as he was, having shelter and food was better than sleeping in her wagon.

"Tyler's bark is worse than his bite."

She jumped and saw Joe Channing standing in the doorway. The rawboned foreman walked in and pulled his hat off, giving her a quiet smile. His politeness was a comforting contrast, but his eyes revealed him to be a poor liar.

"I think you're fibbing, Mr. Channing. I would guess that Mr. Hollins's bark is only a sample of his bite," she retorted.

He smiled again, looking sheepish. "Well, ma'am, not every time," he demurred in his low, rumbling voice. "At least it didn't used to be that way."

Libby was still too busy smarting from Hollins's sharp tongue to wonder what that meant.

"Tyler said you have a job here until we leave for the trail drive to Miles City. The boys'll sure be glad about it. After that, we'll have to play it by ear. He wants me to find someone else to do the cookin', but I know I won't be able to."

Libby wasn't sure if that was good news or not.

"Do you think you could cook out of a chuck wagon, if you had to?"

"Well, I don't—I've never—" Cook in a wagon?

He tipped a look at her that was almost a smile. "The job pays the same as a top hand makes: room and board, and twenty-five dollars a month. The crew draws their wages at the end of the season."

She gaped at him. Twenty-five dollars! Mrs. Brandauer had paid her only room and board, and two dollars a month. At Christmas, she'd received a bar of perfumed soap, or maybe a linen handkerchief.

She had expected Tyler Hollins to be aloof. She

hadn't expected to find him so unlikable. But for that kind of money, she'd figure out a way to manage.

"I've never worked outside of a kitchen, Mr. Channing, but I can certainly learn."

Libby hurriedly flattened out more biscuit dough with a rolling pin while keeping her eye on the simmering gravy she'd concocted from the last of the bacon drippings. Her confrontation with Mr. Hollins had left her badly shaken, but right now, she was too busy to give it much thought.

Though she'd been exhausted, the night passed fitfully for her. Thinking about what she'd seen in the moonlit hall had churned in her brain. After that, apprehension about today, the strange surroundings, and her memories would not let her sleep. Her apprehension, it appeared, had not been unfounded.

She wasn't unaccustomed, though, to getting up in the dark, long before the rest of the household was awake. The chief difference in the Brandauer home was that the family had rarely stirred before eight o'clock. At the Lodestar everyone rose just shortly after she did and worked until she called them to eat.

Considering the fact that twelve men sat in the kitchen behind her, except for the steady clink of silver on the tin plates, she found it surprisingly quiet. If they'd eaten quickly last night, this morning they practically inhaled their food. The first shift had had their breakfast just twenty minutes before and were already hard at work on the western range.

Though she was kept busy pulling hot biscuits from the big oven, stirring gravy, and pouring coffee, she was very aware of the absence of one man.

"Doesn't Mr. Hollins eat breakfast?" Libby asked

when she stopped at Rory's place to fill his coffee cup. The boy turned bright red, and she felt sorry for so embarrassing him. In his haste to answer he gulped down a mouthful of biscuit nearly whole. She swore she could see the big unchewed lump as it went down his throat.

"Oh, yes, ma'am, Miss Libby," he said, tipping his face up to look at her. "But he always takes his meals in the dining room." Rory inclined his head toward the closed door that separated the kitchen from the rest of the house. Her eyes followed the direction he indicated.

Did that mean she was supposed to serve his food to him in there? She imagined him sitting at the table on the other side of this door, waiting impatiently for her to bring him a plate.

"Oh, dear," she murmured, feeling no enthusiasm. "I'd better get him something—"

Rory shook his russet head emphatically. "No, ma'am, no need to do that. Tyler doesn't like to be fussed over. He'll be along when he's ready."

"Oh, but are you sure?" He was already unhappy with her presence. If she didn't perform as he expected, or wanted, it was plain that he'd have her delivered to Heavenly on a moment's notice.

She glanced around at the other men sitting nearby, who'd paused for a moment at the mention of Hollins, their forks and their jaws stilled. It certainly wasn't fear she saw in their faces, but a kind of respectful wariness.

"Mr. Hollins ain't usually much for socializin', Mrs. Ross," one of the men added.

She noted that only Joe and Rory referred to their boss by his first name.

"I saw him out in the barn, lookin' after a new

filly that come while he was gone," Charlie put in. "Most likely, he's still out there. Or maybe in his office." He mopped up gravy with a tender biscuit half and swallowed it almost as quickly as Rory had.

She stood back in amazement, gripping the coffee-pot. It couldn't be good for a body's digestion to gobble food that fast. But they were all doing it. And it seemed that no sooner had the men sat down than Joe Channing was in the doorway, hurrying them out again.

"Let's go, boys. We got work to do around here. That trail drive is comin' soon," Joe said in his low voice. He turned to his top hand. "Charlie, you and Kansas Bob are taking the Cooper boys to the north range to finish cutting out our brand, right?" Kansas Bob Wegner was a slim, rosy-faced young man with wheat-colored hair and, as with most of the others, Libby guessed him to be around twenty. The Cooper brothers had already eaten during the first shift, and were outside saddling their horses.

Charlie stood and drank the rest of his coffee in one swallow, looking morose. "I wish I could send someone in my place, and that's the truth of it. I swear I never seen so many dead cattle in my life as I did on the southern roundups."

"On your way back, you boys might as well bring in the last of those mustangs we turned loose last fall. Rory, you know what you're doing today," the foreman continued.

With a long-suffering sigh, the youth nodded and got to his feet. "Yeah, I know. How long am I gonna have to chase down bogged strays, Joe? That's a greenhorn's job. I'd rather go north with Charlie and Kansas Bob."

"No, you wouldn't, Sass. This ain't a basket social

we're goin' on," Charlie advised him. "Those rotting carcasses stink to heaven on high, and on that last roundup we only found six head of our own. The rest was dead or belonged to the other outfits. And they didn't find much neither. Anyways, most of the cows are so puny, they can't make the walk back. It's a good thing we rounded up our brand early so they could fatten up for the drive to Miles City."

Joe resettled his hat and slapped his gloves against his chaps. "We got to go look just the same. With the herd cut down to a few thousand head, we're lucky to all be working—some of the spreads turned out most of their crews. Tyler wouldn't do that. Besides, I expect you'll be back in just a couple-three days."

"Well, I don't aim to spend any more time on that north range than I can help."

"That's good, Charlie," Joe said, giving him a lopsided smile. "The woodshed still needs a roof."

"Aw, where else could you get a top hand who's a carpenter, too?" Charlie asked.

Joe laughed and shooed him out. "The rest of you boys, off to the southwest line."

Spurs jingled and the bench legs scraped noisily on the plank floor as the men hurried to their feet, some grabbing their hats, others gulping a last taste of coffee. They filed past Libby, shyly murmuring more thank-yous, or touching their hat brims.

Charlie's mouth moved in what she guessed was a smile behind his mustache. "Got to head out, Mrs. Ross. We're losin' daylight. But we'll be back for one of your suppers as soon as we can, maybe tomorrow night."

Libby couldn't help but smile back at him. He was definitely full of himself, but in a sweet-natured,

harmless way. She followed them out to the yard
and waved, watching them ride toward the wide valley under a heavy, pewter-gray sky. The horses blew
steamy clouds in the mist, and the sound of their
hooves was muffled by the newly green, rain-soft
earth. She found herself riveted by the scene. This
was very much different from the clatter of traffic
on the streets in Chicago. Different, too, from the
ceaseless howl of an arctic wind whistling around the
corners of a cold, rough cabin, punctuated only by
a hacking, gurgling cough—

She shuddered at the memory, then turned and
let her eyes scan the dirty kitchen. She'd managed
to clean a corner of it last night, but the complete
scrubbing that it needed would have to wait just a
little longer. The more immediate problem was food.

Charlie had mentioned supper but she didn't even
know what she was going to cook for the noon meal.
After serving a breakfast of more biscuits and gravy,
she needed supplies right away. There was nothing
left to eat.

Much as she'd rather not, she knew she'd have to
talk to Tyler Hollins about it. She leaned out the
open back door and glanced around the yard, looking for a tall man who resembled the owner of the
Lodestar. But she saw only the retreating rumps of
the dozen horses heading across the yard. Their
hooves churned up the sucking mud, and all of their
riders appeared tall from this angle and distance.

Suddenly the door to the dining room swung
open, making Libby jump, and Hollins walked in.
He gave her a double glance, as though he'd forgotten she was there. Then he nodded at her. He was
long-legged and lean, and while Libby knew next to
nothing about cowboys, or cows for that matter, it

was plain to her that he'd been born to this occupation. He looked as though he'd spent his entire life in a saddle. He wore chaps over his jeans, and a plain gray shirt topped with a leather vest. A dark bandanna was tied in a loose knot at the back of his neck, the long tails of which trailed over one shoulder. He was dressed pretty much the same as the men who worked for him, with one chief difference: on his left hip there rested a holster that sheathed a long-barreled pistol. It looked like he had the gun on backward—the butt faced forward. And he seemed even bigger than when she'd seen him earlier.

In Libby's narrow world in Chicago, she'd rarely seen anyone wear a gun except a policeman or a soldier. Her eyes fell to it again, and the dull blue gleam of the trigger was vaguely threatening.

Picking up a clean plate, he went to the stove. He put three warm biscuits on his dish, and ladled gravy over them with her big cooking spoon.

"This could probably save the crew from starving to death," he said, not lifting his eyes to regard her. He poured coffee for himself from the big blue enamel pot, and took a tentative sip.

Libby wasn't positive, but she thought he sounded a bit less antagonistic. Maybe it was a promising sign. Lacing her fingers together in front of her apron, she took a deep breath.

"Mr. Hollins, there are no provisions left. I need to go to town and restock the pantry, or I won't even be able to cook lunch for the men."

He looked around at the empty shelves, and then at her. His eyes were agate blue, intense in their shading and expression, and she couldn't help but study him. The color of his hair reminded her of the glossy red-brown chestnuts that grew on the trees in the Brandauer yard. It was long on top and waved just slightly where it grazed his ears. She guessed him to be about the same age as Joe Channing, although two faint vertical lines already etched the space between his brows. Probably from continuous frowning, by the looks of him. He had a firm jaw and a long slim nose that was positioned over a nicely shaped mouth. And, in a land where huge mustaches seemed to be a requirement of the male uniform, his upper lip was very noticeably bare. His features were strong, even handsome, she conceded. But his was not an open face—there was a remoteness in his eyes, a separateness perhaps—and nothing about him suggested a man who was approachable.

He sat on the edge of the worktable and crossed his ankles while he ate from the plate in his hand. "Yeah, Joe told me we're down to bread and water. Well, you'd better ask him what to buy, and how much," he said, breaking off a piece of biscuit and popping it into his mouth. Upon tasting it, he lifted a brow in faint appreciation, then he took a bigger bite.

But by his very tone he made it clear he didn't think she had much experience with this. Fear of another of his outbursts made her defensive and put an edge on her voice. "I don't need to ask, Mr. Hollins. I used to order food from the grocer every day in Chicago, and I bought vegetables, bread, milk, and butter from the street vendors." Libby drew herself up a little taller, and even allowed the tip of her nose to rise just a bit. She may have been riddled with doubt and regret since the day she'd arrived in Montana, but cooking was one thing about which she felt no uncertainty. "I know everything there is to know about stocking and managing a kitchen, Mr. Hollins. I did it for years before I—"

"Everything, huh?" he interrupted, and pushed away from the table. "Street vendors don't come by very often around here, so we have to buy enough to last for a while."

"Yes, I'm sure that's true—"

"And we don't have much use for French pastry or burgundy wine."

"Maybe not, but—

"Tell me," he interjected, "did you argue this much with your last employer?"

That took Libby aback. No, she would never have dreamed of saying much of anything to Mrs. Brandauer beyond "Yes, ma'am," and "No, ma'am." But that seemed a lifetime ago now, and something about this man standing before her made her forget that she worked for him. His attitude challenged her to respond.

"Well, um . . ."

He went on eating, never taking his eyes off her. "How much tobacco are you planning to get? And kerosene?"

"What?" She blinked.

"What about beans, and dried fruit?" He gave her a knowing look and put his empty plate on the table. "Come on, Mrs. Ross," he commanded.

He turned and walked back through the doorway to the dining room, never once checking to see if she followed. She had to move fast to keep up; his strides were long, and his spurs rang as he crossed the floor. They passed through the parlor to a closed door at the end of the house. When he flung open the door, she saw a room that contained a big rolltop desk, a long table, and lots of empty glass-fronted cabinets. The scent of wood from the peeled log walls was especially strong here, as though the room was often closed up.

Libby stood back as he opened the desk to reveal pigeonholes stuffed with papers that appeared to have no organization. But without hesitation, he reached for one page in particular and put it in her hands.

"That, Mrs. Ross, is what we typically buy when we stock provisions around here."

He'd handed her a receipt from Osmer's Dry Goods. The items and quantities listed there, written with a careless hand in brown ink, staggered Libby. Yes, there was tobacco: thirty pounds of plug and ten pounds of rolling tobacco. And a lot of other—*equipment* was the description that came to her mind: three Colt revolvers and fifteen boxes of cartridges, a roll of rope, twenty boxes of matches, one hundred pounds of soap, and ten gallons of kerosene. But where was the food? she wondered. Oh, there—one hundred pounds of sugar, ten tins of Arbuckle coffee, five hundred—*five hundred*—pounds of bacon and salt pork, five gallons of molasses, three hundred pounds of flour, two hundred pounds of beans, forty pounds of dried apples, two boxes of soda, a box of pepper, and a bag of salt. Civilized people didn't eat like this. What on earth could she make of salt pork? It wouldn't surprise her if they expected her to mix the tobacco with it and create some kind of dreadful stew.

"My goodness," she breathed.

"Not the same as cooking for a family in Chicago?" he inquired, his arms folded over his wide chest. He wore a smug expression that made Libby feel two feet tall.

"My wagon won't hold all this." She gestured feebly at the list.

"Not if it's that wobbly wreck I saw out by the barn, it won't. I don't know how you got this far with it."

"Then I suppose you might have something else I can take to Heavenly? If I'm going to go, I'd better get started. Maybe you could just harness the horse for me—"

He looked at her as though she'd lost her mind. "You're not going alone." The flat statement hung between them.

"Well, yes, I am. It's part of my job to stock the kitchen. Everyone else is busy." Libby twiddled with her collar button, wondering why he found that odd. He so obviously expected all the men to do their part, and she meant to do hers.

He lifted his brows and looked exasperated again. "Mrs. Ross, in the first place, the wagon I'm thinking of needs a team of four horses to pull it. You'll have to get one of the boys to drive you. Secondly, even if you were going to Heavenly just to buy hairpins, someone from the Lodestar would go with you. I won't allow a woman to go anywhere alone around here, especially a city-bred woman."

He said "city-bred" in a way that made it sound as though she wouldn't even have the wits to come in from a rainstorm. "Whyever not? I drove to town by myself from Ben's place, and that was sixteen miles from Heavenly. And anyway, all of your men are—"

He closed up the desk with a soft thud. "Luck got you there, not skill. And you weren't my responsibility then. But you are now, and will be as long as you're at the Lodestar."

His responsibility? She'd left Chicago, heartbroken and disgraced, had traveled thirteen hundred hard miles, survived the horrible winter with Ben, watched him die in that tiny cabin, and buried him by herself. No one had been responsible for her then, or really even worried about what happened to her. She wasn't going to let this man treat her like a helpless child now. "You are *not* responsible for me, Mr. Hollins. I can take care of myself. Besides, there's no one—"

He gave her a look of absolute authority, and his words dropped to a decisive tone. "I am responsible for everyone and everything on this place, from the smallest calf on up to you and Rory and Joe. And that's *my* job, Mrs. Ross—" Libby winced. "What's the matter?" he snapped, seeing her expression.

The impatient note in his voice was intimidating, but she braved it through. "Mr. Hollins, really, I wish everyone here would just call me Libby."

He stared at her, then combed his fingers through his chestnut hair. Just briefly, his autocratic confidence slipped and he seemed almost self-conscious.

"Well, uh—Lib— No, let's just leave things as they are, Mrs. Ross."

She felt her ears and cheeks burn with embarrassment. Certainly, he was right, she thought. Better that they remain as formal as possible. But she wasn't used to it, and oh how she wished her name was still Garrison. It would be again, she promised herself, just as soon as she left Montana.

He gestured at the receipt she still held. "Get what's on that list, and anything else you think you'll need. Nort Osmer will add it all to the Lodestar account. Now go ask Joe to have someone hitch the wagon and take you to town."

"Mr. Hollins, I've been trying to tell you that they've gone, all your men. I watched them ride away just a few minutes ago. I believe I heard Joe say they were going somewhere he called the southwest line. And Charlie went someplace else with three of the others."

"Damn it, that's right," he groused. "The north range." He let out an exasperated sigh and looked around the office, as though he might find a way out of this predicament in the log walls. Finally he brought his eyes back to her.

"Well, saddle up, Mrs. Ross. We're going to Heavenly."

# Chapter 4

Tyler and Libby jounced along without speaking, following the rutted road that led to Heavenly. The silence was broken only by the rattling wagon, and the jingle of harness. The low clouds lifted a bit as the morning and miles passed. But the wind, blowing down from Canada, still held a piercing chill.

Tyler maintained a firm grip on the lines of the four horses, but his mind kept straying to the woman sitting next to him on the narrow seat. It was impossible to ignore her when they kept bumping thighs and hips and knees.

He was accustomed to dealing with the vagaries of nature, from bad weather to the unpredictability of cattle and horses, and everything in between. But to come home and find a *woman* in his house? He felt like he'd been poleaxed. Worse still, it looked like he was stuck with her for a couple of weeks, probably until Joe found someone else to cook for them, both at the ranch and on the drive. But even a week or two would be too long. And she wanted to be called by her first name? Absolutely not. At least, *he* wouldn't do it. That was her first step in establishing herself permanently in the kitchen, and he wasn't about to allow that. His life was arranged precisely as he wanted it, with his privacy and routine intact. The last thing he'd welcome was someone to disrupt it. Or worse, to change it.

The Lodestar was no place for a woman anyway, he reiterated to himself, shrugging deeper into his sheepskin coat. Who could know that better than he did? This one was city-bred, to boot; soft and delicate, and not accustomed to the everyday hardships of life on the frontier. He let a sidelong glance slide to her again. She was small and fine boned, and she sat on that wagon seat like she had a broom handle for a backbone. With both feet planted together firmly on the floorboards, she'd tucked her gray-striped skirt under her to keep it from billowing. Her head was protected from the biting wind by only a thin wool shawl, and her gloves were carefully mended in several places. He could see that she was cold. That she'd made it through the winter surprised him.

He forced his gaze back to the road and wrapped the reins more securely around his gloved fists. A pretty, unattached female would only be a distraction. And she *was* pretty. He'd already noticed the men acting like a bunch of wall-eyed calves when he looked out his office window and saw her waving to them in the yard. Charlie especially seemed to be suffering from calico fever. Damn it all, work was bound to come to a grinding halt as long as she was there. He needed every man's mind on the business at hand, not on this woman with honey-colored hair and big gray eyes.

Even though the Lodestar was in better shape than most of the other ranches in this section, the winter had cost him dearly. God, the snow. Remembering the blinding whiteness, he tightened his jaw. In his thirty-two years he'd never seen anything like it, any-where. It had begun falling on Christmas Eve and didn't stop until the middle of February. During those weeks, the temperature dropped to twenty below. In the house, he wore nearly as many clothes as he did to go outside. And while the winter crew was just across the yard in the bunkhouse, he felt like he was the last person on earth, alone in the bleak, frozen wilderness.

But the wind had been his biggest torment. He'd lost track of the nights he'd lain awake, worrying about his stock, and listening to the wind. It howled like a banshee through the valley, driving blankets of snow ahead that drifted as high as the windows on the second floor. Sometimes, its voice would change. It would wail over ice-hardened cutbanks and through bare-limbed trees like a high, thin scream. Or it would slow to a monotonous moaning for hours on end. One night, he was jolted from a restless doze, panicky and sweating despite the cold, when the wind sounded like a crying baby. In all, his present was enough to contend with—he didn't need reminders of his past.

Now he was forced to sell off part of his remaining herd to raise cash. He shifted on the wagon seat, trying to loosen the tension between his shoulders, and kept his eyes on the cedars and yellow pines that lined the road. Fate seemed to be continuing its war against him—first the winter, now this new cook. With all the ranches in the territory, what stroke of bad luck had dumped her in his lap? On second thought, he really didn't want to know.

Tyler didn't want to know anything about Libby Ross except when she'd be leaving.

*       *       *

The stiffness in Libby's spine eased a bit when she saw the shapes of Heavenly's buildings emerge from the misty valley ahead. She was anxious to be off this wagon and away from Tyler Hollins until she had to return to the ranch. Being trapped with him on that narrow seat in the middle of the prairie was, oddly enough, as confining as a closet. She tried to keep from bumping into him, but every time the wagon hit a chuck hole or a groove in the road, they were thrown against each other. He hadn't spoken one word to her for the entire five-mile journey, but his general displeasure was as hard and uncomfortable as the rough ride.

With far more expertise than she'd shown yesterday, he pulled the team and wagon around to the side of Osmer's Dry Goods. Of course he managed the horses well—he must have worked with them all of his life. But he surprised her when he jumped down, lithe as a cat, and thrust a hand up to help her descend. She'd have expected him to let her find her own way down from the high perch. At least he had *some* manners. But she looked into his upturned face and faltered for an instant, caught by the intensity of his blue eyes. When she didn't respond, he grasped her by the waist and lifted her down effortlessly, setting her on her feet.

"Well, look who's back already," Nort Osmer called from his counter when they walked in. In front of him, a pile of bills was laid out like a hand of solitaire. "Howdy, Mrs. Ross, Tyler."

Libby smiled at the shop owner. It was good to see a friendly face after the tense journey from the Lodestar. "Good morning, Mr. Osmer."

"Say, Ty, wasn't it a fair piece of luck that I found this nice lady to cook for your boys? They sure were in a fix when she came along." Nort poked his pencil behind his ear and regathered the bills into an untidy stack.

Sparing Libby a wry glance, Tyler pushed back his hat and pulled off his gloves. "Yeah, lucky." Within the confines of the dry goods store, she thought his considerable height made him look tall enough to reach up and touch the rafters overhead.

"No, no, don't worry about thanking me. I was happy to help." Nort rubbed his hands together. "Now, what can I do for you today?"

"We need to lay in supplies, Nort." Tyler turned toward her. "Mrs. Ross, you have the list."

"Oh—yes." Libby fumbled in her skirt pocket and brought out the piece of paper he'd given her earlier.

"I'll get my boy to start loading your wagon," Nort said, scanning the list. "How're things over in Miles City?"

Tyler shook his head. "I don't know what's going to happen to most of the ranchers around here after this winter." The two men fell to discussing cattle prices and the fate of neighboring ranches while Nort filled their order.

She let their voices fade to the back of her mind as she looked around at the merchandise. She'd been so tired and distressed yesterday, she hadn't really paid much attention to the curious variety of items that Osmer's carried. On the walls she saw traps with vicious-looking teeth, rolls of wire, tanned animal hides, and rifles. Arranged in a display case were dainty gold thimbles and vanity sets. But in the corner of the store, where the wood stove was stoked with a hot fire, she was drawn to a collection of warm ladies' gloves and wraps. One shawl in particular caught her eye, the one hanging on the shoulders of a dressmaker's dummy.

It was a beautiful dark plaid, black and midnight blue, with a pale green stripe, and a knotted fringe. She reached out a tentative hand and rubbed the thick, soft wool between her fingers. She'd never owned a shawl so fine. Looking down, she pushed off her own thin wrap. Then carefully unwinding the plaid from the dummy, Libby draped it over her own head and closed the ends around herself. Immediately she felt warmer. It was wonderful. Trying it on was a mistake, she supposed, because she couldn't possibly afford it. And even if she could, she wouldn't be able to justify the expense. Its price was marked at six dollars. Saving enough money for a stagecoach ticket was more important than anything else. But . . . maybe it wouldn't hurt to see how it looked on her before she returned it to its current owner.

She craned her neck to search for a mirror when she saw Tyler Hollins watching her. His expression was pensive and troubled, as though he'd caught a child in some disobedient act. Well, she wasn't going to steal the shawl, she thought irritably. Embarrassed, she removed the length of warm wool and hung it on the dress form. When he released her from his blue gaze, he muttered something to Nort Osmer. Then he pulled his gloves back on and resettled his hat.

"I'm going down to the feed store for a few minutes. You can stay here, Mrs. Ross. I'll be back by the time the wagon is loaded."

"All right," she said. As soon as he pulled the door closed, Libby hurried to the side window. She half expected to see him climb onto the wagon and drive away, leaving her in Heavenly. When he passed the horse team and kept walking, she exhaled a quiet sigh. Although he was lean and lanky, his wide shoulders looked even bigger under the sheepskin coat. A woman with a market basket on her arm gave him a double glance as she passed him. Libby didn't wonder why; Tyler Hollins was a very attractive man. But it seemed unfair to her that such good looks were wasted on a man with the personality of a three-day toothache.

"Tyler isn't a bad sort," Nort said, obviously detecting the tension between herself and her employer.

She walked back to the corner to stand near the stove. "Mr. Osmer, you're not the first person to tell me that. But if Mr. Hollins were a *good* sort, I don't think anyone would have to make excuses for him, do you?"

"I reckon it might seem that way, Mrs. Ross. But you'll feel different once you get to know—"

Just then the door opened and Libby was immediately struck by the subtle but very noticeable scent of gardenias. She turned and saw a woman—one who was about her own height, but with a presence and a confidence that Libby herself had never possessed. Her violet taffeta gown bordered on the gaudy, but she was more formally dressed than anyone Libby had seen since leaving Chicago. Although it wasn't raining or sunny, she carried a parasol that matched her gown. This woman made Libby think of a flower that bloomed only in the shade, one that couldn't bear the heat or light of a full sun. And she had a look about her, as though she knew something. A joke, or maybe a secret.

"Howdy, Miss Callie," the shopkeeper said, beaming. "You're out early today."

"You're right about that, Nort," the woman said, and made a face of mild horror. "Isn't it a wonder? I can tell you, I don't like being up with the chickens. I'm not used to starting my day before two o'clock, but I have a few chores to do today. Do you think you could find me three dozen of those beer glasses I use? When the boys from the Circle R visited the other night, they stirred things up pretty good. By the time we got them out of the saloon, they'd broken nearly every clean glass on the shelf behind the bar. They gave my girls the vapors—they were so upset, I had to close early." She pushed at a rust-colored curl peeking from her hat, plainly annoyed by this turn of events.

"Poor old Jinx Malone was feelin' right sorry for himself when he stopped in here yesterday morning, Miss Callie," Nort chuckled, and leaned on his counter.

"Well, two weeks ago I told those Circle R cowhands that I wouldn't put up with one more of them riding a horse into my place." She grinned cheerfully. "I expect the night Jinx spent in jail will improve his memory."

Libby bent her attention to a display of collar pins, and tried not to stare, but her curiosity got the better of her. The woman didn't notice her anyway. She must be the one Libby had heard about yesterday, the one who owned the Big Dipper. Of course, she'd seen concubines a few times in Chicago, but never up close like this. They'd remained behind curtained windows and when they went out, they traveled in closed carriages. They hadn't been so brazen that they walked down the street in the middle of the day to go shopping.

Nort pointed over his shoulder in the general direction of the storeroom. "I've got those glasses in back. I can send my son around with them this afternoon."

Callie smiled at him. "Thanks. I can always count on you. How about that fancy French soap I ordered a couple of weeks ago? Did it come in yet? Some of my regular gentlemen have been asking for it for the bathing room upstairs."

Libby was astounded—this woman was so matter-of-fact about her occupation. Regular gentlemen?

Nort looked at the calendar on the wall next to him, tapping a Friday with his pencil. "Not yet, but I'm lookin' for a freight wagon to come in at the end of the week."

"Say, Nort, you should drop by the Big Dipper some time and try out my new copper tub. I've got the only one in Heavenly, you know." Callie leaned over the rough wood counter a bit, making her taffeta dress rustle ever so slightly, and her voice dropped to a confidential tone. "You're welcome anytime. Why, any one of my girls would be happy to entertain you for an evening."

Libby felt her own eyes widen, and from her vantage point by the stove, Nort Osmer looked to her like he'd swallowed a spoonful of cayenne pepper. Then he turned his eyes her way, as though he'd just now remembered she was in the store, and therefore a witness to this conversation.

Apparently noticing the direction of his gaze, Callie turned to look at Libby, then back at Nort. She lifted a brow, her expression expectant. "I don't believe I've met this lady, Nort, and I know everyone in these parts. Are you going to introduce us?"

Regaining his breath but not his normal coloring, the storekeeper stammered. "Uh—Mrs. Libby Ross, this is Miss Callie Michaels. She's the—uh—Miss Callie owns the Big Dipper."

Libby backed up a step, nodding at her uncertainly. "I'm pleased to meet you." She didn't know what else to say. She'd never been introduced to the owner of a brothel before. The winter she'd spent in the wilderness had provided no hint of what the West was like, except to reveal its raw harshness. Now she wondered what kind of place she'd come to, where a brothel owner solicited business in clear daylight, and a respectable woman was presented to the madam as though she were a member of a church committee.

Callie smiled at her. "I'm sorry, honey, I didn't see you standing in the corner. You must think we don't have any manners at all around here." Her voice softened as she approached Libby, and she looked her up and down, though not in an unkind way. "I'll bet you're the one Ben Ross told me about last fall. He said he was sending for a nice lady to be his wife. I was mighty sad to hear he passed on."

Libby forced herself to lower her eyes. Everyone in this town seemed to have a high opinion of Ben, and it probably wouldn't do to let it show that she didn't share it. "Thank you."

"Now that he's gone, will you be staying on in Heavenly?"

Only for as long as she had to, Libby thought. She wanted to go back to a part of the country where the ways and lives of people weren't so different from what she knew. "For a while. I'm cooking for Mr. Hollins and his men at the Lodestar Ranch."

Callie's brows lifted in amused astonishment. "You're working for *Tyler* Hollins?"

Baffled by her attitude, Libby nodded. "Yes, I am."

"Well, well," she said softly, almost to herself. She contemplated Libby again for a moment. Then she roused herself and laughed. "If he proves to be too ornery, come on over and see me at the Dipper. I can always find room for one more."

Libby felt her jaw drop slightly, and heat flooded her face all the way back to her ears.

"Nort," Callie said, all business again, "I'll be looking for those glasses this afternoon. Send the bill to the boys at the Circle R." With that, she whisked out of the store in a rustle of violet taffeta and a whiff of gardenias, pulling the door closed behind her.

"Now, don't you mind Miss Callie, ma'am," Nort said, obviously aware of her embarrassment. "She's plainspoken, but she means no disrespect. She don't see her line of work as bein' any different from a doctor's or a baker's."

Or a cook's, it seemed. "She certainly is—colorful." She moved to the window to get a final look, and saw Callie on the sidewalk outside, talking with Tyler Hollins. While Nort's son loaded the wagon, Tyler stood with a foot propped on the hub of one of the wheels. Through the wavy window glass she could see his expression clearly—and he actually *laughed* at some remark the woman made. Libby wouldn't have guessed that he had any laughter in him. The grin transformed his face and not only made him seem less like a toothache, it made him look younger, as well. Beyond that, she thought she saw a hint of fondness reflected in his expression for the woman he was talking to. But then he glanced up at Libby, and the smile disappeared. Straightening, he took his foot from the wheel hub, and even his posture looked rigid and uncomfortable, as though she'd learned something he didn't want her to know.

Well, she might have. Maybe Tyler Hollins was one of Miss Callie's "regular gentlemen." What a thought! Libby wasn't so naive that she didn't realize that men, sometimes respectable ones from good families, visited soiled doves like Callie Michaels. She supposed that perhaps even Wesley— But they didn't stand on a public sidewalk and converse with the women.

It was none of her business, she reminded herself, tugging at the hems of her gloves. The less she knew about Tyler Hollins, the better. Her job was to feed him and his men, and nothing more. It shouldn't bother her one bit if looking at Libby had the power to replace his smile with a frown.

But it did bother her, and she didn't know why.

As if to see what caused Tyler's abrupt change of mood, Callie glanced over her shoulder at Libby, and sent her another knowing smile. Then she tapped his arm with her violet parasol, opened it, and made her way down the street.

Tyler pulled out his watch, then motioned to Libby to come outside.

"We're ready to go, Mr. Osmer," she said.

Nort had finished tallying up their bill and was entering the amount in his blue-backed ledger. "It was mighty nice seein' you again. If you think of somethin' else you want, tell Tyler and he can pick it up when he comes into town on Saturday evenin'."

Libby couldn't imagine telling Tyler anything. She adjusted her shawl over her head. "On Saturday?"

He came around to her side of the counter to

open the door for her. "Oh, sure. Ty rides in every Saturday and has supper at the Big Dipper. He's done it for a few years now. Weather allowin', that is."

That was about as "regular" as a man could get, Libby decided. "Then I guess I won't keep a plate warm for him."

Bidding good-bye to Nort, Libby walked out, reluctant to trade the store's warm, aromatic shelter for a cold, hard wagon seat next to a cold, hard man.

Tyler stood at the back end of the wagon box to load some feed sacks. They looked heavy but he threw them into place with little trouble. "Did you get everything you need?" The work was hot and he'd taken off his coat.

Libby watched the fabric in his shirt pull tight and slacken with his efforts. "Yes, I think so."

He pitched the last sack into the wagon, then looked at her and frowned slightly, as though her very appearance displeased him. "Didn't Nort give you—oh, damn it, wait here a minute," he muttered, and jumped down.

Libby gazed at his shoulders as he strode back into the general store and closed the door. Behind her, she heard the horses shift restively in their harness. If she had to put up with his sour attitude much longer, her temper, a deeply buried and long restrained emotion, would slip away from her and she'd tell Tyler Hollins exactly what she thought. And when that day came, she knew she'd better be packed and ready to go. He would almost certainly make good on his threat to bring her to Heavenly and leave her.

Moments later, the door opened again and Tyler

walked out with a paper-wrapped package under his arm.

"Let's get going, Mrs. Ross. It's a long ride back to the Lodestar."

Libby hoisted herself up to the seat and tucked her skirts around her again. "Surely not longer than this morning."

"We can't drive the horses as fast with the wagon loaded down like this."

"Oh." Her heart sank at the news, and she shivered as a stiff gust bit through her wrap. The tree behind Osmer's rattled its bare branches in the wind. Overhead, the sky was growing dark again with heavy clouds.

Tyler climbed onto the seat next to her and put on his coat. Then he thrust the brown paper package into her hands. "Put that on."

"What is it?" She tried to look into his face, but he kept it pointed toward the horses ahead while he wrapped the reins around his fists.

"We've got some cold weather to go through before spring starts to warm up. I figured it—you might as well have this." His voice lost some of its commanding tone.

Libby pulled on the slip knot tied in the string and opened the paper. Inside, she found the plaid shawl she'd admired. Her jaw dropped and she gaped first at the wrap, then at him.

"I can't take this, Mr. Hollins!" It pained her to say it. The shawl was beautiful. It was *warm*. But to accept such a gift was highly improper. Just why, she wasn't sure. Tyler Hollins was her employer. If Mrs. Brandauer had known a moment of uncharacteristic generosity and presented her with such a gift, she'd have accepted it without hesitation. And propriety had never been an issue when Wesley gave her the few small keepsakes she still kept in her trunk: a silver hairbrush, a pair of gold cuff buttons, a sterling buttonhook.

He turned his blue-eyed stare on her. "Yes, you will accept the shawl, Mrs. Ross. Don't forget, you're part of my job."

"What?"

"I take my responsibilities seriously." That said, he flapped the lines on the horses' backs, and the wagon pulled out.

Libby glared at him and pressed her lips into a thin line, tempted to retort. It wasn't very flattering to be viewed in the same light as the calves and dogs and horses he considered part of his domain. She looked down at the package in her lap. She was annoyed by his attitude, but not completely so.

Libby unfurled the length of plaid and wrapped it around her shoulders. "Thank you," she said stiffly.

Early that evening, Tyler sat in his office scratching figures on a piece of paper while he reassessed the winter losses. He paused to adjust the flame in the lamp on the corner of the desk. It was warm in here, but outside, heavy gusts drove sheets of rain against the windows. At least it wasn't snowing. Now and then, the wind pulled the blaze in the fireplace a bit higher, but his dog, Sam, stretched out on the hearth rug, slept on unconcerned.

"Life's pretty good for you, isn't it, Sam?" he asked. He leaned back in his chair, making it swivel a bit from side to side while he considered the big black mongrel.

The dog waved his tail once in acknowledgment, but didn't wake.

"Sure, it's not so hard to have someone feed you and let you sleep in front of the fire. You don't have to worry about cattle, or this damned trail drive we have to make."

Sam put one paw over his head.

Tyler sat up and looked at the numbers again. He wasn't broke, by any means. He wasn't poor. But restocking the herd would take careful planning. If he brought in some new stock from Texas—

At that moment he detected an aroma, a delicious scent that he hadn't smelled in this house for years. It was the scent of baking bread. Not johnnycake, not sourdough biscuits. This was real, honest-to-God yeast bread.

He inhaled again, and closed his eyes. In his mind's eye, he saw a small, raven-haired woman with skin like fresh cream, busy in the kitchen. She was thin—slight, really—and too fragile to endure life in this place. Certainly too fragile for a man's touch. And though she smiled at him, it was a sad smile, and in her face he saw blame.

Just as Tyler began to feel a familiar clenching ache in his chest, the vision dissolved into an unwanted picture of Libby Ross. He imagined her clover-honey hair and white apron as she peeked into the oven to check on the warm, sweet loaves. Her sleeves were rolled up almost to her elbows, revealing pale, slender arms.

Damn it, what made him think of her? he wondered. He laid down his pen and rubbed his eyes. At least she'd quit shivering when she put on the new shawl. It even looked nice on her. He was still uncomfortable that the cook had seen him with Callie today, but for the life of him, he couldn't guess why. Even though he pretty much kept to himself, his relationship with Callie Michaels was no secret. The whole town knew about it and didn't think anything of it. *He* didn't think anything of it. But when he'd looked up and saw a pair of big gray eyes staring at him from Osmer's window, he felt awkward, as though—well, as though he were doing something very wrong.

He closed the desk, unable to concentrate on his task any longer. He hoped Joe found a different cook pretty damned quick.

The last thing Tyler needed around here was another person to make him feel guilty.

# Chapter 5

That night, the crew of the Lodestar enjoyed a stew that swam with cubes of white potatoes, bits of onion, and chunks of beef in a rich broth. Hot bread and honey, and apple crisp drizzled with cream accompanied the main dish. Seconds—and in Rory's case, thirds—were consumed.

Though still trying to accustom herself to cooking on a woodstove again, even Libby thought the simple meal turned out well. The job was made a little easier now that she had everything she needed, at least everything that was available to her at Osmer's. She'd had to bake the bread, and getting the stew beef had required one of the men to butcher an entire steer. It wasn't exactly like going to the bakery and butcher shop in Chicago. But the admiration from the men made the effort worthwhile. And they seemed to be getting used to her—not as many of them blushed like schoolboys when she spoke to them.

Libby made her way down the two long tables to refill empty coffee cups. When she got to Noah Bradley's place, he gestured at his empty dish.

"Charlie and Kansas Bob and the Cooper boys don't know what they missed," he said, scraping his blue enamel plate with the side of his fork. "I almost feel sorry for 'em. Almost. It'll sure be fun to tell 'em all about it."

"Oh, don't tease them too much, Mr. Bradley—um, Noah. I think working in this weather is punishment enough," she said, and glanced at the dark windows.

It was a wild March night, full of lashing wind and rain that tapped against the windows. Now and then, distant thunder rolled down the valley. It reminded Libby of Joe's voice. The kitchen windows were fogged over from the heat of the stove and the wet hats and slickers hung on pegs along the back wall.

Joe wiped his mouth on his napkin and carefully smoothed out his mustache. "I don't envy those boys bein' out on a night like this. Lord knows I've had my share of sleepin' in the rain. Today was hard enough. All day long, I kept thinkin' about comin' back here to the cookhouse for a hot meal and black coffee."

Libby raised her eyes to look around at the unfinished shedlike walls, and the trestle tables and benches. The lighting was provided by big black lanterns, and the dishes were all enamelware. There was a sink, but no running water except for the pump. Even though this was an improvement over Ben's place—and almost anything would have been—in her opinion, this was just one step up from cooking in a tent. At least it didn't have a dirt floor.

Obviously catching her in her critical inspection, Joe laughed. She lowered her gaze hastily, but his dark eyes were kind behind his laughter.

"It probably don't look like much, compared to what you're used to, Miss Libby. But to a bunch of worn-out cowpokes who've been sittin' on horses all day in the rain and the mud, comin' back here, where it's warm and light, and good food is waitin'—well, it's like walkin' into a grand home."

Murmurs of agreement rippled through the room. Libby clutched the handle of the coffeepot and smiled self-consciously. She was unfamiliar with the kind of honest appreciation she received from these men.

There was just one other person who'd yet to taste this supper. She hadn't seen Tyler since they got back from Heavenly. When they'd returned from the slow, bumpy trip, he rounded up a couple of the men to unload the wagon, then he saddled his horse and rode off. She'd heard him come through the front door earlier, but his booted footsteps had gone to the back of the house and stayed there.

"Would anyone like more apple crisp?" she asked. "I have one more pan just about ready to come out of the oven."

"Naw, I guess you should save a little bit for Tyler," Rory said, pushing himself away from the table. "I just hope Charlie fixed all the holes in the bunkhouse roof last week. It's hard to sleep with a tin can balanced on your belly to catch the rain."

The cowboys began drifting outside then, looking well-fed and content. Finally the last of them put on their hats and slickers, and dashed through the rain to the dimly lit bunkhouse across the yard. The wind whipped rain through the doorway and stirred Libby's skirts. After they were gone, she went to the stove and pushed the stew pot to a cooler corner of the stove, wondering how long she should keep it warm for Tyler. Well, he was a grown man. She was hired only to cook, not to keep a restaurant kitchen. She pulled out a plate and got supper for herself.

Libby wasn't completely used to eating alone. Before, she'd had her makeshift family in Chicago: Birdie, the Brandauers' maid; Deirdre, her young kitchen helper; and Melvin, the driver. They'd sit at the big worktable in the kitchen at night, sharing supper, news, and gossip, and laughing—but not too loudly, lest the Brandauers be disturbed.

As she daubed honey on her bread, she remembered the first time she'd seen Eliza Brandauer. It was the third morning she'd spent in the waiting room at Mrs. Banks's domestic employment agency. The foundling home had sent Libby there, giving her the one-dollar fee to pay Mrs. Banks, to find a job. She was fourteen now, she'd been reminded at the orphanage, and it was time she made her own way in the world. Did she suppose that charity would support her forever?

She'd sat in the corner of a room filled with all different kinds and ages of women. Some were younger than she was, some looked experienced, exhausted, or numb. Others appeared as ignorant and scared as she. She didn't own any gloves so she interlaced her shaking hands and buried them in the folds of her thin, dark skirt. Ladies in fine clothes needing servants swept into the waiting room. They looked the applicants over, and sometimes made them stand so they could look them up and down as well. Libby thought it was the most humiliating, frightening experience of her life. She didn't know whether to be relieved or alarmed when she was passed over time and again.

Then Eliza Brandauer had arrived. Cool and imperious in a dark blue serge suit, she chose Libby to be a cook's helper because, she told her, she looked morally upright. Moral purity played a big part in Mrs. Brandauer's view of not only her own society, but the world in general.

Eventually the cook retired, Libby took her place, and was given Deirdre, a cook's helper of her own. It was unusual for a nineteen-year-old woman to hold a position of such responsibility as cook in a wealthy household. And when Mrs. Brandauer decided to promote Libby, she stressed that she was giving her a rare opportunity for which she should be grateful.

As the years passed, Birdie, Deirdre, and Melvin became her adopted family. She'd counted these three people as her friends, dearer than any ever she'd known. Yet, in the end, they all turned their backs to her—

Libby had nearly finished washing the dishes, and was deep in her bittersweet memories when Tyler Hollins thrust open the door from the dining room.

Lost in her musings, his entrance was as sudden and startling to her as a gunshot. With her hand in the soapy water, her fingers slipped convulsively against the blade of a knife she'd been scrubbing in the dishpan.

Gasping, she jerked her hand out of the hot water. She couldn't see the wound but there was so much blood she was certain she must have cut off her finger. Oddly, she didn't feel pain, but red rivulets snaked down her hand and forearm with alarming speed.

"Oh, God . . ." she breathed.

Tyler took two quick steps forward and plucked a clean white towel from the worktable. "Here, let me look." His tone was steady and authoritative. He grabbed her wrist and held her dripping hand over the sink while he opened her fingers to examine them. Soap, water, and blood ran together, concealing the injury. He pressed the towel to her hand, but it was soon soaked through.

"I'm sure I can take care of this myself," she said, trying to pull away. It had been her experience that even sturdy-looking men could be rather faint-hearted when it came to the sight of blood. She didn't want to have to worry about taking care of both of them if he passed out. At least she tried to convince herself that was the reason she didn't want him standing so close, with his strong hand closed around her wrist.

"Stop fidgeting, Mrs. Ross." He clamped her forearm firmly between his elbow and his ribs, smearing her blood on his shirt. Through the fabric, she felt the heat of warm muscle and bone pressed against her arm. Turning them both toward one of the lanterns, he complained, "Goddamn it, I can't see a thing."

"It's bleeding a lot," she offered helpfully.

"Because you had your hands in that hot dishwater." He threw the towel aside and pivoted back to the sink. Working the pump handle, he poured icy water over her hand until her skin was white and the bleeding began to slow.

He stood very close to her, with his head bent next to hers while he cradled her hand in his own. His touch was warm and light. And he smelled good, like leather and fresh air and clean hay. She hadn't noticed it before, she thought, and she'd spent nearly the whole day sitting next to him on that wagon seat. At the moment it provided a welcome distraction.

"Oh, yeah . . . there it is," he said. It was a fierce

slash across the first bend in her little finger, and it looked fairly deep, but the bleeding had dwindled to an ooze. Tyler's forehead was furrowed in concentration as he looked at the cut. But despite her anxiety, she saw something else in his eyes she couldn't readily identify. She thought he looked like he'd remembered something he didn't want to.

He rinsed their hands again, then took her other hand to press her thumb to the wound. "Hold it tight, just like this, and come back to my office."

Libby followed the ring of his spurs without question, partly because she'd learned quickly that Tyler Hollins was not the kind of man who appreciated being questioned. But more than any other reason, she went along because he appeared to know what he was doing.

He filled the office door frame when he passed through it—she thought that his head cleared the opening by little more than a few inches, and his shoulders nearly touched the sides. Given his cold personality, she hated to admit it, even to herself, but there was no getting around it: as a man, his appearance definitely commanded attention, and belied that coldness. His red-brown hair was heavy and thick, with fine coppery streaks running through it that shone in the firelight. His tall, lean-muscled frame cast long shadows across the wooden floor.

"Have a seat over there," he said, and pointed to a pine armchair next to the fireplace. Everything about him, even the way he moved, suggested a man who was capable, invulnerable, always in control. He went to one of the glass-fronted cabinets in the corner and brought out gauze, scissors, and a dark bottle, leaving the doors ajar.

Libby perched on the edge of the chair. From this

angle, she couldn't help but notice the way his close-fitting jeans hugged his legs and slim backside.

Her finger was beginning to throb now. She caught sight of her apron and realized that it, too, was streaked with blood. Between the two of them, they looked like they'd been engaged in mortal combat. With all the trouble she'd put him to, she felt compelled to apologize before he had a chance to scold her. "I'm not usually so clumsy. If you give me the bandage, I can handle this. I don't want to keep you from your supper."

He waved off her concern and dragged his swivel chair next to her. "I'll get it in a minute. Besides, from experience I know it isn't easy to bind your own hand. All right, let go." He put her hand, palm up, across his knee and pulled her thumb away from her finger. Blood pooled in the cut again, but much more slowly.

He cut off a length of gauze and folded it into a pad. Then holding it under her finger, he picked up the bottle and poured a bit of its contents over it. "This is going to sting a bit."

Libby gasped. Reflex made her pull back her hand, but Tyler kept his grip on her wrist. "Sting! It burns like fire. And it smells like it could strip paint," she said, her jaw clenched. "What is that?"

A huff of laughter escaped him, and he actually smiled. She had another glimpse of the younger face she'd seen earlier today when he was talking to Callie Michaels. The mouth that was sometimes pressed into a stern line softened. His teeth were very white, and she noticed that the lower ones were crowded and overlapped slightly. The imperfection made him seem a little less formidable. He leaned closer and blew on her finger to relieve the burn. "Sorry. It's an antisep—uh, something to keep this from festering."

He measured off another length of gauze, and taking her hand into his own, he began wrapping her cut. She watched his hands as he worked. He had good hands, she thought—strong, with long fingers. Inside, across the top of his palm, she'd felt the slight calluses that she supposed came with managing reins and horses and whatever other kind of work he did on this ranch.

She continued to consider him. The October-leaves color of his hair fascinated her, and its texture looked soft and thick. What would it feel like, she wondered, if she were to comb it with her fingers?

Apparently feeling her gaze, he looked up from the bandage, and snared her with his blue eyes. The fire reflected concern in their depths. "What's the matter, too tight?" he asked, nodding toward her finger.

With his face tipped up to hers like that, she had trouble remembering what he'd asked. "N-no, it's fine." Heavens, she'd been staring at him. And wondering what his hair felt like!

After an endless moment, he dragged his attention to the gauze. "Does it hurt much?"

"No, no really, it doesn't," she lied. Libby had the feeling that this man would not tolerate any other answer.

"I'd think that a kitchen expert like you would know better than to grab the sharp side of a knife." Another thin smile dashed across his features.

It might have been a criticism, but the brief grin softened his remark. Yes, she did know better, but she'd been thinking about other things when he barged into the kitchen. About the past, about her conversation with Callie Michaels, about the shawl. She ducked her head ruefully.

"I guess I let my mind wander. I tend to daydream when I wash dishes, but it usually doesn't get me into trouble."

"What were you thinking about?" He kept his attention on his task, but his voice had acquired an interested tone, as though he really wanted to know.

She tried to keep the longing out of her words. "Oh, Chicago mostly."

"Montana's a little different, isn't it," he said.

"A little! More than a little—I mean—" Libby didn't want to insult the man's home territory, but in her view, his remark was an understatement. "Um, have you been to Chicago?"

"Yeah, but it was years ago. There are big stock-yards there, you know. And beef packing plants."

"I know, but I never had any reason to go see them."

Tyler looked up again and considered her for a moment. "Ben must have made it sound pretty appealing out here to make you want to leave your hometown and come all this way to get married."

Libby tensed slightly. "I believe that Ben Ross *exaggerated* a lot of the things he told me."

He shrugged. "Well, try not to hold it against him," he said, and reached for the scissors. "The West is full of old cowhands like him, lifelong bachelors who came up from Texas in the early days after the war. Most of them don't have a lot of experience courting women."

"You seem to be pretty experienced at *this*," she said, twitching her little finger to indicate his skill. She felt easier with him. His manner was almost friendly. She turned to regard the rows of bottles and jars on the cabinet shelves, and ventured a smile herself. "And what a collection of medicines. I'll bet you give the doctor in Heavenly some competition."

Tyler looked up sharply. He snipped the end of the bandage into two strips and tied them in a knot, then put her hand back in her own lap.

"A lot of things can happen on a ranch," he said, suddenly taut and withdrawn again. Standing, he walked to the cabinet and put away the supplies. Then he pointedly closed the doors, making it clear that its contents were none of her business. His watch chain gleamed dully in the firelight, and half of his face was eclipsed by shadow. "If a horse goes lame or one of the crew falls into a barbed wire fence—or if the cook cuts herself—we have to be able to handle it."

Effectively shut out, Libby wondered what on earth had turned the tide of the conversation so quickly, so completely. She felt that she'd overstepped the bounds of propriety with her employer, but couldn't imagine how. Feeling awkward now, she rose from the chair, smoothed her apron and held her white-wrapped finger gingerly. "Yes, well, thank you for your help. I kept some stew and apple crisp warm for you. I'll get your plate ready."

He shook his head and extended his arm toward the door to usher her out. "I'll take care of it. You should probably go and rest. This has been a long day for you." His expression wasn't angry. In fact, it was carefully blank. "And you have to keep that bandage dry."

Libby wasn't used to working for someone so determined to do for himself. But he was right: it *had* been a long day, and if he wanted to get his own supper, she wasn't about to argue with him. She could clean up the sink in the morning.

"I'll say good night, then."

"Good night, Mrs. Ross."

Feeling dismissed, she inclined her head and turned to leave the room. She heard the office door close behind her.

Upstairs in her room, Libby shrugged out of her clothes and into a flannel nightgown. Maybe something had happened to Tyler that had hardened him into the man she saw most of the time, the man who lived behind a wall of coldness. One moment he seemed pleasant, the next he was as icy and remote as the hills on the other side of the valley. She'd think that he truly disliked her, yet he'd bought her that shawl today. It lay across the foot of her bed, and she reached out to smooth its soft wool fringe. And she couldn't have mistaken the concern she'd seen in his face while he bandaged her finger.

Bah, he was probably worried that her wound would hamper her ability to cook, she thought sourly. And anyway, she was too tired to unravel Tyler Hollins's perplexing behavior.

She opened her door a crack to let in the warmth from the hall. Heat generated by the fireplace drifted straight up here and in her mind, it was a shame to waste it. Climbing between the cold sheets, she turned down the lamp next to the bed, and the room was plunged into darkness. She huddled under the blankets, shivering and waiting for her body heat to make a warm pocket. Then she remembered the shawl. She sat up and whipped it from the end of the bed.

As she sank into the feather mattress, despite the throbbing in her finger, sleep crept in to claim her and she told herself that none of it mattered. Not the cold nights, not her cold employer. This job was only a means to an end—an escape from the frontier.

Tyler stood on the edge of the front porch and looked at the clearing night sky. Illuminated silver-gray by a half-moon, clouds drifted easterly across the faces of the stars. At least it had stopped raining. Breaking horses, the job he'd be doing tomorrow, was hard work any day. Doing it in the rain was hell.

But it was nearly midnight, and he couldn't sleep. He'd headed upstairs earlier, planning to go to bed, but almost immediately came down again. He'd no sooner gotten his clothes off than he pulled them back on and went downstairs in his stocking feet.

In the past few years Tyler had carefully established the ordered routine of his life. He usually rose before the crew was up, he worked hard all day, either on the range or in his office, he ate his meals in the dining room. Sometimes he sat in the parlor in the evening, reading stockman's journals, or even less frequently, one of the textbooks from the closet under the stairs. Then he'd go to bed and begin the pattern all over again. The only ripples that fluttered across the even surface of this schedule were his Saturday night trips into Heavenly. He protected this routine by making certain that nothing and no one trespassed on his solitude.

Now it had been completely disrupted by the honey-haired young widow asleep in the room next to his. Upstairs, he'd been nearly as aware of her over there as if no wall existed between them. He'd slouched on the leather sofa in the parlor for hours, staring at the fire, feeling like an outsider in his own home.

Leaning over, he rested his forearms on the porch railing and sighed. In the low yellow lamplight gleaming through the window, he saw his breath as a cloud of vapor. It wasn't that she was a pest, or incompetent, or lazy, he pondered. Hell, even after she'd cut herself, she was ready to go back to the kitchen. And he knew she'd lied about the pain in her hand. He'd seen grown men holler louder over less serious injuries.

Sitting next to her in his office, he'd detected the faint, sweet fragrance of flowers and vanilla. It was innocently feminine, the kind of scent that Callie, with her bright, hard perfume, had made him forget. The loss of that memory had been a blessing.

He'd forced himself to keep his eyes on her hand, but a couple of times he found his gaze straying to her softly rounded bosom. For a small woman she was surprisingly lush-breasted, and her tiny waist and the simple high-necked white blouse she'd worn only enhanced her shape. Her skin, he remembered, was the color of fresh cream with rose petals floating on it.

He suspected that Libby's life hadn't been an easy one for all that she'd worked for a wealthy family in a big house. He'd think that wouldn't be as hard on a woman as life on the prairie. But she had a look to her gray eyes that reminded him of heartache—that nagged at his conscience.

He hadn't meant to snap at her when she'd made the comment about competing with the doctor in Heavenly. She couldn't know how he felt about doctors, or the medical profession in general—

He straightened away from the railing and stretched his spine. His morning was coming up fast; it would be here in just over four hours and he couldn't spend the rest of the night sitting on the parlor sofa. He had to get some sleep.

Turning, he padded back into the house and picked up a lighted candle to see his way up the stairs again. But when he reached the second floor, he realized that Libby Ross's door was ajar. He hadn't noticed it earlier when he'd charged out of his room and down to the parlor.

He took a tentative step, and then another, until he was standing in front of her door. The cut on her hand was a bad one. It would heal well enough, he supposed, but what if it had started bleeding again? He put his fingertips on the edge of her door and hesitated. A long wedge of light from his candle fell through the opening and across the wide plank flooring. Jesus, he must be out of his mind— Finally, he gave the door a push. The candle in his fist wavered slightly.

In the semigloom, and small as she was, she looked like a child in the bed. Her wounded hand lay palm up next to the pillow, the bandage still pristine white. Even in sleep she looked exhausted and vulnerable, but her long hair flowed behind her like a satin drape. He reached out and lightly brushed the backs of his fingers against its softness.

It was then he saw that cuddled to her like a rag doll was the plaid shawl he'd bought for her this morning.

For a moment, he had the wild notion that if he were to lift the blanket, he'd find a pair of angel's wings folded against her body. Tyler backed out of the room more quickly and quietly than he would have thought himself capable. He went to his own room and shut the door, his heart thudding in his chest.

He'd talk to Joe in the morning, he swore with

edgy resolve, jamming his hand through his hair. If his foreman couldn't find a new cook for the trail drive, then by God, Tyler would see to it himself tomorrow night when he went into Heavenly. If it meant he'd have to offer the job to every man standing at the bar in Callie's saloon, he'd do it.

He had to get Libby Ross out of his house and out of his life.

Late the next afternoon, Libby pulled her chair around to sit in a square of pale sunlight at the kitchen worktable. A light breeze from the open door stirred her skirts around her ankles. After dark gray days of soaking rains, the weather had cleared and this afternoon was mild enough to let her open the door to air out the kitchen.

Picking up a rolling pin, she began rolling out a crust for the apple pies she was making. Her finger was still tender, slowing her down and making some chores downright impossible. Handling the pie dough was awkward business with her bandage, and keeping the gauze dry was just a nuisance. But she did as she'd been instructed; she half expected Tyler Hollins to sweep in at any moment and inspect her hand.

She'd seen her employer several times today, but mostly from the distance. He'd spent the day at the corral across the yard, helping to break broncs, as Joe had called them at breakfast. He'd apparently cleaned up her mess in the kitchen last night because this morning she'd found the sink empty and all the dishes put away.

Now and then, she glanced out the window and saw Tyler sitting on the top rail, watching the cowboys on the backs of a succession of wild horses that seemed bent on throwing them off and killing them.

But when Tyler jumped down into the muddy enclosure she put aside the rolling pin, lured to the yard by the absolute power of the demonstration. No one at the corral noticed her—all eyes were turned toward him as he slowly approached a nervous-looking bay. Libby thought that the big horse was the same color as Tyler's hair.

"That filly's got a mad-on now, Mr. Hollins," Noah said from his spot on the rail. "You'd better blindfold her or she'll bite a chunk out of your hide."

"She's not going to bite me—are you, darlin'," he murmured as he got closer to the horse.

The filly reared and gave him a baleful look that supported no such confidence.

"Whoa, now darlin'," Tyler said, and jumped back a step. "She's smart as a whip, you can see it in her eyes. She'll make one hell of a cow horse."

Noah shook his head doubtfully. "Maybe, but not yet. She still don't even like that saddle. You ought to give her another day or so to get used to it before you climb on."

Tyler didn't answer. Instead he reached out and gripped the reins and the side of her bridle. Pulling her head down to his, he spoke in a low, quiet voice. Libby watched from farther down the fence, but she couldn't hear what he was saying. His words, obviously spoken with compassion and tenderness, were meant only for the bay. The mask of his sharp-edged expression fell away, revealing the handsomeness beneath, and for an instant Libby found herself envying that horse.

Only vaguely conscious of it, she put one foot on the bottom fence rail and climbed up so that her head cleared the top. With her lower lip clamped between her teeth, she waited to see what would happen next.

Rory scaled the fence and sat next to her, all gangly arms and legs. "Howdy, Miss Libby."

Libby shaded her eyes against the afternoon sun. "Hello, Rory. Is Mr. Hollins really going to ride that horse? She doesn't seem very inclined to let him. In fact, she looks as though she'd like to trample him." Libby knew the feeling.

"Tyler?" His young face wore a look of mild amazement, as though she'd suggested that the sun might rise in the west tomorrow. "I never seen Tyler get throwed. He sticks like a burr. Anyways, he never asks us to do nothin' he won't do himself."

She imagined that Rory was right. Tyler was a hard, intensely self-sufficient man, obviously without sentiment or any other kind of emotion, except perhaps anger. At least in his dealings with most people, that was the case. Except when he'd patched up her hand.

After his gentling conference with the bay, Tyler, maintaining his grip on the bridle and reins, pushed his hat down more securely. Then he put his foot in the stirrup and hoisted himself to the horse's back.

She immediately made her feelings known about this circumstance. Though the men cheered and whooped, it seemed to Libby that the angry, twisting, snorting beast had no other desire than to shake off the offending rider and stomp him to death. Bucking and diving around the corral, they drew so close to the fence where she stood that Libby expected Tyler to crash through the rails.

"Tyler, look out!" she shrieked.

Hearing her, his head came up and his eyes

connected with hers, blue and piercing. His concentration broken, in the next second when the horse dove again he was flung from the saddle and landed shoulder-first in the mud. Libby heard his breath whoosh from his lungs.

"Oh, my God!" She clung to the rails and gaped in horror, her hand pressed to her mouth. He'd fallen so hard, surely he must have broken something. Could he move? Was he badly hurt? The bay trotted off to the far fence, looking indignant.

Libby's heart started again when Tyler regained his feet. Rory and a couple of the men leaped down to help, but he shook them off. The left half of his shirt and pants were caked with mud.

When he turned to face her, guilt bloomed in Libby's chest. She scampered to the ground and peeked at him between the rails.

He walked over to her through the quagmire, his steps a little stiff but deliberate. Two buttons had popped off his shirt, and the clean side—the one that wasn't glued to his skin—gapped away from his chest.

"Are you all right, Mr. Hollins?" she asked, irked by the puny, scared sound in her own voice. She wasn't afraid of him, although she realized now she shouldn't have distracted him by yelling that way. She shouldn't care if he broke his silly neck trying to get on a horse that obviously had no intention of being ridden.

He removed his hat and briefly considered the wet Montana dirt covering half of its brim. Then he looked up at her.

"Mrs. Ross, shouldn't you be in the kitchen getting supper ready?" He didn't shout. In fact, he spoke with a quiet, conversational tone that reached

only her. He didn't even sound angry. but she knew
better. His annoyance was reflected in his eyes.

"Well, yes, I—"

"The men will be expecting to eat pretty soon."

At the dismissal, Libby pressed her mouth into a
tight line. She inclined her head and turned for the
house. When she glanced back, she saw him watching her, as the bay had watched him. Obviously she'd
worried about his safety for nothing.

Maybe the filly had had the right idea, after all.
Once more, she envied that horse.

An hour later, Libby finished crimping the edges
of the pies, then sat down to peel potatoes for
supper.

Looking at the bandage on her hand again, her
thoughts returned to Tyler. He was so different from
Wesley—Lord, she couldn't believe she'd even considered the two men in the same thought.

Wesley, though nearly the same age, had seemed
far younger than Tyler. By comparison he'd had a
much softer life, she supposed, than had Tyler. The
planes of his face had been more rounded, and his
fair coloring more genteel. And she never once heard
him use the coarse language Tyler uttered every day.
The others swore, too, but not if they thought she
could hear them. Tyler didn't care who heard him.

Yet if she were going to depend on any man
again—and she found that prospect most unlikely—
she'd be more inclined to trust Tyler Hollins than
Wesley Brandauer. Wesley's earnest, honeyed words,
she'd discovered, were nothing but lies—dark, hurt-
ful lies. His confession of love, his promise to stand
by her, all of it had evaporated as quickly as morning
fog along a summer stream. And with them had gone

a lot of the hope she'd carried in her heart since her orphaned childhood.

Libby sighed. She'd tried hard to put Wesley out of her thoughts—even when she'd been snowbound in Ben's cabin, and thinking about Wes had been *preferable* to the reality of her situation. She'd banished him from her heart, but she wasn't always successful at locking him out of her memory. And now, humiliation and Wes would be forever linked—

Just then, she became aware of a vibration in the floor under her. She lifted her head to listen, but there wasn't any sound, really. Not at first.

It began subtly, then increased to a heavier rumble that made the glass in the windows rattle. Floating above that sound was whooping and hollering that grew louder, then fainter, then louder again, as though the wind carried it to and fro. What was that? she wondered uneasily. It felt like an earthquake.

The commotion drew her to the window to investigate. She saw Tyler Hollins step up to the porch, as if to get out of the way of an oncoming train. He shifted his weight to one hip and crossed his arms over his chest. Looking down the road, he grinned. His dog, Sam, ran back and forth, barking his fool head off.

Resting her fingers on the windowsill, Libby leaned forward to look in the same direction. It was then that she saw two riders she recognized as Charlie Ryerson and Joe Channing gallop past the house toward the corral. Both of them were hooting at the tops of their lungs. Charlie's hat bounced on the back of his shoulders, secured only by its bonnet strings, and Joe waved a coil of rope alongside him. Behind them were about twenty horses of different colors and markings. A blur of flying manes and long tails sped past the porch on slender equine legs. The thunder created by their churning hooves all but drowned out the voices of the men following them, who were whooping and hollering, too. The strength and wild beauty of the spectacle made goose bumps rise along Libby's scalp, and she took a deep breath. She'd never seen anything like it.

The men drove the horses into the corral, where Noah and another man waited to close the gates. The animals milled around restlessly inside, snorting and whinnying, their heads lifted high on long, graceful necks.

Joe trotted back to Tyler, as mud-caked as his own horse. Libby saw his big smile peek out from under his mustache, and the rumble of his voice reached her through the open door.

"I was on my way back from Heavenly when I joined up with these boys. I couldn't let them have all the fun."

Tyler looked up at his foreman, and shaded his eyes against the late sun behind him. "I guess they didn't find any of our brand on the north range."

Joe hooked one knee over his saddle horn. "None that was alive, Tyler. But closer in, on Lodestar land, they ran into a few of the One Pine boys, and they told the same story. It's like that everywhere."

"One Pine—God, Joe. They didn't really think we've got their cattle, did they?" Amazement colored Tyler's voice.

Joe shrugged. "Well, Lat Egan is desperate, Ty. He's sent his boys on a wild-goose chase lookin' for their brand over half the territory, thinkin' a few strays that drifted are still alive. He's payin' the crew, but Kansas Bob said they're ready to quit. He lost just about everything, and worse, they think he's gone plumb crazy."

With his back turned to her, Libby couldn't see Tyler's face but she heard him sigh, and he hunched his shoulders, as though a shiver had run through him. "Jesus, isn't he ever going to stop looking back?"

"It ain't likely, Ty. It's been more than five years already," Joe replied.

Just then Rory came running up. "Joe! Did you and Charlie bring those mustangs in?"

"We sure did, Rory. Charlie and Kansas Bob and the rest were feelin' pretty grim about all the dead cattle till they came upon these horses. I found 'em a couple of miles outside of Heavenly, and we brought 'em in from there." He grinned again. "It sure felt good to be with healthy animals runnin' wild through the grass."

"Aw, dang it, Joe," Rory put in. "I wish I coulda gone with Charlie and Kansas Bob." His young face wore an expression of impatience and disappointment, and he scuffed at the porch planking with his boot. "All I've been doin' is pulling balky heifers out of the mud. Are you gonna let me go on the trail drive this time, or do I have to stay home again?"

"You've got to talk to the boss about that, Rory," Joe said, pointing the end of his rein at Tyler. "He's the one who gets final say around here. You know that."

Rory looked at Tyler expectantly.

Tyler gave the boy a mock punch in the arm with his gloved fist. "So you want to go to Miles City with us, huh? Eat dust and get rained on and stay up on night herd?"

Rory nodded so vigorously, Libby, watching him

through the glass, thought he'd end up with a head-ache. "Oh, yessir, I do!"

Tyler rested his chin on his hand and appeared to give the matter grave consideration. "You'll have to ride drags with the Coopers, you know, in back of eight or nine hundred cattle. Charlie and Kansas Bob will be riding point, and Joe and I will be ahead of them."

Rory's eyes shone with wonder, as though he were being offered a grand tour of Europe. "Yeah," he breathed.

Tyler laughed then and slung an arm around the back of the boy's neck. His genuine affection for Rory was obvious to Libby, as real, she thought, as if he were Tyler's own son. So he *did* care about someone. She saw it in his eyes when he turned, and heard it in his voice. And for a moment she felt a twinge of envy for the sense of belonging all these people had, with the land, and with one another.

"All right, you can come with us," he said. "But I'm guessing that by the time we get back, you'll wonder why you ever wanted to go."

Rory let out a whoop similar to the noise Joe and Charlie had made when they rode in. His entire face seemed to be consumed with a goofy grin. "Wait'll I tell Charlie!" he said.

"Tell me what, Sass?" The cowboy in question approached the group, as mud-covered and travel-weary as anyone Libby had ever seen. His one hand was tucked inside his slicker, reminding her of a picture she'd once seen of Napoleon.

"Tyler says I can go to Miles City with the herd!" Although he was trying to regain a careless noncha-lance, Libby could almost feel his excitement through the glass.

Charlie laughed. "Well, I guess every man's gotta try it once before he decides to make it a regular job."

"What's the matter with you, Charlie?" Tyler interrupted, and indicated his tucked-in hand. "Have you got a stomachache or something?"

"No, sir, nothin' that a cup of hot coffee won't cure," Charlie said, and glanced down at his boots as though embarrassed.

"You go on and get the coffee, then take Rory over to the corral to pick out a few horses for the trip." Tyler gave Rory another grin.

"Go over and have a look, Sass," Charlie said. "I'll meet you there in a minute."

Rory, losing his nonchalance for good, whooped again and jumped off the porch. He took off in the direction of the corral.

Libby moved away from the window and watched as Charlie came around the side and appeared in the kitchen doorway, where he lingered. He yanked off his hat, but his other hand was still inside his slicker.

" 'Afternoon, Miss Libby, ma'am."

"Hello, Charlie," she replied, and went to the dish rack for a blue enamel cup. "You look like you could use some hot coffee."

He took only one step forward, as though he were an awkward stranger to this kitchen. He smelled like horses, rain, and hard work. "Well, uh, yes, ma'am."

"You were right—you did make it back in time for supper tonight," she said, prodding the conversation along. Why was Charlie Ryerson who, up to now, had shown her only confidence and charming bravado, acting like a twelve-year-old schoolboy?

He smiled a bit sheepishly. "Me and the boys couldn't wait to get back to the Lodestar and some decent food. In fact, while we were out on the north range, I saw somethin' I thought you—well, they were right pretty, and—here."

He opened his slicker and pulled out a small bouquet of pale purple wildflowers. They were crushed and a little wilted from their journey, but at this place and moment in time, Libby thought they were the loveliest flowers she'd ever seen. He made a vain attempt to straighten some of the broken stems, then gave up and held the bouquet out to her.

"Oh, Charlie," she said, and smiled up into his scarlet face. "I didn't think any flowers were blooming yet. Thank you very much."

He immediately began backing away. "Well, ma'am, I, that is we want you to know that we're— um, glad you're here. It can be kind of hard out here for a lady sometimes—" He backed into the doorjamb, and his face turned redder still. Then he put his hat back on and hurried through the doorway.

She watched him trot across the yard to the corral, then she turned to put the cup back on the dish rack.

Charlie's kind gesture lightened Libby's heart considerably, and as she pumped water into a mason jar for her bouquet, she couldn't help but smile. If only his boss were as kind.

She caught sight of her white bandaged finger, and remembered Tyler's warm, light touch the night before. Well, actually, he could be kind when he wanted to be. But he was as stormy and unpredictable as winter on the Great Lakes.

Libby put the flowers on the worktable, where she could look at them from time to time, and returned to her job with the potatoes. Outside, she heard the discussion continue between Tyler and Joe.

On the porch, Tyler squinted up at his foreman. "How did it go in Heavenly?"

"It's like I told you before, Ty. There's no one left around here who'd be good for this job." He nodded toward the kitchen.

Annoyance, and some other emotion that Tyler didn't want to examine, washed over him. "Damn it, Joe, it can't be that hard to find a cook for a bunch of cowboys. How have we done it before?"

Joe leaned down from his saddle and spoke directly to him. "Before, outfits weren't closing down right and left. I'm tellin' you, Ty, the Big Die-Up finished a lot of ranchers. When there's no place to work, there's no workers." He sat up again. "I don't have to tell you that. You already know it."

In frustration, Tyler plunged his hands into his back pockets. Yes, he knew it, but Joe's answer didn't satisfy him. Joe hadn't sat next to Libby Ross last night, bandaging her hand and inhaling that sweet fragrance, trying to ignore the swell of her full breasts under her blouse. Joe hadn't been the one to peek into the woman's room while she slept, and see her hair spread out on the pillow, or get that foolish notion about angels. Joe hadn't fallen off his horse—something that *never* happened to Tyler—in front of the whole damned crew, just because the woman had distracted him. He idly kicked at one of the porch uprights, then made his decision.

"All right, Joe. I'll take care of it when I go into town tonight." He turned on his heel and strode away.

Behind him, he heard Joe call after him. "Now, Tyler, think about what you're doin'," he warned. "We've already got a cook, and a good one that the crew is happy with. We're eatin' like kings because she's here, and she told me she'd be willing to go to Miles City with us. Don't go stirrin' things up and makin' changes for no good reason."

Tyler stopped dead and turned. "I'll be god-damned and gone to hell before I'll take a woman on a trail drive. And I've got the best reason in the world, Joe. Like you just told Rory, I'm the boss."

In the kitchen, Libby Ross finished peeling the last potato, and slowly wiped her hands on her apron. She reached out and stroked one of the tender petals in the bouquet Charlie had brought her while she considered her next course of action. After she put the potatoes on the stove, she would probably have enough time to pack while they boiled. Sighing, she pushed herself away from the table, carried them to the cook pot, then turned to go upstairs.

# Chapter 6

"Ty, honey, I'm about done in," Callie pouted playfully. The single candle burning on the nightstand gave her an artificial but handsome radiance. "If word ever got around that I couldn't please my very favorite regular gentleman, I'd be out of business for sure." She flipped a corner of the linen sheet over his bare hips and reached for a wrapper so brief and transparent, it seemed nearly pointless.

Tyler felt a dull flush creep up his neck. In his life, this had never happened to him. "Don't worry, Callie. I'm not likely to rush out and tell anyone about it," he muttered.

She gave him that secret smile and idly rearranged a coppery sausage curl that rested on her collarbone. "Of course I know that. You're a better man than to talk about a lady's imperfections. And since you always put me in mind of an unbroken stallion, I know this must not be my night."

Tyler regarded the powdered, naked female kneeling next to him on her mattress, and couldn't help but smile back. She knew exactly what to say to soothe a male ego, even if it did sound a little practiced and overblown.

He suspected that none of Callie's customers ever

felt inadequate in her "boudoir," as she liked to call it. It was a luxurious curiosity in this hard-edged town on the western frontier. Draped in blue velvet and cream-colored lace, it was the most elegant room in all of Heavenly and for miles around. Nothing about the rough confines of the saloon downstairs even hinted at the lavishness at this end of the second floor, and not many men were invited to visit it. And, unless a fight broke out in the Big Dipper, the only sound that drifted upstairs was that of the piano.

For a woman who earned a living with her body—and he knew that had to be difficult—she seemed remarkably well kept, if a man didn't look at her too long or too hard.

"It didn't have anything to do with you," he said and put one arm under his head. "I've had a lot on my mind lately." That was the truth; between trying to assess the winter damages and deal with the matter of Lib—the cook, just falling asleep had become a challenge. The woman had invaded his thoughts continuously since he first set eyes on her, and every minute he'd spent with her after that only made things worse. He saw the soft curve of her cheek, her tiny waist— Why the hell he was thinking about her here, in a madam's bed, mystified him. There was nothing about Callie that could be confused with an angel. Angels! he scoffed to himself. What would he be conjuring up next? Pixies and stardust?

But scoff though he might, when Libby Ross's face had risen in his mind his desire for Callie just sputtered out, despite her most ambitious and creative efforts.

"Isn't that why you come to see me every Saturday night?" Callie asked, leaning over to purr in his ear and give him a closer view of her bare alabaster breasts. "So I can make you forget all your troubles, and ease your . . . mind?"

"That's exactly why I'm here, Callie," he replied, hoping to recover his dignity in this situation.

"And you're leaving again in a few days?"

He reached up and pulled her down to lie against him. "Yeah, I'll be gone for two or three weeks on the trail drive. But there's still tonight."

"Hmm, then I'd better enjoy this while I can," she said, and wriggled her hips against him. He looped an arm around her while she slid her hand under the sheet and ministered to him with professional skill. Her heavy gardenia perfume lay over them like a blanket. It was nearly suffocating compared to the airy, weightless scent of flowers and vanilla. . . .

Across the inside of his closed eyelids drifted a confused image of long honey-colored hair and big gray eyes. She nipped his earlobe, just sharply enough to make him turn his head and try to cover her lips with his own. Callie immediately pulled away and sat up, clutching her silly transparent wrap to herself in a rare show of modesty.

"Now, Ty, you know the rule. I'll pleasure you any way you like, except for kissing. I don't allow kissing. You didn't forget?"

He gazed at her and sighed. "No, I didn't forget." He considered her in silence for a bit longer. Finally, he held out his arm. "Just lie down here and sleep with me, then."

Her sculpted brows rose daintily. "That's all you want? What about—"

"That's all I want, Callie."

He thought she looked almost disappointed. Then

she smiled that cat smile, blew out the candle, and did as he asked. She snuggled up to him, resting her head on his shoulder.

Tyler stared at the ceiling until long after the piano downstairs fell silent.

The next morning, Tyler got his horse from the livery stable and headed back to the Lodestar, tired and frustrated in more ways than one. Trying to find a new cook, he'd talked to every sober man he saw in Heavenly who could drag one foot after the other. Not one was interested. Either they were already working for one of the surviving spreads, they were headed elsewhere, or they didn't know a single thing about cooking. As desperate as Tyler was to replace Libby Ross, he knew he couldn't bring home someone who was as bad or worse than their last cook. The crew wouldn't stand for it, and he wasn't much interested in lousy food himself.

As the bunch grass and sage slipped by, Tyler wrestled with the problem. What was he going to do now? Those cattle had to be in Miles City four weeks from now. That was the deal he'd made with the buyers. But he couldn't take a *woman* on a drive. Women weren't made for the hardships of the trail; they were delicate and easily injured. He'd had to think twice before even agreeing to let Rory go. And he was a strong fifteen-year-old boy, accustomed to working long hours, and in all kinds of weather.

He couldn't allow Libby Ross to go with them. Could he? Tyler pondered his alternatives, and kept coming around to the same truth. He had no alternatives, no choices. To meet the schedule he'd agreed to, and to feed the crew on the drive, he'd have to take her with him. Joe had said she was willing to go. . . .

He turned his horse and splashed through a shallow coulee to cut across the back field behind the ranch house. As it came into view on the valley floor, he saw a plume of smoke rising from the kitchen chimney. The form of Libby Ross rose in his mind's eye again, from her small, fragile-looking shape and softly curved breasts, up to those big gray eyes, where a nameless sadness lurked—

Goddamned and gone to hell, huh? he thought to himself with more than a little irony. It looked as though that vow was no longer an alternative, either.

"So, are you ready for your first trail drive, Sass?" Charlie plunged his spoon into the sugar bowl in front of him while Libby refilled his coffee cup. "Gonna get out there and ride drag and rope strays and go without sleep?"

"Yup, I am," Rory said, grinning. "I can't hardly wait."

The crew was gathered for Sunday lunch. Libby was accustomed to cooking full-blown Sunday dinners, and today she decided to serve roast beef. And since she expected this to be one of the last meals she'd fix here, she wanted to make it special.

Several times during the night she'd caught herself listening for Tyler Hollins's return. Did having "supper" in town mean that he also spent the night? It certainly didn't matter to her how he spent his time, she'd thought primly, or with whom. But after having overheard that conversation between Tyler and Joe, she'd been unable to sleep much. Surely if he was going to make her leave, he'd pay her for the time she'd worked here. And that little bit, combined with her own few dollars, might be enough to buy her that stagecoach ticket.

Finally, toward dawn she grew bold enough, and curious enough, to tiptoe out to the hall to see if his door was closed. But when she looked, it stood open, and in the pale wash of moonlight that filled his room, she saw that his bed was empty.

Charlie shook his head and laughed while he dumped three spoonfuls of sugar into his coffee. "You're sure in a hurry to get drowned or hit by lightning," he teased. "Or maybe you just want to go to Miles City and see what a big town is like, Sass."

Libby had to suppress her own laughter because she suspected that Charlie was serious about his last remark. She'd seen Miles City last fall when she'd arrived in Montana. The minor difference between it and Heavenly was that it had a few more blocks of tall, funny buildings, a real Chinese laundry, a photographer, and a bakery. But to young men who lived their days on the grasslands and in the wide-open hush of the country, Miles City might seem like an exciting place.

"Rory, why do they call you Sass, anyway?" she asked, as she set a spice cake on each of the two tables. "So far, I haven't heard you sass anyone."

"Well, it don't really have anything to do with that, Miss Libby," Rory answered cautiously. His expression made her think she'd unwittingly hit upon a touchy subject.

Low laughter rippled through the men. Joe, who was sitting at a place nearest the wall, turned sideways on the bench and leaned back. Putting one elbow on the table, he idly smoothed his mustache with his finger. A sly grin made his dark eyes gleam. "Charlie, maybe you should tell Miss Libby how Rory got his nickname. You're the one who gave it to him."

Charlie ducked his head, but Libby could see that he was blushing just as vigorously as he had when he gave her the wildflowers. "Aw, shoot, Joe. That ain't a proper story to tell a lady."

"It can't be as bad as all that," Libby said, getting curious now.

"Go ahead, Charlie," Kansas Bob urged, with a laugh. "I don't think Miss Libby will take offense. 'Course, she might not think much of you after she hears it."

Scowling, Charlie turned to Noah who sat at the table behind him. "You were there too, Noah. Why don't you tell her?"

"Nossir, not me," the weathered cowhand said, shaking his head and sinking his knife into the cake. "I was just glad Mr. Hollins never found out about it."

Libby started laughing, too. "Come on, now. How did Rory get his nickname? Will someone tell me, *please*?"

"I will," said a voice behind her, and Libby saw Charlie wince before giving his attention to his plate. All other murmuring in the room ceased as the men became suddenly interested in their food.

Joe grinned, and his chuckle rumbled up from deep in his chest. "Looks like you've had it now, cowboy," he said to Charlie.

She turned to find Tyler Hollins standing in the open doorway. When he walked in, the atmosphere in the kitchen changed. For Libby, the change stemmed from more than just his autocratic manner. He brought with him a physical charge, and the smell of horses, leather, and hay that, for reasons she couldn't define, seemed different on him than any other man present. He carried a shotgun, or maybe it was a rifle, that he propped against the back wall. Libby wasn't at all familiar with firearms; she couldn't tell which it was.

"One day a couple of summers back, Charlie, Noah, and Rory went into Heavenly." He pulled off his hat and gloves, then plucked a clean coffee mug from the table and went to the stove to fill it. "They were supposed to pick up the mail and some wire at Nort's and come back here. But Charlie does love the ladies. And he and Noah got a bad hankering for what goes on above the saloon where Callie's girls work."

Libby glanced away, remembering the woman's swish of violet taffeta and gardenia perfume.

Tyler poured a drizzle of cream into his mug, then continued. "Of course, they realized they couldn't take Rory up there. So they swore him to secrecy, left him at the bar and paid Eli, the barkeep, enough money to give Rory as much sarsaparilla as he could drink. And that was quite a bit. Ever since, Rory's been Sass. At least he has been to Charlie." He took a sip of coffee and shot a glance first at Rory, who scanned the other faces around the table like a cornered rabbit, then at Charlie, who looked as if he wished he were either dead or anywhere else. "At the time, they said Noah's horse had thrown a shoe, and that's why they were so late. I guess you boys didn't think I knew about that."

He sounded gruff, but despite the frown in his voice, Libby thought she saw a glimmer of reluctant amusement in his eyes. Again she was struck by the fact that he seemed to genuinely care about Rory.

"I didn't tell him," Rory whispered frantically to Charlie. "I didn't!"

"No, he didn't," Tyler interjected and leaned

against the edge of the worktable. "Eli told me. He said it was the most sarsaparilla he'd ever sold in one afternoon."

Guilt flashed through Libby. She wished she hadn't pressed to learn this secret. Its disclosure had only made everyone uncomfortable, including her. Tyler turned then and she found herself being scrutinized by those blue eyes.

"Mrs. Ross, I'd like to have a word with you, if you don't mind."

Libby's insides twitched when she heard that familiar, commanding voice. Well, this was the end, she was certain. He was going to tell her he'd found someone to take her place. At least she'd beat him to it this time: she was packed and ready to leave.

As if sensing disaster, everyone in the room suddenly found they had something that needed attending to at that very moment. The sound of benches scraping on the planking was followed by ringing spurs and a jumble of comments.

"The top rail on the corral needs shorin' up—"

"I believe that sorrel is goin' lame—

"I want to take another look at the roof on the woodshed—"

Half-eaten meals and pieces of spice cake with just a bite or two missing were abandoned on the tables as the men hurried out the door into the afternoon sun. Charlie turned and cast a hang-dog, apologetic glance at Libby, then sped outside.

Just before Joe left, he gave Tyler a searching look that she noticed he wouldn't meet. Joe jammed on his hat and shook his head in obvious irritation, slamming the door behind him.

Libby turned back to Tyler, and arched a brow. "You certainly know how to clear a room."

Ignoring her comment, he went to the back wall and picked up the shotgun he'd left there earlier. He eyed her bandaged finger. "How's your hand?" he asked.

"A little better." She took a deep breath and steeled herself for the bad news, then looked at the weapon again. "If you'll just get someone to bring down my trunk, I'll be ready to go in ten minutes. You won't need to shoot me," she quipped dryly, covering her dread with a veneer of wit.

He turned and stared at her. "Go?"

"Well, yes. Isn't that what you want to tell me, Mr. Hollins? That you found a cook in Heavenly to take on the trail drive?" She peeked around him, as though a driver might be standing there. "And that I should get my belongings together because one of the men is waiting to take me into town?"

"No, I wasn't going to say that." Libby saw his grip tighten on the barrel of the shotgun. "As a matter of fact, I want to tell you that we'll be leaving for Miles City in three days. If there's anything you need to get before that, you'd better do it. I'll have a couple of the boys roll the chuck wagon from the barn and chase the mice out of it."

She knew that her amazement must be plain on her face. After what he'd said yesterday, after the way he'd treated her since the day they met—

Something vital stirred in her soul, something that had slept through her lonely girlhood at the orphanage, and all the years of Eliza Brandauer's icy, genteel intimidation. A desire for something she'd never dreamed of having for herself: consideration. This desire roused itself now, and made her speak up.

"Miles City! I believe you swore yesterday, and

bitterly, too, that I wouldn't be going to Miles City. Something about hell—"

For the second time in two days, Tyler, who previously hadn't blushed for a good fifteen years, felt his face get hot. Damn it, but this woman tied him up in knots. He looked at her, small, straight-backed, and dignified as she stood before him. Her soft hair was tied back with a black ribbon and hung in a long fall nearly to her waist. "You weren't supposed to hear that," he muttered, breaking contact with her eyes.

"It would have been hard not to since the door was open," she said, crossing her arms over her chest. "And you and Joe didn't trouble to lower your voices. So I assume you couldn't find anyone else to do this job, and I'm your last and only choice."

He dodged this statement of fact. "We're going to Miles City, Mrs. Ross. Everybody at the Lodestar has a duty. We need someone to cook for us, and that's what you do with this outfit. It isn't easy work, I'll grant that, and the hours are long. But the pay is decent." With tremendous effort, Tyler managed to keep from fidgeting.

Libby Ross looked at him dead-on, with eyes that could have frozen the Musselshell River. "I'm sorry, Mr. Hollins, I won't be going with you."

"What?" He was completely flummoxed.

She drew herself up so tall that though the top of her head just cleared his shoulder, he felt as if she'd be looking down at him any minute.

"I have no intention of following you to the middle of nowhere, with a bunch of cattle and horses and cowboys, only to have you change your mind about me *again*. And maybe dump me in the nearest town we come to if you do find my replacement. I'd rather leave now and take my chances in Heavenly. I'll find a job somehow so that I can go back to Chicago."

He sputtered wordlessly before finally finding his voice. "That's a lousy thing to say. I told you I'd be responsible for you as long as you work for me."

Her nose came up just a notch. "And you can decide to end that whenever you choose. Isn't that so?" She waited as though she expected an answer.

He stared back at her. He couldn't believe this turn of events. Here he'd resisted the very idea of having this distracting woman in his house, with her sad gray eyes and scent of vanilla . . . And now when he'd finally come around to a grudging acceptance of her, when he really *needed* her help, she was refusing!

"Well, damn it, this puts us in a bind. If it's the money—"

She shook her head and smiled. For that instant, it was unsettling how much this smile resembled Callie's: as though she knew something that he didn't. "It's not the money, Mr. Hollins. It's a matter of respect. And I've had precious little of it from you while I've been here. You're more polite to your dog."

Now Tyler shuffled a bit and looked out the window. How the hell was he supposed to defend himself against that? Maybe he hadn't always been as tactful as he should have. It had been a long time since he'd had to deal with any female besides Callie, and she had no particular expectations of him. Plus, she was safe.

Libby Ross, on the other hand, always made him think of that absolute truth lurking at the back of his mind, a hard lesson he'd learned long ago: tender sensibilities got wounded and tender hearts were inclined to break. He knew he'd made some sacrifices over the years in leaving those emotions behind. Sometimes he felt it very keenly that he chose to remain on the outskirts, keeping himself apart from others.

Tyler was not unaware that except for general greetings from the men, he'd silenced all conversation when he'd walked in earlier. The aroma alone had been enough to draw him into the kitchen. The hum of conversation that he heard, and the feminine laughter, only pulled at him harder. He'd hung back for a minute, watching from the shadows on the porch as Libby moved around the tables. It was plain to him, and a little annoying, that without much fuss or bother, she'd fit easily into the daily life of the Lodestar. Without much fuss or bother for anyone but him, he thought. Now she turned those big gray eyes on him, half expectant, half wary.

If politeness would convince her to go with them . . . He held out his hand in an open gesture. "We'd all be much obliged if you'd come along with us on the trail drive, Mrs. Ross. The men work hard and I know they'd appreciate having you cook for them."

Suddenly Libby found herself in a bargaining position. She held the cards. Tyler's cold, impassive mask had slipped again, and more by instinct than any true knowledge of a man's mind or heart, she realized her advantage.

"Mr. Hollins, I'll come on this trip under two conditions."

"Conditions?" He lifted a brow and waited for her to continue, but that long-barreled gun in his hands made her pause a beat.

"I don't belong in Montana. When we reach Miles City, I want to collect my pay so that I can get on the train and go back to Illinois. You should be able to find someone else to take my place there."

The afternoon sun had dropped just low enough in the sky to shine through the window. It made a halo on his chestnut hair and cut a bright path across his lean face. Funny, she hadn't noticed before that his eyelashes were almost blond at the roots, not even when he'd sat right next to her to bandage her finger.

"All right, Mrs. Ross, I agree. What's the other condition?"

She drew a deep breath, feeling as though she were about to ask him for a very personal favor. It was difficult to get the words out above a whisper. "I'd like you to call me Libby. Not Mrs. Ross."

He lowered his eyes and glanced at the floor, and she thought he sighed. He looked up then, and caught her staring. He held her with his gaze just a moment before answering.

"Well then, Libby, I guess you'd better call me Tyler."


"This time wait until I get behind you before you fire," Tyler ordered. He trotted back from the fence where he'd set up a line of tin cans and empty bottles. His watch chain and belt buckle gleamed in the spring sun.

Libby stood in the side yard, his shotgun in her inexperienced hands. From the corner of her eye she could see some of the men lounging around the open barn door, watching the proceedings with great interest. Once she and Tyler had come to an agreement about the trail drive, he'd made her come out here to learn to shoot. It seemed like she'd been at this for hours. First he'd taught her to load this fearsome weapon, and he'd made her go through that several times, once without looking. Then they'd moved on to target practice. But for all her attempts and his instructions, she hadn't improved one whit. She'd missed every one of her intended targets, and blown off some of the top fence rail. Truth be told, she was afraid of guns and didn't like handling this one.

"I really don't think I'm going to get any better at—"

He reached into his front pocket and pulled out a couple of shells. "If you're going with us, you have to learn to shoot. Out on the range, there's no telling when you might need to know how."

"Wonderful," she muttered under her breath, and reloaded the shotgun. She didn't regret her decision to make this trip to Miles City. It might not be the easiest way to get there, but it would do the job. She just hadn't realized what it would entail.

"Now take aim at one of those things," Tyler said, gesturing at the bottles and cans.

She took aim.

"Which one are you looking at?" he asked. He wasn't touching her, but she could feel him standing behind her, and his words were spoken close to her ear.

"That Arbuckle's coffee can on the end." She waved the point of the shotgun in its general direction.

"All right, go ahead."

She squeezed the trigger, the shot blasted from the barrel, and this time, she hit the tree at the end of the fence. A pair of crows, dislodged by the misfire, squawked irritably and took refuge on the woodshed roof. Behind her, Tyler sighed.

"Oh, dear," she said, looking at the smoldering gash in the tree trunk. She glanced again at the men watching her from the barn, who were beginning to make some good-natured but loud remarks. She felt so awkward and incompetent with this.

Following the path of her gaze, Tyler stared at the group until they began to break up. Then with an obvious note of impatience, he said, "This just isn't that hard."

With frightening speed and deftness, he stepped in front of her, pulled the revolver from the holster on his hip, and shattered two of the bottles on the top rail. The quick blasts echoed off the outbuilding with a sharp pinging noise, and made Libby flinch.

"I-I really ought to get supper started," she said. She backed away from him and let the end of the heavy weapon drop.

He considered her, and drew a deep breath as though he were counting to ten. His stern expression smoothed out. "All right. You've got one shell left in there. Just shoot the damned coffee can, and we'll call it good."

Libby pointed the shotgun at the can.

"You're too low," he carped. "You'll hit the fence again." This time she felt the slight pressure of his chest against her back and he reached around to put his hand under hers where she held the long barrel. The instant their hands touched, her heart lurched. She could feel the warmth of his body through his shirt and her shawl. The warm smell of him, of leather and hay and some other scent, new yet familiar, drifted to her, making it very difficult for her to concentrate on the can. The pressure behind her increased, and she found that she was forced to lean back just a bit in order to maintain her balance. At least that was the reason she gave herself. He rested his hand on the small of her back, and the tone of his voice altered subtly. "Um, try it now."

"But I'll probably miss again," she said. Her throat was suddenly dry, and she felt less certain than ever of her marksmanship.

"No, you won't." His mouth was right next to her ear, and his low-spoken words held a faint intimacy. He tightened his hand on hers, holding her aim steady. "I won't let you. Don't be scared, Libby. Go ahead, now—pull the trigger."

She squeezed the metal lever under her finger, and the coffee can flew off the fence rail.

"I did it!" She turned slightly in his half embrace and beamed at him over her shoulder, delighted with her minor success. He chuckled. At this close range, she could see the red stubble in his beard, and when she let her gaze drift up to his eyes, she paused. There was confidence and intense control reflected in their blue depths, but she also saw a hint of feral possessiveness, powerful and elemental.

Suddenly she was as frightened as she'd been at any moment since coming to Montana. This was a fear that had nothing to do with the danger of freezing to death, or burying a dead man, or handling a firearm. This went straight to her heart—

From the general direction of the barn came loud applause and whistling. "Good shootin', Miss Libby!"

Tyler dropped Libby's hand and jumped back.

"You'd better get on back to the kitchen." He was all business again, formal and remote, and the friendly warmth left his voice. "I imagine everyone will be getting hungry pretty soon. We'll—you can practice this again tomorrow." He took the shotgun from her, then turned on his heel and walked toward the barn.

She watched him go, following with her eyes the broad sweep of his shoulders and the way his hair brushed the back of his collar. She realized then what scent she'd smelled on him earlier.

It was the scent of gardenias.

Tyler strode into the barn, hoping that he gave every appearance of purpose. In reality, he was escaping into its dim interior. Escaping from a pair of big gray eyes and the fragrance of honey-colored hair. He could still see her in his mind, the incongruous but common picture of a woman in the West: her apron ties flapping in the wind like kite tails while she aimed his big twelve-gauge shotgun. With her hair pulled back like that, he could see the smooth nape of her neck, and the tender, soft place behind her ear. . . .

Tyler shook his head impatiently. From his point of view, the shooting lesson had gone well enough as long as Libby kept missing the targets. He'd been able to maintain his role as the objective tutor, issuing instructions and drilling her in technique. His mistake was in listening to the discouragement and worry that crept into her voice. The sound of it grazed his heart, and he knew she wouldn't learn if she didn't feel that she'd accomplished something. So he stood behind her to guide the shot. But the second he leaned his chest to her shoulder, his body responded sharply to her warm softness.

The predicament he'd experienced the night before with Callie was immediately and unquestionably forgotten. His arousal had made him wonder what it would be like to press a kiss behind Libby's ear, to hold her to himself in the night. And when he realized where his imagination was taking him, did he break the contact, as a prudent man would have? Oh, no. Instead, like an idiot, he'd cradled her hand in his, under the pretense of helping her hit the target.

Tyler sat down hard on a hay bale with a rag, a cleaning rod, and a tube of Winchester gun grease. When he'd assumed she'd be trouble for the Lodestar, this wasn't the kind of trouble he anticipated.

"So you decided to let her come with us."

Tyler looked up from his task of cleaning the shotgun, and saw Joe's silhouette in the barn doorway.

Tyler shrugged, a bit uncomfortable. "Yeah, well . . ."

"I guess hell is gonna have to wait a while longer for you, then."

He returned his attention to the twelve-gauge. Jesus, was *everyone* going to remind him of that vow he'd made?

The foreman ambled in. "She ain't much of a shot though, is she?" He sat down on the hay bale next to Tyler and crossed his ankle over his knee. Leaning against the wall behind him, he groped around in his shirt pockets for his makin's and began rolling a cigarette.

"She'll improve." Tyler reached for the rag.

"I guess she don't have to be another Annie Oakley," Joe allowed. "At least she finally hit that can. 'Course, she had a little . . . help." He closed his tobacco pouch, pulling the drawstring with his teeth.

Tyler could hear the smile in Joe's voice. He didn't want to discuss Libby Ross, but he knew Joe. If Tyler flat out refused to talk about the woman now, or even tried to sidetrack him, he'd have to put up with joshing that would never end. For a man who'd spent most of his life out on the open plains studying horses, cattle, and weather, Joe could often nail a man's thoughts with surprising skill. He'd had that knack as long as Tyler had known him, since they were just boys, no older than Rory. Maybe that was why Tyler let him get away with it.

"Yeah, I guess she could improve her aim if you work with her every day." Joe struck a match on the sole of his boot, and the dim corner where they sat glowed briefly with its flame.

"It doesn't have to be me working with her," he said. He pointed the long barrels toward the light from the doorway and peered down them. "Rory can teach her. He's as good with firearms as anyone else on this place." God, he didn't want to get into a cozy arrangement with her every damned day.

Joe exhaled a cloud of smoke. "Nope, not Rory. I need him out on the range. In fact, I can't think of anyone I can spare right now."

Tyler looked up and lifted a skeptical brow. "No one? What about Darby, or one of the Cooper boys?"

"Nope. Looks like it'll *have* to be you, Ty."

Suspicious that he'd been maneuvered into this position, Tyler frowned but maintained his silence.

"I don't suppose she'll stay long after we get back," Joe continued with a low rumble that passed for a chuckle. He took off his hat and slouched down on the hay bale to get comfortable. "That is unless Charlie asks her to marry him, and she'll have him. And I wouldn't be surprised if he does ask."

Tyler frowned at him, and pushed the rod down the shotgun's barrel. "What's Charlie got to do with this? I thought he was used to having women chase *him*."

Joe shook his head as if they were talking about a man with a terminal illness. "Worst case of Cupid's cramp I ever saw. A couple boys are a little calf-eyed over her. But Charlie's got it bad. He's real sweet on old Ben's widow. Says it's a goddamned shame and disgrace that such a fine young woman should be left on her own in the world with no man to look after her."

Tyler had already overheard some of the men talking about Charlie and his infatuation for the cook. Resentment had surged through him, although he couldn't say why, exactly. A cowboy with a crush was nothing unusual, especially out here where women were scarce. With a female as close as the kitchen, he knew something like this would happen.

"He does, huh? Well, he'd better not start pestering her. Charlie might be our top hand, but he's tried my patience more than once over the years."

Joe studied the rowel on his spur where it hung near his knee, and gave it a spin. "I don't know, Ty. A woman could do worse than Charlie, and he sounds likes he's ready to settle down. He don't have much but he's loyal, and he'd be good to a wife." He cast a sidelong glance at Tyler.

Tyler stood and leaned the shotgun against his shoulder, his patience with the entire subject at an end. "Well, you'd better tell him to look for one somewhere else. Libby Ross is leaving the drive when we get to Miles City. She wants to go back to Chicago, and I'm going to give her the money to do it."

As he walked away, he heard Joe mutter, "Charlie ain't the only one who'll come to be sorry about that."

# Chapter 7

Under a slate-gray sky, Libby gripped the lines to her mule team, and huddled deeper into the boy's saddle coat that Tyler had bought for her. Actually, she'd insisted that he only advance her the cost of the coat and a new pair of gloves. She fully intended that he take it out of her pay when they reached Miles City.

At the other end of the reins, her four mules shifted and stamped in the cold dawn. Behind her were amassed almost a thousand head of cattle—so Noah had told her. She could hear them bawling, and the clicking of their horns as they bumped into one another sounded like arrhythmic castanets. Above that rose the sound of the cowboys yelling to the stock and to one another, and the nervous whinnying of the horses in the cavvy off to her left. Late yesterday, Joe had switched Rory from the job of riding drag to handling the horses. Even though the position of wrangler wasn't a promotion, Rory was as gravely proud as if he'd been given the job of trail boss. Joe told her that as wrangler, Rory would also be responsible for digging the fire pits, gathering firewood, and hitching her mule team, so at least she'd have some help.

Tyler had ridden by several times, apparently seeing to last-minute details. All the men were wonderful riders, but he looked especially good on horseback, and she drew a deep breath at the sight of him. Slim-hipped and wide-shouldered, he was tall and moved with an easy grace. The low-hanging mist muted and blended the scene around her, making it hard to tell one distant cowboy from another. But she could pick Tyler out of the group with no difficulty at all. She let her gaze wander over him again, taking in all the details of his face and form: his strong hands encased in gloves, his clean profile, his quick, appealing smile. And he *was* smiling a lot this morning, as if the prospect of a cattle drive agreed with him. For at least the hundredth time, she wondered if she'd made the right decision in agreeing to come on this trip. It was a means to achieve her goal, but that apprehension she'd felt during her first shooting lesson was strong upon her.

Over the last three days, her education in frontier survival had been stepped up and she fell into bed at night, too exhausted to dream.

Joe had given her a condensed lesson in driving the chuck wagon, and in building a campfire. Tyler produced another list that told her what provisions to double-sack and load into the chuck box. And she'd endured several hours of shooting practice with Tyler standing next to her, issuing instructions. She'd gained not one shred of confidence that she'd be able to fire the shotgun, much less hit a target, in an emergency. But at least he'd treated her with more courtesy and respect.

After that first lesson, he'd maintained a careful distance between them most of the time, but once or twice he put a hand to her elbow or her shoulder.

She was so undone by the feel of him, it was odd to her that those were the only times she hit her targets. And though she knew she shouldn't, she craved the comfort of his light touch, and found herself wishing for it again.

Then she'd remember the telltale scent of gardenias on his clothes the afternoon she'd first fired the shotgun, and the fear would return, stronger than ever.

Tyler Hollins was her *employer*. Had she forgotten the peril of letting herself become attracted to the master of the house? On top of that, he was engaged in some kind of carnal association with Heavenly's prosperous madam.

No, Libby thought, resettling herself on the wagon seat. This was for the best. The sooner she left Montana, the sooner she could begin her life again. Her lonely, misadventurous trip out here to marry Ben had been a false start. She hadn't really run away from her problems; she'd only brought them with her to a new place. But the same hope and determination that had carried her out here would carry her back. Now her trunk was packed and tucked beneath the seat under her. Within the month, she'd be in Chicago where she belonged.

Libby glanced at the ranch house where it waited in the misty green valley for the day when these men would return to it. The low angle of the dawning sun gave the log building a tranquil hominess that she'd not noticed until now. She felt no particular regret that she wouldn't be coming back after the cattle drive. For all its rugged beauty, Montana could never have been her home. She was almost certain of that. Almost.

"All right, Miss Libby," Joe called as he rode by

at a trot. "Give those mules a slap and let's get going." He took a lead position next to Tyler at the head of the procession, then stood in his stirrups and whistled back at the men behind him. Waving his hat in a wide arc over his head, he lifted his deep voice. "When we get to Miles City, the first round of beers is on me."

Libby took a long, final look at the ranch house. Then she flapped the reins on the mules' backs and the chuck wagon rolled forward toward the sunrise.

"Got any hot water going?"

Libby recognized the voice, but didn't bother to look up. The fog had burned off and the sun was bright in the spring sky, but the firewood Rory had gathered for her was damp. She poked at her sputtering, smoky fire, already feeling beleaguered and drained, and it was only noon.

With a bit of effort she hoisted a Dutch oven, heavy with water and beans, onto the rack suspended over the fire. The beans probably wouldn't be ready to eat until tomorrow morning. She realized she'd be able to cook them only during the short time they stopped for the lunch. Then she'd have to pack up the iron kettle, and put it on the fire to simmer again at their next stop. If she'd thought the Lodestar was primitive, cooking out of the back of a wagon beat all.

"Hot water for what?" she muttered. "Afternoon tea and scones?"

She didn't mean to be abrupt, but Tyler sounded altogether too peppy to suit her. And why shouldn't he? What had he done besides ride ahead of her to scout out this stopping place, and lope alongside the cattle making mooing noises while he waved a coil of rope to urge them along? On the other hand, she had struggled with these balky mules. With a seemingly perverse sense of direction, the animals had led the rough chuck wagon over every bone-jarring rut and hole on the prairie. Inside, everything that could make noise clattered: the cast-iron cooking utensils, the tin plates and cups, the shovel, the shotgun, her teeth. And they'd come only *six* miles. She realized that this job would be much harder than she'd anticipated. But she wasn't about to let Tyler know that. He already thought she was a puny, helpless Easterner.

And now he wanted hot water.

"Not for tea, Libby. I want to shave."

She lifted her eyes then and saw him standing there, holding his razor, a mug, and a shaving mirror. He'd slung a towel over one shoulder.

"Oh," was the only reply she could make. He'd unbuttoned his blue-striped band-collar shirt, pulled out the tails, and rolled up his sleeves. The sun fell across his lean face and the shadow of his one-day beard that sparkled with blond, red, and dark brown bristles. She let her eyes follow the line of his throat down to his uncovered chest. Something about that display of skin and muscle between the edges of his gaping shirtfront was more intimate than outright nakedness. Her gaze dropped past the waist of his pale buckskin chaps until the glint of his silver belt buckle made her realize what she was looking at.

Libby felt her cheeks grow hot and she looked away, but not before she saw his expression. It was the same one she'd seen the day she shot the coffee can off the fence: controlled, powerful, territorial. "Th-there is no warm water. I'll put some on to heat." She turned to get a kettle from the wagon, but she was stopped when his hand closed on her arm.

"No, that's all right, I'll use water from the barrel. I just thought I'd ask. Um, do you have a basin?"

"Well, yes ..." Basin, Libby thought blankly, basin. Where had she— Suddenly she couldn't think of anything except the way his hand felt on her arm. She glanced up at his eyes, an act that just about completed her discomposure.

He released her forearm and lifted his brows. "Maybe there's one under the chuck box?"

She stepped back, feeling silly and tongue-tied. "Yes, of course, yes." She rummaged around in the compartment beneath the wagon bed, and withdrew a white enamel basin. Taking it, he nodded his thanks, and walked around to the other side of the wagon to fill it at the water barrel. Now that she was so acutely conscious of him, his spurs told her every step he took, reminding her of a cat with a bell on its collar. Libby released a deep, quiet breath, and bent over the beans to give them a stir.

She pushed a long lock of hair back over her shoulder. Why the devil should he have that effect on her? she wondered impatiently. Just because he was attractive? That wasn't a good enough reason. In fact, it might be the worst reason. Wesley had been handsome. Actually, not as. Tyler was rugged, harder hewn. But the true measure of a man was in his deeds, not his looks. Libby straightened and looked back at the boots on the other side of the wagon box.

Maybe that was where the biggest difference lay: Wesley Brandauer had felt no sense of responsibility at all.

Tyler seemed to have taken the whole world onto his shoulders.

Tyler turned the spigot on the barrel, and called himself an idiot. He never used anything but cold water to shave, not even at home. He'd only dreamed up that excuse to talk to Libby, to see how she was doing, to see *her* . . .

He propped up the mirror on the lid of the barrel and raked his hair back from his forehead. While he lathered his face, he continued to silently berate his reflection. He'd meant to stay away from her on this trip, hadn't he? He lifted the razor and began its downward stroke just below his left sideburn. Sure, circumstances had forced him to bring her along, but Joe, Noah, *Charlie*—all of them were looking out for her, he argued with himself. Maybe, but ultimately he was responsible for her; she was just a helpless greenhorn. Well, not so helpless, he was beginning to realize. For someone who'd never set foot in the country—and Rory said she'd told him that—she was managing surprisingly well without anyone's help. Just the fact that she'd traveled all the way out here from Chicago, and come through the winter, said a lot about her. She'd make a good wife for some man.

Then there was the way she lit up when the men complimented her cooking; it was as though no one had ever shown her respect or appreciation before now. And it made him want to protect her. It didn't take much effort on his part to imagine her lying safe in his arms in his big four-poster back at the Lodestar, her soft, full curves limned in a wedge of moonlight while she granted him the pleasure of slow, moist kisses and the solace of her body. . . .

Tyler realized that his shaving had come to a complete stop. Impatiently, he scraped at the rest of his beard, and in his haste, nicked his chin.

"Damn it all," he mumbled, and pressed a corner of the towel to the cut. The woman stirred emotions in him that he'd buried long ago with a mahogany coffin on the green bluffs above the ranch house. And he aimed to keep things that way. He wasn't about to get all moony over Libby like some line shack cowboy who hadn't seen a female in four or five months. Not that it could happen, he reassured himself. He had his arrangement with Callie, and it suited him just fine.

He took a final look at his reflection, then he glanced up at Libby's very feminine shape as she crossed the camp with a coffeepot.

At least it had suited him until now.

No sooner had Libby fed the crew and washed the dishes than she was back on the wagon seat again, driving the mules to the night campsite. The herd was far behind and wouldn't catch up until late afternoon. That would give her time to make enough sourdough biscuits to go around at tonight's supper and tomorrow's noon meal.

All the men, including Joe and Tyler, were back with the herd. After Tyler selected this spot, only Rory had come along with her to put the cavvy in the rope corral and dig her fire pit. He rode in dragging a dead branch he'd lassoed for fuel.

Libby was glad for his help. It didn't matter how determined she was to prove her ability and avoid Tyler's displeasure—she couldn't pretend that she wasn't tired. Her skirt was damp to the knees from dragging it through the wet grass. She wasn't accustomed to hauling water to wash dishes, or cooking food in progressive shifts. By the time they finally got to Miles City, she hoped she'd have enough energy left to step up to the railroad platform.

Now she stood at the dropleg worktable in back of the wagon. She had to admit that this was a pretty clever arrangement. Tyler had told her that cattle baron Charles Goodnight invented the chuck wagon twenty years earlier, and that its best feature was the chuck box itself. Its hinged door served double duty as a work space. She sprinkled the surface with flour and began rolling out the sourdough. The sound of Rory's shovel digging into the earth gave her a chill, reminding her of the day she'd dug Ben's grave.

She glanced up from the dough, and watched the youngster for a moment. He looked strong and healthy. Working at the Lodestar was obviously good for him, but he seemed so young to be away from his home and family.

"Rory, have you been at the Lodestar very long?" She dipped her biscuit cutter in the flour.

He straightened and dragged his arm across his sweating forehead. " 'Bout five years, I guess," he said.

"Five years! Goodness, you were really young when you came to the ranch."

He shrugged and sank the shovel blade into the dirt again. "Joe was fifteen when he went to work for Tyler's pa. Kansas Bob came to the Lodestar when he was fourteen."

"But you were ten! Did you run away? Lose your family?"

"Naw, my old man knows where I am." It wasn't longing or regret she heard in his answer, but rather a weary bitterness that momentarily aged the very timbre of his young voice. "Anyway, Tyler says there ain't no such thing as an old cowboy. He says this is a young man's job."

Libby smiled. She could understand that—ranching was hard work. "No old cowboys? What happens to them?"

"No one's sure, Miss Libby." He looked at her from under the brim of his hat and gave her a big grin. "Sometimes they become cranky old cooks."

She laughed and put her biscuits into the bottom of a Dutch oven. "Maybe because they have cranky bosses."

By the time the crew arrived at the night camp, the sun was low in the sky, and the coffeepot was on the fire. Given her rough working conditions, Libby thought she had put together a reasonable meal.

The men ate in two shifts, and between serving big portions of beans, pork, and biscuits, she watched for Tyler to come in. But he didn't. She spotted him on the western range, just beyond the perimeter of camp, riding against the yellow-orange sunset like a sentinel. What drove Tyler Hollins? she wondered as she slapped a scoop of beans onto a plate. What substitute had he found for friendship that made him such a remote, solitary man?

She was still watching the chestnut-haired rider—and she could well imagine his hair though it was hidden by his hat—when Charlie Ryerson came to her for his supper. He'd lagged behind, waiting until the rest were busy with their own meals to get his plate.

He glanced at the group gathered around the campfire, obviously hoping for a measure of privacy.

"Evenin', Miss Libby. Did you fare all right today?" It sounded like polite conversation but he spoke gravely, as if the words hid a greater meaning.

Libby tightened her plaid shawl against the late afternoon coolness. "It's a little harder than I thought it would be," she admitted, pulling out a dish and coffee mug. Soreness was beginning to settle into her arms and shoulders from her daylong struggle with the reins. "I'd always thought that 'stubborn as a mule' was just a saying. But they really *are* stubborn."

He laughed, and his big mustache stretched across his face. "Yes, ma'am, they can be. I reckon that's why mule skinners learn to cuss so good."

Libby laughed, too.

His expression grew serious then. "But drivin' a chuck wagon ain't a job for a lady. It ain't right that you should have to be out here trailin' cattle. I-I s'pose I got no right to say so, but you ought to be livin' on a nice little spread with some young'uns to look after and a man to come home to you at night."

Libby felt a twinge in her heart. That was what she'd believed waited in Montana when Ben had sent for her. She curbed a sigh, then smiled into Charlie's sincere face. "Things don't always work out the way we hope, I guess. But I'm only driving this wagon to Miles City. Then I'm catching the train for Chicago."

"I know, Joe told me." He glanced around again, then leaned forward, suddenly earnest. "Miss Libby—" He swallowed. "Miss Libby . . . I-I've got a little money put by. It ain't much, but it would give us a start. That is, if you—" He left the sentence unfinished and turned a vivid shade of red.

Libby gaped at him. "A start?"

He pulled in a deep breath and went on, his words
urgent. "I've got my eye on a piece of land up by
Mosby. It's in a real pretty little spot, with a creek
and lots of pines. It would be a good place to grow
cattle and kids—y'know, make a life." He shifted and
looked down at his boots, then up at her again. "I've
had some wild ways in my past . . . uh, I s'pose you
probably figured that out. And I know this ain't the
courtship you deserve, but our time is short. I want
to give you a few days to think about—well, bein'
my wife." He reached out as if to touch her arm,
then let his hand fall. Instead, he whipped off his
hat and withdrew a blush pink flower. He laid it
gently on the worktable. "Miss Libby, ma'am, I'd be
honored if you'd think it over."

"But we don't know each—Montana isn't—I—"

"Hush, now." He spoke to her in the same soothing tone she'd heard him use on skittish horses. "Just
ponder it a spell." He turned and hurried away with
his plate and cup before she could find her voice to
say anything.

Her hand at her throat, Libby stood in the gathering dusk and stared at his retreating back, then at
the bloom in front of her. Had Charlie Ryerson just
asked to marry her? That was what it had sounded
like, but she could hardly believe it. After he'd
brought her wildflowers that afternoon in the
kitchen, she suspected he might be smitten with her.
But she'd had no idea that he was truly serious. She
picked up the blossom by its slender stem and held
it to her nose, then flexed her aching shoulders.

Maybe she shouldn't find it so strange. After all,
she was in Montana because she had answered a
newspaper advertisement for a wife. Maybe out here,
a proposal coming from a man she'd met barely a

month earlier, and hardly knew, wasn't unusual at all. The difference was that being a mail-order bride— marrying a total stranger as soon as she'd stepped off the stage—had been mainly a business arrangement.

In Charlie's honest offer, she sensed something much more substantial. Yet only a little more appealing.

"How was your first day?"

Startled out of her thoughts, Libby turned and saw Tyler walking toward her. An electric jolt shot through her, and to her utter dismay, she realized that surprise had very little to do with her reaction.

His height gave him long strides and her eyes were drawn to the chaps covering his jeans. His shirt-sleeves were rolled up to his elbows, and his gloves were cuffed at his wrists. The lantern hanging from the side of the wagon picked up blue-green glints in his eyes, and he wore the faint, troubled frown that she'd grown accustomed to seeing at the Lodestar. He smelled of horses and the coming night air, and he brought with him the same palpable physical intensity that she always felt in his presence.

"Fine! Uh, just fine. I didn't have a bit of trouble," she lied, and put down the flower. "I've never done this before, but I've always worked. I'm used to it. Where I grew up, if we didn't work, we didn't eat." Picking up a tin plate, she put two big spoonfuls of beans on it, but when she stretched for a biscuit she pulled up short with a wince. The muscles in her arms and shoulders were stiffening like leather left in the rain.

Tyler looked at her and lifted one brow knowingly. He took off his gloves and tucked them into the waist of his chaps, then reached for the biscuit himself. He knew she was lying about the way she felt. He could see fatigue in her face, and her hobbled movements weren't lost on him.

Neither had been Charlie's proposal. God, Joe had been right—Charlie was serious. Tyler hadn't meant to eavesdrop. But he'd reached the front end of the wagon in time to hear the last words of the cowboy's plainspoken request for Libby's hand. And he'd lurked there like a thief, waiting for her reply, wondering why his stomach was in knots.

"Where did you grow up that you had to work so hard?" Tyler took a bite of the tender biscuit. The evening breeze carried Libby's faint scent of flowers and vanilla.

A scent that now sometimes made him think of warmth and home.

No matter that he impatiently rejected the idea as soon as it would occur; it kept returning. Wispy tendrils of hair blew across her eyes and she brushed them back, then turned away and busied herself with searching for a fork. She was slow to reply, and then her words were barely audible.

"Erie Foundling Home."

A foundling home. Tyler clenched his jaw. No, damn it, no. He wouldn't ask anything else. Her response created more questions than he wanted answers to. She'd be on her way back to Chicago in a few more days. Then the Lodestar would return to normal, he could go back to his Saturday nights at the Big Dipper, and everyone's thoughts—including his own—would return to the business of work and responsibility.

Libby tensed, wishing she'd kept her mouth shut about the orphanage. Talking about it brought back painful memories. Of a young, dying mother who, she now realized, had been little more than a child herself when she'd left behind four-year-old Liberty. Of the years of aching loneliness that had followed. Tyler gave her a long, searching look, and she braced herself for the inevitable questions that surely hovered in his mind.

Instead, he took his plate from her outstretched hand and turned to go. But then he stopped and reached for the flower on the worktable. "I've never known these to bloom this early in the year." His voice had a pensive edge, as though he were remembering another time and place himself.

"Do you know what kind of flower it is?" she asked, grateful for the change of subject.

He looked up at her and a smile pulled at the corners of his mouth. "Yeah. They grow along the porch back at the ranch house." He pressed the bloom back into her hand. His touch was warm, vital. "It's a wild prairie rose."

Libby watched him upend a keg, away from the rest of the men, to sit and eat his supper. Seeing him like that, with the last of the day's sun streaking his hair with auburn and copper threads, more than anything she wanted to go sit by him. But that was ridiculous, it was out of the question.

As soon as she'd eaten her own supper and washed the dishes, in exhaustion Libby struggled to climb into the wagon. But over the last few hours, her cramping shoulder muscles had almost locked, and pulling herself up to the wagon bed proved to be futile. She stepped on the wheel hub and reached for the side of the wagon box, but had trouble getting any farther. After several unsuccessful attempts, frustrated and weary, she stood by the front wheel and looked up at the seat that seemed as high as a mountain. Gingerly, she moved her shoulders.

"Having a little trouble?" Tyler asked. Carrying an empty cup, he was apparently on his way to the coffeepot. Light from a nearby lantern accented the fine-boned structure of his handsome face and cast shadows on his chest where the collar of his shirt gaped open.

"Trouble? No, no. I was just going to settle in for the night." Why did she get that funny, restless feeling inside whenever he came near her? "Did you need something?"

He considered her for a few seconds. "No, but I think you do."

He put down his coffee cup, and with an effortless agility that she admired, he sprang up to the wagon box. "All right, step on the wheel hub."

With dubious hope for success, she scrabbled for a grip on the side, and stepped up. Just as she felt her strength slipping, Tyler reached out and grabbed her by the waist. He lifted her up to the seat as though she weighed no more than a child.

He pushed back his hat. "You're as stiff as an old rawhide rope, aren't you?" he said.

It was hard to deny. "A little, maybe," she admitted, flexing her shoulders again.

He pointed over his shoulder. "I have something for that. I'll be right back."

With the same nimble grace, he jumped down and disappeared around the corner of the wagon. She couldn't imagine what he had that would fix her twitching, throbbing muscles, but she was willing to give him the benefit of the doubt. Tired though she was, she knew she'd have trouble sleeping with this discomfort, and she had to get some rest. Out here their days would begin even earlier than at the ranch.

Tyler reemerged from the darkness carrying a bottle. He handed it to her and climbed back up and sat down next to her. "Okay, in you go," he said, indicating the interior of the wagon.

She looked at the bottle label. "Four-H Horse Liniment? You're giving me horse liniment?"

"Sure, why not? Aches are aches. Hell, I knew one old-timer who used it to stretch his whiskey."

"You mean he drank it?"

A chuckle got away from him. "Yeah, but I wouldn't recommend that. It's mostly for external use, and anyway, I thinned it down a little."

She looked at the label again. "But don't you have anything for people that I can use?"

"It doesn't matter if it's for a horse or a human. Besides, you're not going to put it on. I am."

She gaped at him. Either she'd misunderstood him, or he'd lost his mind. She wasn't about to allow him that kind of intimate access. "You certainly will not! I can manage very well, thank you."

"Liniment only works if it's rubbed in. You can't reach your own shoulders to do that."

"I can reach them well enough," she reiterated, her face so hot—and probably so red—she was grateful that the lantern was behind her. She tried to scoot away from him on the seat, but there was no place to go.

Tyler frowned at her. "If you don't let me do something about it now, by morning you won't be able to move at all."

"I simply don't think this is proper—"

"You're arguing again, Libby," he said in a louder voice.

She lapsed into indignant silence, gripping the bottle in tight hands.

He continued more quietly. "When problems come

up, it's my job either to see that they get fixed, or to fix them myself. That's what I'm doing." He stared at her. "And that's *all* I'm doing. Now, please—get into the wagon. Unless you don't care about privacy."

She stared up into his face, and pressed her mouth into a tight line. She could refuse, but Tyler Hollins wasn't a man who accepted being told no. And worse, she knew he was right. She wouldn't have much luck reaching around to her shoulders. Damn it, she thought, borrowing one of his turns of phrase, he was always right. Furious with both him and his arrogance, she climbed over the seat. He ducked his head and followed, bringing the lantern with him. He set it down and threw his hat onto a flour sack.

Looking around, he found two sturdy crates and put one in front of the other, then took the liniment from her. "All right, sit down here, and"—he waved a hand at her—"you know—uncover your shoulders." He plowed a hand through his hair. For an instant, he looked not quite as autocratic and sure of himself.

She felt her eyes grow as wide as saucers, and she whirled around to face the back of the wagon. With shaking hands she unbuttoned her blouse to her waist and untied the ribbons on her camisole. Then she shrugged them back, gripping the edges together, and pulled her hair around to the front to move it out of the way.

"Come on, Libby. Sit down."

Keeping her back to him, she reached out a hand and felt behind her for the crate, her face burning with embarrassment. She lowered herself to sit, cursing fate for letting him see her hindered movements in the first place. It made her feel very vulnerable that he was behind her, and that she was blind to whatever he was doing.

Tyler swallowed hard at the picture presented to him. In the lantern light, Libby's honey-colored hair gleamed where it swept over her right shoulder. The exposed nape of her neck, and the four inches of her back revealed below it, were smooth and pale. She looked beautiful, like an artist's model posing for a painting. He could see the back edge of her plain camisole and was amazed at how arousing he found it to be. Callie's outright nudity didn't kindle that kind of fire in him.

He sat down right behind her, so close that his knees bracketed her hips. The warm scent of her hair and skin reached him, and he felt a sudden, intense urge to wrap an arm around her waist and bury his mouth against her neck. He could imagine her pressed to the length of his torso, with her bottom between his legs, nestled against his crotch. God, maybe this wasn't such a good idea after all. But he'd insisted upon it, in fact, he'd practically bullied her into it, and he had to see it through.

Uncorking the liniment bottle, he set it on the floor. Then he pushed her sleeves a bit farther down her arms. The instant his fingertips touched her soft, bare skin, she gasped and jumped, and he did, too.

"It's all right, Libby, I'm just getting your sleeves out of the way."

"Sorry," she said.

She was as skittish as a wild mare, and if she'd been able to see the images in his mind, he supposed she'd have good reason to be.

He probed gently along the muscles that stretched from her neck to the points of her shoulders. She flinched but said nothing. "Pretty tender, huh?"

"Yes," Libby admitted. "I didn't expect to be so sore."

"It's okay, we'll take care of it." He poured a little into his palm, rubbed his hands together, and began massaging her muscles. He could feel her pulling away from him. "Take a couple of deep breaths and try to relax," he murmured. "This stuff doesn't smell too good, but it works."

Libby exhaled a long sigh, and let her head tip forward. Tyler was right: the liniment had a strong, pungent odor, and that helped diffuse some of the tension she felt at being partially undressed in front of him. But it also generated heat beneath his deft, gentle touch that was infinitely soothing. He gripped her hips between his knees, as though anchoring her in place, and rubbed her shoulders and arms with deep strokes.

As the spasms in her muscles began to dwindle, he pressed a little harder with his thumbs, kneading and loosening the tightness, bringing back the blood.

Utter relaxation spread through her limbs and she realized dimly that she was listing backward, held upright by his knees and hands. A pleasant lethargy washed over her, crowding out her nervousness.

"Do you do this for your horses, too?" she asked drowsily. Her eyelids were growing heavy.

"Sure, sometimes."

"Lucky horses," she said, nearly hypnotized.

He chuckled. "Like it?"

"Hmm." She was content to admit that he'd been right. His ministrations were much more effective than any awkward maneuvering she could have managed on her own.

He continued the slow, firm strokes for several minutes. When he finally stopped, she felt a rush of greedy disappointment. Being touched was an uncommon experience for Libby, one that she found she liked very much. She nearly forgot that she'd been afraid to have his hands on her, afraid of the sensations that he would awaken. Now she felt as limp as a rag doll.

"That should take care of it," Tyler said near her ear. He said it quietly, feeling his blood pounding through him, bringing heat to his groin and his heart. With the feel of her warm, smooth skin under his hands, it was very easy for him to imagine what the rest of her felt like. And if he didn't stop now, his imagination would demand satisfaction.

It took all the self-control he had to keep from turning her around and pulling her hand away from its death grip on her blouse. He wanted to press kisses to that tender place behind her ear, to take her soft coral lips with his own, to feel the weight of her breast in his hand—

Puzzled by the strained sound of his voice, Libby turned slightly on the crate to look at him. His eyes were smoky blue, as though a fire smoldered behind them, and he searched her face with an intensity she'd never seen before but recognized easily.

The scent of him, leather and horses and clean air, knifed through the harsh odor of the liniment. He sat so close . . . she watched, captivated, as he let his gaze touch the shadow of her cleavage and her breasts, then travel up her throat. When he lifted his eyes to consider her mouth, the tip of his tongue emerged to moisten his lips. He leaned a bit closer and took her chin in his hand to hold her as he had the filly in the corral. She could feel his breath on her cheek and eyelashes, warm, intimate. His lips grazed the corner of her mouth, as if in preparation for the full taking of it—

Suddenly, from just outside the thin canvas wall, she heard spurs clanking and Rory's voice.

"I ain't seen him. Maybe he's off ridin' by himself—he does that sometimes."

Tyler released Libby's jaw and pulled back, like a man awakened from sleepwalking, only to find himself doing something improbable. He picked up the bottle of Four-H and jammed the cork back into its neck.

"That should help," he said, feeling damned awkward and aroused at the same time. He knew she'd see the evidence as soon as he stood, but there was no other way out of the wagon. His only option lay in moving fast. Grabbing his hat, he muttered, "Good night, Libby," and jumped down from the wagon bed.

Libby heard him stalk away into the clear night, then rummaged in her trunk for a nightgown. Tyler had been about to kiss her, she thought. And she'd been about to let him! Had she learned nothing? It had been all that shoulder-massaging business that distracted her. It had felt so good that she nearly forgot everything—time, place, and who she was with. That wouldn't happen again, she vowed. It couldn't.

She had only to get to Miles City, then she'd be on the train and away from here. Away from Montana, and Tyler Hollins.

But when she turned down the lantern and hurried into the snug pile of quilts that made her bed, the view of the clear night sky made her pause. Even Libby had to admit that there was a wild beauty to this land she'd not seen until she came to the Lodestar. Through the arched opening of the wagon canvas, she saw stars so bright she was certain their light was enough to see by. Out here, time and schedules took on completely different meanings. Sunrise and sundown were the timekeepers. In fact, she hadn't seen anyone look at a watch all day. Except Tyler Hollins, of course.

Libby rolled to her side and pulled the quilts up around her chin. The sound of the nightwatch singing to the cattle floated to her on the night breeze, punctuated now and then by the howl of a coyote.

Tonight Chicago seemed as remote as the stars overhead. And perhaps just a bit less bright in her memory.

# Chapter 8

The next couple of days passed in a blur of Dutch ovens, campfires, water hauling, and dish washing. Libby's sleep was interwoven with the smells of cattle and wood smoke, and the sound of distant voices singing to the herd. She couldn't say anyone had lied to her; both Joe and Tyler had told her the work would be hard, and they were right. She rose around four every morning, and washed in cold water. The skimpy privacy of the wagon made her think of the orphanage. But the worst part was bathing from a bucket.

Montana water was rock hard, and no matter what she used, even her treasured bar of French milled vanilla soap, Libby had trouble raising a lather. Dishes, her stockings and underwear, herself—they were washed in water that all soap turned milky white. She thought back to Callie's discussion of her copper bathtub with a feeling akin to jealousy.

After her bath, she hurried into her clothes in the cold dark, then climbed out of the wagon to stir up the fire to cook breakfast. Strangely enough, it seemed that no matter what time she emerged from her canvas bed chamber, she always found Tyler awake already, sipping coffee poured from the pot that stayed on the fire all night long. He was the last one asleep and the first one up. God, did the man never rest? she wondered. She had to admit, though, that it was very comforting to see him there.

Following breakfast, with the herd stretched out behind her, she would drive the chuck wagon on to the next stop that Tyler had selected. When the fire was going, he'd ride in, ask for a basin—which she now filled with warm water—and he'd wash and shave.

On the fourth hushed spring noon, she stood at the worktable rolling out a pie crust when she heard him call her.

"Libby."

He spoke her name so quietly, it sounded as if he were saying it to himself, experimenting with the feel of it. She peeked around the corner of the chuck box and saw him standing next to the wagon. He'd taken off his shirt and slung it over a low bush. She couldn't help but admire the long, graceful plane of his bare back as she looked at his profile, the way it curved out slightly at his shoulders and in at his waist, then disappeared into low-slung jeans.

He stood perfectly still, as though he were chiseled from stone. The only movement she detected was his wind-ruffled chestnut hair. Shaving soap covered the lower half of his face, a slim contrast to his own coloring that had turned suddenly pale. His razor dangled from his hand at his side, its shiny blade gleaming in the noon sun. He wasn't looking at her. Instead his gaze was fixed on some object not far from his feet.

"Libby, where's Rory?" His tone was the same, calm, steady, almost inaudible. But something about it frightened her.

"He's off looking for firewood."

"Get the shotgun, then."

"Sh-shotgun?"

Still he didn't look at her. "Get the damned shotgun and come around behind me from the left side. Be quiet, and be *quick*."

Galvanized, she grabbed the weapon from the wagon. Despite all the target practice he'd made her endure, the smooth, cool stock felt foreign in her hands. Following his terse instructions, she moved as swiftly and as quietly as she could, approaching him from the left.

"Stop right there. You're close enough."

She paused about ten feet off to his side. Her heart had begun to thud in her chest with rapid, heavy beats. "What—"

"Hush," he ordered, whispering now. "*Don't talk.*"

She only heard it at first, a strange whirring noise. But then she saw the object of Tyler's intense scrutiny, no more than three feet from his boot. A thick snake, coiled among some sun-heated rocks next to the wagon wheel, poised to strike. The end of its tail rose slightly above its sinuous length, sounding the warning rattle.

She swallowed a gasping shriek that crept up her throat. The aim would be awkward, and she knew she was a terrible shot. This wasn't like firing at tin cans and old whiskey bottles on the fence back at the ranch. When she'd missed those, all that had been injured were her pride and Tyler's patience. In this desperate situation, she was positive that she would hit Tyler's foot—there just wasn't enough space between him and the reptile. Her heart pumped harder and her hands grew damp on the stock and barrel. Oh, God, why couldn't someone more competent have been here to help?

"But—"

"You're close enough not to miss. Goddamn it, don't think, just shoot!"

The hissing grew ominously louder and Libby knew instinctively that the huge creature had issued its final warning. In another second it would strike, sinking its fangs deep into Tyler's leg.

With that image in her mind, her fear fell away and a kind of angry, protective reflex came over her. She raised the shotgun, took the best aim she could, and squeezed the trigger. The blast of fire kicked the stock back into her shoulder, and vented a puff of sulfurous blue smoke that momentarily clouded her view.

The silence that followed was so complete, not even the grass rustled in the low wind. She looked frantically back and forth between Tyler and where she'd last seen the rattlesnake. She couldn't tell if she'd hit it, or Tyler, or if he'd been bitten. It happened in the blink of an eye, but she felt as though time and events were moving as slowly as in a dream. All the details of her surroundings stood out: the gray-white canvas, the glint of Tyler's razor through the smoke, the bandanna sticking out of his back pocket.

"Tyler!" she called. "Are you all right?"

He turned to face her, the light streaks in his hair gleaming under the sun. "Yeah," he exhaled.

Relief made her arms and legs feel like lead. She held the shotgun in a death grip; she could even detect the metallic smell of the long barrel.

He walked over and touched her arm. His eyes

were startlingly blue against his pallor. Sweat ran from his temples into the lather on his face.

"Pretty good shooting, Libby." He waved a shaky hand in the direction of the decapitated snake.

Libby looked at it and swallowed. Reaction was beginning to set in and chills rushed over her body in waves, making goose bumps rise on her skin. For no reason she could think of, tears welled in her eyes.

Tyler peered into her face. He wiped the soap off his jaws with the towel slung around his neck. Prying the weapon out of her hands, he leaned it against the wagon wheel. Then he put an arm around her shoulders.

"I-I didn't know if I c-could do it—" She turned and dashed her hand across her eyes. Her voice shook, her limbs shook, and she couldn't conquer either one. He'd think she was just the flimsy, inept female he'd believed her to be all along. But it was infinitely comforting—and just as disturbing—to stand in his loose embrace. "I always m-missed before—"

"Shhh . . . it's all right, Libby." The timbre of his voice had changed, and he spoke right next to her ear. "Shhh . . ." It was the same reassuring tone he'd used when he bandaged her hand that night in his office. Then he pulled her closer and put both arms around her. She melted against him. She'd had so little comforting in her life. Growing up with dozens of other children in the orphanage, she'd been fed, clothed, and provided with a basic education. But hugs had been few and far between.

When he pressed her cheek to his warm, bare shoulder, she thought she felt his lips graze her temple.

"B-but I might have shot you instead."

Backing up a bit, he lifted her chin to look at him, and smiled with honest admiration. "Yeah, but I was willing to take the chance. Besides, I'd bet on you over a snake any day. And see? You *did* hit it. Took its head clean off."

She glimpsed at the creature again. "I guess I did."

He shifted her to one arm, keeping her close to his ribs, and gave her shoulder a squeeze. "Sure you did. You know, you earned that snake's rattle, if you want it."

She shook her head vehemently. "God, no."

He smiled again, as nice a smile as he gave to Rory and Callie. "If we were back in Texas, we'd be having rattlesnake stew for supper."

"Snake stew!" She made a face. "N-no, we wouldn't, not if I were doing the cooking. I-I wouldn't have that thing in my kitchen."

"Noah Bradley will be disappointed when he hears that. So will a couple of the others from south Texas." Lifting his closed razor, he looked at it wobbling slightly in his grip, and a wry chuckle escaped him. "Maybe I'll wait until tonight to shave. Right now, I'd probably slip and cut my own throat."

Tyler counted himself lucky. He'd had close calls with rattlesnakes before, but he'd always been wearing his revolver, or had a weapon close by. He felt incredibly stupid now for taking off his gun belt with his shirt. Where the hell had his head been? If Libby hadn't been here—

"You know, you probably saved my life." He admitted this a bit grudgingly. To be defended by a little city woman like her—damn, Joe would *really* give him hell for this.

"I only shot the snake instead of you," she reminded him with a little laugh. "It could have been lots worse." The color was returning to her face. For a minute, he'd worried that she might faint. But probably not Libby. He was beginning to believe that Joe had been right about her: she was stronger than she looked.

"Well, you saved me from being bitten anyway. And saved yourself from the job of cutting open the wound." He sketched the mark of an X in the air with his razor, then tucked it into his belt.

Shifting his gaze to her again, his smile faded. He searched her face. It was small, smooth, and pretty under the mild April sun. Her eyes were fringed with long lashes that were much darker than her honey-colored hair. Like a reflex action, he tightened his arm around her and slowly brought his fingertips to her cheek. Her breasts, pressed to his side, felt soft and full. He let his eyes drop to her moist mouth, which also looked soft and full, and tried to remember the last time he'd kissed a woman. It seemed like a silly thing to wonder about, considering the fact that he regularly slept with a female who gave him blithe, uninhibited access to her body. But Callie would not let him or any other man take her lips in a kiss. For reasons known only to her, she thought it too intimate an exchange, whether or not he was one of her "regular gentlemen."

Tyler had never understood that. To him, it was just another physical act. But now, holding Libby in his arm, he thought that perhaps he did understand. To cover her mouth with his own would mean much more than a casual meeting of lips, and he ached to do it. But it scared him.

Their association would end one of two ways: she would get on the train in Miles City, or she would marry Charlie. Either way, she would be gone soon, and so be it. He wasn't even foursquare positive any more that her going was a good thing. But he knew it was the right thing.

"Well, I guess you'd better get back to whatever you were doing," he said, and released her.

Libby wished he hadn't. No matter how inappropriate the notion was, she felt she could stand with his arm around her all afternoon. He was strong, unyielding—like a rock—and she found more reassurance in that than she would have guessed. And while her knowledge of such things was limited only to Wesley, she swore he'd been about to kiss her. The thought was warm and tantalizing, and brought fire to her cheeks.

No! Enough of that foolishness, she scolded herself, and pulled away from him, backing up four or five paces. It wasn't just that she and Tyler Hollins would be parting company in a few days. He was her employer, *her employer*, just like Wesley Brandauer. Well, maybe not exactly like him. He'd been selfish, and haughty sometimes, and had known how to charm and cajole her to achieve his own gains.

But Tyler was not warmth and security, not for her, anyway, and she didn't need his strength. She'd gotten this far on her own; she could manage the rest of the way, too.

She tucked her hands into her apron pockets, suddenly feeling awkward. "Yes, I'm sure the men will be expecting their lunch soon. I-I'd better get busy." She bent to retrieve the shotgun. "I'll put this away."

Rory rode in then with a bundle of firewood tied to the back of his saddle. "I thought I heard a shot," he said, looking at her, then at Tyler. "Have you been target practicin', Miss Libby?"

"I guess you could say that," she said with a shaky laugh.

Tyler, putting on his shirt, gave her an even look. "And her aim has improved, Rory. It's improved a lot."

The incident about the shooting spread quickly through the men. Having witnessed Libby's misfires at the ranch fence, they all congratulated her on her marksmanship, and made jokes about the danger of a sharpshooting woman. Joe offered to make a hat band for her out of the diamond-patterned snakeskin, but she declined.

"Well, dang—ain't we havin' it for supper?" Noah Bradley inquired of her that evening. He looked down at his tin plate of pork belly, fried apples, and biscuits. Though the sun was low in the sky, his hat cast a shadow over his eyes. "I've been lookin' forward to rattlesnake ever since I heard about it this afternoon." A couple of disappointed murmurs had carried the news to him at the back of the line, as Tyler had predicted.

"Sorry, Noah." Libby shook her head. "I'm trying to learn to make coffee you men can stand a spoon in, if that's what you want, and biscuits nearly as big as stove lids. But I refuse to cook a snake for supper."

"No disrespect, Miss Libby, but we ain't used to such civilized cookin' in Texas." Like a lot of the cowboys, Noah was very sure of himself, although he lacked some of Charlie's easygoing good nature, or Joe's mannered dignity. But he was generally respectful in the few dealings she'd had with him. And she knew that he and Charlie were friends. "Down on the Nueces River we ate snake and lizard." He smiled, and his face fell into weathered creases that looked out of place on a man so young. "I'll tell you all about it if you go for a walk with me after supper."

That was the last thing she wanted to do, but before she could refuse, Charlie, who was getting a drink from the water barrel, jumped in.

"Miss Libby don't want to take a walk with you, Noah." He stepped closer, his usually friendly face clouded over like a storm hovering above the mountains. Immediately the air crackled with tension between the two men.

Noah gave him a cold look. "Maybe she does. Who died and made you the boss man, Charlie?"

Libby had no intention of going anywhere with Noah Bradley, but could imagine the scene becoming ugly, and she refused to be argued over like a bone between two dogs. Charlie's infatuation, or whatever it was, had robbed him of his sense. "Excuse me, if I could say something—"

Both men ignored her. Charlie jabbed a finger into Noah's shoulder. "Miss Libby ain't one of those dance hall dollies you're used to. She's a lady."

Noah's face flushed with anger, and he jerked his shoulder away. "The *lady* can decide for herself if she wants to take a stroll. What do you know about ladies, anyhow, Charlie? You've had to pay for your pokes for years now," he said, shoving back.

"Charlie—Noah, stop it!" Libby demanded, but if either of them heard her, she saw no indication of it. She backed up. They were nose to nose, and she saw Noah's right hand close into a fist. Around the campfire behind her, she became aware that all conversation and eating had ceased. She looked around for Tyler or Joe, but didn't see either one.

Suddenly, Charlie's hand flew up under Noah's plate, launching pork and apples into his face and down his shirtfront.

After his initial shock, fire flamed in Noah's eyes. "You son of a bitch!" With the raging energy of humiliation, he flung himself at Charlie and they fell to the ground, rolling and grappling like a pair of tomcats, neither one able to pull an arm back far enough to deliver an effective punch. A hat tumbled across the grass, carried by the wind.

Every man present abandoned his supper to watch the brawl, and to egg on the combatants.

"Watch out for eye-gouging, Noah!"

"Swing with your left, Charlie, your left!"

Even Rory, wide-eyed and grinning, yelled, "Git him, Charlie! Show him how it's done!"

"Rory!" she exclaimed. "Don't encourage them!"

Occasionally, a successful punch got thrown and the sound of a fist connecting with a face made a sickening noise. She hovered on the outside of the group, a horrified witness, until she managed to elbow her way between a couple of cowboys.

"Will someone please pull them apart?" she demanded, trying to make herself heard over the whooping and hollering of the onlookers. They made as much enthusiastic racket as spectators at a prize fight. "Hickory, do something about it!"

"Aw, they're just havin' a little fun, Miss Libby," Hickory Cooper said, pantomiming jabs without looking at her.

Frustrated with being ignored, and jostled back and forth, she shouted, "Isn't *someone* going to stop this before they kill each other?"

"Yes, goddamn it all! I'm going to stop it right now." An angry voice thundered through the camp, and Libby turned to see Tyler coming on like a locomotive with long legs and spurs. Joe was right behind him.

Tyler looked weary and thoroughly disgusted, as though this bothersome thing was the last straw at the end of a particularly trying day. Fury poured off him in waves that scattered the men like grain in a hailstorm. Even Libby thought he was a terrifying figure.

"Goddamned harebrained idiots," Joe barked in his low voice. "You get your asses up from there and have done, or both of you will be riding away from here tonight with your pay." He and Tyler yanked the two men up by their shirt collars.

"But, Tyler—" Rory protested.

"Rory," he replied warningly, indicating by his tone that the youngster would be wise to maintain his silence. "Charlie, aren't you supposed to be with the herd?"

"Yeah," he grumbled between breaths, and jerked his dirty, grass-stained shirt back into place. Then he took his hat from Bean, who'd retrieved it, and put it on. His eye was already swelling; apparently one of Noah's fists had made contact.

"Noah, you get on with whatever you're supposed to be doing," Tyler ordered. "The rest of you do the same."

With his nose bleeding down the front of his shirt, Noah stormed off across the field.

Libby went back to her post at the chuck wagon, both shaken and angry with Noah and Charlie, wishing she could give them a piece of her mind. She couldn't believe those two had rolled around on the ground and punched each other like—like savages! She'd never seen anything like that in Chicago. Yes, it probably had happened all the time, but not right under her nose. Then she decided that being bawled out by Tyler and Joe was punishment enough.

She poured hot water into the dishpan and began washing the plates and utensils with soap that wouldn't lather. And for the first time since they'd left, she found herself thinking about the Lodestar instead of Chicago.

Tyler eyed his cook. Despite all the difficulties that he'd dealt with today—the rattlesnake and this fight had been only two of several—he realized that coming back to cow camp and seeing her here had lifted his spirits a bit.

"Those boys are good friends. What the hell do you suppose that was about?" Joe asked as he and Tyler walked to the remuda.

Tyler glanced back at Libby's small aproned figure as she handed Rory a hot biscuit and what appeared to be the beginning of a lecture. "I have the feeling I know *exactly* what it was about."

He didn't add that he was starting to understand just how Charlie and Noah felt.

Later that night, Tyler pulled off his boots and spread out his bedroll next to the chuck wagon. The campfire had burned down to low flames, popping softly now and then. Around him, eight other exhausted men slept and snored and dreamed, but Tyler was conscious only of the woman up in the wagon next to him.

Living on the trail was hard on anyone—staying clean was just about impossible, the conditions were rough and comforts were few. Men didn't mind so much; they could sleep almost anywhere, anytime. If a week or two passed without a bath, it wasn't the end of the world to them. Tyler shucked his clothes every morning and scrubbed down in an icy creek without a second thought.

Women, on the other hand, weren't inclined to like this life. Somehow though, despite all of those obstacles, Libby managed to stay sweet-smelling and shiny-haired. As though the picture in his mind had invoked it, he heard the splash of water from within the wagon and knew that she must be washing.

So far, Libby Ross had not proven to be the physical burden he'd envisioned. She'd learned to manage that mule team without much training or practice, she fed the men good food and on time, under conditions he knew she wasn't used to. She'd done her best to try and stop that fight this afternoon, even though the numskulls wouldn't listen to her. He smiled in the darkness when he thought of her with his twelve-gauge pointed at that rattler. He couldn't bring himself to tell her that he'd half expected to take a load of shot in his foot, and hoped the blast might scare off the snake.

No, she carried her weight and did her job, there was no denying it. He found his wary resentment of her surrendering to growing respect. It was her vulnerability, the whisper of tragedy he sensed in her, that gave him pause.

Thinking about the fight again, and the reason for it, made his stomach clench. What if she did marry Charlie? He'd seen nothing pass between them—no girlish blushes, no shy glances from her—to indicate that she'd accepted him. That Charlie was behaving like a lovesick calf also told him nothing. He'd felt like that himself a time or two in his life. Fortunately, he'd recovered.

When he lay back against his saddle and looked

at the night sky, a deep sigh escaped him. Whether it was from the relief of finally lying down after a hell of a long day, or from the weight of his thoughts, he wasn't sure. Plain old cowboying on the trail was the hardest work he knew of, due mostly to the lack of sleep that went with the job. Once, years ago now, an old-timer had told him that if he wanted to trail cattle, he'd better learn to do his sleeping in the winter.

Except Tyler hadn't wanted to be a cowboy. He'd had a much different life mapped out for himself, but time and fate intervened to put him on this path.

He wasn't sorry, exactly. He loved the Lodestar and he'd given it everything he had, including beautiful, fragile Jenna. And something inside him had died along the way. He watched a pair of stars overhead sparkle blue-white. On that silent, snow-covered November dawn five years back, it had felt as though grief and the stars, distant and cold, were all he had left. And he'd felt like that for a long time—a hard frost had lain upon his soul that shut out everyone. Eventually, he grew tired enough of his solitude to take comfort in Callie Michaels's company.

That had been enough until now. But he was beginning to realize that the breezy simplicity of his relationship with her might also be its drawback. Idly, he touched a spoke in the wagon wheel behind his head, and looked up at the canvas.

The layer of ice on his spirit was beginning to shift. What lay beneath after all this time, he had no idea.

The following morning Charlie came to Libby and apologized for his part in the brawl, saying that he hoped it hadn't diminished her opinion of him to such a low degree that she would no longer consider his proposal. She didn't have the heart to tell him that she'd considered and rejected it a half hour after he'd made it.

Still, whether or not she wanted to, Libby couldn't stay mad at him. He looked so dejected standing before her with a first-class shiner, twisting his hat brim in his hands, that she had to forgive him. His face lit up immediately.

"But, Charlie," she cautioned gently, "I think it's only fair to tell you that I still plan to get on the train in—"

He put up his hand to stop her words. "Now, now, Miss Libby, this trip ain't over yet. You keep on thinkin' about it till we get to Miles City." Then smiling, he put on his hat and swaggered to his horse. As she watched him walk away, she had to smile, too. It wouldn't be easy telling him she couldn't marry him.

Noah Bradley, on the other hand, was cross and silent at breakfast. He didn't speak to Libby and maintained an obvious distance from Charlie whenever the two were in camp at the same time. While she'd done nothing to encourage their attentions, it bothered her to know that their friendship had been jeopardized because of her, especially when she had no interest in either of them.

Libby didn't see much of Charlie or Noah after that. The herd was nervous and on the edge of panic, she'd heard Joe tell Bean. It took all their efforts to keep them in line.

One thing she had noticed, though, was Tyler watching her. It seemed like any time he was within her own sight, if she glanced in his direction, she'd find him looking at her until he realized he'd been detected. For some reason, catching a glimpse of those blue eyes on her made her cheeks heat in a way that Charlie's sweetness—or Wesley's selfish groping—had not. And despite the stern, ongoing lecture she conducted in her mind, she found herself searching out Tyler, as well.

Late in the afternoon following the fight, Charlie trotted up to the side of Libby's wagon, and motioned for her to stop. "There's a storm comin'. A bad one." He pointed over his shoulder.

She pulled on the lines to half the mules and leaned forward to look at the northwestern sky. The air had turned deathly still, and a wall of greenish black clouds was boiling up on the horizon. Behind her, she could hear the cattle bawling nervously, and the horses were skittish. Although sundown was still an hour away, the land grew darker by the minute, and Libby could smell rain. An immense angry force was gathering strength in those black clouds.

Joe and Tyler rode up then, and looked at the herd.

"Damn, just what we need," Tyler complained, his expression grim.

"What should I do?" Libby asked. She was the only person who didn't have a job in this pending emergency. "Should I stop here?" She knew she sounded scared, but she couldn't hide the tremor in her voice.

Tyler never looked away from the herd and the threatening sky. "You'd better get into the wagon. You won't be able to cook in the rain that's coming." Then he spurred his horse back toward the point.

Joe tugged at the hems of his gloves. "Well, come on, Charlie, let's get them steers together and try to keep 'em that way. I'm sure glad we crossed the river this morning. After this rain, it'll be runnin' faster than ever." He wheeled his horse and followed Tyler.

Charlie leaned toward her from his saddle, and in that moment, he wore his whole honest heart on his face. No man had ever looked at Libby that way. "I wish I could stay here and see after you. It ain't right that you should have to fend for yourself—"

From the distance, Libby heard Tyler's tense voice. "Charlie!" he bellowed. "C'mon, goddamn it! We've got to keep this herd together."

Just then a zigzag of lightning arced down from the sky with a sizzling buzz, briefly illuminating the countryside in a glare. Libby jumped, gasping at the close proximity of the bolt. Pandemonium erupted among the cattle behind them. The rumble of bovine hooves competed with the following clap of thunder as they began running, taking a general turn off to Libby's right.

Charlie glanced over his shoulder, then back at Libby in an agony of regret. If she'd learned one thing from these men, it was that the welfare of the herd came before anything else, including their own lives. "God, they're runnin' toward a cliff. I *gotta* go help turn 'em. I'll see you when this is over," he yelled over the din. "Stay safe!" He pushed his hat down tight and galloped off to join the crew to help turn the panicked cattle.

Libby watched until he and his horse disappeared behind her wagon canvas.

Suddenly, another fork of lightning snaked down from the clouds, closer this time, and her mule team lurched forward and started running, too. A peal of thunder shook the earth and the sky opened, loosing torrents of rain driven by a fierce wind. Her sight dimmed by the lashing downpour and the ink-black clouds, Libby pulled frantically on the reins to halt the runaway mules. But they charged on. Water ran in streams from the brim of her hat, further obstructing her vision.

"Whoa! Stop! Please, stop!" she yelled, her heart pounding at the base of her throat. The team bounced her and the chuck wagon over ruts and bumps at a speed that the vehicle was never intended to travel. It creaked and rattled as it flew over the rough terrain, and behind her, Libby heard cans and jars thumping around in the chuck box. Caught by a gust of wind, her hat flew off her head, and for an instant its bonnet strings pulled tight around her throat. A couple of times, the wagon tipped precariously to one side, almost toppling over. Her heart nearly paralyzed with gnawing fear, Libby struggled to keep her seat without dropping the reins. She had no trouble imagining herself thrown from the spring seat, and her life ending abruptly with a broken neck.

Finally, with a burst of strength born of utter terror and the instinct to survive, she hauled on the lines with every fiber of her will and body. Her arms felt as though they would disjoint at the wrists and elbows, and despite her gloves, the leather reins bit into her hands.

"Stop, damn you!" she cursed the mules, her voice a cross between a snarl and a scream. But it worked; the team stopped, their rain-drenched sides heaving.

Her own breath coming in harsh, sobbing gasps, Libby stared at them. Oh, dear God! she thought. She set the brake and wound the lines around it, then wrapped her arms around herself for a moment. Her entire body felt shaky and boneless from the adrenaline coursing through her. She peered through the gray veil of rain, trying to figure out where she was, but nothing looked familiar, and nightfall was fast approaching. How on earth would she find her way back to cow camp? She couldn't even tell east and west—the sky was the same dark gray in every direction she looked. But she couldn't just sit out here. She had to try.

After she and the mules caught their breath, Libby took up the lines again and turned the wagon in the direction she believed she'd come from. She had to get back to the crew before sunset. They'd be hungry after this hellish day, and more than that, she didn't want to be out here in this vast, wild country, alone in the dark. But there were no defining landmarks that she recalled from her first breakneck ride past here. And the low clouds and sheets of pounding rain shortened the horizon considerably.

She scanned the soaked grassland for a chestnut-haired horseman; surely even if this storm presaged the end of the world, Tyler Hollins would still be out here, riding the range and tending to details. It was his way: he was strong, capable, immutable, like granite. While those very traits made him seem annoyingly remote and unemotional, she also took comfort from them. As the miles and days of this trip rolled by, more and more often Libby would lift her gaze from the ears of the mules to search for his straight back up ahead. And he was nearly always there.

But now she found only the sky touching the land. She couldn't tell where the sun was setting. Nowhere did she see the herd or even one cowboy. Libby felt as though she were the last person on earth. She'd known this particular kind of desolation only once before, and it had been here in Montana, when the wind moaned and the snow was deep . . .

She let the mules slow to a halt. There was no point in going on now. She'd just get herself more hopelessly lost. Her only recourse was to wait until morning. Maybe the weather would clear by then. But right now the rain turned to a stinging, wind-driven hail, and she scrambled over the seat into the shelter of the wagon. She'd taken off her saddle coat earlier and thrown it into the back, lulled by the mild spring afternoon, and her clothes were soaked through.

Falling into the pile of bedrolls, Libby shivered in the gathering darkness while hail and rain pelted the wagon canvas. The shotgun—she should have the shotgun, she thought nervously. Just in case. She pulled off her gloves and hat, and crawled over the bedding, looking for the lantern that hung on the back of the chuck box, hoping it hadn't bounced off its hook. When her hands closed around the glass globe, she prayed that at least one match in her apron pocket was still dry.

The sulfur head blazed and in the glaring kerosene light, she grabbed up the shotgun and a box of shells with hands that trembled. Thank God Tyler had insisted that she learn to shoot this thing. She still thought that hitting the rattlesnake had been far more luck than anything else, but having the gun on her lap would make her feel a little safer.

The lightning had moved on, but the storm continued to howl around her. Her hair hung in limp, wet hanks on her neck and back. Picking her clammy, cold skirts away from her legs, Libby tried to think of a convincing reason why she shouldn't feel sorry for herself. But given her miserable circumstances and her growing fear, she couldn't come up with even one.

Hot tears welled up in her eyes, and she let them come because she could think of no reason to stop them, either.

Tyler looked at the milling, tightly herded cattle with a sense of profound relief. They might have to round up a few head—there hadn't been time to count them yet. But at least they'd turned them before they plunged off the cliff.

"Jesus Christ," Joe exhaled next to him. "That was a little too close for me." Rain continued to pour down on them, but the noisiest part of the storm had passed west toward the mountains.

Tyler nodded and tipped his head down to drain the ring of water that had collected in his hat brim. At least he'd been able to grab his slicker from the back of his saddle before he started chasing the cattle, so he wasn't as wet as some of the boys.

"I'd hoped we could get through one drive without a stampede. I should have known better." He watched as Rory cut across the range to rope a steer that was attempting an escape.

Joe leaned forward and rested his forearms on his saddle horn. "Yeah, and that herd is still pretty nervous. I think we're all gonna have to sit up with 'em tonight. Maybe if it quits rainin', Miss Libby can get the coffeepot goin'."

Tyler finally found a reason to smile. With some resistance Libby had learned to make the kind of strong, tar-black brew the men wanted. She'd refused to budge, though, when Hickory's brother, Possum, asked her to toss in a rusty nail for "flavoring."

"Coffee sounds good. I wonder how far we ran from the chuck wagon." He glanced around in the waning daylight, looking for the wagon's white canvas cover. "I don't see it," he said, an odd sense of dread coming over him.

Joe turned in his saddle and looked, too. "We didn't go far at all. We were able to swing the herd back almost to the place where the stampede started." He stood in his stirrups and scanned the flat prairie again. Their eyes locked, and he shook his head. "She ain't here, Ty."

If Joe said it, he knew it was true. Joe had spent his life in the open and could see practically to the Badlands, it sometimes seemed.

"The mules might have spooked in the storm and set to runnin'," Joe suggested. "I'll go look for her."

A troubling picture formed in Tyler's mind of an overturned wagon, of delicate bones broken, of clover-honey hair spilled out across the wet grass—

"No!" he blurted. "Uh, no, you stay with the herd, Joe. She's my responsibility, I'll search for her." But in the quietest corner of his heart, Tyler knew that his sense of duty had nothing to do with it.

He reached down and felt for his rifle in its scabbard, then checked the rounds in the pistol on his left hip. He was lucky that he still had both weapons. Huh, he was lucky they hadn't killed him. Even the greenest greenhorns knew to leave their firearms and anything else metal in the wagon during an electrical storm. In the rush, he'd forgotten. Damn it, he should have realized that something could happen to her. She had no experience controlling a runaway team. But the truth of the matter was that this same thing could have happened to Rory, to anyone.

Now he tried to keep his fear for Libby's safety

from robbing him of his good sense. His feelings for her ran deeper than he wanted to admit, even to himself. That scared him, too. He felt Joe's eyes on him. He had the very uncomfortable feeling that his friend could read his thoughts.

Tyler shrugged, trying to act casual. "It's likely that she just got turned around. You know city people can't find their way to Sunday if you put them on the range."

Joe shot him a shrewd look. "Yeah. I know. Well, you'd better get to it while there's still light. Maybe she left tracks."

"Maybe." Tyler tugged at his hat brim in farewell and spurred his horse into a trot. "Hang on, Libby," he muttered to himself. "I'll find you."

# Chapter 9

Libby sat on a low pile of bedrolls in the back of the wagon, leaning against the chuck box with Tyler's shotgun across her knees. Her muscles were tight and cold, and her teeth chattered. She couldn't leave the mules harnessed to the wagon all night, so she'd hobbled them. But unhitching the team in the rain had soaked her to the skin. When she'd tried to open her trunk to find dry clothes, she discovered that the dampness had caused the lid to swell tightly and firmly closed. No matter how she pulled and pried, she couldn't open the trunk.

She wasn't sure how long she'd been here; the sun had gone down long ago, and time felt as though it had stopped. The bedrolls and sacks of flour and cornmeal cast tall, angled shadows that seemed to bend toward her like creatures from a fever dream. Rain continued to buffet the canvas, and heavy wind gusts rocked the wagon. The storm played tricks on her ears, too. Sometimes she thought she heard someone calling her. She shook herself. Of course, that was impossible.

It had crossed her mind that one of the crew might look for her—Charlie or Joe—but that was out of the question, too. They probably had their hands full with the herd in this storm, and who would search for her in the dark and the rain? She'd be expected to take care of herself, for a night anyway.

She thought of the Lodestar and a hysterical little sob crept up her throat. For most of the time she'd spent at the ranch, she'd wished she were in Chicago, even though her future there was uncertain. But now she understood what Joe had meant when he'd spoken of the ranch house seeming like a grand home—a safe, lighted harbor in this sea of grass. God, she yearned to be there now, dry and comfortable, instead of stuck in this wagon—cold, miserable, and lost, prey to bears or any other hungry animal that came down from the hills.

Just then, she heard a noise outside, right next to her. She sat up, her back stiff. What was that? she wondered. It sounded like something—or someone—had bumped the wagon box. She strained to hear, her breath stopped in her chest. This time she knew it wasn't her imagination, but her heart was pounding so loudly in her ears, she couldn't tell what direction it had come from. She lifted the shotgun and pulled back the hammers. Her hands were damp on the stock and barrel. Aiming at the dark front end of the wagon, she sat as rigid as a mannequin, waiting, listening, her throat chalk-dry.

A man's head and shoulders appeared in the arched opening behind the seat. He was nothing but a dark, unfamiliar silhouette framed in that arch. Already edgy and frightened, Libby swallowed a scream and her heart doubled its pace. She leaned forward. She'd lived through too much and come too far to let this man harm her.

"You come closer and I'll shoot you," she choked out with straightforward intent. "I swear I will!"

"Libby, it's me!"

That voice. "Tyler?" she asked, her own words suddenly small. She lowered the shotgun, so surprised her jaw dropped. He was the last person she expected to see. "Is it really you?"

"Jesus, I've been looking for you everywhere." He climbed over the seat into the wagon and stooped to make his way to her. She could feel the cool dampness of the night radiating from his clothes. He knelt and took her hands in his. His gloves were damp, but warm from his body heat. The lamplight fell across him and her surprise grew when she saw the expression of naked worry on his handsome face. His blue eyes reflected some emotion she couldn't identify.

He opened his slicker and with a muffled cry she launched herself against his chest, trying to keep her chin from trembling. It really *was* Tyler. He smelled of wet horse and clean, storm-washed air. He hesitated a moment, then he closed his arms around her. She shivered. It was good to feel the solid wall of him under her cheek, to know that someone stronger was with her now. "I'm so glad to see you," she said against his shirt.

"I'm pretty glad to see you, too," he murmured, briefly pressing his cheek to the top of her head.

She sat up, embarrassed by her own forward behavior. "Excuse me. I didn't mean to be so—I was kind of scared—"

He held her back and looked her over in a quick inspection, running his hands up and down her arms. "Are you hurt?"

"No, I'm so cold." Libby tried to keep her voice from quivering, but chill, fear, and exhaustion had taken their toll. "H-how did you find me?"

"I was beginning to think I wouldn't. It got dark so damned fast." He released her hands and pulled off his hat and gloves, throwing them on a bundle in the corner. "Finally, I saw a faint glow up ahead in the mist. It was the light from this lantern. It made this canvas look like a lamp shade." He indicated the top of the wagon.

She shivered again.

"You shouldn't be sitting here in wet clothes," he said, frowning. "That's a good way to get sick, and we can't afford that out here." He took the shotgun from her lap and leaned it against a box of dried apples.

No, of course not, she thought, her joy at seeing him dimmed a bit. Who'd cook for him and his men if something happened to her? Who'd drive this wagon if she should fall ill? The tone of her voice flattened. "I couldn't get my trunk open. The rain swelled it shut."

Tyler made his way to the trunk and pulled on the lid. It didn't budge.

"There isn't any hot food," she said. She watched him shrug out of his slicker and readjust his grip. "But there are sourdough biscuits left over from lunch. And I think I have some preserves left." She watched the muscles in his back flex and contract under his shirt while he wrestled with the trunk. "I didn't expect you to come looking for me."

He glanced at her over his shoulder. "Don't forget, Libby, you're my responsibility."

When he'd first told her that, she resented being thought of as a bumbling idiot who needed protection from herself and everything else. Now when she heard this designation, her heart objected for a different reason. Had it been only his sense of responsibility that made him come after her?

Swearing a blue streak, he tugged and struggled with the stubborn box, but it wouldn't yield, not even for him.

"Damn!" he finished with an exploding exhale. "I'd shoot the son of a bitch if I thought it would help!" He turned back to her then and pulled his bedroll out of a stack. "Well, come on, get those wet things off. You'll just have to wrap up in one of my blankets."

"I *beg* your pardon, Mr. Hollins—" His brusque command made her lapse into formality, and she felt her cold cheeks flame. She wouldn't have supposed she had the energy to blush, but this set her back on her heels. "This makes twice now that you've ordered me out of my clothes."

Tyler looked at Libby. She made a sorry picture. Her gray eyes were wide with indignation and her teeth chattered while she clutched her damp blouse collar close to her throat. He sighed. Fatigue and worry made him sound abrupt with her. He'd searched so long, he'd begun to worry that he'd be lost himself in the darkness. The nightmarish vision of the wagon overturned had played again and again through his mind.

"Come on," he repeated, more gently this time. He held up a blanket. "We can't go anywhere until morning, and you can't sit in those wet clothes all night." This time when his eyes traveled over her, he couldn't help but notice the way her wet blouse molded itself to her breasts. A surge of heat coursed through him, but he felt awkward, too. This wasn't Callie standing here. She was a young widow who, unlike the madam, hadn't lost her ability to blush.

Still gripping her collar, she dropped her eyes self-consciously, and another spasm of chill shook her. She didn't move. Her voice wasn't much more than a whisper. "You don't really expect me to undress in front of you—"

Tyler felt a flush color his own face. He handed her the blanket and turned toward the front of the wagon. "Uh, no, no—are those biscuits out in the chuck box?"

"Yes."

He heard the relief in her voice. "I'll unsaddle my horse and get the biscuits while you, um, change. Give me the other lantern."

She handed it to him, and he lit it, facing away from her the whole time. Then he grabbed his hat and slicker again, and scrambled down into the rain. Suddenly he felt as green and inexperienced as Rory. Hell, he'd seen enough undressed women in his life—why this one should have him stumbling all over himself was baffling. No, it wasn't, he admitted. This was completely different from those other times, and he knew it.

After he lifted the saddle off his mare, he put it on the wagon seat. Then he splashed over the soggy ground surrounding the wagon, holding the lantern in front of him, and opened the chuck box. After rummaging around, he pulled out the biscuits, wrapped in a napkin. He didn't see the preserves but he found half a cherry pie. It had suffered having a can of condensed milk fall on it, but it would serve. He pawed through dark drawers for two forks and two cups. Hot coffee would have been welcome on a bitch of a night like this, but water would have to do. Balancing supper and the lantern, Tyler started to get his canteen from his horse when he glanced up at the wagon canvas. He faced it slowly, transfixed by what he saw.

The lantern in the wagon, the one that had led him here, now cast Libby Ross's very feminine silhouette upon the wagon canvas. She peeled away the wet blouse and hung it on something in the wagon box. Then she stepped out of her skirt, and dried her arms with what he assumed was a towel. She still wore her petticoat and camisole; he could see the edge of the ruffle on her bodice when she turned, and the swell of her breasts beneath. In response to this very feminine display, his body answered swiftly with a hard, heavy ache.

Tyler clutched the canteen to his chest and took a deep breath, temporarily forgetting that the wind and rain lashed his face, that he was hungry, that he was tired beyond his capacity to measure. He forgot everything except the beauty of the light and shadow in front of him. When Libby untied her petticoat and pushed it down her legs, he turned away and leaned back against the wagon wheel, a torrent of lust pulsing through him.

How the hell was he supposed to get back into the wagon and pretend that it was like any other evening around the old campfire? That she wasn't wrapped in just a blanket? This would be even more trying than the episode with the liniment. At least that night he could leave. He should have shot the lid off her damned trunk so she could get dressed. But there was no help for it now.

After waiting a moment or two, he went to the front of the wagon and called up, "Are you—" But his voice came out as a strangled croak. He cleared his throat. "Are you decent yet?"

Decent, Libby thought, and looked down. In her

camisole and drawers? Why had nakedness been added to the predicament she was already in? But she couldn't make him stand outside in the rain any longer. Silently cursing her trunk as vividly as Tyler had aloud, she grabbed the blanket he'd given her, and flung it around herself. She was immediately enveloped in the familiar scent of him, an undefinable combination of leather, soap, and clean air. "All right. Come in."

As soon as he climbed into the shelter, he paused with the food cradled in his hands and stared. The wagon felt charged with his presence, and his eyes deepened to turquoise as his gaze swept over her. From another man, such a look would be vulgar. Not so with Tyler. It was straightforward and powerful, and made her suck in her breath. Her apprehension stemmed as much from her own reaction to him as what she read in that look. She backed up a step and felt the chuck box against her bottom.

Breaking the silence and eye contact, he showed her the biscuits and pie. "I brought supper." He took off his hat and slicker, and plunged a hand through his hair. "I don't know about you, but I'm starving."

He was obviously waiting for an invitation—or was it permission?—to sit in her presence.

"Please," she said, and waved at a vacant spot on the floor. She felt a tremendous disadvantage in having only her underwear and a blanket for clothes. She had to hold the wrap shut with one hand while taking the cups and forks he handed to her.

"I didn't bring plates," he said. "It was too dark and rainy out there to do much searching." When he sat down, he slowly leaned against a pile of bedrolls and stretched out his long legs. Libby heard him sigh tiredly.

"That's all right. We can eat out of the pie pan." Cautiously, she lowered herself to the only place available—next to him, shoulder to shoulder. "It's been a hard day, hasn't it?"

He sat motionless for a few seconds, as if too exhausted to do anything else. Then he crossed his ankles, brushing her thigh with his own as he moved. Libby tried to ignore the fire that raced up her leg.

"I've sure had better."

"Me, too."

He chuckled, then they sat in silence for a few moments, their attention focused on the food. Libby hadn't realized how hungry she was until she tasted the sourdough.

He waved at the pie with his fork. "You know, I've been meaning to tell you, you're one hell of a cook."

Libby gaped at him. Tyler did not seem to be a man who lavished praise on people. "Thank you. The men told me you've had a run of bad luck with cooks in the last couple of years."

He smiled while he chewed and swallowed. "Yeah, I suppose we have. But this—my old man would have called this 'a little taste of heaven.' That's what he used to say when something tasted really good—if heaven had a flavor, it would taste like this." He grinned at her.

Libby ducked her head and smiled, too. He'd never mentioned anything about his family before. "Your father sounds like he had a touch of poet in him."

"Mostly he was just a cattleman who brought us up here from San Antonio. Someone told him the sweetest grassland on earth was in Montana, free for the taking, and that a man could raise a herd better than any in Texas." He speared a cherry on the tines of his fork. "My mother didn't want to come at first. She said if he made a go of it, he could send for us. If he didn't, we'd be waiting for him. She was a strong-willed woman. But my old man ..." He shook his head. "His word was law. He told her we were his responsibility, and it was her duty to follow her husband. So we came. I don't think she was ever happy here."

"Has she been gone a long time?" Joe had told her both of Tyler's parents were dead.

He poured water for both of them from the canteen. "Yeah. She died of influenza our second winter here. I was eleven years old. I think my father always felt guilty about it. But life up here isn't always easy. I guess you've figured that out."

"Yes, I have." Libby glanced at her hand. The cut had been healing well, but pulling on the reins this afternoon had partially opened it again.

"How's that finger?" Tyler asked, watching her.

"It was getting better, but after today with the mule team ..." She shrugged.

"Let's see," he said, and held out his open hand.

She hesitated just a beat before laying her hand, palm up, in his. His touch was warm as he held it toward the lantern light. "I probably should have put a stitch in this."

"Oh, no," she warned, pulling back a little. There were limits to the amateur, ranch-house medicine she'd allow him to practice on her. But the sensation of her hand in his warm grip made her think it might almost be worth the risk to let him try.

"Can't now, anyway. It's too late for it to help." He released her hand. She tucked it into the folds of the blanket, telling herself that it hadn't really been as comforting as she'd imagined. She was just tired and being foolish.

He gave her an even look. "I know you came out here to marry Ben," he said, taking a bite of sourdough, "but I've wondered what it was that made you want to leave Chicago to begin with. I don't get the feeling it was a pioneering spirit."

Libby heard the same polite, caring interest she'd heard that night in his office. Underlying that was encouragement to talk, and a lulling assurance that he would listen. She supposed it was only fair—he'd revealed more about himself than she'd expected.

She pulled the edges of the blanket more tightly around her shoulders and leaned back against a sack of flour. With a little food in her stomach and his warmth next to her, she let herself relax a bit. She began by telling him the story of going to work for the Brandauers when she was fourteen.

"They had a big, fancy house with deep carpets and a fireplace in every single room. I'd never seen anything like it. And Melvin, Birdie, and Deirdre, we were close. They became my own family."

Tyler kept his eyes on the blue enamel cup in his lap. "It sounds as though you were content there. Why did you leave?"

*Why.* Libby's memory fell back to a warm evening the previous August, to Wesley's bedroom, and his impatient, groping hands, to the sensation of utter horror when Eliza Brandauer, presumably visiting friends out of town, had flung open her son's door with only a cursory knock, before he took the cook's virginity—

Absently, she pleated a fold of the blanket. "My life there became ... impossible," she replied, and by her tone, asked him to press no further. Wesley

Brandauer was her own private hurt. "I couldn't stay any longer."

Tyler nodded, turning the cup in his hand. "You're not the first person to come west for a new start."

Overhead the rain slowed to a steady tapping, now only occasionally driven by buffeting winds.

She resumed her story. "I saw Ben's advertisement for a wife in a newspaper in Chicago. He said he was looking for a woman to come to Montana and live on his ranch with him. I needed to, well, put some distance between me and what was going on in my life. Do you know what I mean?"

"Yeah. I know." A tinge of bitterness colored his answer.

"So I answered his advertisement. He wrote back and told me he had a successful ranching operation, and that he'd advertised for a wife because there are so few women in this area." She gave him a little smile, then she looked at her lap. "He also said that he was thirty years old. I told him to send the train ticket. It seemed like a good choice at the time."

Tyler stared at her. "Thirty years old! Jesus Christ, Ben Ross was over seventy. Both his health and his ranch were long past their prime. Did he think you wouldn't notice?"

Libby shrugged. "I can't begin to guess. When I got to Heavenly and learned the truth, I wanted a ticket to get right back on the stage and leave. I'd have gone anywhere. Anywhere. But I didn't have any money and neither did he. I didn't have a choice, either. I was alone and scared. I realized I'd have to make the best of things. So we were married in the sheriff's office, and then we made the trip to his place. It was strange to be in such a vast, open country, and yet have to live in a one-room cabin so cramped I had to turn sideways to squeeze around my cot." She took a drink of water.

"Then winter set in. He took sick the first night it snowed, and pretty soon he had pneumonia. The cabin seemed even smaller after that." She shifted on the hard wagon bed, and tucked her feet inside the blanket. "I think Ben Ross knew he wouldn't live out the winter, and he didn't want to die alone. He wanted someone to keep him company. I can't blame him, I suppose, but I wish he'd chosen a different way to get it."

She fell silent, lost in the memory of the night Ben took his last breath.

Tyler prompted quietly, "So as soon as he was gone, you went to Heavenly?"

She shook her head. "No, not right away. When he died, there was still a lot of snow on the ground and it was frozen solid underneath. I found that out when I tried to bury him." Her voice faltered, and she took a breath, waiting to regain control. She felt Tyler's hand on her blanket-covered forearm. "So I sewed him into an old quilt and dragged him to the porch. H-he didn't weigh much by the time he died. Some—sometimes at night, I'd wake up because I thought I heard him wheezing. But it was only the wind ... God, that wind. He was out there for a month before it warmed up enough for me to dig his grave. I was never really his wife—" She faltered for a moment. "Not in any way that a woman can be a wife, but I guess I owed him that much."

His hand on her arm tightened and he sighed, but she was afraid to look at him. Afraid that whatever she saw in his eyes—and she wasn't sure what that might be—would crumble her remaining strength and make her start blubbering again like the day she'd shot the rattlesnake.

But she felt a sense of relief, too. She hadn't told anyone about Ben. She'd carried the ordeal, locked in her heart and head, while she relived it at night in her dreams. Maybe now it would give her peace.

She felt his gaze on her while he considered her. She had the odd sensation that he was seeing her for the first time. "You've had a hell of a time, haven't you?" he murmured.

Finally she gathered enough courage to glance up at him. She saw something very like tenderness written in the lean planes of his face, and in the way his eyes smiled, even though it didn't reach his mouth.

"Well, it wasn't a picnic in the park, but I have to keep hoping everything will work out. How can any of us survive in this world without hope?"

Tyler switched his gaze to the opposite canvas wall as if there were something of great fascination to be found there. "Does that mean you're going to marry Charlie?" he mumbled.

"Charlie! How did you know about that?" She stared at his cleanly defined profile: the slim nose, wide brow, full lips, and sharp jaw.

"There isn't much that goes on with my ranch or my crew that I don't know about. So—are you?"

She thought about the expression she'd seen on the cowboy's face earlier, when the storm hit. She wished she could care about him; she suspected that he was a good, decent man. "No, I'm not. If I ever marry again, it will be for love. I like Charlie, but that isn't a good enough reason to get married. I'll make it on my own in Chicago, even if the only work I can find is scrubbing floors."

Tyler felt two feet tall. He'd thought she was a

helpless city-born woman. He'd thought she'd be a timid burden on this trip, who'd have to be watched over and hand-fed every mile of the way. That she wanted to go back to Chicago because it wasn't soft enough here for her, or refined enough. And every mile of the way, she'd proved him wrong.

What he couldn't understand was why he felt even more protective toward her now that he knew how capable she really was.

The night he'd bandaged her hand, she'd said with some bitterness that Ben Ross had exaggerated a lot of the things he'd told her. She'd been kind in her understatement; he hadn't realized just how flagrant the old man's lies were.

"You're a pretty amazing woman, Libby Ross. You're braver than a lot of people I know."

She tried to give him a wobbly smile in return, but she couldn't completely suppress the tears that threatened. Turning away from him, she dashed a hand across her cheeks. It was her brave front more than anything that went straight to Tyler's heart.

He took the cup out of her hand and put his own down with it, then pulled her into his embrace. Bundled up in his blanket like that, she reminded him of a child. With her forehead resting against his jaw, he couldn't see her face. But her hair, drying on the ends, fell in soft unruly waves over her shoulders, highlighted here and there with lantern light. It smelled like rain and vanilla. He could feel her tension, though, as she leaned against him. She sniffled a couple of times.

In the last few years, he'd had more practice soothing upset horses than upset women, but in his experience, what worked for one, worked for the other.

"Come on, darlin', hush now. It's all right," he

intoned as he rocked her a little and rubbed her back. "You're safe. You're not alone."

Libby couldn't ignore the solace in Tyler's embrace. He was warm and strong, a reassuring presence in the cold darkness of the night. She knew she should resist the comfort, but dear God, it was so difficult.

That was how Wesley had gained her trust—by appearing to care. By making her feel like a duchess instead of a domestic. Until that nightmarish August night when, on top of the raging humiliation of being discovered in his bedroom, she'd learned that "Mr. Wesley" was to be married in a month's time to the daughter of a prominent Chicago family—

But this man holding her in his arms was not Wesley Brandauer. This was Tyler Hollins, a plainspoken man. A man she sensed might be carrying a heart full of regret, too. Under the gentle strokes of his hand on her back, she felt her tight muscles begin to loosen. His murmured words next to her ear were reassuring. She wasn't sure what to make of this new unsuspected side of him, but she liked it. Very much. So when his hand slid from her back up to her jaw, as though he'd willed her to do so, she tilted her head and received his kiss.

Instantly a fierce heat sprang up between them. His lips were lush, warm, thrilling. The stubble from his beard rasped softly against her chin. She nestled closer to him, and immediately he deepened the kiss. He tightened his arm around her and she felt a vital, restless urgency throbbing in him and in herself. His breathing grew heavier and her own heart beat like a rabbit's. She told herself to resist, to end this now, but her body refused to obey.

The instant their lips touched, a fiery jolt zigzagged through Tyler's body. His arousal was swift and sharp. Libby's mouth under his was soft, yielding. Her delicate fragrance filled his head and he heard the low, anguished groan that came from his own throat.

Such a simple thing, a kiss. But it had been so long since he'd tasted one, to him it felt like his first—as if he were a kid again, as if this were the kiss he'd always waited for. Gently, he touched his tongue to her upper lip, then her lower. He was pleased to feel her quick inhale. Her hand emerged from the folds of the blanket to press flat against his chest, just over the place where his heart thundered. He reached up and quickly unbuttoned his shirt halfway down, then tucked her hand inside and held it against his bare skin.

"Tyler," she whispered, and another chink opened in his ice-bound spirit.

He pulled back to look at her, beautiful and fragile in the lantern light, and he knew this was what he'd wanted to do since the first morning he saw her. Greedily he drew her to him and took her lips again. The inside of her mouth was hot and slick, and an intense desire burned in him to lay her down on a pile of blankets. To shelter her with his body and press kisses on her smooth, naked skin, while he pulled her hips to his to surround himself with her warmth. And afterward, to sleep with his head on her breast while the rain poured down around them—

No. He couldn't do that. He wouldn't be able to share that with her, then put her on a train in Miles City. That one fact brought him crashing back to the present.

Tyler swiftly kissed her forehead and cheek. "We'd better get some sleep, Libby. Morning will be here sooner than we want." He shifted slightly, trying to ease the throbbing ache in his groin, and tucked her against his side.

Although her head told her she shouldn't allow it, Libby's heart was content to let her lie in Tyler's arms. It was dangerous: she knew she'd never see him quite the same way again. The edgy desire he'd begun to kindle in her was bound to keep her awake, at least for a while. But his embrace was also too comforting, too secure to refuse. His heart was a steady timekeeper beating under her ear.

If anyone had told her even twenty-four hours earlier that she would find herself in this situation, she'd have called the person a liar. The distrust fostered by Wesley's betrayal had only been compounded by Ben Ross. But she *was* here, with her head pressed to Tyler's chest. He hadn't charmed her with pretty words or false promises. In fact, it seemed that he'd gone out of his way to keep her and everyone else away from him.

But she'd learned tonight that Tyler Hollins was not as angry and aloof as he'd wanted her to believe.

When Libby awoke, it was to the sound of voices outside the wagon. She was lying on Tyler's bedroll on the floor of the wagon, with his blanket thrown over her instead of wrapped around her. Apparently, he'd put her down here in this makeshift bed. She glanced down at her underwear, realizing that he must have seen her in this state of undress. The sun was just coming up, and what she could see of the sky was a clear, pale blue.

The first voice she recognized was Joe Channing's low rumble. She pulled up to her elbow. Once again, she wondered if Tyler ever slept.

"We came upon him about an hour ago. Hell, there wasn't any way to look for him in the dark last night. And I figured he'd find his way back."

Tyler replied, "I know ... I know. It didn't stop raining until way after midnight." He breathed a heavy sigh. "I'll finish getting these mules hitched and we'll be along shortly. Tell the boys breakfast is coming."

Joe mumbled something, then she heard the sound of creaking leather and horse's hooves pounding across the turf and off into the distance.

Tyler climbed up and stuck his head in. "Awake yet?" He looked tired and preoccupied, but he gave her a brief smile.

"Yes, I didn't mean to sleep so late." Thinking about the night before, and all that had transpired between them, Libby felt self-conscious now. Had she really lain in his arms and kissed him? Had she actually let him put her hand inside his shirt so she could caress him? It brought hot blood to her cheeks just to think about it.

"I managed to pry this damned trunk open so you'd better get dressed while I hitch the team. Do you think you can drive the wagon back to the herd if I lead you?"

She nodded and looked at him a bit more closely. Was it just the light that gave his face a slightly gray cast? "Of course. Are we far from them?"

"About three miles. Are the shovels in there with you, or under the wagon bed?" He looked down for a moment and squeezed his temples.

"They're back here. Tyler—is something wrong?"

He ignored her question and once again became the remote, responsible leader. "All right, let's get going then. We've got a crew to feed. And a cowboy to bury."

# Chapter 10

Libby felt as though a great weight had descended upon her chest that only grew heavier as they neared cow camp. The West, in her opinion, was fraught with such cruel violence, loss, and perpetual mourning, that she wasn't sure why anyone would want to come here. It was a hard place that stole men's lives and women's dreams.

Yet as she considered the span of emerald green plains, covered with a sky so enormous, so breathtakingly beautiful, she almost understood the attraction of this cursed paradise.

All traces of last night's storm were gone, and the sun began the job of drying out the sodden earth. She looked over the mules' backs to the horizon. Where had she seen that particular shade of blue before? It was clear and flawless, different from any spring sky she'd seen in Illinois. Then she realized it was exactly the color of Tyler's eyes.

He rode ahead of her, his shoulders drooping slightly, his back not quite as straight as usual. But when cow camp came into view, he sat up, as though he didn't want anyone to realize that he was susceptible to human frailties.

Joe came forward to meet them when they arrived.

A pall of bereavement hung over the camp, but more than ever, she felt a strong sense of family with the Lodestar crew.

"Where is he?" Tyler asked, climbing down from his horse.

"Over here," Joe replied. Tyler handed his reins to Rory, and patted him on the shoulder, then he and Joe began to walk away.

Libby scrambled down from the wagon and, lifting her skirt a few inches, ran to catch up. "Tyler, wait—please, may I come, too?"

Joe and Tyler exchanged a look, and Joe nodded. "Yeah. It's not too bad."

Tyler waved her forward. "All right. Come on."

They crossed the wet grass, and along the way were greeted by several of the men. They saluted Libby and Tyler quietly with tips of their hats, falling back on the respectful formality that disaster sometimes brings out in people.

Outside the campground against the shelter of a boulder, Libby saw a man's form covered by a slicker. His boots and twelve inches of chaps stuck out, and his hat had been placed over his chest. Tyler stood beside the body for a moment, then crouched to pick up the hat and slicker.

She approached, then drew a deep breath and stared at Charlie Ryerson as he lay there. She hadn't known what to expect. Tyler told her that Charlie had been struck by a bolt of lightning. It seemed a very brutal way to die—she'd once seen a tree split into two smoldering halves—but he looked as if he were sleeping. His hair and big mustache were wet, and she remembered that he'd lain in the rain, undiscovered, until this morning. The thought of that tore at her heart.

"Oh, Charlie," she whispered, and blinked back hot tears that scalded her lids. She would *not* begin crying again. She couldn't. Weeping left her feeling drained and defenseless.

Tyler gazed into the still face for several seconds, then pulled off his glove and brushed the cowboy's hair off his forehead. "Give me a hand, Joe," he murmured, and they turned him over.

Libby gasped. A large, jagged rip in his shirt ran down his left shoulder blade. The fabric along the rent was scorched, and when Tyler lifted one edge she saw that the skin underneath was blackened as if someone had held a flame to it.

Tyler examined both of Charlie's hands, front and back, and glanced down at his boots. She couldn't imagine what he was searching for.

"Here it is," he said then, and showed them Charlie's right elbow, where his sleeve was also torn and blackened. "Here's where it came through." He looked at the unnaturally peaceful face again. "Does his mother still live in Wichita?"

"I believe she does," Joe said.

Tyler nodded. "I'll wire her when we get to Miles City." He propped his own arm on his knee, then he looked up at Libby. All traces of the frown she knew so well were missing. His expression was open and unguarded, betraying his sense of loss. "We'll need a blanket from his bedroll for a shroud. Could you get that?"

She nodded with her shaking hand pressed to her mouth, her throat constricted. "D-do you want me to sew him into it?"

Tyler gave her a small, tired smile. "No, we won't do that. He'll be all right." He reached out and patted her foot. "Go on, now. Get the blanket, and then we'd better eat. Joe, you go with her, and talk to the crew. See which of them would like to dig Charlie's grave." He made no effort to move beyond taking off his hat.

"Ty?" Joe prodded.

He glanced up again. "I'm just going to sit here with this boy for a minute."

It was the first time she'd ever seen him express any real emotion. No, she corrected herself. It was the second. Last night, there had been *something* in his kiss, his tenderness . . . that feeling. But it had to have been due only to the circumstances, she told herself. Thrown together like that in a frightening situation—it couldn't have meant anything more.

Joe nodded and put a hand on his shoulder. Then, as she and the foreman walked away, she glanced back and saw Tyler gently fold Charlie's hands across his chest. She turned her head and inhaled, pushing down her persistent urge to cry.

When they'd put some distance between themselves and Tyler's privacy, Joe spoke.

"Maybe it don't seem like the right time to say this, but I think I should. Charlie was in love with you." He said it quietly; it was a very personal thing to discuss. "I don't suppose he told you that. He said he couldn't work up the nerve."

"Joe," she said, her voice trembling again, "h-he hardly knew me—"

The ring of his spurs was comforting as they walked along. It was a sound that she'd learned to listen for, the men's jingling spurs, and one that had become familiar to her, like the soft tick of a clock. She'd miss it when she went back to Chicago.

"He knew enough to suit him, Miss Libby. I don't think he could have given you an easy life—not too many people out here have easy lives. But he would've done everything he could to give you a happy one." He sighed. With his head bent, he looked every bit as downcast as Tyler. "He couldn't tell you any of that himself, but I know he wished he could. I'm not sayin' this now to make you feel bad—" He kicked at a tussock in his path. "Aw, hell, ma'am, I don't know why I said it."

Listening to him, her chest had grown tight again. "Maybe it's a way of telling me that Charlie was a kind, good-hearted man."

He turned and gave her a pleased smile, as though grateful that she understood. "Yes, Miss Libby, I expect it is."

After she retrieved Charlie's blanket to give to Joe, she put together a quick meal of bacon and fried potatoes while Possum Cooper and Noah Bradley volunteered to dig the grave.

Even though the men hadn't eaten since the day before, breakfast was somber and orderly, and the group around the campfire very quiet. Death and exhaustion had silenced their good-natured bantering. Now and then, she lifted her gaze to the distant boulder and saw Tyler still crouched next to Charlie. No one intruded on his solitude.

When Rory came to get his food, he gazed blankly at the plate she offered him.

"Miss Libby, no offense, ma'am, I ain't really hungry. Tyler says I have to eat, but I don't want anything."

Pale as snow and despondent, his misery was so obvious that Libby's heart ached for him. The Lodestar seemed to be the only family he had, and Charlie had been his hero. She knew he'd take his death hard. She patted his arm.

"He's right, Rory," she agreed, putting back most of the potatoes and half the bacon. "But I think he just wants you to eat a little."

He took the plate and glanced across the flat, un-timbered range at the hole Noah and Possum had dug for Charlie's final resting place. Two shovels were stuck in the pile of dirt they'd excavated.

"I wish they could've found a tree to put him under—you know, so he wouldn't have the weather beatin' down on him year after year. A man ought not to have to spend the rest of eternity bein' frozen and rained on."

"He prob—" Libby cleared her tight throat, "he won't mind, Rory," she said just over a whisper. He hung his head for a moment, then nodded and scuffed away with the dragging steps of an old man.

Tyler didn't follow his own advice about eating. When he came to Libby, he took only coffee. "We'll be having the funeral in a few minutes. Do we have enough cups to go around?" His face still wore its faint gray cast. In some ways he looked worse than Rory: the hint of emotion that he'd shown earlier was under firm control again, but she sensed that it required considerable effort to keep it there.

"Yes, shall I make another pot of coffee?" she asked.

He shook his head. "Just make sure everyone has a cup."

Several minutes later, with the exception of a couple of men who held the herd, the Lodestar crew assembled to bid farewell to one of their own. They gathered in a semicircle around the grave in which Charlie had been laid. Libby stood between Rory and Kansas Bob Wegner.

Each of them held a tin cup as they waited for

Tyler, their hats removed and their shifting feet stilled under the morning sun. It was the first time she'd seen them bareheaded as a group. No one spoke. The only sound to be heard besides the far-off bleating of the cattle was the wind in the grass. She kept her eyes averted from the bottom of the grave; it was too similar to her experience with Ben just a few weeks earlier. Feeling her eyes well up again, she reached into her apron pocket for her handkerchief.

Down the line, she saw Noah Bradley staring at Charlie's blanket-wrapped body, looking grief-stricken and remorseful.

Finally, Tyler rode up to the graveside. The smudges under his eyes were noticeable even from where she stood, and his face mirrored his exhaustion. But still, he was so handsome she couldn't help but stare at him. He dismounted and reached into his saddle-bag for a bottle of whiskey. Walking around to face the semicircle, he put the bottle down at his feet, then let his gaze rest on each face.

When he spoke, his voice had an unhurried, intimate tone, as though he were talking to each of them individually.

"Charlie Ryerson worked at the Lodestar for seven years. He was always cheerful, brave, and helpful. His life ended before it should have because his luck ran out first. But he always did the best he could, and it was an honor to know him. He was a good cowboy, and a good friend, too. I'm going to miss him."

A couple of bandannas came out of back pockets as his words rolled over the Montana prairie, carried away on the wind.

He picked up the whiskey bottle. "All of you know

I don't hold with drinking on the trail. Hardly any cattleman does. But burying a friend is a damned hard thing to do, and I don't think any of you would object to drinking to Charlie's memory." He scanned the circle, stopping at Libby and Rory. "That includes both of you."

He handed the bottle to Joe, who poured a measure into his tin cup and passed it along. When it reached Kansas Bob, he poured a sip for Libby and a full drink for Rory.

At last the whiskey made its way back to Tyler and he gave himself a healthy share. Then he extended his cup, and the rest raised theirs. In the distance, a lone bird twittered.

"Some people die in their beds, but Charlie, you died doing a man's job, and doing it well. Now we're going to put you into the arms of the land you loved. I hope you find tall grass and good water." His voice grew rough with emotion and he paused. "You were one of the best."

Tyler bolted the whiskey in one swallow. Around the circle, the men followed suit. The silence was punctuated with a few coughs and gasps. Libby wrinkled her nose at the strong smell, but the occasion seemed to warrant drinking the thin layer of liquid fire at the bottom of her cup. She let it trickle into her mouth and tried to swallow before she tasted much of it.

Imitating Tyler, Rory gulped his, then coughed until she thought he would choke. She clapped him on the back until he got his breath.

Then, one by one, each of them filed past the grave and threw in a handful of dirt. When Rory's turn came, he froze, the mud clenched in his fist.

"Mr. Hollins is right, Rory," Kansas Bob said in

a low voice. His usually rosy face had gone quite pale. "Burying a friend is one of the hardest things a man can do. It takes a lot of grit. And that's what you are today—a man."

Libby watched to see if Kansas Bob's words would make the youngster feel better, but his chin still trembled. His effort to hold back his tears was obvious. "I sure don't feel like a man. I wish I could wake up and find out this is all just a bad dream."

Tyler, who'd been watching this, stepped forward and took Rory out of line. His tired face was shadowed with concern.

"I need you to do a favor for me," he said in a confidential tone. Rory stared at the gaping hole with wide eyes and said nothing. Tyler put a hand on the back of his neck and gently turned him away. "Rory, listen to me, now. I need you to escort Miss Libby to camp. I can't go with her because I have to finish up here and Joe needs to see to the herd. We don't want to make her walk back all by herself—it wouldn't be right. So could you take her?" He looked for Libby over the boy's head.

She stepped forward. "I'd really appreciate your company, Rory. This is a bad day for me."

He wouldn't meet her eyes, but he turned and offered her his arm, the dirt from Charlie's grave still clamped in his hand. His voice suddenly sounded much older than his years. "It's a bad day for all of us. Come on, Miss Libby, I'll walk you back."

As he led her away, Libby saw Tyler leaning on one of the shovel handles, considering her. She thought he looked for all the world like a man who'd just seen his own life go by.

\*　　\*　　\*

After the night they'd all had, and this morning's sorrow, Tyler decided to make it a short day. He rode ahead to choose the night campground, while Joe stayed back with the herd and took over Charlie's place at the point.

Tyler rode alone. He wanted some time to think, to be by himself. Feeling as though he hadn't slept in a year, he kept a slack grip on the reins and let his horse find its own way. In the void, his thoughts turned to things that had happened in the last day or so. The image of Charlie's lonely grave out there on the grassland behind them kept returning to his mind. He'd helped Noah fill it in and ended up doing most of the work himself. Noah had become so unraveled he could only push feebly at the dirt with his shovel while he swiped at his streaming eyes with the back of his hand.

When a man lost someone, he was inclined to think of all the things he wished he'd said and done for that person, and felt guilty for any petty human grievance or grudge he'd ever held. That's what was bothering Noah. And Tyler's conscience pecked at him for the day he'd embarrassed Charlie in front of Libby Ross.

He shouldn't have told her the story about the afternoon Charlie and Noah had spent upstairs at the Big Dipper. He knew he'd done it on purpose. He'd been highly annoyed when his top hand appeared to be setting his sights on Libby, and he'd had no reason to be. At least no reason he'd been willing to admit to. Now he wasn't so sure.

Losing a friend also made a man prone to review the regrets of his own life. Tyler was no stranger to disappointment and grief, although he'd learned to shut them out. But in many ways, that left him with not much more than the icy shell that encased his heart. Libby, with her scent of flowers and vanilla, her modest blushes and her courage, had warmed the shell in a way that Callie, all fire and proud brassiness, could not.

When he'd held Libby in his arms last night and kissed her, it took every bit of self-control he had to keep from pulling the blanket away from her and burying his face in her breasts. He'd wanted to *make love* to her, hot and sweet, to join his body with hers, to fall asleep in her arms. He didn't make love with Callie. He satisfied a physical need. Oh, he wouldn't for a minute say that he didn't enjoy it. But a hunger in his soul was left wanting by their encounters.

Tugging on his hat brim, he kicked his horse into a trot through the buffalo grass, driven by the urge to be near Libby. Not to touch her or kiss her—though he couldn't forget how good that had felt: her soft body in his arms, her lips under his, moist, warm. No, right now he just wanted to be around her, to look up from his shaving mirror and see her rolling out pie crust or stirring beans. He was beginning to realize how good that felt, too. He was setting himself up for trouble, and he knew it. But, God, it had been such a lousy day. . . .

He spotted the chuck wagon sitting on a gentle rise up ahead. Yellow flowers bloomed in the grass around it, and he wondered why that wagon made him feel as though he'd come home. Maybe because *she* made it seem that way—

He pulled on the reins and slowed his horse. God-damn it, but he was getting all sappy and soft, he thought crossly, and tried to derail the contemplations. It was just because he was tired. A decent night's sleep would help get this weight of gloom off his shoulders.

Riding toward the chuck wagon, he continued to scold himself. He should count himself lucky that a lightning bolt hadn't sent *him* to an early grave. So his soul was unsatisfied—so he was scared sometimes, and lonely most of the time, and weary of the burdens he carried by himself—well, so what? Life was hard but it went on.

Yeah, life went on, but now and then it left unlucky ones behind, buried on green bluffs in a mahogany coffin, or quilt-wrapped in a windswept prairie grave. It could happen to anyone.

It could happen to him.

When Libby and Rory arrived at the night camp, he went about his usual routine to stake the rope corral and dig the fire pit. But she was concerned about him. She watched him from her spot at the drop-leg worktable as she cut lard into flour for pie crusts. He was still chalk-pale, and his movements were as listless as those of a sleepwalker. And though she didn't expect him to be his customary outgoing self, it worried her that he'd stopped speaking altogether. As soon as the coffee was boiling, she called him to the back of the chuck box.

"Rory, have some coffee and a biscuit. You've hardly eaten today."

Obediently, he came and took the cup she held out to him. When she looked at him, her heart contracted. His freckles stood out in stark contrast to his pallor, and he gazed back at her with an uncomprehending hurt. The wind ruffled his sandy hair, and at that moment he seemed very young.

She wiped her hands on her apron. "I think I'll

take a break myself. Do you want to sit down with me over here?"

He only nodded and followed her to the side of the wagon where Libby had put Tyler's keg. She sat, and he sank down on the ground next to her, staring into his cup.

Suddenly he looked up at her, and his pale mask cracked. "Miss Libby, I keep askin' myself why that lightning bolt hit Charlie, instead of a stupid cow, or the saddle band, or the ground. But I can't figure it out."

"I don't think there are answers to those questions," she said. "Maybe that's why accidents like Charlie's are so hard for us to accept."

When Tyler got to cow camp the fire was going, and he smelled biscuits in the Dutch oven, but he found neither Libby nor Rory. Dismounting, he walked around to the chuck box and paused.

Tyler saw Libby sitting on an overturned keg down by the front wheel. In the afternoon sun, her hair gleamed in shades of ripe wheat and whiskey, lifted by the breeze to fly around her shoulders. Sitting on the ground next to her was Rory. Tyler heard the tremor in the boy's voice.

"One minute he was alive, just doin' his job, tryin' to save the herd. Then come dawn I found him out in the grass—f-face down with that burned h-hole in the back of his shirt."

"You were the one who found him?" Libby asked.

He nodded, and his face crumpled.

"Oh, Rory, Rory—I'm so sorry," she lamented, and drew his head to her lap. He gripped a wad of her apron in his fist, and sobbed out his heart while she stroked his hair. As if feeling his eyes on her, Libby turned and glanced at Tyler.

He drew a deep breath, backed up and walked away. At that moment he wished to God that he could rest his head in Libby Ross's lap and cry, too.

The next few days on the trail were busy but, to everyone's relief, uneventful. Libby, tired, but oddly enough, growing stronger, had settled into a routine that made her job bearable, if not easy. She still silently cursed the primitive conditions: she had little privacy, and no washing facilities beyond a bucket of warm water and a bar of soap. But that would all be over soon. Tyler said that barring any more problems, Miles City was two days away.

After the cause of Charlie's death had been dispensed with once and for all, at night around the campfire the men would fall to reviewing funny things he'd done or said, heroic deeds he'd accomplished, the nobility of his spirit. Overall, it was decided that Charles Ryerson had been a cowboy's cowboy, embodying every good thing that was expected of a man who earned his pay in the saddle.

After Rory had poured out his grief the day of Charlie's funeral, Libby supposed that he'd feel uncomfortable around her now and would avoid her. Instead, he was more solicitous, and she noticed that he walked and rode with a bit more dignity. Perhaps he had indeed become a man, she thought.

But foremost on her mind, ahead of Rory, or the day-to-day chores, or the end of this journey, was Tyler and the night she had spent with him in the chuck wagon. He didn't try to kiss her again, and she was distressed to realize that her disappointment far outweighed her relief. But she thought that maybe it was on his mind, too, because more often than not, when she looked up from the mules' backs, she'd see him. He rode close to the wagon, pointing out the very vastness of the sky, the heartstopping vistas of land, and its rugged beauty. Once, they even saw a bear on a far hillside. Libby was relieved when the animal showed far less interest in them than they did in it.

Sometimes Tyler galloped out ahead of her, executing tricky roping maneuvers and breathtaking displays of horsemanship. His skill was both surprising and impressive. She couldn't imagine what he was up to, except that it helped pass the hours from one cow camp to the next.

She couldn't help but admire his straight back and tall form. He was the most attractive man she'd seen in Montana. In fact, she was beginning to believe that he was the handsomest man she'd ever seen in her life.

He smiled more often, revealing white teeth that gleamed in the spring sun, and once, to her complete astonishment, he actually winked at her from the back of his horse. She'd laughed with delight and a blush of shyness, and nearly dropped the lines.

Sometimes, though, he looked at her with a hot, piercing gaze that held such raw, intense need, she felt both frightened and enkindled, as if she needed to respond somehow. At night, when she lay in the wagon waiting for sleep to overtake her, she'd remember the way his lips had felt upon hers, how he'd unbuttoned his shirt and put her hand inside. Nothing she'd experienced with Wesley Brandauer accounted for or made her comfortable about the restless yearning that thoughts of Tyler produced in her.

But he performed his most amazing deed on the

afternoon that he brought her a handful of wild-flowers.

Tyler Hollins wasn't such an ogre after all.

Tyler stood outside the rope corral with his pinto's foreleg in his hands, checking the hoof for rocks. About an hour of daylight remained, and on the western horizon the low sun lit the underside of the clouds with vermillion fire. It was one of his favorite times of day, sunset. Sunrise was the other one. Something about the way the sky looked—a ball of fire on one horizon and stars on the opposite side—appealed to his soul and gave him a sense of peace. In good weather, he loved to sit on the porch at the Lodestar, a cup of coffee on his knee—or a drink of whiskey, depending upon the time—and watch the days begin and end. Three weeks had passed since they left the ranch, and Tyler was glad that the drive was almost over. Fairly glad, anyway.

Now and then he'd look up at the chuck wagon, watching Libby's white-aproned figure as she moved from the chuck box to the fire to the water barrel. She wore her plaid shawl with the ends tucked into her waistband, and looking at it, Tyler thought it was the best six dollars he'd ever spent. Even on clear days like this one, the breeze that blew over the grass was chill and sharp.

Before he'd gone out of his way to avoid her; now he found himself more preoccupied with her than his job. More than once he'd caught himself acting like a goofy schoolboy around her.

"Looks like we made it, after all. We should be in Miles City tomorrow afternoon." Joe ambled up, but Tyler heard his approach before he spoke; he had the noisiest spurs of any of them. "Sometimes I had my doubts." He crouched next to Tyler and pulled up a blade of spring grass.

Tyler glanced down at him, surprised. "You? You've never worried about much of anything."

Joe ripped the blade into long, thread-fine strips. "I guess what happened to Charlie sort of made me back up and take a look at things."

Tyler pulled a hoof pick out of his pocket. "Yeah?"

"Sure. A man never knows when his time is gonna be up. That's why he has to keep lookin' forward, and not let things from the past drag at him."

Tyler sighed and rubbed his nose against the back of his glove. He had the feeling that he knew where this line of conversation was going, but figured he might as well play along. "What's dragging at you?"

Joe squinted up at him, the late-day sun golden-bright in his face. "Me? Nothin'. I'm not talkin' about me."

"Uh-huh."

"I was thinkin' of Rory."

Tyler let the pinto's hoof drop, and looked at Joe. This wasn't the response he was expecting. "What's the matter with Rory? I talked to him about Charlie. He was upset but he seems to be doing all right."

Joe pointed the grass stem at him. "That's just my point. Think of what that boy has been through. He lost his ma and his sister, he's cut off from his old man. Now, this week, his hero got killed by a lightnin' strike. But he ain't gonna let it dry him up and turn him into a bitter man."

"If you're comparing him to me—he's—how the hell—" Tyler spluttered, then found his voice, "For chrissakes, Rory is only fifteen years old!"

"Yessir, he is. That's a lot to happen to someone in such a short lifetime. If he was like his pa, he could blame you for Jenna. 'Course, I guess he don't need to—you blame yourself enough to cover everyone."

Tyler gave him a hard look and didn't respond.

A cold, stiff breeze flattened the grass around Joe. "Are you gonna let Libby Ross get on the train in Miles City?"

He picked up the pinto's hoof again. Even within the confines of his own heart, he wasn't willing to consider how her leaving would change his life. " 'Let' doesn't have anything to do with it. She wants to go. And she should."

"Not accordin' to what I've seen lately. Even the boys have noticed it." Joe reached into his jacket pocket and brought out a bent cigarette.

Tyler felt a flush creep up his neck and he kept his face tipped down toward the hoof as though it were the most fascinating thing he'd ever seen. "There's nothing to notice," he mumbled. He felt the foreman's gaze on him.

"Ty, some men spend years lookin' for somethin' that'll make them happy, never knowin' it was right under their nose the whole time."

"I've got the years to spend," Tyler snapped, beginning to feel badgered.

Joe stood and threw the grass stem aside, and started to walk away. As if thinking better of it, he turned and looked at him across the horse's back. Lighting his cigarette with a kitchen match, he held it out and gazed at the flame for a moment. Then he lifted his dark eyes to consider Tyler. A humorless smile spread his big mustache across his lean face.

"I'll bet Charlie thought the same thing." He blew out the match with an exhale of cigarette smoke, and went back toward camp.

# Chapter 11

The sky was dark with the threat of rain when the Lodestar crew arrived at the Miles City stockyards early the next afternoon. Tyler climbed onto the wagon seat next to Libby to drive her into town, and she bid farewell to the men there as they saw to the delivery of the cattle. Saying good-bye was much harder than she'd expected.

She waved to most of them from the chuck wagon while they stayed in their saddles, herding their charges through the gates. Rory stood in his stirrups and waved his hat. Joe, however, rode his horse to her side. He leaned over and kissed her cheek, tickling her face with his huge mustache. His smile held genuine fondness.

"Miss Libby, ma'am, thanks for lookin' after us old cowhands—we never ate so good till you got here," he said in his voice of low, rolling thunder. "I hope you find the best of everything back in Chicago. But we're gonna miss you."

"Thank you, Joe." Her throat tight with emotion, it was all she could do to get the words out. "You'll find another good cook."

"Maybe. But I doubt it." He sent Tyler a brief scowl that she didn't understand, then wheeled his horse around to rejoin the others. Next to her, she heard Tyler sigh, then he slapped the reins on the mules' backs and turned the wagon toward town.

Driving down Main Street, they passed saloons, shops, a bank, the blacksmith, and all manner of business offices. Libby's eyes and ears were assaulted by the buildings and people and horses. How quickly she'd grown accustomed to the wide-open and the quiet of both the Lodestar and the range. And this was just a small town in eastern Montana. Chicago was a hundred times busier and noisier than this. But she'd get used to it again, she told herself. The traffic and the crowds would become so familiar she wouldn't really notice them after a while.

Tyler had been pretty quiet sitting next to her, and it reminded her of the day they'd gone to Osmer's and he bought her the plaid shawl she now wore.

"Will you start back for the Lodestar tomorrow?" she asked, studying the clean lines of his profile.

"Yeah, in the afternoon. It'll give the boys a chance to sober up. I imagine they'll get going on a pretty good drunk once they finish at the stockyards and clean up."

"I hope not Rory," she exclaimed. "He's too young to be going into saloons and drinking."

"Oh, Joe will buy him a beer or two," he said, maneuvering the mules around a wagon with a broken wheel. "I don't think sarsaparilla is going to do the trick this time."

A gap of silence opened as they both remembered Charlie.

"Well, maybe not," she agreed softly.

"It was good for Rory, having a woman around," he continued. He kept his eyes straight ahead, but a brief smile pulled at the corners of his mouth. "I don't suppose we've taught him much about how to behave around a lady. Or how comforting a woman's heart can be. I meant to thank you for sitting with him after Charlie's funeral. Joe hadn't had the chance to tell me it was Rory who found Charlie's body."

She dropped her gaze to her lap. "He just needed someone to talk to." She'd been good for Rory, she thought. And for Tyler Hollins? She cast a sidelong glance at him. "And are you going to get drunk tonight, too?" They passed a busy saloon and she couldn't help but remember Callie Michaels and the Big Dipper.

He turned and looked at her. The smile was gone. "No, I've got to find another cook."

Not for the first time during the course of the trail drive, Libby caught herself wishing that things had turned out differently. Just a few short weeks ago, she'd smugly believed that her plan to return to Illinois was a good one. She'd wanted to leave Montana, an uncivilized wilderness thinly populated with people whose standards and ideas were completely alien to her. Why, the first time the Lodestar crew had invited her to sit and eat supper with them, she'd been aghast. Mrs. Brandauer would have happily starved before she invited Libby to dine at the same table with the family. But after spending time in the West, she'd begun to value the absence of pointless formality that separated people into such rigid stations.

Tyler stopped the wagon in front of what passed for a hotel in these parts—another narrow, two-story clapboard structure that reminded her of the buildings in Heavenly. Four rooms and a tiny bath, reached by a staircase on the side, were built over a restaurant downstairs. After he'd paid her, duly subtracting the cost of her saddle coat and gloves as she'd insisted, they stood on the busy sidewalk in front of the restaurant.

Tyler was dirty and tired, and he smelled like cattle, horses, and hard work. But he remained unforgivably handsome, formed as he was with long bones, and lean, powerful muscles. It ought to be illegal for a man to be that attractive, she thought. With a sense of resignation, she knew that he would look good to her no matter what the state of his appearance. A brief gleam of afternoon sun sparkled on the blond stubble in his one-day auburn beard.

"Well, Libby, you made it." He shifted his weight from one long leg to the other, and pushed his hat forward and then back. An awkwardness sprang up between them.

She laughed nervously. "You didn't think I would, did you?"

He shrugged, obviously a little embarrassed by the direct question. "I guess not—not at first. But I was wrong. I knew it as soon as you killed that rattlesnake." He met her gaze then, and jammed his hands into his tight front pockets. "Oh, hell, I knew it before then."

Staring up into his lean, attractive face, Libby felt a catch in her heart. Why? Just because they'd shared a kiss on a stormy Montana night? That had been a stupid, dangerous thing to do. Ever since, she'd wished she could live that night again, to feel his hands and lips on her. Even now she felt a despairing, wistful urge to step into his arms and hide her face against his neck, to hear him ask her to stay.

But it was best all around to tell him good-bye

right now, right here on the sidewalk, and be done with it. He'd helped her, grudgingly, and she'd helped him. Now it was over. He didn't want her here, and she didn't want to be here. At least not very much. She'd come here from Chicago because she'd had no place else to go. Now she was going back for the same reason.

She gave him a wry smile. "The next time you meet a rattlesnake, you'll have your gun with you. You wouldn't want to have to depend on someone whose aim is as bad as mine." She broke the connection with his eyes. "Thank you for everything. I guess I'd better see about my room. Well . . ." She extended her hand.

Tyler looked at it, then hurriedly pulled off his glove. The moment his hand touched hers, a heated, vital current passed between them. She looked up into his sky-blue eyes again. There was something in them that drew her, a heat, a yearning—something—that she didn't want to identify. No, she saw nothing, *nothing*, she agonized. She tried to pull away, but he maintained his grip and steered her to the edge of the sidewalk, out of the path of pedestrians.

Tyler gazed at the small woman standing in front of him, at the nose that turned up slightly, the silky brows, her clover-honey hair. She wasn't helpless or cowardly; in fact, she was a tough little scrapper. Still, he was beginning to understand what Charlie had felt: it bothered him that she had no one at all to look out for her. But he didn't know what he could do or say. He had nothing to offer except farewells. Besides, she was doing what she wanted to.

"Listen, I didn't mean to—well—" He glanced at the planking under his boots. "I guess I was a little hard on you at the beginning. You did a damn good job for us." He raised his voice to be heard over a passing freight wagon. "If you ever need anything . . ."

"Chicago is a long way from Montana." His stomach knotted at the forlorn expression that crept through her smile. "But thank you."

A heavy mist began to fall, the kind of soft, soaking drizzle that occurs only in spring. "I guess you'd better get inside before you get wet," he said. Getting wet under a little rain seemed laughable when he thought about what they'd just come through. He had no talent for good-byes, but he couldn't seem to end this.

"B-be careful going back to Heavenly," she said, and started to turn away.

"Libby, wait—" He gripped her arm. It was the last time he'd ever see her, touch her. Urgently, he pulled her into his embrace and pressed his mouth to hers, brief and hard. She smelled so sweet, despite her travel dirt and fatigue. He felt her stiffen with surprise. It wasn't the kind of kiss he would have wished for. But once more, time and circumstances were working against him.

Tyler released her suddenly, and Libby stared up at him, flabbergasted. The expression she'd seen once or twice before—open, longing, regretful— flashed over his handsome features. She was vaguely aware that people on the street were looking at them but at this moment, she didn't care. She pulled up the plaid shawl to cover her head.

"Go on inside now," he said hoarsely. He turned and leaped up to the wagon seat. With one last look, he urged the mules forward and drove away.

Pressing a shaking hand to her mouth, she stood in the rain and watched the wagon until it disappeared in the jumble of other horses and vehicles at the far end of the street. With a tight throat and leaden feet, she turned and climbed the outside stairs to her room.

"You look like you could do with some fun, cowboy. How about if I sit down here and you buy me a drink?" A saloon girl in a blaze of red satin and black lace dragged Tyler's attention away from his thoughts.

After a dinner at one of the chophouses, he'd tracked his crew down to the Briar Rose. Full of smoke, cowboys, and card games, it was as loud and rowdy as a cow town saloon could get short of brawling, gunfire, or horses being ridden in. But he didn't feel like joining the fun. He sat at a side table with his feet propped on the chair across from him, considering the untouched glass and whiskey bottle on the table. He'd been considering them for twenty minutes.

"What's your name?" he asked the girl. Hell, she was just a kid under all the paint she was wearing, probably not much older than Rory. She had the same look that Callie did; as though she never saw the sun. But if he closed one eye and squinted the other, under the harsh kerosene light her hair was almost the same color as Libby's. Her perfume wafted to him, a heavy, oppressive essence.

She dragged her fingertips along the back of the chair that served as his footstool, and gave him a lazy, practiced smile. "Rebecca."

He leaned back in his chair and put his elbow on the arm. "How is it that a girl your age is selling favors in this place, Rebecca?"

She straightened and gave him a hard look. "Listen, mister, I'm not interested in a lecture—"

"And I'm not giving you one. I really want to know. Was this the only work you could find?"

She hesitated a moment, then answered in a much younger voice. "My pa left me in this town two years ago. Sally, the owner here, took me in. I couldn't find anything else to do."

"You don't have family somewhere else?"

"I don't have any family at all. Pa got killed in a card game over in Rosebud, and he was the last of my kin."

He looked at the young face that was already aging before its time. She might be telling the truth, or she might be making up a sad story to gain his sympathy. He didn't know, or care. Either way, he doubted that she really wanted to be here. His mind drifted to Libby again, and her sad gray eyes.

He pushed his change from the bottle across the table to her. "Here, Rebecca. I'm going to drink alone tonight, but you take this for your trouble."

The girl gave him an even stare, then scooped up the money so fast he wasn't sure where she put it. The straggling feather in her hair dangled on her bare shoulder, and she gave him a crooked smile. "Thanks." She turned to walk away, then stopped. "Mister, I hope you find the woman you lost."

That took him aback. A wry, humorless chuckle huffed out of his chest. "Thanks, Rebecca, but I didn't lose anyone. At least, not lately."

She shrugged and moved on to a more likely looking prospect two tables over.

Tyler shifted in his chair, and he took the cork from the bottle and poured a drink. He'd spoken the truth to Rebecca, as far as he knew. Yet, he had to admit that a vague, uneasy sense of loss had plagued him since the minute he'd left Libby Ross standing on the sidewalk this afternoon. The image was fresh in his mind of her draping her shawl over her head while the rain poured down on her. And nothing—not the long soak in a tub at the bathhouse, nor falling asleep in the barber's chair with a hot towel on his face—nothing had taken the feeling away. If anything, it had only been made worse when he started inquiring around town about a new cook. He'd talked to a few promising men, former cowboys who'd been thrown a few too many times and were already developing rheumatism. But he'd found some problem with each of them; he suspected that one might be a drinker, another one didn't seem like he'd fit in with the crew, still another one just grated on his nerves.

Up at the bar, Joe and his crew were well on their way to getting pleasantly, fatuously drunk. He envied their ability to put problems aside and laugh. Even Rory was smiling again, thank God. Tyler had been concerned about him—the boy's solemn expression was too much like the one he'd worn when he first came to live at the Lodestar. The fun took a melancholy turn only when some of the Lazy J crew blew into the Briar Rose and learned that Charlie Ryerson had been killed.

After relating the details, in a moment of beer-tinged eloquence, Joe, with his elbows on the bar behind him, said, "I imagine every man gets a naggin' little ache in the pit of his belly about things left unsaid and undone. I wish Charlie was here with us now, but that accident of his—well, it was out of our hands. All's we can do is fix whatever things we have the power to fix. And try to leave this life with a tally of more joys than regrets." His audience murmured in agreement and lifted their drinks to Charlie's memory.

Tyler stared unseeing out the window. Joe's words had a chilling effect on him, more profound than any of the uninvited counsel delivered to him over the past few years. He tossed back the shot of whiskey he'd poured—it burned like fire all the way down. Shaken, he refilled the glass, sloshing a little over the rim. He knew if he were to die in his sleep tonight, the weight of his regrets would anchor his spirit to this earth for the rest of eternity.

After Jenna's death, he'd withdrawn into his safe, orderly existence. It didn't matter that he sometimes hungered for more; he'd felt he didn't deserve more and he still wasn't sure he did.

But damn it, he'd let life and happiness pass him by while he did nothing. That wouldn't bring back his wife. And despite whatever kind of man he might be, good or bad, Tyler Hollins was not one to do nothing.

He sat up and pushed himself out of his chair. First thing tomorrow, he'd set about balancing his tally. He couldn't change everything, but he had the chance to fix one thing, and he was going to do it, as Joe had advised.

Tonight, though, he was going to have a couple of drinks with his crew.


"Well, ma'am, your timing is nigh on to perfect. The only train for Chicago this week will be here at eleven, sharp."

"Oh," Libby faltered. "So soon?" Why wasn't she glad about this? she wondered. She'd wished for escape from Montana since the moment she set foot in the territory last fall.

"Yes, ma'am, unless you want to wait until next Thursday."

"No, no, I can't do that. I'll take the ticket." She put the money on the counter.

Looking very official in his porter's cap and sleeve garters, the young station clerk glanced at the clock behind Libby. "That gives you almost an hour if you want to get some lunch before you leave."

"If I can hire someone to bring my trunk from the hotel down the street, I believe I'd rather just sit here in the station, if that's all right," she said. She felt no appetite.

"Right as rain with me, ma'am. Choose any seat you like. I'll send a boy to fetch your luggage." She gave him her name for the delivery boy, then he pushed a ticket across the counter to her. She put it carefully in her pocketbook.

Crossing the deserted little station, she sat on an empty bench that faced the clock. The place smelled of ink, wood, and old paper. She smoothed the skirt of her plain traveling suit; this was the same one she'd worn to come out here, the same one she'd gotten married in. She didn't want to stay here a minute longer than she had to, but her reasons were not as clear as they'd once been.

She peeked inside her pocketbook to look at her ticket again, and caught a glimpse of five double eagles within the purse's leather folds. She'd been baffled, then outraged last night when she opened her trunk and discovered the hundred dollars. What on earth had Tyler Hollins been thinking, paying her off like that? Oh, he hadn't left her a note, but there was no question that the gold coins had come from him: she'd found them tied in one of her handker-chiefs with a twelve-gauge shotgun shell. Was he so relieved to be rid of her? She'd wished she could track him down to whatever saloon or restaurant he was sitting in and give him back his money.

But as she'd sat on the narrow bed in the hotel room, ripping her brush through her long, tangled hair, reason crept in and cooled her offended pride. Money was security, a hedge between herself and destitution. Pride, she realized, was a very fine thing, but it wouldn't protect her from starving, or put a roof over her head until she found work. Reaching down, she touched her pocket that held the shot-gun shell.

Libby tried hard not to think about Tyler, but the soft ticking of the clock over the door was lulling, and she lapsed into the world of daydreams where time stopped. The lines between the planks of the wooden flooring in front of her blurred and grew indistinct—

*A horseman with chestnut hair and agate-blue eyes galloped his pinto across the juncture of earth and sky, silhouetted against a crimson sunset. He rode toward her where she waited on the Lodestar porch for him to come home to her. And when he dismounted and approached her, alive with the intense passion of a man at one with the land, he bore her back into the house and up the stairs. On the big four-poster bed that they shared he laid her down, his hands impatiently opening the buttons of her bodice, impatiently seeking the heat under her skirt. His mouth was warm and moist on her throat and breast, and she longed to touch his bare skin. "Libby," he whis-pered thickly, "you're mine—I'll never let you go, do you hear? Never. I love—"*

"Mrs Ross! Ma'am, are you asleep over there?"

Libby was jolted back to the four drab walls of the railroad station. She turned sharply on the bench, and saw the young clerk frowning back at her from behind the counter. "I'm sorry, I must have dozed off," she lied. Her face felt as hot as a branding iron.

"Ma'am, your train is boarding now. You don't want to miss it."

She looked out the window and saw the huge, gaseous beast that would carry her back to Chicago, and grim reality set in.

She was not Tyler's. He was not hers.

Rising from the bench, she adjusted her new hat, the one small luxury she'd permitted herself. Then she went outside into the mild spring sun. Montana was never meant to be her home. She had to keep reminding herself of that, because the hope that had carried her all these months was now failing her. Her heart was as heavy as a millstone.

She walked down the crowded platform, passing men in suits, women, children, and cowboys. Apparently they were all coming home. She, on the other hand, didn't have a home anywhere. At this realization, her throat became so constricted she feared she'd begin weeping right here in public.

And now her ears were playing cruel tricks on her, too, much as they had the night of the storm. Somewhere above the racket of human voice, horses, wagons, and the hissing locomotive, she thought she heard someone calling her name.

She put her head down and hurried toward the conductor, who was helping an elderly man make his way up the steps of the passenger car.

"*Libby!*"

With each passing second, her eyes burned with

tears, and she felt panic enveloping her. The old man ahead of her was making little progress. Was she asking so much to put this place behind her with her dignity intact? She inched closer to the steps.

"Libby, wait!"

Reflex made her turn toward the direction of the voice, but she was completely unprepared for what she saw. Bearing toward her were Tyler Hollins and Joe Channing. They dodged pedestrians and freight goods, and despite the din on the platform, she heard their boot heels and spurs. She gaped at both of them, but her eyes fixed on Tyler. The urgency in his expression was unmistakable, and her heart began pounding. Something must be wrong.

Joe hung back a step, looking relieved, but Tyler plowed forward and grasped her shoulders in his big hands. He was a little breathless and he swallowed.

"Jesus Christ, we've searched all of Miles City for you. I went to the hotel, Rory and Possum went to all the restaurants, Kansas Bob and Noah stopped in every goddamned shop on Main Street—"

"Why? What's wrong? Has there been an accident?"

"Uh, no—" Tyler ground to a halt. He turned and glanced at Joe, but the foreman only backed up against a hitching rail and took out his makin's.

"You're on your own, cowboy," Joe advised, and crossed his ankles.

Tyler released her shoulders and searched her face, then he drew a deep breath. "Look . . . I know that Heavenly isn't Chicago. God, it isn't even Miles City." He gestured around them. "But I was thinking, well—" It was the first time she'd ever seen him so tongue-tied. Even his ears were tinged with red. "The boys like your cooking and you don't have anything in particular to go to. And—it wasn't so bad having someone to look after us. Anyway, do you still hate it in Montana? Would you consider coming back to the Lodestar? The pay is the same as on the trail."

"All aboooarrrd!"

Libby looked behind her at the train. "But they have my trunk," she replied, as if that settled matters.

"Will you come home with us?" Tyler asked again, louder this time.

Home. The peaceful hush, the sense of family and belonging, this man—"Well . . . yes! Yes, I'll come." She felt almost faint with relief.

"Joe!" he fired without taking his gaze from hers. "Get Libby's trunk from them."

Joe jammed his half-rolled cigarette into his pocket and bolted off in the direction of the baggage car.

Tyler grinned down into Libby's face, then leaned forward and put a quick peck on her forehead. His broad smile was one he'd rarely shown, and she thought she'd never seen anything so good. His blue eyes seemed more alive, his face more rested. He was the best-looking cowboy in this town.

"I don't hate Montana anymore," she said. "It just took me awhile to appreciate it."

He kissed her forehead again. "Come on, let's go find those boys before they wear themselves out from searching for you. Most of them have headaches I wouldn't wish on anyone," he said, and put his arm on her shoulders to turn her toward the center of town. "It's a good thing you said yes."

"Why?"

He grinned again, this time a bit sheepishly. "Well, because I promised them that you would."

She pulled away slightly and gave him an arch look. "So sure of yourself, were you?"

His smile faded slightly, and he shook his head. "Not at all, Libby. Not at all."

Once more Libby found herself on the high seat of the chuck wagon, but this time Tyler drove. When they'd finally rounded up the crew, they met down at a stand of cottonwoods on the edge of town where the horses waited in the rope corral. The men were so glad to see her she knew she'd made the right choice to stay.

"Miss Libby, what are we havin' for supper tonight?" Rory asked, his face lighted up.

"Maybe she'll give in and fix us rattlesnake," Noah chuckled. He ran a brush through his sorrel's mane.

"If it means I have to be the bait again, forget it," Tyler said. They all laughed.

Libby grinned and held up her hands. "No, no, as much as I like you all, you'll have to settle for something less exciting."

Joe leaned forward and put his forearm on his pommel. "I looked in the back of that chuck wagon—we might be down to snake tonight if we don't stock up for the trip home."

"Libby and I will do that," Tyler volunteered. "We'll meet you back here in an hour, then we'll head for home."

There was that word again, Libby thought, tucking her skirt around her. Home. It gave her a warmth she'd felt very seldom in her life. And the scent that had been so noticeably absent a few weeks ago, of spring and things newly green, was strong in the air today.

Tyler turned the wagon and they drove down to the general store, where they loaded up on enough provisions to see them through the seven or eight days it would take them to get home.

"Seven or eight days!" Libby exclaimed, as they headed back to the wagon. "It took us almost three weeks to get here." She listened to the drumming of his boot heels on the plank sidewalk, and the clink of his spurs, and she smiled. She liked the feeling of walking next to him, but she wasn't fooling herself. She knew better than to think of her return to the Lodestar as more than a job. Disappointment loved to visit people with lofty expectations. No one was more aware of that than she was.

"Our work will really be cut out for **us** when we get back. And I think we'll have some extra calves to brand. I'm not sure how many but—"

His words cut off so abruptly that Libby turned to look at him. He was staring straight ahead at an older man who approached on the sidewalk and blocked their path. Though she wasn't touching him, she sensed that every muscle under Tyler's shirt and jeans was tight. If he'd been a wolf, the crest of fur on the back of his neck would have bristled. Almost unconsciously, he pulled her back and put his shoulder in front of her.

They stopped within ten feet of the man.

"Tyler?" she said. He didn't respond, but she felt blood climb into her own cheeks when the approaching stranger looked her up and down with insulting contempt.

He appeared to be in his fifties, with a fringe of gray hair that was visible beneath his hat, and a red, jowly face. His sizable girth was most obvious in a big belly that overhung his belt.

"Well, well, Hollins," he said, and raked Libby again with narrowed, bloodshot eyes. "Got a replacement lined up for my little girl?"

Tyler stared at the wreck of a man standing in front of him, both repelled and angered. "You're drunk, Lat," he said, keeping his voice low. He could smell the whiskey from where he stood.

He laughed. "Drunk? Yeah, I am. But, then, Jenna was only your wife—guess you don't know what it's like to mourn a dead child, Hollins. It makes a man drink."

Tyler felt his hand close into a fist. He knew that nothing the man had to say was valid, but the accusation infuriated him. He'd grieved for his wife until grieving was nearly his undoing, and all he had left. In the end, he'd settled for blaming himself for her death.

"I mourned her, too, but it didn't bring her back. It only made me crazy." Maybe the rumors were true, Tyler thought. Lat Egan did act like he was unhinged.

"It wasn't enough that you let my Jenna die," the older man raged on. "You turned my only living son against me, too. That boy never comes to see me— I bet Rory wouldn't even talk to me now that you've poisoned his mind against me."

Tyler took a deep breath to keep control of his temper, and wondered why he continued with this conversation. Libby was pressed against the back of his arm, and he could feel her shock. Goddamn it, why had this happened now, in front of her? He hadn't seen Egan in more than two years. "Rory is free to leave the Lodestar any day he chooses." He grabbed Libby's hand and pulled her past his former father-in-law. "He's just never wanted to."

Behind them, Egan yelled, "Lady, if you're his wife, I feel sorry for you."

Tyler pulled her along toward the wagon. His stomach was in knots and, unthinkingly, he squeezed Libby's hand so hard she cried out. He let her go but pushed her ahead of him. A couple of people on the sidewalk turned to look first at them, and then beyond them to Egan.

When they got to the wagon, Tyler vaulted into the seat and pulled Libby up next to him. He flapped the reins viciously and the mules took off with a startled lurch. She stared at his granite profile as she clutched her hat. His face was fixed as though cast in stone.

Her heart pounded so hard in her chest, she could feel it against her breastbone. She tried to make sense of what she'd just heard but her mind was whirling. Jenna? He'd had a wife named Jenna? And how did Rory fit into this?

"Tyler, who was that?" she asked, feeling oddly winded. She'd never seen him so angry or so frightening, not even on the first morning he found her in the kitchen.

"I'm sorry that happened, Libby," he said. His words and voice were tightly controlled. "I would have prevented it if I could have."

"But who was that man?"

He wrapped the reins around his gloved hands. "Lattimer Egan. He's got the spread next over from the Lodestar, about ten miles east. His daughter, Jenna, was my wife. She died in childbirth five years ago."

She struggled to get her breath. "A-and Rory—Rory is—"

"Her brother," he finished.

He lapsed into silence then, and as much as she wanted to, Libby dared not ask any more questions. As they left the buildings of Miles City behind them, Libby realized how very little she really knew about the man sitting next to her. Still, though a lot about Tyler was a mystery to her, it was clear that pain lay beneath his gruff exterior and hard manner.

The crew was still lively and joking when she and Tyler reached them.

"About time you two got back," Joe teased. "We were near ready to come lookin' for you."

Tyler ignored the remark and tied the lines around the break handle. Pulling his bedroll out of the wagon, he jumped down.

"Rory," he called. "You climb up here and drive the wagon for Miss Libby. Possum, you and Hickory can see to the horses." He strode over to a cottonwood where his pinto waited, saddled and nibbling on the new grass. After tying his bedding behind the cantle, he mounted the horse and wheeled it around. "I'll see you at the ranch."

He spurred the pinto and took off at a gallop across the field.

"What the hell is wrong with him?" Joe demanded of no one in particular. Then he turned to study Libby, apparently searching for an answer to Tyler's abrupt mood change. She knew she looked as startled as everyone else who'd watched him ride away.

Staring openmouthed at Tyler's diminishing form, Rory walked around and got into the seat next to Libby. "What's ailin' him?"

"Rory, I think I met your father in town. I didn't

know that you were Tyler's brother-in-law." She recalled a conversation they'd had their first night on the trail. He'd said his father knew where he was. Now she understood why.

Rory let his hands rest on his thighs. "Aw, dang," he sighed, and offering nothing more, unwrapped the lines.

"Oh, Jesus," Joe added. "That explains it all. Well, we'd better get movin'. We've lost most of the day as it is." The contingent moved forward out to the open grassland.

Libby sat in baffled silence, watching the buffalo grass and sage roll by. The information she'd provided about Tyler and Rory's father explained the situation to everyone but her.

# *Chapter* 12

The trip back to the Lodestar was shorter, and easier for Libby with Rory driving. But it seemed strained by Tyler's absence. During the day, as she and Rory bounced along in the chuck wagon, she tried to learn the reason for the malevolent animosity between Tyler and his father. Why on earth would he blame Tyler for letting his sister die? But Rory, in a departure from his usual outgoing friendliness, proved as unwilling to discuss the situation as his brother-in-law.

Rory considered her question, then shook his head. "Tyler can tell you if he's a mind to, but I doubt he will. No offense, Miss Libby, but it's been a sore spot with him for a long time, and we just don't talk about it. None of us." Then to the mules, he yelled, "Heyup, you knobheads, keep movin'! Keep movin'!"

Libby spoke no more of the incident, not to Rory or anyone else, and simply withdrew to her original role as camp cook. At night, though, when she lay in her makeshift bed in the wagon, she missed knowing that if she were to peek out under the wagon canvas she'd see Tyler staring into the flames of the campfire, or watching the last minutes of a sunset.

The wound Wesley had left on her heart was beginning to fade into a scar, and she no longer missed Chicago.

But she missed Tyler Hollins.

Libby was relieved when they arrived at the ranch. Except for one night in the hotel in Miles City, she'd slept in the back of the chuck wagon and bathed from a bucket for almost a month. She hadn't been able to wash or iron her clothes. To top it off, she'd grown heartily sick of pork belly and beans.

And she wanted to see Tyler.

They rode in with the same fanfare and whooping as the day Charlie and Joe had driven the wild horses to the corral, and she and Rory laughed and made as much noise as any of them.

When she caught sight of Tyler's tall, slim form leaning against one of the porch uprights, her heart flip-flopped. The sun glinted off the rich auburn strands in his hair, and he stood with his arms folded over his chest. Right now, she was too glad to see him to tell herself that he was her boss, and that her shameful daydreams were improper.

After the first rush of greetings, Rory stopped the wagon in front of the house, and Tyler stepped forward to help her down. Although he still looked tired, she was reminded all over again what a handsome man he was, how blue his eyes were, how lush the curve of his mouth.

"Take the wagon on to the barn, Rory," he said. Then he smiled at her and she saw a faint spark in his eyes before his familiar cool mask dropped into place. "Welcome back, Libby. The trip went well enough?"

She smiled, too. "Yes, but I'm glad to be back. It'll be good to sleep in a bed again and cook on a stove. I just wish we had a copper bathtub like that hotel in Miles City. And tonight, thank God, we'll have something besides pork." Without thinking, she put her hand on his arm.

He took a step back. "Then you'll want to settle in." He started to walk back into the house.

She was stunned by his coldness. "Tyler, wait. Is that all you—um, I mean are—are you all right?"

The faint frown she knew so well drew his brows together. "I'm fine, Libby. It's not your job to worry about me. Your job is to cook." He left her standing on the porch, and the screen door slammed behind him. A moment later, she heard his office door close at the back of the house.

Her face was hot with embarrassment, and she looked around to see if anyone had witnessed his curt dismissal. Fortunately, the crew was busy with the horses over by the corral.

Oh, that man, she stewed. He was every bit as rude as on the morning she met him. She hoped she wouldn't be sorry they'd cashed in her train ticket.

One night a week later, Libby woke with a start. She didn't know what time it was, but the moon had crossed the sky to lay a slash of light across her bed from the window. It was a mild night and a soft breeze fluttered the lace curtains. A noise, she thought, something outside had awakened her.

She pushed back the covers and went to the open window. The full moon lighted the yard and surrounding buildings but she saw nothing. The horses in the corral were quiet, the bunkhouse was dark—

*Thwuck!*
*Thwuck!*
*Thwuck!*

She looked down then, and just beyond the edge of the porch roof she saw Tyler chopping wood. There was no mistaking his identity. He'd taken off his shirt and his sweating torso gleamed in the gray light—she remembered very well the contour of his shoulders and straight back. The ax blade gleamed silver on its upward arc before it plunged down again to bite into a log.

Chopping wood! At this hour? She was certain it must be far past midnight.

Sighing, Libby crept back to her bed. She lay awake a long time after the noise stopped, cursing the cruel moment of fate that had allowed Tyler to meet Lattimer Egan on the sidewalk in Miles City. No matter how she tried not to, her mind kept returning to the other side of Tyler Hollins that she'd glimpsed so briefly—Tyler massaging her shoulders, kissing her in the wagon the night of the storm, searching for her at the railroad station. She'd liked that man very much.

She didn't know much about him, but she knew enough to realize one thing: grieving for his wife was his prison. It kept him from sleeping, and it crowded everyone else out of his heart.

For that, Libby was resentful. And very sorry, indeed.

Fresh from a sluicing on the back porch, Tyler slowly climbed the stairs in the darkness and made his way down the hall. An inexpressible weariness dragged at him. That was good; he hoped it meant he'd finally be able to sleep now. It was nearly two o'clock, and the sun would be up in only another three hours. When he reached Libby's closed door, he paused. He thought of her, with her long honey hair and gray eyes. He saw comfort and redemption in those eyes whenever he looked at them. He'd told himself often enough that the idea was just so much bushwa, but he couldn't banish it from his mind. After a long moment, he reached out and gripped the knob. It was cool and metallic beneath his touch.

He wished he had the right to open her door and go to her, to leave the burdens of his heart out here. But he had no right at all.

He released the doorknob and went to his own bed.

Early the next afternoon, Libby stood in front of the ranch house in her oldest clothes, hands on her hips, and considered the ratty tangle of vegetation that had once been flower beds. She recognized the prairie roses that Tyler had said were here, but they were practically consumed with choking weeds and well-established grass.

"Well, maybe I can't fix anything else around here, but I can sure fix you," she muttered to the plants. She turned back her sleeves and put on her gloves, intent on reclaiming the beauty of these beds. She knew she was in for a lot of hard work. But it was a beautiful, cloudless day, and she welcomed a task to take out her frustration with Tyler, and to distract her from the vague gray mood that hung over the Lodestar.

Since their return Tyler had been withdrawn and irritable, reminding her of what he'd been like when she first came to the ranch. He disappeared for hours at a time while he rode the range alone. Thank God his horse knew the way back. A couple of nights she'd heard him stagger up the stairs and knew he was drunk. Her chief worry was that he'd tumble over the gallery railing before he got to his own room. She'd even heard the cowboys grumbling about how much they'd enjoyed the "new" Mr. Hollins, the one who laughed and joked and drank with them at the Briar Rose. Too bad it hadn't lasted.

Tyler stopped at the parlor window and watched as Libby dug at the flower beds in front of the porch. Or rather, what had once been the flower beds. The land had pretty much reclaimed them in the seven years since his father died. Tyler hadn't had the time to keep them up, and Jenna had not cared about them. His father had planted them for his mother, hoping to make her feel more at home at the Lodestar. Tyler didn't think they'd done the trick, not for his mother or for Jenna.

Now a beautiful little cook from Chicago, who in many ways was much braver than he was, apparently planned to give the wild roses new life. Armed with only a sharp-clawed weeder and a spade, she set to reversing years of neglect.

Kneeling on a pad of old newspapers, she yanked out a winter-bleached clump of grass and threw it into a bushel basket next to her. Long strands of hair had escaped the loose knot at the back of her head and trailed on her shoulders. A smudge of dirt marked her forehead, and she was dressed like a refugee, but once again, the image of an angel crossed his mind.

He walked out to the porch and considered her progress as he leaned on the railing. It seemed like a nearly hopeless enterprise to him—it was impossible to tell where the beds ended and the scruffy yard began. But she'd erected a substantial pile of grass and weeds.

"You don't have to do this, Libby," he said.

"Oh, it feels good to be out here with the sun and digging in the soil. I've never had the chance to do that before." She paused and locked her gray eyes on him. "Are you going to tell me that this isn't part of my job here?"

"No, of course not," he mumbled, and self-consciously slapped his gloves against his thigh. When he'd heard the wild commotion of the crew coming home from Miles City, he'd been so anxious to see her he'd had to stop himself from running out to meet the chuck wagon. He'd wanted to pull her down off the seat and kiss her soft, pink mouth until she was limp in his arms, and carry her up to his bed and make love to her. Then, as if he were a dog on a short rope, the memory of Jenna had pulled him back, and he remembered the one truth that Lat Egan had spoken: Tyler was responsible for her death. Because of that, any real happiness wasn't to be a part of his future. So he'd walked away from Libby with a curt dismissal. He looked down at her now, kneeling among the weeds. "But I can't spare anyone to help you with this, and it'll take weeks."

Libby sank the weeder's claws into the two-foot square of dirt that was finally clear after an hour of work, and churned up rich, dark soil. "That's all right. I'm in no hurry, and I think it will probably be beautiful when it's finished." She rose from her knees and flexed her back. Tyler felt his gaze drawn to her breasts and tiny waist. "Besides, if I work hard enough during the day, I might be able to sleep through the wood-chopping at night." She gave him an even look.

Tyler felt himself flush. Damn it, he thought, no other woman had ever made him do that as often as she did. He didn't know what to say. To offer the excuse that he was catching up on chores seemed ridiculous. Telling the truth—that his thoughts wouldn't let him rest, that he'd wanted nothing more than to lie down with her and just hold her in his arms—wasn't an option.

Fortunately, he was saved from offering any explanation because Joe rode in at that moment. His expression was as dark as a thundercloud.

"How did it go?" Tyler asked.

Joe climbed down from his horse and threw the reins over the hitching rail. He tipped his hat and smiled at Libby, then trudged up the front steps. Tyler waved at the pair of chairs on the porch, and Joe sank into one.

"That old bastard and his vigilantes tried to blow my head off, Ty." Astonishment colored his deep voice. He crossed his ankle over his knee.

"Vigilantes! When did Lat hire them?"

"I don't know, but that ain't all. He's got his boys sinkin' posts and stringin' bob wire. They said they'll shoot anyone who even comes near that damned fence."

Tyler sighed and shook his head. Barbed wire— that was bad. A lot of the territory had already seen the end of open-range grazing, but it went against all of his cattleman's instincts. He tipped his chair back against the wall. "I wonder what's gotten into him now. Did you talk to him at all?"

Joe lifted his hat and resettled it. "Yeah, but hell, it wasn't what you'd call a friendly conversation. I only got as close as the road that leads to the ranch house. Lat came out wavin' a rifle, and said he'd put a bullet in my hide if I came any nearer."

"Jesus—did you tell him about the fifty head we want to give him?"

"I told him. It just made him madder. His face turned nearly purple, he was so damned mad. Said he don't need our charity."

Tyler let his chair fall forward with a bang. "Oh, goddamn it, I was just trying to help him out. Everyone lost so much this year, not just him."

Joe lifted a hand. "I know, I know. But he fired over my head and told me to take our goddamned cattle and—" With a glance at Libby, he left the sentence unfinished. "Uh, well, you can probably guess the rest. I didn't need any more encouragement to leave, so I met the boys back down the road and we brought those steers home."

Silence fell between them for a moment. Only the rasping sound of Libby's clawed weeder filled the void. From her secluded place next to the shrubbery, she listened to this exchange.

Then Joe said, "You might as well give it up, Tyler. You're wastin' your time tryin' to please that old man and ease your conscience."

She couldn't see Tyler's face, but his words suddenly exploded with anger. "That wasn't why I did it, Joe. My conscience has nothing to do with this, and I don't need you to second-guess my decisions."

Sounding just as furious, Joe said, "I ain't second-guessin' nothin'. But I ain't gonna take a bullet between the eyes from Lattimer Egan, either." She heard his boots hit the porch flooring as he stood. "You'd best remember who your friends are, Tyler, and stop chewing at 'em like they've got nothin' better to do than take it."

Joe thundered down the steps, spurs clinking madly, and snatching up his horse's reins, pulled him none too gently toward the corral.

With her brows raised and eyes wide, Libby stood and looked at Tyler. She read the chagrin in his face when he realized that she was still there, and a witness to the heated exchange.

She threw her garden tool and gloves on top of the grass pile and climbed the steps. He still sat in the chair where Joe had left him. Crossing the porch, she sat next to him.

"Tyler—"

"Don't *you* start," he muttered, exhibiting great interest in a sliver on the edge of the chair seat. His lean, handsome face was beginning to show the strain he was under.

Libby wasn't sure why she bothered. She knew she shouldn't care. In fact, she didn't want to examine her feelings too closely, but the feelings were there, nonetheless, and she couldn't deny them.

She put her hand on the arm of his chair, and leaned toward him. "To keep grieving for someone until you make yourself sick, and sacrifice your own happiness, why, you're throwing your life away. I don't think Jenna would have wanted you to do that, no matter what her father says. You can't let his bitter heart become yours."

His blue eyes met hers sharply. "Libby, you don't know what you're talking about here," he warned.

She squeezed the chair arm until she felt the square edges dig into her fingers. This was so difficult for her to talk about, but it was the only example she could think of. "Yes, I do. My mother left me at the foundling home when I was four years old. Years afterward, I-I found out that she died a week later in a doorway, alone. Tuberculosis, they said." He said nothing but his frown knitted more tightly, and he put his hand beside hers on the chair arm. She took a deep breath to continue. "*Everybody* loses someone, Tyler. We live and we die, some of us sooner than others. You have to go on and make the most of your time on this earth. Otherwise, grief will eat you up."

He studied her for a moment, then shook his head and stood up. "Like I said, Libby—you don't know what you're talking about." He went down the steps and headed toward the corral without a backward glance.

Libby watched him walk away, and tried to pretend that his words hadn't hurt. But they had. Moments later, she saw Tyler gallop out of the yard on the bay filly that he'd finally tamed. The two of them streaked across the field toward the hills, as if he thought he could outrun the demons that were chasing him.

That night Libby stood before the mirror over her washstand, brushing her hair and thinking. She was alone in the house again; she hadn't seen Tyler since he'd left that afternoon. When he'd asked her to come back to the Lodestar, she never once envisioned being lonely. She was now, though.

Her position here was an odd one. She certainly wasn't friendless, and there wasn't the class distinction she'd always known. But she didn't have the closeness she'd had with the little domestic staff at the Brandauers'. The bunkhouse was no place for a woman, and the men were not inclined to hang around the kitchen merely to keep her company.

Foolishly, perhaps, she'd once imagined sitting in the parlor with Tyler on an occasional evening, reading or talking. Not for any romantic purpose, she assured herself, but simply for the companionship of another person. And it might have come to pass, if—

Just then she heard a noise with which she was becoming unhappily familiar. It was the sound of Tyler, staggering his way up the stairs. He was back earlier than usual—it was only about nine o'clock. His progress was a bit halting, as if he were trying to keep his balance, and even from behind her closed door, she could hear his spurs. When he finally hit the landing, she let out the breath she held. At least he hadn't toppled backward down the steps. But now the gallery lay ahead of him. If he fell—

With an irritated sigh, she flung her shawl over her shoulders and went to the door. Why hadn't he decided to come home before she'd changed into her nightgown? she fumed. But she couldn't leave him to plunge into the parlor below and break his silly neck. When she pulled open the door, she saw him in the half-light of the lantern on her night table: disheveled, his eyes starkly blue and bloodshot, his hair a windblown tangle. She stepped into the hallway with her arms crossed over her chest.

He wobbled to a stop and squinted at her with woozy surprise. "Whassa matter?"

She would not lecture him, she told herself. Not only was it not her place to do so, this certainly wasn't the time. But she couldn't refrain from pursing her mouth and frowning slightly. "I can smell the whiskey from here."

"Oh, don' pucker up like a persimmon," he said, waving her off with a loose-jointed arm. He tottered sideways to the railing.

Gasping, she lurched forward and grabbed him by his sleeve. His balance was so poor, it wasn't difficult to pull him back to her side. She looped his arm over her shoulders. "Come on, Tyler. It's time you were in bed."

"R-really? Libby, really?" His voice held a relieved thankfulness, and horrified, she knew he'd misunderstood. He sort of fell into her arms, and then tried to steer them back into her room. He was much too big for her to control, and before she knew it, he'd succeeded in pushing her as far as the bed. She felt the mattress pressed against the backs of her legs.

"Not in *my* bed, you big lummox!" she grunted, struggling with his weight. "Yours, in the next room."

"Thass all right, we can sleep here. Iss big enough." He nuzzled her neck, all the while muttering something about "angelheart." Sliding both hands to her bottom, he pulled her tight to his hips. She was alarmed to feel the very real, very hard proof of his arousal pressed against her abdomen.

"Tyler, stop it!" Libby tried to put her shoulder to his chest to push him away from her, but she was no match for his big, relaxed body. In another second, he'd have her pinned to the mattress, and then she wouldn't be able to get him to his feet again. The one advantage she had was speed; he moved as slowly as a bear in a tar pit. As soon as he lifted one hand to caress her breast, she ducked out beneath his elbow and escaped to the doorway. He looked down in front of him, as though he wondered where she'd vanished to.

"You come away from there," she insisted in her firmest tone. She wasn't really afraid of him, but her anger was increasing by the minute.

Turning, he stumbled over to her. "Aw, Libby, come on. Don' make me leave. Lemme sleep here with you." And then sounding abruptly and uncannily lucid, he added with a deep sigh, "I'm so tired."

For the space of a breath, she thought her heart would break. "I know you are," she said. "That's why it's time to go to your own room."

He went along agreeably, and with some tricky maneuvering she managed to pilot him down the hall to his own bed. It took only a single push to flop him onto his mattress—boots, spurs, gun belt, and all.

When she reached over to wrap his blankets up

around him, his hand suddenly shot out and grabbed her wrist. He pulled her down with a strength that she hadn't anticipated, and her face was inches from his.

"Don' I getta kiss g'night?" Putting his other hand on the back of her neck, he forced her mouth to his and gave her a hard, sloppy kiss that tasted like stale whiskey.

With a muffled shriek, she wrenched free and backed away, disgustedly scrubbing her mouth with the cuff of her nightgown.

Tyler was already asleep.

Libby was in the kitchen kneading bread dough the next morning after breakfast when Tyler came in. He came through the door, and with an offhand acknowledgment to her, picked a cup from the dish rack and went to the coffeepot on the stove.

He'd changed his clothes and washed, but he moved a bit slowly, as though in pain. She just bet he was. Dropping her gaze back to her work, she ignored him and went on punching her dough with furious vigor.

Grabbing a sugar cookie from a plate on the table, he finally looked at her. "What's the matter, have you decided to stop talking?"

She sprinkled flour on her work surface. "After last night, you shouldn't be surprised."

"Last night?"

She scowled at him. "Yes, you have some memory of it, don't you?"

A hint of recollection crossed his puffy face, followed by a sheepish expression.

"Besides, as you pointed out yesterday, I don't know what I'm talking *about*. Remember?"

He sighed impatiently, and he pushed his hand

through his hair, slowly, as if to avoid aggravating his monstrous headache. "Oh, damn it, Libby, that isn't what I meant, exactly—"

She glared at him. "No? What did you mean, then? You can't say that my life has been all soft cushions and cream cakes, and that I don't understand what it's like to be lonely and scared." She gripped the dough in her hands until it squeezed out between her fingers. Looking at it, she shook it off. Like a slow-boiling kettle, her anger steamed—at him for his behavior, and at herself for worrying about him. Was this what her job here would become? Caretaker to a man who seemed bent on destroying himself?

"Libby, this is none of your business."

"Oh, yes, it is! I can see what you're doing to yourself, and everyone around you. You made me care about you—um, the way, well, the way I care about everyone here," she amended hastily. "And now you've shut me out. You snap at all of us, *including* Rory. Tyler, that boy loves you as if you were his father, and you know he just lost his best friend." Her rage grew. "God, you make me so angry sometimes, I could, oh, I could sock you!"

"Miss Fix-it wants to take a poke at me?" Tyler seemed genuinely amused and his laugh was mocking. He put down the coffee cup. "Come on. I dare you," he taunted. Walking around to her side of the worktable, he put his chin out and tapped it with a forefinger. "Put one right here."

Her outrage had reached a rolling boil. All of the frustration and worry and uncertainty of the past few months came churning to the surface. It might be worth jabbing that arrogant chin just to interrupt the smirk he was wearing. Though she was hardly aware of it, her fingers began to tighten into a fist.

He glanced down at her hand, and his bloodshot eyes gleamed. "Go ahead, *Miss Libby*," he pressed sarcastically. "You want to hit me." He stretched his chin out farther. "I'd like to see you try."

Even though his hangover made him feel as though he'd been horse-kicked, Tyler trusted his reflexes. He could handle this *girl*. He briefly pictured holding her off with one hand while her arms windmilled ineffectively, and he chuckled. But he was prepared to catch her fist as it flew toward his face, not into his stomach. When Libby's hand connected hard with his body, his breath woofed out of him. His arms closed around his middle and he snapped forward at the waist like a ballroom dance master. He couldn't talk, he couldn't even breathe.

Libby's wrath was instantly replaced with horror and she reached for his shoulders, thinking he might collapse. "Oh, my God. Tyler, I'm so sorry!"

At that moment, Joe walked in and leaned a hip against the worktable, a huge grin on his face. Obviously a witness to the event, he said, "Don't be too sorry, Miss Libby. He's been actin' like a mule's rump."

What had she done? Never in her life had she struck anyone. Why had she let him goad her like that? As it was, he barely suffered her presence these days. And now he was bent over like a fishhook, trying to get his wind back because she'd punched him in the stomach. If he'd been looking for a reason to get rid of her, she'd just given one to him. A reason no one could find fault with.

Tyler shrugged off her hands and straightened slowly, revealing a big round spot of flour her fist had left on the front of his shirt. His chest expanded as he pulled in a full breath. He was greenish-white and sweaty, reminding her of the shadowed side of an ice block, but beyond that, she couldn't read his expression.

"I'm really sorry," she repeated miserably, but even to her own ears, the words had a hopeless sound. She knew her fate had already been decided. She looked up at him, waiting for the ax to fall. If only he'd say *something*.

Instead, he pushed past her, obviously trying to muster his dignity, and walked outside.

Joe winced, and shook his head, unable to stifle a rumble of low laughter.

"Oh, how can you laugh?" she asked, watching Tyler's back as he went to the barn. Her heart pounded in her chest. "I did a terrible thing!"

Completely unconcerned, he lifted his head to peer at Tyler. He shrugged and picked up a cookie. "He ain't pukin' yet, so you didn't hit him that hard. Besides, you only did what we've all been itchin' to do. We wouldn't be able to get away with it. You can."

He patted her arm and gave her a sly smile. Then he took another cookie and headed out the door, leaving Libby to ponder his words.

That evening after the crew ate, Tyler sat in self-imposed exile in the shadows on the front porch, a glass of whiskey resting on his knee. It was a soft spring evening that gave no hint of the hotter summer he knew would follow. The kitchen door was open, and a rectangle of golden light fell across the porch planks. A familiar aroma of chicken stew floated to him, and he could hear the clink of Libby's silverware. When he'd sat down out here, he caught a glimpse of her through the window, eating alone at one of the long tables. She wasn't actually eating much. Mostly she poked the food around on her plate.

As hard as it was for him to admit, he knew he'd really deserved that punch. Oh, he'd been madder than hell—after he got over his surprise, anyway. And his stomach had protested with wrenching spasms for an hour afterward. He'd had the rest of the afternoon to think about everything she'd told him; there were things she didn't know, that he couldn't tell her, but she was right in many ways. For years, he had shut himself away from everyone, and then in Miles City, as soon as he'd thought it was time to begin living again, he saw Lattimer Egan.

An ache crept up Tyler's chest to his throat and made it tight. It was a sensation he hadn't known in a very long time—at least five years. But he recognized it. Tyler felt like crying. For himself, for a little girl left at an orphanage by a tubercular mother, for a good cowboy who'd lost his life working for the Lodestar.

His eyes started to burn. Goddamn it, he thought. He swallowed hard and pushed the feeling back to the smallest corner of his heart, where it belonged.

He drained his glass, then pushed himself to his feet, and looked through the kitchen window again. It seemed like there was only one person in the world tonight who could make him feel better.

Libby glanced up to see Tyler standing in the doorway. Why did he have to be so handsome? she wondered irritably. Even in his current state of dissipation, he looked better than did most temperate men. It would be much easier to ignore him if he were ugly, or even dirt-plain.

Getting a plate, he walked to the stove and

spooned up chicken stew from the big pot on the stove, and brought it to the table.

"May I join you?" he asked, and waited for her answer.

She stared at him with her jaw slightly open. He was going to have his supper with her? She'd never seen him eat with anyone, except for that stormy night in the wagon when they'd shared biscuits and tender, fevered kisses. It seemed like years ago, now.

"Yes, of course."

He took the seat across from her. She caught a faint whiff of whiskey, but he wasn't drunk, or even tipsy. A kind of fatalism had settled on her shoulders in the hours since their last encounter. Despite Joe's confidence to the contrary, she assumed that Tyler was about to deliver her dismissal.

He poked his fork into a piece of chicken. "That's quite a right arm you have."

A scorching blush sizzled up her from her neck to her hairline, and she began babbling. "I really apologize. I can't imagine—I don't know why I—"

"Yes, you do," he said, capturing her eyes with his. "And so do I. Joe was right. I haven't been so easy to get along with. As for last night, I don't remember it very well, but I'm sure I made a jackass of myself."

It wasn't exactly an apology, but it sounded like one. And to her own amazement, Libby found herself making excuses for him. "Well, I guess a lot has happened lately," she said. "There was the drive, and the storm, losing Charlie—" She still got a catch in her chest when she remembered the unnatural peace on his face that morning.

Tyler picked up a piece of bread from the plate on the table. "That's not good enough. Those things happened to all of us. Anyway, this goes back a lot further."

"To your wife?" She felt as though she were putting her head in the lion's mouth by asking.

He sighed slightly. "Yeah."

Tyler had said that she'd died in childbirth. "Maybe if she'd had a doctor to take care of her?" she posed. Libby thought of the night he'd bandaged her hand; he'd said there hadn't been one in Heavenly for a long time.

His tone turned flinty. "A *doctor* let Jenna die. A doctor who was supposed to know how to save lives, not let them slip away."

"Oh, dear." That would explain, then, why he seemed to think so little of physicians. She knew they were heading into dangerous territory with this conversation. Fortunately, he turned its direction.

He put his hand on the table, close to hers. "Anyway, I'm sorry for the way I acted. I know you were just trying to help."

She glanced down shyly at her plate. "Actually, you can be pretty charming when you want to be."

Whatever response he might have expected from her, clearly it hadn't been this one. He smiled self-consciously, and then he laughed, reinforcing her comment, but refuting it at the same time. "Yeah, charming like an abscessed tooth."

She laughed, too. "No—well, sometimes . . ."

With that, the tension of the afternoon eased, and they talked of inconsequential things: summer chores on the ranch, the rhythm of the land and the seasons, her progress with the flower beds.

"I don't think you'll want to be digging out there tomorrow," he said, and popped the bread crust into his mouth. "It's going to rain, probably most of the day."

"What makes you say that?" she asked, somewhat doubtful. "There isn't a cloud in the sky. The stars are so close and bright."

"Yeah, but it'll rain. I can smell it coming." He gestured at the open doorway. She lifted her head and sniffed, then shook her head. "Can't you?" He sounded surprised that she couldn't.

"This is all a lot different from the city," Libby said, getting up for the coffeepot. "It would take a lifetime of living here to learn everything there is to know. You're so much a part of the land and the animals—it suits you."

He held out his coffee cup for her to fill. "It didn't always, though. For a while, I wanted to get away from here so bad, I thought I'd bust. And I did leave for a few years to go to school. I came back when my father got sick. I wasn't planning to stay, but I ended up promising him that I would." He laid his knife and fork across his empty plate. "It was the last thing he asked of me. He said it was my responsibility to steward this land, to keep it for my own son just as he'd kept it for me."

Tyler fell silent for a moment. He wasn't sure that there would be sons to inherit the Lodestar when his own life reached the end of its days. But the idea of children made him think of the act that created them, and he looked at the woman sitting across the table from him.

Despite the events of this morning, regardless of the times they'd clashed, and the conflict that raged in him, his desire for Libby had not dimmed. If anything, it had grown stronger.

He remembered just enough of last night to recall

holding her to himself, with her soft breasts pressed against his chest. More than ever Tyler wanted to lay her on his bed and find out if hearts could be mended in the joining of bodies and spirits. He could imagine her, soft and aroused with the timid fire that he'd felt coursing through her that night in the wagon.

That she was a virgin was almost a certainty—she'd admitted that she and Ben Ross hadn't consummated their marriage of convenience, and her inexperience had been obvious when he kissed her. But what sweet pleasure it would be to gentle her and coax her from her shyness . . .

He shook off this daydream. It was impossible, out of the question, and he'd just make himself crazy if he didn't stop thinking about it.

"I've got to check on that bay filly." He pushed himself away from the table and Libby stood to pick up their dishes. He took them from her hands and carried them to the sink. When he turned, he couldn't quite stop himself from walking back to her.

"Thanks for dinner, Libby," he said, allowing himself the treat of looking down into her delicate face. He let his gaze roam over her soft, coral mouth, her smooth brow, her gray eyes. "And, well, everything else."

She blushed, the color staining her cheeks with an innocent beauty that tugged at his heart and made him smile. "You're welcome, Tyler. I-I hope you'll be feeling better."

Unable to resist, he pressed a kiss to her cheek and the corner of her mouth.

"I do, too."

Tyler didn't return until later that night. He'd ridden the open range in the moonlight until both he and his horse were exhausted. When he finally came home, he'd sat on the front porch, hoping that would take his mind off Libby Ross. But it hadn't worked.

In all his life, he'd never had to deal with the conflicting emotions that were at war within him now. His life had been simple: work and sleep. Problems were met head-on and solved. Even his Saturday nights at the Big Dipper were figured into his routine.

Now he climbed the steps in the dark, carrying his boots to avoid waking Libby, and praying for the oblivion of sleep. As he neared her bedroom door, though, his steps slowed, and once more he found himself stopped in front of it. As he stood there, he got the stupid notion that she was the only one who could make him feel better. The only one who could redeem his spirit from the lifeless void into which it had fallen.

He gripped the doorknob again, and this time he turned it. The door swung open and he saw her lying there. Her hair flowed loose behind her head, and the front of her nightgown had opened to reveal the swell of a perfectly curved breast. A shaft of light from the half-moon cut across the bed. She looked so beautiful, he thought, swallowing. Like an angel. He put his boots down in the hallway and padded into the room.

It was a stupid, dangerous thing he was doing, he told himself, but that didn't stop him. Fully dressed, he eased himself down next to her on top of the blankets, and had but a moment to inhale her sweet vanilla scent before sleep overtook him.

# Chapter 13

Libby stood at the kitchen window, looking at the clearing skies and wet yard through the wavy glass. Tyler had been right—it had begun raining steadily just after dawn and now, at three o'clock, the sun was finally drying things out.

She felt restless. It wasn't that she didn't have enough to do here in the kitchen. But she missed her work in the flower beds. It was good to get out in the sun, and after a few hours of weeding and digging, she slept like the dead at night. Not only that, but it gave her something to think about besides Tyler.

Tyler.

Today, it seemed that she'd been able to think of nothing but him and the beautiful, disturbing dream that she'd had last night. In the way of dreams, it had been a confusing jumble that made no sense. Why would a man lie down to sleep with a woman on top of the blankets, with all his clothes on? At the same time, it was so vivid, she'd sworn that she could smell the clean scent of horses and hay, even after she'd awakened and realized she was alone.

This morning when he'd come into the kitchen for coffee, she could hardly look him in the face, she felt so self-conscious. He, on the other hand, had looked a little better than he had lately. His eyes were brighter, and he smiled more.

Sighing, she went to the oven to baste the roast she was serving for supper. One good thing about living on a cattle ranch was that she never lacked for beef or had to worry about how fresh it was. She knew exactly where it came from, and when.

From outside, she heard running footsteps and jangling spurs; it sounded as though someone were dodging the puddles between the barn and the house. Suddenly the door flew open.

She froze, basting spoon in mid-drizzle.

"Miss Libby!" Rory gasped, charging into the kitchen. His color was high and he was breathless, and he was as mud-spattered as she'd seen any of them.

"What?" Oh, God, what had happened now? she wondered, her heart lurching to a full gallop.

"Miss Libby, Joe says to get yourself prettied up because—" he huffed, "because we're goin' to the grange dance tonight."

"A dance?"

"Yes'm. One Saturday night a month, there's a dance at the grange in Heavenly. Joe said if it quit rainin', we'd go. Well, we're goin'! Right after supper!" He turned around and raced out again, slamming the door behind him.

A dance! That meant music and socializing. She hadn't been to a dance since Mrs. Brandauer had donated Libby's services to an event sponsored by one of her pet charities. Even then, Libby had worked in the kitchen at the dance, not attended as a guest. She wasn't even sure she could remember the few simple steps she'd learned as a girl.

Hurriedly, she shoved the roast back in with the hem of her apron and closed the oven door. She hoped she had something nice enough to wear. Pushing on the swinging door, she raced through the parlor and up the stairs, all the while mentally reviewing the skimpy contents of her wardrobe. Granted, this was the frontier, but she wanted Tyler to be proud of her—

Well, what a ridiculous notion, she scolded herself. She wasn't dressing to please him. Not exactly . . .

In her room, she stood before the wardrobe, considering and discarding possible dresses, until she finally saw the one that would be perfect.

At supper, the crew offered to serve themselves so that Libby could wash and dress. She was so nervous, she had trouble turning the handle on her curling iron without burning herself. When she put on the pale blue gown she'd selected, she was surprised to discover that it was a bit loose now. Apparently hard work and worry had taken a few pounds from her. But she was able to hide the fact with the cream satin sash, and the sweetheart neckline was still flattering.

Finally, she stood before her washstand mirror, twisting this way and that, trying to see the results of her efforts. Her hair, tied back with a blue ribbon, hung down her back in big curls that caught a gleam of yellow sunlight from the window. She dabbed a bit of lavender water on her throat and behind her ears. Then leaning closer to the mirror, she pinched her cheeks and bit her lips until they stung like fire. Nodding at her reflection, she drew a breath, then left her room and went down the stairs.

At the bottom, Tyler and the Lodestar cowboys waited, including the ones who weren't even going tonight, to see what their cook looked like when she was dressed up. Their hats clutched to their bellies, they stared at her in amazed silence that reminded her of her first day here. The smell of bay rum hovered in a cloud above them. Everywhere she saw shined boots, water-slicked hair, and dressy shirts.

"Miss Libby, I have to say that the boys from the other outfits are gonna be so green with jealousy when they see our cook, they'll probably try to steal you away from us," Joe pronounced. "But you have to promise that you won't let 'em."

Libby laughed at the sweet, honest flattery. "I promise. After all, I've just gotten you boys figured out." She locked eyes with Tyler then and thought, *all except you.* He said nothing, but she read his compliment in his eyes and his quiet smile.

"All right, everybody, let's get going," Joe said, in his best trail boss voice.

Wrapped in her plaid shawl, she followed them outside to the wagon that would take them into Heavenly. Only Tyler rode his own horse.

Perched on the seat next to Joe, who was driving, Libby heard all the good-natured ribbing and laughing going on behind her as they rolled toward town. Their high spirits and excitement were contagious.

"Joe, you remember old German Sam," she heard Noah say.

"I remember him," Joe said. "The glass eye and those false teeth give me the creeps every time I see him."

"Yeah, and what about the wig?" Kansas Bob put in.

Libby's brows rose at the description.

Noah went on. "He was a miner for a time over around Virginia City, and he was in an explosion before he gave it up to drive a freight wagon. That's why he lost so many parts. Anyways, a few years ago when Custer got the Sioux all stirred up, German Sam was drivin' that wagon and some braves stopped him and was tryin' to decide if they should kill him. But old Sam knew some of their lingo, so when he heard one of the braves talk about scalpin', he took that derned wig off and handed it to him."

"Oh, my," Libby said.

"Well, Miss Libby, I 'spect that brave was thinkin' the same thing when he got a look at that bald head. Next, Sam took out his false teeth, and gave them to the Indian. He stood there, Sam said, petrified and sayin' nothin'. But when he took out that glass eye, those braves skedaddled—"

Groans, laughter, and Libby's gasp drowned out the rest of the account.

"Good heavens, what a story!" she laughed.

Riding next to her, Tyler laughed, too. "I don't know. I'd think twice about anything German Sam told me."

Tyler looked so handsome on his pinto, silhouetted against the May sunset. She was surprised that he'd decided to come with them. A dance didn't seem like the kind of event that would interest him. She wondered if he'd ask her out to the dance floor, or if he'd just lean against a wall and watch everyone else.

But when they arrived in Heavenly, the answer was one that Libby hadn't contemplated. The Big Dipper came into view, and Tyler tipped his hat at the group, avoiding her eyes all the while.

"Have a good time at the grange," he said, and trotted ahead to put his horse in the livery stable next to the saloon.

"Guess Callie will be keepin' him all night again," Hickory chuckled in the back. "Ow! Dang it, Kansas, watch out who you're jabbin' with those bony elbows."

Somehow the brilliant glow of the evening dimmed a little for Libby. She wouldn't see Tyler again until tomorrow sometime. And would he smell like gardenias? She gripped the edges of the shawl and wrapped them around herself. It shouldn't matter to her what he did. He was her boss and nothing more. She had no claim on him or his whereabouts.

But as they drove by, she saw him come out of the livery and head to the Big Dipper, and Libby could think of nothing but the dull ache in her chest.

"Ty, honey! You're back!" Callie Michaels hailed him from across the smoky interior of the Big Dipper. She hurried to him in her dark blue taffeta dress, with the fabric swishing like ten acres of wheat. Twining her sinuous white arms around his neck, she tipped her face up to his.

He was immediately enveloped in a cloud of her heavy perfume. Funny, he'd never really given it much thought before, but now it seemed suffocating.

"I was beginning to think you'd forgotten your favorite gal, you were gone so long. Why, darlin', you look downright peaked. I guess it's because you missed me so much, isn't it?"

He'd ridden along with the wagon to Heavenly for the express purpose of letting Callie take his mind off his problems. It was a talent at which she usually excelled and one she was quite proud of. Right now, though, that idea had lost its allure. Maybe because of a pair of sad gray eyes that he'd been unable to look at when he and the crew parted company. . . .

He unwound her arms and led her by the hand to an empty table. "We had a hard trip, Callie."

"Oh, really?" She called to Eli to bring them a bottle and two glasses.

He nodded. "We lost Charlie during a thunderstorm. He's buried about forty miles from Miles City."

She stared at him. "Oh, damn and hellfire."

Eli brought the whiskey and Callie poured two drinks.

Tyler leaned back and bolted the shot in one gulp.

"How'd that little cook hold up? What was her name—Lacy? Leah? Nort told me she was in a dither to get back to Chicago. Can't say that I blame her, especially after Charlie's death. She was a sweet thing, but really, Ty, she looked like she wouldn't know a steer from a jackrabbit." She perched on her chair and leaned toward him in a way that gave him an unobstructed view of her plump, powdered bosom.

"Actually, Libby turned out to be a lot of help. She worked hard, she didn't complain." He held his glass out and she gave him another drink. "She even saved my life." He related the story of the rattlesnake.

"Well, she was a wonder, wasn't she?" Callie drank half her whiskey. "So now you boys are without a cook again. I'm sure you'll find some old cowhand here in town."

"No, Libby came home to the ranch with us. She decided she didn't have anything waiting for her in Chicago, and I—we realized it would be a mistake to let her go."

"Oh—that *is* good news," she said, and gave him that knowing smile of hers. She rose from her chair and wriggled her taffeta fanny into his lap, reminding him of a hen settling on her nest. "You know, Ty, you haven't been upstairs to my boudoir in ever so long now." She leaned in and quickly nipped his earlobe, and adjusted her seat a bit more. "If I remember it right, I have some unfinished business to conduct with you."

Tyler's arousal felt more like a basic reaction than the real fire that Libby could spark. He chuckled. "Still shameless, Callie."

She smiled again. "Why, honey, if I changed you'd be so lost, you wouldn't know what to do. Now, come on. Let's go upstairs, and you can tell me all about your trip."

Oh, what the hell, Tyler thought. "All right."

Giggling, she stood up and took his hand. They wove their way through the busy saloon and up the staircase to Callie's blue velvet and cream lace boudoir on the second floor.

"Now, then," she said, leaning against the closed door. Her whiskey eyes gleamed. "Let me show you everything you've missed."

Like a magician, she slithered out of her dress. It happened so quickly, he wasn't sure how she'd done it. But she stood before him wearing nothing but her shoes. Leaving the dress in a puff of taffeta on the floor, she walked up to him and brushed her breasts against his chest. He swore she was purring like a cat.

Reflex made Tyler run his hands along her bare skin. Using the same deft skill with which she'd undressed herself, she pulled out his shirttail and unbuttoned his pants. When her nimble hand closed around him, he drew a sharp breath and leaned into her grasp. Without thinking he put a finger under her chin to lift her mouth to his. Immediately, she pulled her head back.

"Now, now," she warned playfully, continuing the artful massage, suddenly to no avail. "You know I don't hold with kissing."

He sighed and gripped her wrist to stop her hand. "But I do, Callie." Their eyes locked for a moment, long enough for Tyler to ask himself what the devil he was doing here. This wasn't what he wanted anymore. He knew it, and his body was telling him, as well. In his mind rose the image of a young widow in a simple, pale blue dress and long honey-colored curls.

Stepping back, he tucked in his shirttail and buttoned his pants. A look of panicky comprehension crossed Callie's powdered face before she recovered her breezy nonchalance. "Tyler—darlin', you just got here. Are you leaving?"

"It's not you, Callie. It's me. Things are . . . different, I guess."

"Well, I know it's not me," she agreed, attempting a joke. She grabbed a thin wrap from a blue velvet chair and threw it around herself. Then in a voice that was barely audible, "Does *she* kiss you?"

He gave her a keen look. Her obvious jealousy surprised him, even though she tried not to let it show. Without replying, he reached into his pocket and withdrew a double eagle.

"I can't charge you, Ty," she said, laughing uncertainly. "I didn't earn it."

Smiling, he lifted her hand and pressed the coin into it. "Then call it a good-bye gift," he said, kissing her forehead, "between old friends."

"Good-bye?" Her voice was shaking now. She held the money on her open palm and clutched her wrapper.

Walking to the door, he opened it and nodded. "Good-bye, Callie."

After looking in all the shop windows, Tyler had nothing to do. He could have gotten his horse and ridden back to the Lodestar, but that held little appeal. Finally he ambled down the twilit street to the grange hall. Sitting on a bench outside, he crossed his ankle over his knee. From within, he could hear music and whooping and the faint rumble of dancing feet.

This sure wasn't how he'd picture his Saturday night. Usually by this stage in the evening, Callie would have pulled some new trick out of her repertoire that left him so exhausted and sweat-soaked, he could barely walk. But his association with Callie—the gardenia perfume, the smoky saloon, the ostentatious "boudoir"—none of it seemed right for him anymore.

When she'd opened his pants tonight, giggling and purring, he'd never felt as low and coarse as he did at that moment. It wasn't Callie's fault. She'd done nothing different—he was the one who'd changed. He no longer found solace in physical satisfaction that was nothing more than a business deal, no matter how imaginative. Hell, she wouldn't even kiss him and *pretend* to like it. He couldn't pinpoint the moment this change had occurred, but he knew who was responsible for it.

Just then the door swung open, and Tyler looked up to see Joe Channing.

"Well, don't this beat all?" he said, surprise in his

voice. "Are you too cussed and ornery even for Callie?"

"Come on, Joe," he mumbled. "Not tonight, okay?"

Joe looked him over, then sat down next to him in the near-darkness and started rolling a cigarette. "What happened?"

Tyler shrugged and twiddled with the rowel on his spur. He didn't know how to explain it, so he told him about the scene in Callie's bedroom. "It just isn't the same."

Joe gave a low whistle accompanied by a thin line of smoke. "Callie could stir a man three years in his grave. If that don't interest you anymore, you've got it worse than I thought."

"Got what?" he asked dully.

"Why, you've got it bad for that little gal inside."

"Aww, Jee-zus—" Tyler uncrossed his ankle.

Joe shook his head and spoke sharply. "Now, there ain't no point in denyin' it. I've seen it with my own eyes, and in my opinion, you couldn't do no better. She's a fine woman, and I believe she likes you— despite the rocky path you've made her walk."

"You're imagining things," Tyler said, with a little less vigor.

"Oh, I am, huh? Then why the hell did we run all over Miles City like a flock of hens looking for one lost chick, then drag her back to this piss-ant town to cook for a crew of rough cobs like us? Especially when you said, if I rightly recollect, the Lodestar ain't no place for a woman."

"I thought you and the boys wanted her to stay!"

"This ain't about me and the boys. It's about you."

"It was my responsibility to take care of the crew. And she needed a job."

"Give it up, Ty. That horse just ain't gonna run."

Tyler heaved an exasperated sigh, but offered no further argument.

Rightly interpreting his silence, Joe flicked his cigarette away, and stood. "All right, then, come on." He reached for Tyler's arm.

He looked up at him. In the dark, Joe's most prominent features were his hat and his big mustache. "Come on where?"

"You get your ass into the grange hall and ask that lady to dance before some other cowboy wins her. They've been linin' up to spin her around the floor all evenin'."

"I don't like to dance."

"Then why did you come down here? You could have gone back to the ranch instead of hangin' around out here like a sulky, empty-handed kid in front of a candy store."

Tyler grumbled, but he let Joe pull him off the bench and steer him into the dance.

After they got inside, Tyler waited for his eyes to adjust to the light. He scanned the people on the dance floor, but didn't see her.

Joe nudged him. "She's right over there, drinkin' punch with Gabe Swanner."

Tyler took one look at her, beautiful in her simplicity, and knew he was a doomed man.

Sitting by an open side door, Libby listened with polite interest while Gabe Swanner related the story of the trail drive he'd worked on the summer before. It was stuffy in the room from the hot, exercised dancers, and the mingled scents of bay rum, perfume, and beer. She fanned her face with her handkerchief. She was surprised at the number of people here. They must have come from miles around.

"One day the whole danged—uh, beg pardon, ma'am—the whole blessed herd turned and stampeded over the ten miles we'd just traveled, so's they could get back to the last water hole."

"Oh, dear! I'm glad we didn't have trouble finding water."

Libby stifled a giggle that ballooned in her chest over Gabe's worry about saying "danged." What would he think if he knew the inventory of Tyler's vocabulary that she heard on a daily basis? But she sipped her punch—her sixth cup, for her would-be suitors had been very attentive—and smiled. In her life Libby had never been paid so much attention. And when the cowboys learned she'd gone with the herd to Miles City, they thought she was just a marvel. It helped take away a bit of her disappointment about Tyler. But only a bit.

Even the other women in the hall were beginning to put their heads together about her. She couldn't help it if almost every man present had asked her to dance. And anyway, none of them was the chestnut-haired, long-legged cowboy she wished had stayed with them instead of—

"You'll excuse us, Gabe?"

Libby whirled at the sound of the familiar voice.

"Mr. Hollins, yessir, sure." Gabe looked as though he'd been caught red-handed committing some wicked offense.

Tyler took the punch cup from her hand and gave it to the cowboy. "Mrs. Ross, may I have the pleasure?"

A clutter of feelings bumped around inside her: relief, the joy of just looking at him, the femaleness that pulsed in her whenever he was near, and, much as she hated herself for it, jealousy. Still, he was here, and he'd asked her to dance.

"Of course," she replied. She reached for his extended hand, and he escorted her to the floor. But as soon as he took her into his arms, she smelled gardenia perfume. Not much else could have forced her to comment tartly, "This is a surprise. Hickory guessed that we wouldn't see you until tomorrow."

He flushed back to his ears. "Yeah, well, Hickory doesn't know everything. Besides, I had to come back here and see how everyone is faring. Joe tells me you've been the belle of the ball tonight."

She shrugged innocently. "I guess the men think I'm interesting because I went on that trail drive. Most of them said they'd never heard of such a thing before."

He gave her a riveting look that made her breath catch in her throat. "I can guarantee you that isn't the reason they think you're 'interesting.'" He searched her face, letting his intense gaze touch lightly on her eyes and rest on her mouth. Though they still moved around the dance floor, jostled by other couples, she no longer heard the music. She stared back, her lips slightly parted.

Tyler inhaled the light scent of Libby's shining hair, and it went straight to his head like a shot of whiskey. She was beautiful in the pale blue dress. It hugged her slender waist and its neckline hinted at the soft swell of her breasts. She felt so right in his arms, it almost scared him. Baffling and guileless, innocent and wise, she bewitched him without even trying. Desire surged to life within him, pounding back with twice the yearning he'd felt before. And suddenly, it bothered him a lot that any man thought she was "interesting."

"It's so hot in here," she murmured.

He felt edgy and restless himself. "Let's go outside for some air."

She agreed and he took her hand to pilot her through the crowd in the hall. There were quite a few people outside, too, and he led them to a shadowed bench on the side of the building, away from eavesdroppers and harsh lantern light.

The night was fragrant of late spring, and overhead a starkly white crescent moon mingled with the stars.

"Oh, that's much bet—" Libby began, but Tyler immediately pulled her into his arms and tried to kiss her.

"Tyler!" She pushed him away and jumped to her feet. "How dare you come to me from that—that woman's bed," she demanded in a low, shaking voice, "smelling of gardenias, and expect to kiss me?" His face was in the shadows, and she couldn't read his expression. In the awkward silence that followed, Libby felt foolish for revealing her jealousy.

He sighed. "I'm sorry." He reached for her hand, but apparently thought better of it, and indicated the seat next to him. "Please—sit down."

She stared at him for a moment, then relented. "Well . . . all right." Cautiously, she sat on the end of the bench and huffily arranged her skirts.

"I want you to know that I didn't—well—I only had a couple of drinks at the Big Dipper. Nothing else."

"And I suppose that every man who goes in there for a beer comes out smelling like that?" She knew she sounded like a shrew, but she couldn't stop herself.

"No. Callie sat in my lap," he admitted. He leaned back against the wall and looked at the expanse of night sky over them. "I've been going to see her every Saturday night for three or four years. After Jenna died, all the women around Heavenly with eligible daughters invited me to their spreads for supper. Oh, it just boiled their beans to see me without a wife. They were bent on fixing that." His huff of laughter was humorless. "I wasn't interested in being maneuvered into marriage. Callie asked nothing of me. Our arrangement was straightforward and uncomplicated." He turned his head and looked at her. "But that's not what I want anymore. When I left the Big Dipper tonight, I told her good-bye. I won't be going back."

Libby was afraid to ask what he did want. The implication of his decision made her mind spin foolish, heartening possibilities. But she knew better than to get her hopes up. She had been burned twice, and badly, by pledges made and not kept. Still, Tyler made no promises. It was the trace of yearning in his voice that touched her.

He lifted his sleeve to his nose then. "That perfume is pretty strong," he allowed. "Maybe I should burn my shirt?" He sat up and started unbuttoning it.

"Don't be silly," she said irritably, but he had the front open, and one cuff undone. Her eyes were drawn like magnets to his broad chest and flat belly. "Tyler!"

He stopped to rummage in his pockets. "I think I have a match here someplace. Of course, you'll have to let me wear your shawl home."

Much as she didn't want to, she burst out laughing.

"I guess I might have to burn my jeans, too. Hoo-eee! I stink like a saloon girl." He stood and reached for his belt buckle.

"Now, Tyler, stop it!" she ordered, but her giggling canceled the weight of her words. She'd never known him to act silly, just for the fun of it.

Once they got started, they couldn't seem to stop, and each round of laughter fed the next until they were weak and winded.

Finally, Tyler flopped down on the bench again in a sprawl of long arms and legs. "Oh, Libby, gal, it feels good to laugh with you. We haven't done much of that, have we?" He fastened his cuff, and to her secret disappointment, rebuttoned his shirt.

Her mirth subsided but her smile remained. "No, we haven't," she agreed. "A lot of serious things have happened."

He put his arm on the back of the bench and brushed her sleeve with his hand. "Yeah, I know. But life is so damned short. I've had time to think since we got back from Miles City." He gave her a wry smile. "I did more than just get drunk out there in the hills. And I realized I have enough regrets in my life for the things I've done. I don't need any more for the things I didn't do . . . am I making sense?"

She leaned her shoulder against his hand just a bit. It felt hot through the fabric of her dress. "Yes, you are."

He looked into her face again and plucked at her hand where it rested in her lap. Turning it over, he lifted it to his mouth and kissed it.

The feel of his warm, soft mouth in her palm sent

shivers rippling through Libby. Her fingers curved around his cheek and rested against the light stubble of his beard.

"Cold?" he murmured into her hand, pressing another kiss on the base of her thumb.

"No," she whispered, leaning closer. Beneath the fading miasma of gardenias, his own familiar scent began to emerge—fresh air, leather, horses. She felt a wild temptation to weave her fingers through his thick hair where it broke over his collar.

His kiss advanced to the inside of her wrist, and she felt his tongue touch the spot where her pulse throbbed as fast as a bird's. She shouldn't permit this, but he was so difficult to resist. Sometimes, when she'd lain awake in the moonlight and shadows crossing her bed, she'd thought of that rain-drenched night in the wagon. He moved his arm from the back of the bench and wrapped it around her shoulders, turning her toward him.

"Tyler—"

"Shh," he urged, kissing her throat, and proceeding to the corner of her jaw and the sensitive place behind her ear. He slid his big hand along her midriff up to her breast and, to her chagrin, drew a quiet moan from her. She should pull away, she knew. But his quickening breath ruffled the fine, downy fuzz on her cheek and raised goose bumps all over her body. Her heart thundered inside her ribs. When his teeth closed gently on her earlobe, Libby breathed a soft gasp and arched against his chest.

Tyler pulled back and gazed at her. The ache in his groin was so damned uncomfortable, he was torn between the wish that he'd never started this, and a raging desire to lay her down on this bench right now. As he'd suspected, under her sweet, prim exterior, a low fire burned. But he wasn't even going to kiss her mouth until the essence of gardenias no longer stood between them.

He shifted on the bench. "What do you say—have you had enough of this dance?" he asked.

She cleared her throat. "Yes, I believe I have," she said, and smoothed her skirt.

He leaned over and kissed her cheek. "Then let's go home, Libby."

# *Chapter* 14

The changes that occurred between Tyler and Libby after the grange dance were subtle but distinct. He didn't try to kiss her again, and she was glad: the intense feelings he stirred in her heart and body took her breath away, leaving her unable to think straight. But they circled each other, watchful, curious, aware. In the next few days, she noticed it in the way his eyes followed her when he thought she wasn't looking, especially when she worked on the flower beds.

She found herself searching him out, too. When he was working in the corral or near the barn, she'd drift to the kitchen window every few minutes to admire his long-legged stance, or the way the muscles in his forearms flexed when he reached for something. One day she lingered at the open door, mesmerized by the sight of him stripping off his shirt to pump water over his head. The rivulets sparkled like crystals in the sun as they ran down his torso and into the low-slung waist of his pants. As if feeling her gaze on him, he glanced up suddenly, and sent her a look of such fevered yearning, she jumped back and leaned against the rough-timbered wall.

He joined her for supper every night after the crew had eaten, and sometimes even brought wildflowers for the table. He became the easier-going man Joe had described on her first day here, quicker to laugh and joke with the men. She was pleased to see him spend more time with Rory, too, and give him greater responsibility. Rory was so puffed up with pride, she thought he'd float away.

The Lodestar was definitely a happier place.

One afternoon, Libby was in Tyler's office to talk about a shopping trip to Heavenly when they heard Joe's footsteps thunder through the house.

He appeared in the doorway, and one look at his face told her something was wrong.

"What's the matter?" Tyler said, rising from his chair.

"It's the new man, Jim Colby." Joe had hired him to take Charlie's place. "That stallion threw him against the side of the stall. It looks like Jim busted his arm."

"Goddamn it!" he erupted. "I knew we should have cut that horse. What the hell good is breeding stock if we can't even get close enough to feed the mangy bastard? Well, how bad is it?"

Jim shrugged. "I would have liked Doc Franklin to take a look at it, but I sent Kansas Bob to Heavenly for him, and he ain't in his office. I can set it, but I thought maybe you'd want to give it a try."

Tyler blanched, and he shook his head. "No. You boys can take care of this. You've done it before." Taking a key from his desk drawer, he went to the glass-fronted cabinet that held the bandages and dark-brown bottles she'd seen the night she cut her hand. "I can give him something for the pain, though." He plucked a bottle off the shelf and handed it to Joe with instructions about how much to give Jim.

"You sure you don't want to handle this? You could give it a try."

Tyler glanced at Libby, then back at his foreman, and lowered his voice. "You know how I feel about that. You'll do fine."

With an oddly resigned expression, Joe gripped the bottle in his gloved fist and strode from the room.

Puzzled by what she'd just seen, Libby looked at Tyler. His face was still a flat, unreadable mask. "You did a great job with my finger. I thought you handled the injuries around here." She held her hand up and waggled it for his inspection.

"Not me—*we*," he said. "Joe has set lots of broken bones in his life. He doesn't need my help." Walking to the window, he lapsed into a reflective silence while he stared at the green bluffs beyond the valley.

She looked at his broad-shouldered back. The conversation seemed to have reached an end. "Um, maybe we can talk about the provisions?"

"Make the list, Libby. I trust you to know what we need."

"But—"

"Go on, now," he said, looking over his shoulder at her. "We'll talk about it at supper, okay?"

She left the room, quietly closing the door behind her. Whenever he withdrew into himself, Libby knew he was thinking about Jenna. She couldn't fault him for mourning his wife, but—but oh, God, it made her feel like she was competing with a ghost.

Everything about that idea was wrong, she told herself as she walked back to the kitchen. It was wrong of her to envy a dead woman, a woman whose tie to him had been much stronger than her own. After all, despite the brief, heated moments they'd shared, Libby was still Tyler's employee, just like Kansas Bob or Possum Cooper.

At least she trusted him enough to stop comparing him to Wesley Brandauer. She realized that there were things about Tyler she didn't know, but she felt he'd always been honest with her. That he'd never led her to believe he was anything other than what he said.

She looked out the kitchen window at the nearly completed flower beds. The rich, dark soil was tilled, and free of choking weeds and grass. Now the prairie roses, climbing on trellises that flanked each end of the porch, were visible in all their delicate beauty. The only task that remained was to line the edge of the beds with stones. She took her gloves from an apple crate next to the door, and walked outside into the sun.

It seemed like a good job to get her mind off the one fact about her relationship with Tyler that frightened her the most. She might work for him, like Kansas Bob or Possum, but it was a safe bet that she was the only one on this ranch who was in love with him.

That night, Tyler brought no wildflowers to put on the supper table. He was distracted and quiet, and responded to her attempts at conversation with one-word answers. When she asked him to pass the gravy, he handed her the bread. Libby realized that sitting with him under these circumstances was lonelier than having supper by herself.

"Tyler," she said at last, getting up for the gravy, "keeping things bottled up isn't good. I've seen what it does to you."

After a pause, he lifted his sky-blue eyes to hers.

"I don't talk about myself much. You should know that by now—it's not my way."

She put her elbows on the table and leaned toward him. "What I know," she said earnestly, "is that the troubles you're keeping to yourself eat you up and make you miserable. It's not as if it doesn't show."

He put down his fork and pushed away his empty plate. She could see him grappling with the decision to tell her what was on his mind.

"I-I know that somehow Jim Colby's broken arm made you think about Jenna." Libby's voice trembled slightly, and she cleared her throat to steady it. Putting her hands in her lap, she dropped her gaze to her half-eaten meal. Daring and desperation forced her to candor. "I can imagine that you miss her but—it's been so hard knowing that when we— when you kissed me, you wished I was her."

His head came up sharply. "Libby, I never wished that for one minute. *Never.* And I don't miss Jenna."

"You don't?" She was surprised.

Tyler tossed his napkin onto the table and wearily ran a hand through his hair. Maybe he should tell her. She was right about one thing: keeping this to himself wasn't doing him any good. Or her either, for that matter. But where to start? At the place where everything changed, he supposed.

He straddled the bench. Putting his feet up, he leaned back against the wall. "I'd been away from Heavenly for six years when my father got sick and I came back to run the Lodestar. One day I went into town, and I saw Jenna in front of Osmer's." A faint smile crossed his face. "She'd grown from the scrawny kid I remembered into a beautiful, delicate woman. Almost ethereal, I guess you could say. I knew she was suited to a more gentle life than ranching. But I took one look at her and I proposed to her right there, right on the street in Heavenly."

That she was already engaged to a lawyer from Helena didn't deter Tyler. He courted her with all the passion and heartfelt ardor of a foolish young man, never once seeing that she wasn't really the right woman for him. Winning her wasn't easy: she'd never liked living on a ranch. She'd attended finishing school in the East and wanted a more civilized life.

But Tyler was in love with her, and her father, Lat Egan, was his ally. Lat admitted that he saw more status in having a lawyer for a son-in-law than a doctor. But that was outweighed by the even bigger advantage of a marriage between their two spreads, the Lodestar and the One Pine.

"You're a doctor?" Libby asked, barely above a whisper.

He glanced at her startled, wide-eyed expression, then looked away again. "I *was* a doctor. Anyway, I was so persistent and promised her such an ideal life, she finally broke her engagement with the lawyer. I suppose she regretted that because she wasn't happy here, not even from the first day, I don't think. She didn't like horses, cattle, or cowboys. And even though I wanted her to be happy, I worried that I'd made a terrible mistake in marrying her. When she got pregnant, I was certain of it."

He stood and went to the window, bracing his hands on either side of the frame. Purple dusk gave way to moonless night across the landscape, and the barn loomed as a dark mass in the distance. "It was a bitterly cold evening in November when she went into labor. Late the next afternoon, the baby still hadn't been born when she started hemorrhaging.

Rory was visiting with us, but I'd sent him out to stay with Joe, you know, to get him out of the house. Jenna grew weaker and weaker—finally she asked me to send Rory for her father so she could see him one more time. God, I tried everything I could think of to stop the bleeding." He turned and looked at her then. "She was gone before they got back."

Libby listened to this with tears in her eyes. "The baby?"

"Stillborn."

"B-but you told me a doctor let Jenna die."

"That's right. *I* was the doctor."

"Tyler, you didn't *let* her die!"

He leaned against the rough log wall and gave her a little smile, full of regret and self-doubt. What frightened Libby most was the utter lack of emotion in his voice. It was as if he were dead inside, too.

"I didn't save her, either, did I? Logically, I could tell myself that women die in childbirth every day. But that didn't ease my guilt when I put Jenna in the coffin that Charlie built for her. Or when I laid our son in her arms."

She pressed her hand to her mouth to stifle the sob working its way up her throat.

"Jenna's father holds me responsible, too, but you know that. And he blamed Rory for not coming soon enough so that he could see Jenna before she died. I couldn't do anything about what he thought of me. But that kid was only ten years old. For the guilt he heaped upon him, I never forgave Lattimer Egan."

"Oh, God, poor Rory," she choked.

He flopped down on the bench next to Libby, as though suddenly too tired to stand any longer. She wished she could take him into her arms, but his icy mask and voice stopped her.

"Rory wanted to stay here—I sent him home. I thought his place was with his father. But he kept running away and coming back to the Lodestar. Finally, I gave up and accepted the responsibility of raising him. He's been here ever since. Lat was furious about that, too."

"But you gave up medicine? Tyler, that's such a waste."

He sat hunched on the bench, his elbows on his knees, staring at the floor between his boots. He squeezed his temple between his thumb and second finger. "I just lost my nerve, and now I'm afraid I'd freeze. That's why I didn't want to set Jim Colby's arm. Anyway, there's a doctor in Heavenly, Alex Franklin. God help him." His back heaved with the deep breath he drew. "So, Libby—it isn't grief I feel for Jenna. Not anymore. It's guilt. I persuaded her to give up the life that she wanted in Helena for one she hated here. And when I should have saved her life, I couldn't. After we buried her up on the bluffs I came back here and sat on the porch, trying to figure it all out. The only thing I knew for certain was that I was responsible. But as evening began to come on, I saw two stars right next to each other, a big one and a little one. I asked them to forgive me. And I have lots of times since."

Her heart contracted with anguish for him, and she understood why he'd walled himself off from everyone. Never once had she guessed how dark a burden he carried. Yet she knew she should have realized that Tyler was a doctor. It all made sense: his skill with the cut on her hand, the medical supplies in his office, his compassion in the face of suffering.

"Tyler," she whispered, because that was all she

could do over the constriction in her throat, "Jenna doesn't need to forgive you. You need to forgive yourself. I wish you'd told me about this sooner."

"So you'd know what a fraud I am?" he asked, his face still pointed at the floor.

"You're not!" she said emphatically. "I-I knew a man who was a fraud, a selfish liar."

"You mean Ben Ross?"

"No, not Ben. Someone worse, back in Chicago. You're nothing like him. There's so much goodness in you—you're just afraid to let it show." That was what she'd responded to all along—the goodness in Tyler—no matter how she tried not to, no matter how he tried to put her off.

"You think so, huh?" he scoffed.

She put her hand on his shoulder. It was tight and tense. "Yes, I do, Tyler."

Tyler sat up and looked at her, the big gray eyes, the silky, vagrant strands of hair that framed her face, the lush coral mouth. But more than anything, he saw honesty, and his cynicism faded. She meant what she said.

He pulled her into his arms and rocked her slowly. That sweet, faint scent of flowers and vanilla came to him, and he kissed her temple. "Libby," he murmured, "bringing you to the Lodestar was the best day's work those boys ever did."

"You didn't think so at the time." He heard the smile in her words.

"It just took me awhile to admit it to myself. But I wasn't so lonely after you got here." He rubbed his cheek against her hair. "Those long days here at the ranch and out on the trail—knowing that I would come back and find you in the evenings, it felt more like home ... at night, knowing that you slept in the room next to mine, I wanted to come to you ..."

Libby heard the subtle change in his voice, and she pulled back to look at him. She recognized the low, blue flame in his eyes that she'd seen once or twice before. Entranced by his words, by his touch, she inhaled his clean scent. "And did you?" she asked softly.

He stared at her lips, then let his gaze drift over her face. "Once. I lay beside you for a few hours." He made it sound like the most intimate, personal thing that had ever taken place between two people.

Her face grew warm. "You slept on top of the bedding ... I thought it was a dream."

He lowered his mouth to hers. She felt his breath mingle with her own. "It wasn't."

When his lips met hers, it was as if they'd never kissed before—all the passion and lonely, urgent longing between them now suddenly flowered in the low-lit kitchen. He teased her mouth open and she felt his tongue against hers, warm and seeking.

Breaking away, he whispered, "God, I love kissing you." His fervent honesty fanned the timid spark he'd ignited in her, and her pulse jumped its tempo. He buried his mouth against her throat, leaving a trail of heat as he worked his way up to her lips again.

With deft agility, Tyler turned her around on the bench and lifted her to his lap. Again, he was struck by the certainty that this virgin widow, with her brave spirit and banked fire, could make him forget the desolate years of regret and emptiness. He wanted to claim her as his own in every possible way. But he couldn't make himself tell her that. Maybe his breezy association with Callie had cost him his ability

to court a woman, to gentle and honor her with his
body and his heart.

"I don't know how to say what I want to say," he
muttered against her neck. "It's been a long time
since I've asked ... Libby, I need you...." He
wound his hand in the folds of her skirt.

"I know," she whispered. She stood up and extended her hand. He looked at it, and then at her
face. He saw acceptance there, and maybe the same
desire to fill the emptiness she'd known.

Tyler lifted her hand to kiss it, then tucked it
inside his own. Lighting a candle, he led them
through the swinging door and up the stairs to his
room at the end of the gallery.

Libby stood in the doorway with her hands
clasped in front of her and looked at the four-poster
she'd daydreamed about in the train station. Were
they doing the wrong thing? In the eyes of polite
society, perhaps. In the peace and beauty of Montana
Territory, she didn't think so. Looking at Tyler, she
knew in her own mind that making love with this
man was indeed the right thing to do.

Tyler set the candle down on the bureau and came
to her where she waited. He ran his hands up and
down her arms, rucking the fabric of her sleeves. He
pulled the ribbon off the end of her braid and
combed his fingers through the plait. The light
strokes sent waves of delicious shivers over her.
Though his touch was tender, she sensed powerful
desire coursing through him.

"Save me, Libby," he whispered thickly. "And I'll
save you. We've had too many years of heartache,
I think."

With those words, any last-minute trepidation fell
away from her. "I think so, too," she replied. He

drew her into his embrace, and she clung to him, feeling the warm muscle and bone of him through his light shirt.

He grasped her buttocks and pulled her up against his hips, murmuring unintelligibly. She felt the hard length of him through her skirts. He made a noise in his throat and kissed her again, hot and slow, his lips moving over hers with sweet urgency.

When his hand slid up her back and around to her breast, she pulled in a deep breath and leaned into his palm. Her heart pounded in her chest. Surely he must feel it, she thought.

With hands that trembled slightly, he reached up and opened the buttons on her bodice, one by one, then he untied the ribbons on her camisole. His warm hand on her bare breast was electrifying. Her nipple hardened instantly under his touch.

Feeling that, Tyler's flimsy grasp on his resolve to go slowly diminished considerably. He wanted to pull her clothes away and lay her down, to look at the beauty of her nakedness, and to feel her against his own bare skin. He wanted to watch her pretty face when he joined his body to hers.

Impatiently, he unbuttoned his own shirt and opened it wide. As if by instinct she pressed against his chest, and the feeling that ripped through him was so consuming, he wondered how he'd ever thought that even the most talented madam could replace this.

She shrugged out of her dress, letting it lie where it fell with a click of buttons on the hardwood floor. She stood before him, small and shy in her drawers and open camisole, her hair draped around her like a young girl's. Obviously bashful, she couldn't lift her gaze from the rag rug under her feet.

Seeing her like that, he swallowed and hurried to kick off his boots, and shed his pants and shirt. Then he stepped forward and swept her up into his arms.

"Angelheart, you're so beautiful."

*Angelheart.* Libby remembered him calling her that the night he was drunk and wanted to sleep with her. At the time, she'd written it off as the rambling of a whiskey-soaked brain. But he'd really meant it.

He laid her on the mattress. In the low flicker of the candle, she saw the testimony of his arousal, and quailed a bit. She'd never seen a man completely undressed before. He was beautifully built, with long legs and a flat belly. The red-gold hair on his chest picked up highlights from the candle, and she stretched out a hesitant hand to touch it. But when Tyler lay next to her and began a trail of kisses from her jaw down her neck, she lost track of everything else. He rested his palm between her breasts for a moment, then smiled.

"See what you've done to me," she said. "My heart is hammering away."

"A healthy sign," he said, grinning. "See what you've done to *me*." His smile faded and he guided her hand to him, wrapping her fingers around himself. Intuition rather than experience told her what to do, and when he moaned into her neck she knew she'd discovered what pleased him.

He gripped her wrist. "Whoa, stop, honey. I'm not as strong a man as you think."

She didn't know what he was talking about but as he gazed at her lying before him, his expression grew serious and he lowered his head to gently suckle at her breast.

Libby gasped and arched against him, and passion

exploded between them. The feeling of his hot, moist mouth tugging at her nipple sent arrows of fire through her belly to her womb. He reached for the tie on her drawers to loosen them, then jerked them off her hips and down her legs. He ran his fevered palm up the insides of her thighs, stopping to touch his fingertips to the place between her legs that had grown liquid with readiness. His strokes were like the beats of a hummingbird's wings against her swollen, throbbing flesh.

"Tyler," she whimpered, writhing under his hand. Blindly, she groped for him.

"I know." He dropped his head to suckle her other nipple.

She wasn't sure if she wanted him to end his ministrations or increase them, but this torment could not go on. The heat, the need building in her was excruciating, and she didn't know what to do about it. When he stopped, she was consumed with frustration.

"Oh, no, please—"

"Hush, angelheart, I won't leave you this way," he whispered hoarsely.

Tyler covered her with his body and nudged her legs apart. Take it slow, he told himself, but it wasn't easy when he wanted to bury himself in the hot center of her. His need was as punishing as hers. He probed her flesh, and finding the opening to her femininity, pushed against its portal. He felt the resistance. Beneath him, Libby tensed.

He gazed down at her. Passion had made her eyes heavy-lidded and even in candlelight, he could see the rosy flush that colored her cheeks. He took her hands and laid them on either side of the pillow, then interlaced her fingers with his own. "Just this once, Libby, I promise—" He clamped her earlobe between her teeth and claimed her virginity in one smooth stroke, then lay still, waiting for her body to accommodate him.

A cry escaped her and she gripped his hands.

"I'm sorry," he murmured, putting swift, soft kisses on her forehead and cheeks and eyelids. He wasn't happy about hurting her, but it felt so good to be surrounded by her.

For her part, Libby was surprised and disappointed by the sharp twinge of pain. But then he began moving inside her with a flow and rhythm that transcended the moment, and harkened back to the most primal drive of life. Though she had no experience to draw upon, she found herself lifting her hips to complement his movement. Inevitably, the throbbing heat she'd felt moments earlier returned to burn higher and hotter than before.

"Tyler," she moaned, her breath whooshing out of her with each pounding stroke. She felt like crying, like dying. Every muscle was rigid with the wanting of something that eluded her. Hearing her, Tyler whispered reassurance and endearments, and increased this sweet agony, moving faster, harder.

At last, when she was sure that her death must be imminent she teetered on the knife-edge of a breathless suspended moment. And he pushed her over with a thrust that triggered spasm upon spasm of intense, overwhelming pleasure. He smothered her wail with a searing kiss.

Tyler quickened the fast, hard thrusts. His breathing was heavy and labored, and sweat poured off him. "Sweet angel," he mumbled like a man in delirium. "My sweet angel—" The last word dissolved into a groaning sob that sounded as though it were being ripped from his soul. He pushed into her while his straining body convulsed, and white hot jets poured into Libby.

He let his forehead rest on the pillow next to her, waiting to get his breath back. Finally rolling to his side, he tucked her against his chest and wrapped his arms around her. It felt so natural, so right having her here in his bed. It was as though she'd always belonged here.

With a deep sigh, he kissed her forehead, and hugged her to him. "Are you all right? I hope I didn't hurt you too much."

"No, you didn't."

He uttered a satisfied noise. "That's good."

Libby lay in his embrace, sated and awed and desperately in love. Her heart was so full, she could barely speak without telling him.

It had not come easily to her; the Tyler Hollins she'd first met was a difficult man to love. Stubborn, cold, and self-sufficient. That had been only a shell. The real man who hid beneath that was uncertain and vulnerable. She wished she could tell him how she felt. But this wasn't the time. She had no way of knowing whether he'd come to her merely out of loneliness, or genuine affection. She wanted to think it was the latter. But she'd revealed her heart once before and had lived to regret it. Though Tyler wasn't Wesley Brandauer, she wasn't ready to take that chance again.

For now, though, she nestled against him. The morning might bring with it aching regret for this night, or for things left unsaid. Tonight, though, she was content to lie with him in his bed, her head pillowed on his shoulder.

Watching the rise and fall of his chest, she heard

his breathing slow and deepen. She turned to look at him. Sleep smoothed out the tired lines that years of worry and guilt had etched into his handsome face.

She put a protective arm over his waist. "I love you, Tyler," she whispered.

In his sleep, he pulled her closer.

Libby poked her head out of the covers the next morning with the feeling that something was different. She opened her eyes and realized that she was not in her own room. She was in Tyler's bed, naked. She liked it in here, she thought, stretching dreamily. The room was warm with sun, and a clean, fresh breeze from the open window fluttered the curtains. Then the memory of the night before came rushing back to her, and she pulled the sheet up to her chin.

She rolled over and looked at his side of the bed, disappointed that he was already up and gone for the morning. The things that they had done last night! The passion and fire that had coursed between them—had it really happened? Yes, undeniably.

She had sensed that impatient urgency in Tyler all along, simmering behind a facade of rigid self-control; she'd had no idea how it would reveal itself. Closing her eyes against the glaring sun, she pulled his pillow over her head and smiled sleepily as she inhaled the familiar scent of him. It hadn't been a dream this time. It was real.

Glaring sun? she thought with a start, and threw the pillow off her face. Oh, God, why had he let her sleep so late? The men would have been waiting for breakfast for hours. She scrambled to the side of the bed, the sudden movement bringing a sharp ache to muscles she'd not used until last night.

Quickly plucking her discarded clothes from the floor, she opened the door a crack to make certain no one was in the hall, or the parlor below, then dashed for her own room.

After dressing hastily, she sped lightly down the stairs, braiding her hair as she went. When she walked into the kitchen, she found Rory drying dishes. The faint odor of burned bread hung in the air.

"Rory, heavens, I must have overslept. Did everyone eat?"

"Yes, Miss Libby. Tyler had me and Kansas Bob cook this mornin'. I still ain't figured out how to make toast without burnin' it." He wore an old flour sack for an apron, an accessory that she felt certain clashed with his aspiration to be a top hand. "I was hopin' to air the place out." He nodded at the open door.

"Oh, dear, I'm sorry. Here, give me that." She took the dish towel from him and applied it to a wet tin plate on the counter. "Why didn't Tyler wake me?"

"He said you were up late last night and he was lettin' you sleep in. Were you sick?"

Libby could only hope that her face wasn't as red as it felt. But at the same time, she was extraordinarily pleased that Tyler had thought of her. "Uh, no, I just couldn't sleep. You can take off that flour sack and go be a cowhand again. I certainly appreciate your help, though. You did a wonderful job cleaning up. Someday, your wife will be glad you know your way around a kitchen."

He discarded the apron with a horrified expression. "Wife! Thanks, Miss Libby, but if it's all the

same to you, I'd rather stick to horses and cattle."
He smoothed back his hair and put on his hat.

She laughed. "You might change your mind later
on. For now, I'm sure that Joe can find something
more interesting for you to do out on the range."

Rory walked out the open door and trotted toward
the corral, presumably in search of the rest of the
crew and a manly occupation.

Libby looked at the clear blue sky as she dried the
last of the dishes. Had it always been that blue, she
wondered, or was it different today? She inhaled a
deep breath through her nose. Despite the lingering
trace of burned toast, the breeze blowing in from
outside smelled fresher and more invigorating than
it had just yesterday.

In fact, Libby couldn't recall the last time she'd
known such a sense of happy well-being. But the
man responsible for it came into her view then, leading the pinto toward the road and talking to Joe. A
flush of love and excitement filled her just to look
at him, and she had to stop herself from running out
to meet him.

He was so handsome, and this morning he looked
downright beautiful to her. His hat rested on his
back, hanging by its bonnet strings, letting his chestnut hair glimmer with brown and copper fire under
the morning sun. She couldn't see his eyes but she
knew that they matched the endless sky above him.
His long legs were wrapped in buckskin chaps, and
his shirtsleeves were rolled up nearly to his elbows,
showing off lean, muscled forearms. Now and then,
he reached up and absently stroked the pinto's neck,
and she remembered how gentle and comforting his
hands could be.

He and Joe were walking slowly, apparently deep

in some conversation. When they came abreast of the kitchen door, their words floated to her. Tyler's dog, Sam, bounded around his feet, his pink tongue lolling.

"Not this time, Sam. You stay here."

"How long you figurin' on bein' gone?" Libby heard Joe ask.

"Well, you know how far it is to Billings. Three or four days at the most. I shouldn't have any weather to contend with."

"You sure you want to do this?" Joe asked. "Things are goin' just fine."

"I can't very well have her cooking for us anymore, Joe. Not now."

"I s'pose you're right. Bring back someone decent, then. We've gotten kind of spoiled with Miss Libby's cookin'."

Tyler said good-bye, then Libby heard the jingle of bridle and the pounding of hooves as he set off across the turf.

Adrenaline flooded her, making her hands shake and her heart thunder like a herd of runaway horses. Pulling out the chair at the worktable, she sat down, fearing she would either faint or vomit. Her breath came in jerky gasps, and she pressed her trembling fist to her mouth. It was happening again, she thought wildly. Scalding tears welled in her eyes and spilled down her cheeks. Stupid, stupid woman, she cursed herself. Why hadn't she learned her lesson with Wesley?

Oh, because she'd thought Tyler was *different*, she sneered, that was why. He wasn't any different at all. Not really. She doubted that he had a wealthy, society fiancée waiting in the wings. But he'd revealed his innermost thoughts to her, he'd made love with her, and now, of course, he regretted it bitterly. So much, in fact, that he was going all the way to Billings to find someone to take her place.

A wailing sob crept up into her throat, and she clapped her hand over her mouth to muffle it. Oh, Tyler, why? she mourned.

He hadn't had the guts to tell her what he was planning. He'd simply sneaked away while she slept, without even saying good-bye.

Well, this time, she wasn't going to pack. This time, she'd make that detestable coward tell her to her face that she was finished here.

And she had three or four days to work up the nerve to listen.

# Chapter 15

Tyler had pushed the pinto as hard as he dared, trying to eat up the miles of sage and grass between the Lodestar and Billings. Every time he thought back to the fire and tenderness Libby had summoned in him, born out of raging desire and desperation, he urged the horse on. Now, after a day and a half in the saddle, he finally saw the town emerge on the horizon.

It was one of the toughest things he'd ever done, leaving his bed at dawn yesterday morning. He woke with Libby asleep next to him, her arm looped around his middle, and the sheet barely covering her full, soft breasts. Her face was buried in his neck and she lay with one leg between his, the front of her pelvis pressed tight against his hip. All he'd wanted to do was spend the morning making love to her again.

But the night before, she'd whispered those words to him in the instant just before he fell asleep. Hell, maybe he wasn't even supposed to hear them. It had seemed so far from his consciousness that it was almost like a dream. But it wasn't a dream, and he knew what he had to do. Nothing else could have forced him from her side and set him on this trip.

So he'd left a note on his pillow, and kissed the angelheart good-bye.

Up ahead, the buildings began to take shape. Saddle-sore and exhausted, he nudged the pinto into a canter. Yeah, leaving her was definitely one of the hardest things he'd ever done.

Libby woke with a start, and found she'd been hugging her pillow again. She glanced around the walls of her room. It was still dark, she thought unhappily. The last two nights had seemed endless. Disentangling herself from the twisted bedding, she went to the window and rested her forehead on the cool glass. How quickly—in a heartbeat, or with the utterance of a few words—joy could turn to despair.

Below, the Lodestar slept in the quiet darkness, contrasting with the turmoil that churned within Libby's heart. During the day, she crept around the ranch house like an injured bird, feeling sick and empty inside. In front of the men, she made a valiant effort to appear as though everything were normal. She believed she succeeded, but only because Joe had gone to the northern range shortly after Tyler left. Although he'd have said nothing, Joe would have seen through her pretense, making it difficult for her to maintain it. His sharp jet eyes missed very little.

At night, sleep eluded her and at best, she only napped, falling into a troubled doze for brief periods. Keeping Tyler from her thoughts proved impossible. Over and over, her treacherous memory would drift back to the night he had held her in his arms, his skin warm on hers. Finally, she had closed Tyler's bedroom door, leaving the bed unmade, so that she wouldn't have to look at it and remember the way he'd touched her, or the things he'd whispered to her—he'd sounded so sincere.

But he'd spoken even more candidly to Joe the following morning. *I can't very well have her cooking for us anymore, Joe. Not now.* No matter how Libby analyzed it, there could be no mistaking his meaning and intent. And Joe had agreed with him, so that meant that he probably knew what had transpired in Tyler's bed, too.

She gripped the edge of the windowsill. Despite her resolve to face Tyler when he returned, she wished she hadn't returned the hundred dollars that he had given her in Miles City. If she still had it, she'd fly away across the prairie, away from the man with sky-blue eyes who'd taken her heart.

About an hour before sundown the next evening, Libby stood at the sink, with her hands submerged in hot, soapy dishwater, and her thoughts on a gloomy path. She listened for the muffled strikes of Rory's ax, but she didn't hear them yet. Although he was certain that a top hand wouldn't split firewood for the kitchen, it wasn't too hard to get his help with the proper inducement. The chore might be beneath the dignity of a top hand, but cookies apparently were not.

The door opened behind her, and spurs rang across the plank floor.

"When you finish out there, I've got some peanut butter cookies for you," she said.

"Cookies aren't going to do the trick, Libby. I've got an appetite for something else altogether."

Her breath trapped in her throat, she whirled and saw Tyler standing there. She froze like a doe caught in lantern light, a sopping dishrag clenched in her hand. The kitchen always seemed much smaller when he was in it.

He was dirty and he looked dead-tired but, oh, damn him, he wore it so well. His eyes turned smoky-blue with desire, and he gave her a wicked grin that told her exactly what his appetite demanded.

"Well, Jesus, honey, you don't look very happy to see me," he remarked ruefully. He took off his hat and threw it on one of the tables. Then pulling off his gloves, he tucked them into the waist of his chaps, and walked toward her, arms open. "I rode fifty miles today to get home to you. I just about wore out that pinto. Can't you even say hello?"

A slow-burning rage erupted in her, fueled by humiliation and heartache. She squeezed the rag until soapy water ran through her fingers and down to her elbow. Backing away from him, she nearly fell over a low stool trying to put distance between them.

He dropped his arms and his smile died. "What's the matter with you?"

Libby found her voice, and it shook with righteous fury. "*What's the matter with me?*" she repeated incredulously. She looked down at the wet cloth in her hand and threw it at his face with all the strength that anger put into her arm. The rag hit its mark with a *slap*, then tumbled down the front of his shirt, leaving a wet trail before it landed on the floor.

A black, forbidding scowl contorted his features, but she didn't have the presence of mind to feel fear, or anything else but betrayal.

He kicked the rag to the far wall and rubbed his face on his bare forearm. "Libby, what the hell is going on? I did some hard riding to get back here to see you," he barked. He took two more steps forward, as if to clutch her arms.

She scrambled back, putting the worktable between them, eyeing him warily. "You stay away from me, you liar!" she ground out, her heart thudding in her chest. "I thought you were better than him, but you're not. You're the same. He made me think he cared about me, too, but I was only an—an amusement." She heard the hysterical edge in her words, but she didn't care how she sounded. With a voice that began to tremble, all the pain and bitter anguish that she'd never been able to vent on Wesley came pouring out in a torrent. "To him, I was just the cook in the kitchen, n-not even a real person with feelings to hurt, or a heart to break."

Tyler was so damned confused and mad himself, he could barely follow what she was talking about. Of all the accusations she'd hurled at him, though, he grabbed the one that sounded familiar.

"What are you talking about? Does this have to do with something that happened in Chicago? Maybe you'd better tell me the real reason you left!" He stayed on his side of the table, but he put his hands on its surface and leaned toward her.

She wrapped her arms around herself. "I told you—I just couldn't stay there anymore."

He pounded his fist on the tabletop, once, making everything on it clatter. Libby jumped, too. "God-damn it, that's not good enough. I have the right to know who you're comparing me to!"

She glared at him, then lowered her eyes. "I suppose you do," she said. Weariness crowded out the wrath in her voice, and she told him about Wesley, Eliza Brandauer's spoiled, handsome son who made Libby believe that he cared about her, and even went so far as to promise eventual marriage. One night, when his mother was supposed to be out of town, he brought her to his room on the pretense of stitching a rip in his shirt.

Libby kept her gaze fixed on the table. "If he'd been anyone else, I would have worried." She shook her head, as if still trying to understand. "But I trusted Wesley. As soon as I was in the room, he closed the door."

His gentle, affectionate kisses rapidly escalated into rough, insistent groping that frightened and offended Libby. "I'd never thought about a woman being raped by someone she knew. But that's what he would have done to me. I guess I should be grateful that Mrs. Brandauer came home when she did."

With a single knock on the door, Eliza Brandauer walked in, outraged by the sight of her son rolling around on his bed with the cook, whose skirt was hiked up to her thighs.

Libby tipped her face down. "Oh, God, I wanted to die. Wesley said nothing in my defense—*nothing*. Mrs. Brandauer called me a whore and dismissed me on the spot. I was to be packed and out of the house by morning—she wouldn't abide a whore sleeping under her roof, she said. Moral propriety was very important to her." Her voice quivered with the tears that coursed down her face unchecked. "I ran from the room and I heard her scold Wesley, asking what he supposed his fiancée's family would think if they learned he'd been dallying with 'the servants.' Fiancée . . ." She repeated the word, as though it were beyond her comprehension.

Word of Libby's discharge and Wesley's upcoming wedding spread quickly through the house. That kind of news always did. Even her adopted family of

Melvin, Birdie, and Deirdre shunned her because she'd committed the grievous sin of forgetting her place and consorting with Mr. Wesley, and him newly engaged, too.

"After ten years, I suddenly found myself on the sidewalk with nowhere to go, no one to turn to. I had barely any money. I walked all day trying to find a job, but I didn't have any luck. I looked disreputable, I guess. Finally I knocked on the kitchen door of a church. The pastor's housekeeper let me stay in exchange for work until Ben sent me the tickets to come out here."

Tyler stared at her. The picture in his mind of Libby wandering the streets of Chicago made his eyes burn. His throat was so tight with suppressed emotion, it felt as if there were a whole sourdough biscuit in it. "And you thought that after the other night—"

Her head came up then, and so did the volume of her voice. "Oh, well, what about the other morning, Tyler?" she demanded, her hands on her hips. "What about telling Joe that you couldn't let me cook here anymore? You can sleep with a whore in Heavenly, but you won't have one cooking for you, is that it? No, you had to go to Billings to find someone to take my place."

His heart clenched in his chest. "Sleeping with me makes you a whore?"

Ignoring his question, the razor-edge of her voice broke, and in barely more than a whisper she uttered, "You just rode off. I watched you go from this window right here. You didn't even tell me good-bye. Even Callie Michaels got a good-bye from you."

Tyler gaped at Libby, stunned. Her face was colorless, but her gray eyes had darkened to charcoal. She folded her arms across her chest, withdrawing into herself.

"But I never told Callie that I loved her," he shot back, feeling persecuted now.

"How nice, do you want a reward?" she snapped, her eyes full of pain and fire. "You never told me that, either."

"Then what did I write in that note? I don't know how much plainer I could have put it!" He was shouting now, too.

"What note? You didn't leave me a note."

A muddle of feelings closed in on Tyler—exasperation, fury, and distress for what the Brandauers had done to her, hurt, grinding fatigue, harassment. He put the heel of his hand to his forehead and took a deep breath.

"I thought I was being *considerate* by not waking you. Goddamn it, now I wish I had. I left you a note on my pillow the morning I left."

"I don't believe you."

Abrupt silence fell in the kitchen and they stared at each other, entrenched and breathing hard. Libby wore an expression of utter distrust.

Breaking this stalemate, Tyler strode around the end of the table and grabbed Libby's wrist. "Come on." He pulled her along toward the door to the dining room.

Libby caught a glimpse of glittering anger in his eyes, and for the first time she felt real terror. Though she tried to free her arm, it was useless— she couldn't break his grip. In the space of a breath, she'd lost command of the situation and Tyler, with a hot, feral energy, seized it. She'd never seen him so furious, or so dangerous.

She looked up at his straight back, and narrow waist and hips as he dragged her up the stairs. His chaps slapped softly against the legs of his jeans, his spurs clinked with each thunderous footfall. "Tyler, let go of me. You can't mean to do this."

He didn't answer, but proceeded to the end of the gallery and his own closed bedroom door. Libby trotted behind, afraid to envision the magnitude of the punishment awaiting her.

Finally, he turned to her. "You've punched me in the stomach, slapped me with a dishrag, and lashed me with that tongue of yours more than once. I took it—sometimes I guess I even deserved it. But to call me a liar, to say that my word is no good—" He twisted the knob, nearly yanking it off, and flung the door open. It banged off the wall and bounced forward.

The room stood as they'd left it four days earlier, with the window open and the bedding in a tangle. The hard, gold sundown cast a long rectangle on the floor and wall. Tyler pulled her into the room and kicked the door closed behind them. Libby hung back, but he hauled her to the bed, and she recoiled. Twisting and struggling, she tried to get away.

"Hold still, damn it!"

"Tyler, God, please—don't do this—" She closed her eyes, feeling as though she stood before a firing squad, and expected him to push her to the mattress.

Instead, he reached out and threw the pillows aside, and began rifling through the sheets and quilts. All the while he kept her wrist locked in his fingers. Baffled, she watched as he impatiently stripped the bed down to the bare mattress. Cursing violently, he flung that against the wall as though it were weightless. Then, through the slats she saw a piece of paper, folded once, resting on the hardwood floor underneath. He bent down and snatched it up. Releasing her arm, he unfolded it and shoved it into her hands, crumpling it with the force.

"Here," he said. "Read it."

Libby lifted her gaze to his face. Beneath his anger, she saw pain. "But it was under the bed. How could I—"

"Read it!"

She dropped her eyes to the pen strokes.

*Dear Libby,*
*Nothing could have forced me from your side this morning but an errand in Billings that just won't wait. I'll be back as soon as I can.*
*I love you, too, angelheart.*
*Tyler*

The words blurred as tears welled in her eyes. *I love you, too* ... He'd heard her the night she whispered to him. She pressed a shaking hand to her mouth and looked up at him again. "Tyler, I'm sorry—"

His anger seemed to drain away all at once, apparently taking with it whatever energy he'd had left. He walked to the mattress where it lay and sat down heavily, sprawling his long legs and leaning against the wall.

"Not exactly what you were thinking?" He looked suddenly haggard. He scraped his hair back with both hands.

She took a step closer to him, and held out the note. "But—but if this is how you feel, why are you firing me?"

Sighing, he dug two fingers into his front pants

pocket and pulled out a tiny box that he closed in his hand. "I sure pictured this moment differently," he muttered with a trace of regret. "Come and sit down." He patted the mattress next to him.

Libby approached gingerly, and perched two feet away, clutching the paper to her breast.

"It's true that I don't want you cooking for the crew anymore. That's one of the reasons I went to Billings. But I'm not firing you, Libby." He edged closer to her and took her hand in his. "I want to marry you."

She couldn't quite get her breath. "Marry me?"

He looked at her fingers laying across his palm, and ran his thumb along the length of each one. "Yeah, if you'll have me. I'm not always the easiest man to get along with—huh, I guess you already know that. But you make me feel good whenever I'm around you. You gave me back my life." His tired face was full of emotion, and tears edged his blue eyes. "God, woman, why do you think I turned Miles City upside down looking for you? Just because I like your biscuits and gravy?" He pressed her hand to his mouth and kissed it. "I love you so much, it scared me to death when I realized it. I didn't want to love anyone again—I didn't think I could. But I don't know how I'd have stood it if you'd gotten on the train back to Chicago."

"Oh, Tyler, I'm sorry for the things I said," she whispered, her own eyes wet. She reached up and brushed her hand through his hair. "It was just that—maybe you realize just a little why I misunderstood when I overheard you and Joe the other morning?"

He nodded. "And *I'm* sorry as hell for what those damned Brandauers did to you." He opened his hand

and held out the tiny black velvet box he'd pulled from his pocket.

Slowly, she took it from his palm. "For me?"

"That's the other reason I had to go to Billings. Nort Osmer has wedding bands, but he doesn't sell diamonds."

She opened the spring-hinged box and found a beautiful engagement ring inside.

"I can't change the past, but I'd like to make up to you some of the things you missed, if you'll let me. Will you, Libby? Will you marry me?"

With a cry, she flung herself into his embrace and threw her arms around his neck. "Yes, oh, yes, I will!"

He buried his face in her hair. "Thank God," he mumbled with a voice that broke. He held her tight for several moments, rocking her. She felt a deep, shuddering breath wrack his body, and she knew without looking that his tears were wetting her hair.

They remained entwined for a while in the hush of the sundown, not moving. From the open window, she heard the last of the day's larks call out as they winged to their nesting places for the night. Libby had never felt such peace and security.

Finally, Tyler took the ring from the box and slid it onto her finger. Pressing a kiss to her knuckles, he looked up from her hand and murmured, "You're mine, Libby, now and forever. Don't forget that."

The timbre of his voice changed, and a delicious shiver flew down her spine. "And will you claim what is yours?"

His eyes, now smoky-blue, locked with hers. "I didn't ride fifty hard miles today for any other reason." He looked down at the front of his dusty shirt. "I'm not too clean though."

"I don't care. I'll take you clean—or dirty." She cupped his face in her hands, feeling the scratch of his day-old beard, and drew his mouth to hers. "I love you, Tyler," she said softly, her lips less than an inch from his.

Tyler groaned. "I love you, too, angelheart." He consumed her soft, pink mouth in a kiss, while he sank his fingers into her hair. Her innocent seduction sparked a fire in his blood that made him grateful this was not their first time together. Fierce hunger drove out some of the forbearing gentleness that he'd needed for taking her virginity.

Now a hot, predatory instinct licked through him, a powerful desire to possess her and make her his. To take her here, now. He deepened the kiss and laid her down on the bare mattress. His tongue sought the slick warmth of her mouth as his lips moved over hers with rising urgency. Each little noise that rose from her throat only made the flames in him burn higher.

He rose on one elbow and tried to open the buttons on her bodice, but in his impatience, he only popped off the first two.

"Here, let me," she said, and he watched with ravenous eyes as the front of her dress parted to reveal her camisole underneath. Reaching for its pale blue ribbons, he pulled on them to open the garment, and swallowed hard at what he saw. Smooth, full breasts with dusky rose nipples. Soft, white shoulders. A long creamy throat. Her body warmth coursed her sweet vanilla scent to him in waves.

"God, Libby, you take my breath away," he said thickly. "I just can't . . . help myself—"

Supporting her breast with his hand, he dipped his head to close his lips on her nipple. Libby gasped softly, shattered by the nearly unbearable pleasure of suckling him. She threaded her fingers through his thick hair, quickened by the slight rasp of his beard on her tender flesh.

He pulled back and she greedily reached for the front of his shirt, but he grasped her hand and pulled it lower to his fly buttons. Behind them, Libby felt the proof of his arousal, and his heat. Drawing a ragged breath, he pressed into her palm, pushing hard, and an answering hot pulse began low in her abdomen.

As if sensing that, Tyler reached beneath her skirt, trailing his fingers up the inside of her leg, past the top of her stocking and on to the thin muslin of her drawers. He put his hand between her thighs, and she knew he must feel the damp heat gathering under the fabric.

"Tyler," she moaned.

"Yes, angelheart," he answered.

He sat up then and kicked off his boots, the spurs digging into the hardwood floor. His shirt he threw to the other side of the room. Shucking off his chaps, he unbuckled his belt and opened his pants. Libby was mildly surprised to see that he'd not bothered to put on underwear, but that fact was curiously arousing.

He lay down beside her, naked, fully erect, and beautifully male. The clean, carved lines of muscle and bone were as graceful as any sculptor had ever dreamed of.

"Touch me, Libby," he whispered urgently.

A bit timid, she reached for his hard fullness and closed her hand around him, repeating what he'd liked their first night together.

A hard-edged moan rose from his throat, and she

felt quite pleased with herself and his response. She continued for another moment, until he pushed her hand away. "In you, honey, not on you."

Garment by garment, he pulled off her remaining clothes, replacing them with trails of flushed, urgent kisses on her bare skin. Only dimly did she realize that she rocked her pelvis against him.

"I know what you want," Tyler muttered in her ear.

He let his hand drift down her belly to reach for her wet, throbbing flesh again. His gentle, probing touch evoked sensations that were almost painful in their intensity. Libby gasped as his fingertips caressed the delicate, swollen tissues, and she pushed up to his hand. Instead of withdrawing as he had last time, he continued the slippery, rapid strokes until she thought her heart would burst from her chest. It was as if a coil in her wound tighter and tighter, and just one touch would release the constricting pressure.

"Tyler—oh, God—please, please—"

Tyler knew. The strokes came faster. He crooned to her in a breathless groan. "This is what you need, right here. Right . . . here."

Suddenly, her muscles constricted and hovered on the brink of quivering silence. Then the one touch she'd been waiting for tripped the tight coil and her body convulsed with spasm upon spasm of excruciating pleasure. Libby turned her face against Tyler's chest and sobbed his name in a high, thin cry.

Ready to explode, Tyler gave Libby no time to catch her breath before he pulled her under him and parted her legs. He entered her with one smooth stroke. She drew a sharp breath, and lifted her hips to receive him. He wanted to keep his thrusts long and slow; as soon as he sank into her warmth, he knew he was lost to her. He'd mark her soul with his body, if he could. But he knew she'd already marked his.

The acute heaviness low in his belly and groin grew more fevered with each passing second. He gripped Libby's buttocks and canted her to reach into her more deeply. Her fingers bit into his hips and she pulled him toward her as he pushed.

He looked at her lying beneath him—beautiful, tender. Her eyes were charcoal with rebuilding passion, and her wordless murmuring only increased his need to relieve this aching, exquisite torment.

He devoured her mouth with a moist, hot kiss, "I'll never let you go," he ground out.

"Then take me, Tyler," she pleaded fervently. "Make me yours."

"Libby—angelheart," he muttered against her neck. He quickened his pounding strokes, and sweat popped out all over his body.

Suddenly she arched against him with a wailing sob, her climax vanquishing her. He felt the paroxysms within her that began a chain reaction in his own body. He pressed his forehead to hers and plunged forward, as swift, hot pulsations overwhelmed him.

Libby wrapped her arms around Tyler and held him close while a shuddering groan was torn from his chest. They lay still then, both spent and breathing hard.

The evening breeze from the open window swept over their damp bodies, cooling them and raising goose bumps. Limbs entangled, they fell into a brief, languorous doze, still joined. Finally, Tyler slowly roused himself and pulled her over to lie against him.

He rubbed a hand over his face, and the scrape of his beard bristle on his palm sounded like sandpaper. A wry chuckle escaped him. "I probably look like hell, but I sure feel great."

Libby propped herself on one elbow to consider his handsome, drowsy face in the twilight. Maybe he wasn't at his best. He smelled of horses and road dust. His lean jaws were shadowed by stubble, and his sweat-soaked hair stuck up in a couple of places where he'd run his hands through it. But he couldn't have looked better to her if he'd been wearing a Sunday suit. "You're the handsomest cowboy I've ever seen."

He raised his brows, obviously struggling to keep a straight face. "That's a real compliment coming from a city gal."

"You always made that sound like a disease," she complained with a laugh. "I'm sorry to have to tell you this, Miss Libby," she went on with a deep, mock-stern voice, "but you have a bad case of . . . city-born."

He laughed, too. "All right, all right—I agree you fared much better than some who've come West."

She lifted her chin with an air of feigned arrogance. "Besides, I'm not a 'city gal' anymore."

He gazed at her with quiet reverence, and combed his fingers through her tangled hair. "No, you're not, angelheart. And below that soft, pretty surface, there's a strong, brave woman. That was one of the reasons I fell in love with you."

She traced her finger across his lips. "I fell in love with you because I discovered the tender man hiding underneath a tough, hard mask." She arched a brow at him. "It took some work to find him, though."

He chuckled again and pulled her back down to his shoulder. "I'm glad you didn't give up."

She snuggled against him. "Well, you're stuck with me now."

Now and forever. Tyler turned his head to press kisses to the outer corner of her eye and her cheek. He'd sworn to her that he'd never let her go.

How could he, he thought, a bit ruefully, when she had such a tight grasp on his own heart?

# Chapter 16

The next morning, Tyler surprised Libby by coming into the kitchen while the crew was making short work of her pancakes. When he walked in, conversation ceased abruptly. She raised her brows and smiled at him. It would take a little more exposure to his easygoing side to get them used to this new Tyler Hollins—a man who smiled more than he frowned.

She could not keep her eyes off him. Had there ever been a man so handsome? His blue eyes had a wicked sparkle in them this morning, and he looked far more rested even though she knew that he'd slept only about three hours.

Catching her gaze, he winked at her and she blushed hotly, remembering how they'd spent the rest of the night. After she'd helped him put his bed back together, he washed and shaved, and came to her again in her room. This time, they made love slowly, exploring each other's bodies with curious, gentle caresses.

Tyler stood at the worktable and faced the men. "I don't mean to interrupt your breakfast, and I know Joe has that schedule he likes to keep, so this will take only a minute." He smiled at the foreman, and a quiet chuckle rippled through the group; everyone knew that Tyler was the schedule maker at the Lodestar.

"You boys probably heard that I went to Billings. I found a new cook there. He used to work for the DHS outfit over in the Judith Basin, and he'll be here in about a month's time to take over this kitchen."

All eyes shifted to Libby, with some awkward stirring and throat clearing. Rory watched Tyler, and a slight frown creased his brow. Only Joe grinned.

Tyler paused a beat before going on, obviously enjoying the suspense. "I fired Miss Libby last night when she agreed to marry me."

Libby stared at him with her mouth open. He was such a private man, one who shared his thoughts and feelings with nobody—this was the last thing she expected him to say. He winked at her again, and suddenly she realized what he had done. By making this public announcement of their engagement, he'd expanded the scope of his commitment to her. It wasn't a secret, or an unsubstantial promise made in the dark. It was real. And he wanted everyone to know it.

The cheers and whistles and applause that erupted in the room were deafening. Tyler held his hand out to her and she joined him at the worktable, blushing and laughing.

Joe stood up and came to pump Tyler's hand. "So you did it, you stubborn bast—son of a gun."

"Yeah, I did it." Tyler held up Libby's left hand and showed him the ring.

Joe kissed Libby's cheek, grazing her with his big mustache. "He said he was gonna ask you, but . . . I'll tell you, Miss Libby," he rumbled in a confiden-

tial tone, "I nearly wrung this boy's neck a time or
two, waitin' for him to come to his senses."

She whispered back, "If I'd known, I probably
would have helped you."

His dark eyes gleamed and he laughed again, then
he shook her hand. "Welcome to the Lodestar, Miss
Libby. We're sure glad you're here to stay, even if
Tyler is takin' the best damned cook we ever had."

Rory came up then and offered his hand to Tyler
in a very grown-up gesture. His young face was serious and dignified. Libby had seen him wear that
expression from time to time since the day Charlie
died. It was as though he'd buried the last of his
childhood with his friend.

"What do you say, Rory?" Tyler asked, slinging
his arm around the back of the boy's neck. "Does
this sound all right to you?"

Libby realized then what significance Tyler's re-
marriage might have for Rory; after all, his sister had
been Tyler's first wife.

Rory nodded. "Yeah, if it'll keep Miss Libby here
so we don't have to worry about her leavin'
anymore."

Tyler replied, "That's exactly what it means."

A bright smile lit up his face. Then he asked in a
wheedling tone, "Miss Libby, ma'am, do you think
you'll still bake cookies once in a while?"

"Peanut butter?" she asked.

"Oh, yes, ma'am!"

"I think that's one job I'd better keep, then."

One by one, the men approached the informal
receiving line to congratulate them—Kansas Bob,
Noah, the Cooper boys, and all the rest, including
Jim Colby.

Jim was a big man with a lantern jaw and quiet,

solitary ways—the complete opposite of the man he'd replaced. There wasn't much he could do around the ranch with his arm in a sling, but both Joe and Tyler had insisted on keeping him on at full pay.

As she received their sincere best wishes and good-natured teasing, Libby basked in the well-being that washed over her. She might not have blood relatives to witness her marriage to the man standing next to her, but she had the people at this ranch.

And that counted for a lot.


Plans went forward for the wedding, and Libby's days were busy. No formal invitations were sent. Rather, news of the event was spread by word of mouth, and Nort Osmer was counted upon to do most of the broadcasting. The ceremony would take place at the Lodestar, and there would be a cookout feast afterward.

Libby forced herself to remember that while it felt otherwise, this was not her first marriage. And she was a widow on top of that, marrying after a disgracefully short period of mourning. In Chicago, where rigid Victorian etiquette held sway, even a domestic would be expected to wear black for at least two or three years. Things might be more relaxed in Montana, but a white dress for Libby was still out of the question.

When Tyler took her into Heavenly to buy the fabric for her wedding gown, with a trace of regret she passed over a bolt of fine white lawn in favor of lavender shadow stripe.

"Was that nine yards, Mrs. Ross—uh, Miss Libby?" Nort asked, measuring off the stripe.

"Yes, that's right," she said, watching him unroll the fabric on the counter.

"I swan, who'd have dreamed when you came here last September that you'd be marryin' *two* of our boys within a year's time?" Nort pondered tactlessly. He looked up from his yardstick. "I guess this was what you could call one of them whirlwind courtships."

Just then the door opened behind Libby, and she turned, hoping that Tyler had finished his business with Sheriff Watkins. She doubted that Nort would feel quite so reflective if he were here. Instead, she saw Callie Michaels.

"Hello there, Nort. And if it isn't Mrs. Ross," she exclaimed, smiling, and looking around the store. "I thought that was Ty's wagon out front. Where has he run off to?" She swept in with a rustle of emerald brocade and gardenia perfume.

"Oh, he's down talkin' to the sheriff," Nort said.

Callie walked up to the counter and rubbed the lavender shadow stripe between her soft, plump fingers. "Running up a new dress?" she inquired of Libby. "Except for church and those dances at the grange hall, there aren't many places around Heavenly to wear a nice dress." She looked down at her own brocade and laughed broadly. "'Course, I don't go to church and we've got dancing every night at the Big Dipper."

Libby smiled and backed up a step, the perfume starting a headache at her temples. "Mr. Osmer, you'll put in a spool of matching thread, too, please?"

"I guess Montana didn't scare you off, after all. Ty said you'd decided to stay on and work for him in his kitchen."

She heard the barb hovering under Callie's remark. She found it unnerving to be in the company of this woman who'd spent more time touching her future husband's body than Libby had herself.

"Actually, I've been promoted," Libby began.

"That's right, Callie," Nort jumped in. "Tyler and Miss Libby here are gettin' married. We're just now measurin' off the dress goods for her weddin' dress. And Ty is talkin' to Jack Watkins about performin' the ceremony."

This time, Libby silently blessed Nort for his gabbiness.

Though her expression did not change, the madam's face paled beneath her powder. "Well, is that a fact?" she said a bit too brightly. She turned her knowing smile on Libby, and looked her up and down. "Then I probably won't be seeing him—for a little while, anyway. Nort, I'll come back when you're not so busy."

She left as she'd arrived: with a swish of brocade and a choking cloud of gardenia.

When the door closed, Libby let out a low, angry breath and released her clenched fists.

"By dang, that Callie," Nort laughed and shook his head. "If she don't take the cake."

Libby knew it wasn't cake that Callie Michaels was interested in taking.

That night, Libby lay in Tyler's arms, quivering in gasping astonishment at the pleasure he summoned from her body. After a climax that had left her weeping and exhausted, she rested in his strong embrace, her own pulse still echoing faintly in her womb.

"Are you all right?" he murmured, slowly smooth-

ing her hair. She could hear the smile in his voice—
he knew very well what her answer would be.

"Yes. You're pretty pleased with yourself, aren't
you?" she said.

"Well, maybe a little. It's more important that
you're pleased." His big hand ran up and down her
bare back.

She stretched against him languorously. "I am, but
you have an unfair advantage over me. You learned
in school how to—um, how this works."

He laughed softly and kissed her forehead. "Trust
me, honey, this isn't something you can learn from
a book. It's mostly instinct and practice."

Practice. It made her think of Callie Michaels and
all the "practice" he must have gotten in her bed.
Telling herself that it shouldn't bother her was not
very effective.

"Uh, you mean like when you went into Heavenly
on Saturday nights . . ." Her voice trailed away. She
didn't have the courage, or even the right, she supposed, to ask what his life had been like before.

Rolling her to her back, he turned on his side to
face her and propped his head on his hand. The
vague shape of him loomed over her in the darkness,
and he interlaced his fingers with hers.

"What's this about, honey?"

After an awkward start, she told him about seeing
the woman at Osmer's that afternoon.

He sighed. "Libby, what was between Callie and
me, that was mostly business. It might be hard to
understand, because here in this bed, it's so personal
with us—" He paused, as though searching for the
right words. "I guess I was friends with her. I went
to her looking for forgetfulness more than anything
else. You know . . . I *paid* her. She and I never had

real intimacy, not like this. Hell, she wouldn't even kiss me—she thought it was too familiar or something."

"Oh." This cheered Libby enormously, although she couldn't say why. But it probably accounted for the reason Tyler liked to kiss her now. She squeezed his hand.

"And anyway," he continued, "after you got here—well, things were never the same. I couldn't— it didn't—" He stumbled to a halt.

Libby waited, trying to puzzle out what he meant. "What?"

He took her free hand and pressed it to himself, that particular part of his anatomy now in repose. "It was like this the whole time." He sounded self-conscious, a rarity for him.

"Really?" she asked. The brief touch of her own palm, though, was apparently enough to revive him. Now she was very happy. She remembered Callie, with her cloying smell of gardenias, and that complacent, secret smile.

He leaned over and nuzzled her neck. "When that happened, I knew I wanted only you. That was why I told Callie good-bye," he said simply. "And it seems the more I get of you, the more I want." The kisses he left behind were warm, soft.

She couldn't suppress her giggle when he touched a ticklish place.

"Are you going to let me see the material you chose for your wedding dress?" he asked, working his way down her shoulder.

She turned her head toward the window. "I didn't get white, if that's what you're wondering."

"Did you want white?"

"It really wouldn't be appropriate."

He was up on his elbow again. "Why the hell not?" he demanded.

"For one thing I'm a widow. Plus, well, Tyler, you should know better than anyone. I'm not a virgin—"

He put a finger to her chin and brought her face back to his. "You were a virgin when you came to my bed and I'm going to be your husband, the only man you'll ever sleep with. If you want to be married in white, there's no reason why you shouldn't be." He smoothed her hair back from her forehead and chuckled. "Besides, I've seen a few pregnant women go to the altar in white. It's not illegal, you know."

She reached up to pull him back down to the pillow. "I don't give a damn what color the dress is as long as you're there."

He laughed. "That's the spirit. You're starting to sound like me. Now let's see," he said, kissing her throat, "where did I leave off?"


The golden days that followed were the sweetest that Libby had ever known. In love, Tyler Hollins was a very happy man. When they were alone, they couldn't keep their hands off each other. And he seemed to find so many reasons to come to the kitchen.

"I'm just checking to see if you'd made cookies again, angelheart."

"Libby, could you sew this button back on before I lose it?"

"Did you call me? I was down at the barn and I thought I heard your voice."

One noon, Joe pulled her aside and teased, "Ty is just about useless—I can't give him a job to do that he'll stick with. I never seen a man so lovesick in my life."

For her part, Libby could hardly look at Tyler without smiling and blushing. Between their nights of heart-stopping passion, and the affectionate, laughing companionship of their days, she was left almost breathless. Now and then she'd notice the crew watching them with good-natured amusement, but if anyone suspected that they were doing more at night than sleeping chastely in their own beds, no hint of it was dropped.

On an evening a week before the wedding, Libby and Tyler sat on the front porch after supper, watching the sunset. He had his feet propped up on the porch railing, and a drink on his knee. Libby sat next to him, mending a rip in one of his shirts. This quiet peace and contentment seemed like a miracle to her after the winter she'd endured. Even when she'd envisioned a life with Wesley, her imagination had not shown her a picture as mellow as this.

Across the yard by the bunkhouse, Noah Bradley was showing off some tricky roping maneuvers to Joe, Hickory Cooper, and Kansas Bob Wegner. Tyler watched them, shading his eyes against the low-angled sun.

"Dr. Franklin stopped by today while you and Joe were out on the east range," she said.

Tyler turned his head to look at her. He didn't think he'd had more than two brief conversations with Alex Franklin in the four years that the doctor had lived in Heavenly. "Yeah? What the hell did he want?"

She shrugged, snipping a length of thread from a spool. The fire of the sun turned her hair and lashes to gold. "Nothing special. He looked at Jim's arm. Then he stopped by the house to say he'll be at the wedding if no emergency comes up—he said there's really too much work for one doctor. He seems like a very nice man."

Tyler grunted noncommittally and returned his attention to Noah's roping. Sure, nice man—let him deal with the heartache of losing patients, he told himself.

"Tyler?"

"Hmm—"

"Have you ever thought you might practice medicine again?"

His breath stopped in his chest. "Libby—"

She leaned forward in her chair. "Don't get angry. I'm just curious."

He looked at her delicate, pretty face and sighed. How could he explain it to her—the nightmares ... waking up in cold sweats that in his dreams had been rivers of blood ... listening to frigid winter winds that had echoed through his brain like a woman screaming. Even now, sometimes he heard it. What could he say about the cold hand that closed around his heart whenever he thought of watching helplessly while another patient died? How could he make her understand any of it? He barely understood it himself.

"I'm not angry, honey." He drained the glass in his hand. "Once, there was nothing more important to me than being a doctor. Taking care of the land and the stock, taking care of people—those things were so interwoven, I couldn't have told you where one ended and the next began. But all of that changed when Jenna died. I'm not a doctor anymore, and I'm glad for that." He dragged his feet off the railing and stood up. "I think I'll wander down there and show Noah a thing or two about that hooley-ann throw he's trying to make. His loop isn't big enough."

Libby watched him as he crossed the yard. He might look more like a cowboy than a doctor—the way he walked, the lift of his head. And he might claim to prefer it that way.

But Libby wasn't so sure. He was still trying to outrun the demons that haunted him.

"You boys try to stay clear of that bob wire fence of Lat Egan's," Joe warned at breakfast the next morning. "His vigilantes have nailed signs to the posts with skulls and crossbones, and 3-7-77 painted underneath. I heard in town yesterday that one of his men took a shot at the J Bar J crew after those boys wouldn't let 'em inspect their cattle for a brand. The way things are right now, it wouldn't take much to get a range war goin'."

Tyler looked up from the coffee Libby was pouring for him at the stove. It had taken all the willpower he had to make himself get out of bed today. The temptation to lie in the linen sheets with her in his arms had been almost impossible to resist. Hearing Joe's words made him wish he'd given in to it and pulled the quilt over their heads—trouble was brewing on the plains. He could feel it.

"What does that mean?" Rory asked, loading his own coffee with three spoonfuls of sugar. "What's 3-7-77?"

"I ain't seen it around here for years now, but it stands for three feet wide, seven feet long, and seventy-seven inches deep." Joe leaned back against the wall, popping half a biscuit into his mouth.

Possum chuckled a bit nervously. "Sounds like the measurements for a grave."

"That's exactly what it means," Tyler put in. He propped his foot on Libby's low stool and leaned his forearm on his knee. "It's a death threat. What is going on over at the One Pine? I haven't heard about rustlers in the area. Lat has water holes over there, but we've all got water." He was about to suggest that Lattimer Egan had lost his mind altogether, but he didn't, not in front of Rory. Rory never saw his father, but respecting the ties of blood, Tyler tried not to say too many disparaging things about him when the boy was around.

Joe shook his head. "Honest to God, Tyler, I don't know. I just don't want any of our people getting shot."

"We might have to take this up with the sheriff and some of the other ranchers around here. We've managed to avoid a range war all these years—I sure as hell don't want to see one start now."

"Me, either." Joe put his cup down on the table then, and put on his hat. "All right, we got a lot to do, and the sun's up. Let's get going." He reviewed the assigned jobs for the day, then grinned at Tyler and Libby. "*If* you decide to join us and earn your supper, Mr. Hollins, we'll be doin' a little brandin' down by the creek. Your fancy ropin' ability would be appreciated.

Tyler felt his face grow warm, but he just laughed. "I'll be along in a minute."

At the tables, last gulps of coffee were downed and Noah grabbed a biscuit to take with him. After a moment of pounding boot heels and jingling spurs, the lovers were left alone.

Libby gave him a puzzled, worried look. "Tyler, a range war?"

He opened his arms to her and enfolded her in

his embrace, resting his chin on the top of her head. Her softness against his chest and the scent of her honey-colored hair made him think again about sneaking back upstairs with her and closing the door. Closing out trouble, closing out the rest of the world.

"Don't worry," he murmured to her. "I'm beginning to believe that Lat *is* crazy, but we're safe. Nothing can happen to us here. He's just a bitter, mean bastard whose own life is so miserable that he wants everyone else to be miserable, too."

She backed up and gave him a meaningful look. He nodded ruefully and kissed her. "Yeah, maybe that could have happened to me. But I was saved by an angel."

That afternoon, after making sure that Tyler was at the corral, Libby went upstairs to her room to put some finishing touches on her wedding gown. She'd been certain to work on it only up here, and only when he was out of the house. Her dress might not be white, but that was no reason for the groom to see it a week before the ceremony.

Lifting it from the hooks in her closet, she had to admit that the gown had come together beautifully. The high neck and huge gigot sleeves made her already small waist tinier still, and the bodice came to a point on her abdomen over a circular skirt that fitted smoothly over her hips. In a way, she was glad that this dress was lavender—it would be a shame that a garment so lovely could be worn only once. Tyler had said that they might be able to get away for a trip to Helena before fall roundup. She smiled as she imagined wearing this gown to supper in a hotel dining room, with her handsome young husband sitting across the table from her.

Pulling a chair to the open window, she settled in a square of mild June sun, looking out now and then at the sea of grass that rippled in the breeze. Though she was not likely to forget the previous winter, she'd come to love this place in a way that she had never foreseen. The expanse of land and sky, the songs of red-winged blackbirds and finches, the riot of wildflowers—it was a place of wild contrasts. Just like the men it bred: tough and tender, peaceful and violent. She'd seen Tyler rope a calf and wrestle it to the ground for branding, and at night, had felt his hands caress her with infinite, wondering gentleness.

Just as she took the first stitch to attach a hook and eye on the gown's collar, she heard a thud downstairs, like the front door had banged open.

"Hollins! Where are you?" a man's voice bellowed. Filled with fury and panic, it seemed to shake the very rafters.

Libby jerked upright in her chair.

*"Hollins!"*

A shiver of alarm rippled through her, raising goose bumps all over her body. Jumping to her feet, she threw the dress on her bed and ran out to the gallery to look down over the railing. What she saw froze her heart. Lattimer Egan stood in the parlor, as blood-smeared as a butcher. In his arms he carried Rory, and struggled to keep from dropping the boy's sagging, unconscious body. A slow, steady drip of blood ran from Rory and puddled on the floor.

"Oh, my God," Libby uttered. "Dear God in heaven!" She ran through the gallery and hurried down the stairs.

"Where's Hollins?" Egan demanded again. His usually florid face was as pale as his son's.

With wide eyes she looked at Rory's lifeless form and touched his cold face with a shaking hand. "My God," she cried again. "Is he dead?"

"He needs a doctor and Franklin is gone to the Wickersons' farm—hellfire, woman! Do something!"

Her heart thundered so hard in her ears, it impaired her hearing. "T-take him into the kitchen and put him on the table. I-I'll—" She turned and ran out the front door, screaming as she went. "Tyler!"

Tyler was in the barn, hoisting feed sacks with Kansas Bob, when he heard Libby's high, distant scream. The absolute horror it carried raised every hair on his body. The cowboy looked at him uneasily.

*"Tyler!"*

"Jesus Christ," Kansas Bob murmured.

Tyler dropped the sack in his arms. It burst on the hard-packed floor, spilling oats over his boots up to his ankles. He turned to run outside, with Kansas Bob close behind.

They emerged from the barn and Libby plowed straight into Tyler. He gripped her by the arms to keep her from falling. Her hair hung wildly around her ashen face, and she was out of breath. The terror he saw in her eyes scared the hell out of him as little else ever had.

"What—what?" He couldn't seem to string his words together.

"It's—it's Rory. His father—brought him—he's hurt—bleeding a lot—"

Tyler felt as though a horse had kicked him in the chest. He was suddenly as breathless as Libby. He turned to Kansas Bob. "Get Joe and tell him to come up here. He's still down at the creek. Th-then ride like hell to town and bring back Alex Franklin."

Libby put up her hand and shook her head. "Egan already—looked for him. He's out on a call some-place—the Wicker-somethings. I told him to put Rory on one of the kitchen tables."

Tyler tipped his head. "Shit! Well, go on and find Joe anyway. Take the bay—she's saddled and tied up at the back gate. Then ride for the Wickerson place and bring Franklin back here."

Kansas Bob took off at a dead run.

Tyler grabbed Libby's hand. "Come on," he said, and pulled her along toward the kitchen, past Egan's wagon.

They trotted up to the porch and Tyler kicked open the door. But when he saw Rory laid out on the table, a blanket of silence fell over the rough-hewn room.

He slowly approached Rory, his heart pounding double time against his breastbone. The first thing that struck him was the smell of blood. It was strong in here. His visual field narrowed--his peripheral vision, oddly, seemed lost. He knew that Lattimer Egan hovered at the end of the table, but he couldn't see him and he ignored him. At this moment in time, he saw only the young man he'd come to think of as his own son. At fifteen, he'd grown to about five-foot-ten, but lying there he seemed no bigger than a child. His face was blue-white and misted with sweat. Tyler put his fingertips to his throat and felt a pulse that was rapid and thready. And he saw the right leg of his tan pants, saturated with blood from thigh to ankle, and a gaping hole ripped in the fabric at the inseam just above his knee. Beneath that was a large, ugly wound. He touched Rory's clammy forehead, brushing his hair out of the way.

Libby hung back to stay out of the way, her arms wrapped around herself. She was too scared for tears, too shaken to wonder how Rory had gotten hurt. Behind her she heard hooves pounding in the yard. Turning, she saw Joe ride to the porch. He jumped down from the saddle and trotted into the kitchen, then skidded to a stop next to her, obviously stunned by the scene in front of him.

"Jesus God." The words rumbled like low thunder carried on a breath.

"Did one of your men do this, Egan?" Tyler asked, not taking his eyes from Rory. His voice was frighteningly, deathly quiet.

Visibly shaken, Lat Egan dodged the question. "I'll handle my business, Hollins. You just patch up my son—or are you going to stand there and watch him die like you did my Jenna?"

Like lightning, like the blink of an eye, Tyler grabbed Egan by his bloody shirtfront and had him trapped against the log wall before either Libby or Joe could react.

Both of them were the same height, but the older man easily outweighed Tyler by fifty pounds. Fury gave him the advantage, though, and he had one hand around Egan's jowly neck. In the other he held his revolver with the barrel jammed under the man's chin.

"He's not your boy, you filthy, no good son of a bitch!" Tyler snarled in a voice more animal than human. "Rory is *my* business. And the hole in his leg was made by a rifle shot, and judging by the angle, I'd say it came from behind—"

Libby gasped, and clapped her hand to her mouth.

"My guess is that one of your hired gunmen shot this boy, or maybe you did. What happened, did he get too close to your goddamned fence?" Tyler's eyes glittered with terrifying, murderous rage—his hand tightened around Egan's throat, and he cocked the revolver. "I wonder how much of your face I'd blow off at this range?" Egan began to gasp for air and his face reddened.

"Tyler!" Joe roared, and jumped to pull him off. He got the gun away from him, but he couldn't break his squeezing grip. Egan was gurgling now. "Damn it, let him go!"

Tyler held him for just an instant longer, then pushed him away. "You make me sick," he said with complete disgust.

Joe hustled Egan outside, sputtering and swearing, and left Tyler and Libby alone with Rory. She went to the table and looked at the wound. What she could see of it was a raw, vicious-looking hole that oozed blood, and she cringed at the sight of it.

"What shall we do next? D-do you stitch something like this or wh—?"

"We'll wait for Franklin."

She took in Rory's clammy pallor and shallow panting. "But—he doesn't look very good at all. Should he be breathing like that?"

When he didn't answer, she turned to look at him and was worried by what she saw. His white-hot rage had left him, and now he stood gazing at Rory with his arms crossed over his chest and his shoulders hunched. She had never seen such naked pain and anguish in a man's face. "Tyler—you have to help him."

He pushed a shaking hand through his hair. "Libby, I'm not a doctor anymore."

"Are you saying that you don't remember what to do?"

He wouldn't meet her eyes. "No, I remember. But if everything I know still doesn't work, I don't want to be responsible for killing Rory, too. I'll wait for Alex Franklin."

Then Libby recalled the night that Tyler had explained why he'd given up medicine. He'd lost his nerve, he said. And now he stood here paralyzed, frozen with the fear of losing this boy.

"What if Dr. Franklin doesn't get here in time? What if Kansas Bob can't find him at all?" His very expression told her that he had already thought of these same possibilities. "Just saying that you aren't a doctor doesn't make you stop being one." She jumped around in her mind, trying to think of some way to budge him. "Don't doctors make a pledge? Don't they promise to help?"

He took Rory's limp hand in his own, and gazed down into his slack face. "Huh, yeah, the Hippocratic Oath. And the first thing I promised was to do no harm."

She felt helpless. "But if you don't do something, he might die. Isn't that harming him? Tyler, please, you have to try. I love you and we both love Rory. I believe in you—I *know* you can do this. And I'll be right here with you."

"Libby, damn it—"

Frustration over his stubbornness and fear for Rory sharpened her words. "You have a moral obligation to help this boy! You just told Egan that he's your business. Will you abandon him when he needs you?"

Stung, he glared at her. "I'm not abandoning him! I sent Kansas Bob for the doctor."

"Tyler, *you're* the doctor here." She paused, and her stomach clenched with apprehension over the next words that formed in her mind. But she carried on with a low voice that shook. "If you do nothing but hold his hand while he dies, you are far less than the man I believed you to be. I'll never forgive you if you don't try."

He looked stricken. "Maybe you're right," he barked, "maybe I'm not the man you think."

Suddenly, Rory's breathing became noisier and more shallow.

She gestured at the unconscious body. "Tyler, for God's sake," she begged, her voice breaking, "give Rory a chance. He's already had a bumpy ride into town in Egan's wagon. You're the only hope he has. I promise I'll stand here with you and we'll work together. It's all right to be scared, but damn you, don't be a coward!"

Tyler looked at Libby's sew face across the table. He was scared to death, but he saw her faith in him. Where it came from, he couldn't guess, but her words hit hard. Did he have the courage, the guts to do this? On his own, no, probably not. But Libby, Libby, who had always been braver than him—she'd be here. She'd had the daring and the backbone to save *him* when he'd done everything possible to discourage her.

He gazed down at Rory again and sighed. She was right. He had to reach down deep, to act, to save Rory, to redeem himself. If he didn't, he knew the doubts that plagued him now would be just pinpricks to what lay in store for him. With that decision, some of his uncertainty fell away.

He took a deep breath. "All right," he said, his voice sounded strained to his own ears. "Get the fire going in the stove and put on a kettle of water to heat so we can boil the instruments. We'll need soap, towels, and a lamp, and bring your scissors so we can cut these pants off. I'll get everything else."

Libby's face lit up with his words, and he felt a little better still. She flew through the house to get what they needed. Tyler ran back to his office and unlocked the glass cabinets to bring out bandages, carbolic, his stethoscope—all the things he had not laid his hands upon in more than five years.

They met back in the kitchen. With everything washed or boiled, Tyler sprayed the whole area down with carbolic from an atomizer. Then they cut Rory's pants off and he got his first good look at the wound Egan's vigilantes had inflicted. He winced— it was serious enough. The bullet hadn't lodged in Rory's leg, but it had torn off a piece of flesh that left a crater inside his thigh just above the knee. It was about three inches wide and an inch deep. The structures that had been damaged—muscle tissue, ligaments, tendons—

"Goddamn, what a mess," he muttered, more to himself. "At least the femoral artery isn't nicked. If that happened, we'd be in real trouble." He glanced up at Libby across the table, where she held the lamp for him. Her gray eyes were huge in her sud- denly paper-white face. "You're not going to faint, are you?"

"No!" she said. He saw her throat work convul- sively as she swallowed, and she gave him a watery smile. "I'm fine."

"Good girl. If I'm going to be brave, you have to be, too." Tyler decided that even though Rory was unconscious, the work he needed to do on his leg would be pretty painful. He gave Libby the job of administering the chloroform on a piece of gauze over Rory's nose and mouth.

"Just a few drops," he said, watching as she poured.

She looked up at him for confirmation, and he nodded. "Okay, let's get started."

As the minutes passed, Tyler gained more confidence. Knowledge that had lain fallow these past years came to him as he needed it, steadying his hands and guiding them.

He washed out the wound with lots of cooled boiled water, then cut away the dead and dying tissue. With forceps he plucked out pieces of fabric that had been embedded by the blast.

Next he cauterized the wound to stop the bleeding, using a scalpel he'd held over the open lamp flame.

"A-are you going to sew it up?" she asked, clearing her throat.

He dragged his arm across his sweating forehead. "No, there's nothing to sew with this kind of injury. We'll pack it with more clean water and gauze, and keep close watch over it for the next few days. And hope to God that it doesn't get infected."

After Rory was bandaged and cleaned up, Tyler lifted him off the table. "I'm going to put him in my bed, then I'll come back down and help you clean this up. He should be coming around in a while, but he sure as hell won't be going anywhere."

Libby heard the hope and confidence in Tyler's voice, and saw his smile.

Relief washed over her, making her feel weak and shaky. Maybe Rory wasn't the only one who'd been helped in this last hour.

\*          \*          \*

After the kitchen was cleaned up and the crew had been fed their supper, Libby came to the doorway of Tyler's bedroom to look in on both doctor and patient. The room was dark except for a single candle burning on the nightstand. Rory lay sleeping in the four-poster, wearing one of Tyler's old nightshirts. They had put pillows beneath his injured leg and folded the blankets away from it.

For the last several hours, Tyler had slouched in a chair beside the bed, with his feet propped up on the windowsill. He'd changed his clothes, but the meal she'd brought to him sat untouched on the table next to his chair. She tiptoed into the room and put her hand on his shoulder. He reached up and covered it with his own.

"Tyler, love, you have to eat," she whispered. "It's nearly eleven o'clock, and you haven't had anything since lunch."

He patted her hand. "Leave the tray. I'll get to it pretty soon." He dragged his boots from the windowsill and sat up, patting his leg. "Sit down for a minute."

Libby perched on his knee, and looked at Rory. "How's he doing?"

"I think he's going to be just fine. He'll probably limp for a while, but I don't think there was any permanent damage. We'll just have to keep an eye on him."

Tyler looked weary in the low light, and his handsome features were drawn with concern. "Do you want to take a nap on my bed for an hour or so?" she asked. "I'll sit with him."

"No, but thanks, honey. I think I'm just going to stay here tonight. If he's doing well by morning, I'll sleep for a while then."

Just then, Joe tapped on the door frame. Libby stood and Tyler turned in his chair. "We must be getting tired if we didn't hear your spurs."

The foreman grinned behind his mustache, but it didn't mask the worry in his face. "I took 'em off for now so's I wouldn't wake the boy."

Tyler rose from his chair with creaking stiffness and flexed his back. Then he motioned them out to the gallery. "Let's talk out here." When they were out of Rory's earshot, he asked, "Where's Egan?"

Joe took a match from his pocket and stuck it in his mouth like a toothpick. He leaned against the railing and crossed his ankles. "I convinced the old man to go home hours ago."

"Did you get him to tell you how this happened?" Tyler asked, the embers of his anger stirring to life.

"Yup. That was the first thing I pried out of him after we left the kitchen. It was like you figured— Rory was shot by one of Egan's hired guards. The boy was tryin' to free a cow that got stuck in that damned bob wire. The lowdown snake shot him from behind while he was rasslin' with it. Egan was there when it happened. I honestly don't think he even recognized his own son till they got closer."

Libby gasped in horror. "Oh, God—"

She looked at Tyler and saw the muscles working in his jaw, and his low voice quivered with fury. "Goddamn it, Joe. I'll get that mercenary bastard if it's the last thing I do."

Joe shook his head and gave him a meaningful look. "He's already disappeared. I guess when he found out he'd shot his boss's son, he took off."

Tyler eyed him. "What about the rest of those hired killers Lat Egan has working over there? They're taking their orders from him."

Joe's brows rose speculatively. "I wouldn't be at all surprised if they find themselves out of work. Especially now that one of 'em is gone. And 'course, I told Lat that we'd be talkin' to the sheriff and the other ranchers about this."

Worn out by the long day and the stress of the afternoon, Libby stifled a yawn.

Tyler turned to her and put his arm around her shoulders. "You'd better go on to bed now."

"Oh, but I'm not tired," she protested. "I want to help with Rory."

"It's all right. I'll let you know if anything changes." He hugged her close and whispered so that only she could hear. "Angelheart, I'll come and tuck you in after a while."

Blushing, she looked at Joe as if he'd heard this, but he just continued to rest his forearms on the railing and gaze down at the parlor below while he chewed on the match.

"Well, if you think—"

"I do. Now go on." Tyler pecked her cheek and put a guiding hand on her back to nudge her toward her own room. More than anything else, she thought Tyler wanted to talk to his friend alone.

Tyler waited until he saw her door close, then he turned back to Joe.

"Where's the man who shot Rory?"

"You know, a couple of the boys saw a new grave on the east range late this afternoon. It's over in that draw where you and me used to shoot at prairie dogs when we were Rory's age." Joe reported this as if he were talking about a new brand of tobacco at Osmer's.

Tyler pulled in a deep breath. "A couple of the boys?"

"Yeah," Joe said, turning toward him, "but I'll be damned if I can remember which ones."

He didn't know what to say. He couldn't condone what they had done, yet when he glanced over his shoulder and saw Rory in that bed, shot from behind . . . It could have been his boy in a grave on the green bluffs overlooking the Lodestar if that bullet had struck an artery. Hell, if Libby hadn't grabbed him by the scruff of his neck and shaken him, this still might have ended differently.

Joe put out his hand. "Tyler, I'll be sayin' good night."

Tyler took the hand and pulled Joe close for an instant in a backslapping embrace. "Thanks, Joe. And—if you remember who those two men were, you thank them for me, too."

He smiled and started toward the stairs. "That I'll do." He gestured toward Libby's closed door. "Don't keep that gal waitin' too long."

Just before dawn, Libby rolled over when she felt the empty side of the mattress sag beneath Tyler's weight. Even though it was dark, she knew it was him; despite the day and night he'd had, he still smelled like fresh air and clean hay.

"Tyler?"

"Sorry, angelheart. I thought I'd be able to sneak in and get into bed without waking you." His bare skin was cold and he sounded exhausted. She pulled him over to rest his head on her shoulder.

A tired groan escaped him. "God, you're nice and warm." He burrowed against her and she tucked the quilt up around his neck.

"How is Rory?"

"He'll be fine. He's young and strong. I forced

some salt water into him and I changed the dressing on his leg. The wound looks good. It's clean and as long as we take care of it, we should see proud flesh forming in a few days. And I expect him to be strong enough to attend our wedding."

Libby was relieved it had turned out so well, but she felt a twinge of conscience for some of the hard things she'd snapped at him in the kitchen. "Tyler?"

"Hmm."

She stroked his thick, soft hair. "I-I'm sorry I said those awful things this afternoon. I don't really think you're a coward."

He sighed and was silent for a moment before answering. "Libby-girl, I didn't think I was either, until you forced me to take that hard look at myself. But over the last five years, I got scared. Mostly I was afraid of the shadows and ghosts deep inside. I guess the part of me that was the strongest got broken somehow. I didn't know how to fix it, so I just kept backing away from anything and anybody who tried to get too close. Including you."

The echo of desolation in his voice brought tears to her eyes and they ran from the corners of her eyes to the pillow. "I think you're the finest man I've ever known."

His voice was light and a bit slurred with exhaustion. "If I am, angelheart, it's because you made me that way. You gave me back my soul.

As he drifted away into sleep, Libby whispered, "It was a fair trade, Tyler. My heart for your soul."

"And do you, Tyler Michael Hollins, take this woman to be your lawfully wedded wife, for better, for worse, for richer, for poorer, in sickness and in health, as long as you both shall live?" Sheriff Jack

Watkins peered over his reading glasses at Tyler, fixing him with a stern look.

"I do."

Libby felt Tyler squeeze her hand as he spoke. Although he tried to keep the emotion out of his voice, she heard it quaver just a tiny bit. He looked so handsome in his dark gray frock coat and black silk tie. She never would have dreamed that the man she'd seen dressed only in chaps and jeans could be so breathtakingly handsome. No Chicago gentleman ever looked finer.

Beaming at Tyler's answer—as if he might have responded another way—Sheriff Watkins said, "Well, then, by the power vested in me by Montana Territory in this Year of Our Lord eighteen hundred and eighty-seven, I now pronounce you husband and wife." He gestured at Tyler. "All right, son, you can give your gal a kiss now."

Tyler took Libby into his arms and gave her a short, tender kiss that held the promise of something much more exciting and intimate later. One glimpse at his blue eyes, eyes that matched the endless sky over them, vowed the same. He dipped his head to take her mouth again. Just before his lips touched hers, he whispered, "I love you, angelheart."

"All right, all right," Sheriff Watkins said, clearing his throat. "That's enough, Ty." He put his hands on their shoulders and turned them toward their guests. "Friends, I'm pleased to introduce to you Mr. and Mrs. Tyler Michael Hollins."

They were greeted with cheers and whooping the likes of which Libby had never heard, but then, there were people present from five ranches. She and Tyler laughed like youngsters and held hands as they stood on the front porch of the Lodestar to meet the people who had become so dear to Libby.

She let her gaze scan the sea of cowboy hats. There was Rory, who was healing well, and Joe, the Cooper brothers, Noah, and all the rest. She dabbed her damp eyes with her handkerchief. Finally, she had the family she'd yearned for.

Finally, here in Montana, Liberty Garrison Hollins was home.

# *Epilogue*

Joe ambled over to Rory, who paced in front of Libby's flower beds. Most of the men had found some excuse to stay close to the house this June morning. And for once, Joe couldn't find a better reason to pull them back to work, especially since he was slacking off as much as the rest of them. Jim Colby was showing Noah how to improve his hooley-ann throw—Noah just couldn't seem to get the way of that roping trick. Hickory and Possum were showing Kansas Bob the finer points of mumblety-peg.

"Heard anything yet?" Joe asked Rory.

"No, dang it, and I'm just about worn down."

Joe laughed. It was good to see the boy back to normal again. It had taken awhile, but he was young and strong. When he thought of that awful day a year ago, and Rory stretched out on the kitchen table, more dead than alive—

Joe pushed back his hat. "Maybe we should tell Tyler to hurry things along. We've got work to do out here."

Just then, the front door opened.

Tyler walked out on the porch, drying his hands on a towel. Looking at the men gathered in the yard, he chuckled. "What is this? Somebody's birthday or something?"

Joe called back with a grin, "I don't know, Tyler. Is it?"

Tyler flung the towel over his shoulder and let his eyes rest on each face turned in his direction. Unable to keep them in suspense any longer, his laughter rang free then. "Yes, by God, it is! We've got a new man on the place—Charles Joseph Hollins. His mama is doing fine and he'll be out here teaching Noah that damned hooley-ann before we know it."

The laughing and cheering that followed brought tears to Tyler's eyes. To have such friends and such a wonderful wife, he felt like the luckiest man on earth.

He felt like a man who'd been allowed a taste of heaven.

# WE NEED YOUR HELP
To continue to bring you quality romance
that meets your personal expectations,
we at TOPAZ books want to hear from you.
Help us by filling out this questionnaire, and in exchange
we will give you a **free gift** as a token of our gratitude.

- Is this the first TOPAZ book you've purchased? (circle one)

     YES          NO

  The title and author of this book is: _____

- If this was not the first TOPAZ book you've purchased, how many have you bought in the past year?

     a: 0 - 5    b 6 - 10    c: more than 10    d: more than 20

- How many romances in total did you buy in the past year?

     a: 0 - 5    b: 6 - 10    c: more than 10    d: more than 20 ____

- How would you rate your overall satisfaction with this book?

     a: Excellent    b: Good    c: Fair    d: Poor

- What was the main reason you bought this book?

     a: It is a TOPAZ novel, and I know that TOPAZ stands
        for quality romance fiction
     b: I liked the cover
     c: The story-line intrigued me
     d: I love this author
     e: I really liked the setting
     f: I love the cover models
     g: Other: _____

- Where did you buy this TOPAZ novel?

     a: Bookstore    b: Airport    c: Warehouse Club
     d: Department Store    e: Supermarket    f: Drugstore
     g: Other: _____

- Did you pay the full cover price for this TOPAZ novel? (circle one)

     YES          NO

  If you did not, what price did you pay? _____

- Who are your favorite TOPAZ authors? (Please list)

- How did you first hear about TOPAZ books?

     a: I saw the books in a bookstore
     b: I saw the TOPAZ Man on TV or at a signing
     c: A friend told me about TOPAZ
     d: I saw an advertisement in_____magazine
     e: Other: _____

- What type of romance do you generally prefer?

     a: Historical    b: Contemporary
     c: Romantic Suspense    d: Paranormal (time travel,
        futuristic, vampires, ghosts, warlocks, etc.)
     d: Regency    e: Other: _____

- What historical settings do you prefer?

     a: England    b: Regency England         c: Scotland
     e: Ireland    f: America    g: Western Americana
     h: American Indian         i: Other: _____

- What type of story do you prefer?

  a: Very sexy  b: Sweet, less explicit
  c: Light and humorous  d: More emotionally intense
  e: Dealing with darker issues  f: Other

- What kind of covers do you prefer?

  a: Illustrating both hero and heroine  b: Hero alone
  c: No people (art only)  d: Other_____

- What other genres do you like to read (circle all that apply)

  Mystery  Medical Thrillers  Science Fiction
  Suspense  Fantasy  Self-help
  Classics  General Fiction  Legal Thrillers
  Historical Fiction

- Who is your favorite author, and why?_____
  _____

- What magazines do you like to read? (circle all that apply)

  a: *People*  b: *Time/Newsweek*
  c: *Entertainment Weekly*  d: *Romantic Times*
  e: *Star*  f: *National Enquirer*
  g: *Cosmopolitan*  h: *Woman's Day*
  i: *Ladies' Home Journal*  j: *Redbook*
  k: Other:_____

- In which region of the United States do you reside?

  a: Northeast  b: Midatlantic  c: South
  d: Midwest  e: Mountain  f: Southwest
  g: Pacific Coast

- What is your age group/sex?  a: Female  b: Male

  a: under 18  b: 19-25  c: 26-30  d: 31-35  e: 56-60
  f: 41-45  g: 46-50  h: 51-55  i: 56-60  j: Over 60

- What is your marital status?

  a: Married  b: Single  c: No longer married

- What is your current level of education?

  a: High school  b: College Degree
  c: Graduate Degree  d: Other: _____

- Do you receive the TOPAZ *Romantic Liaisons* newsletter, a quarterly newsletter with the latest information on Topaz books and authors?

  YES  NO

  If not, would you like to?  YES  NO

  Fill in the address where you would like your free gift to be sent:

  Name: _____
  Address: _____
  City:_____Zip Code: _____

  You should receive your free gift in 6 to 8 weeks.
  Please send the completed survey to:

Penguin USA•Mass Market
Dept. TS
375 Hudson St.
New York, NY 10014